VOLUMN **6** WATCHER

WATCHER
OF THE
DAMNED

BY R.H. SNOW

Rosa De Oro. A Texas Publishing Company.

— ◆ —

DEDICATED TO THE TREASURES OF MY HEART:

God my Father, David my Love, Roxanne my Heart, Danny my Soul
— and Texas, my Texas!
We Will Be Free!

— ◆ —

Dear Reader,

Is survival or the treatment of the people around us more important? Many argue that is what makes us human, yet both have played that role in the history of our species.

Lonestar Libre! is the sixth in the Watcher of the Damned series, encapsulating the struggles of human life after the biological apocalypse. Post-apocalyptic source material, like graphic novels, video games, shows, and other books, have inspired the series, which deals with multifaceted divisions along biological, societal, moral, and religious lines. Though some have argued that the cultural fascination with mutants and the apocalypse is indicative of an overall fear of globalization, the fear is not that we could become an animal with lesser humanity; rather, that we already are.

Thank you for picking up the book, and enjoy.

Arthur DeVitalis

Table of Contents

I

High above the wild Texas Prairie, an all-seeing eye raced towards its mission.

Whirling through branch-tunnels of yellow Ash and brown Oak leaves, above twisting hog trails of limestone rock and sandy soil, the earth flew by, glimpsed though misty veils of concentrated jet fuel. Panoramas of forests and savannah rolled their imagery into data banks, the long-forbidden realms at last revealed for current analysis:

#ALTITUDE 40M
#SPEED 60KPH
#SCAN: INFRARED, FULL SPECTRUM

Bursting through the branches and into the open sky, they soared above a sea of waving silver bluestem and pink Muhly grass. They scanned a bear and her cubs fattening on acorns in the post oak grove, the cougar crouching above her in the high branches, and beyond them, the great lowing herd of spotted Longhorn Cattle, trampling a golden prairie beneath the blue October sky.

#TURN 45 DEGREES SE
#PLOT NEW COURSE: FOLLOW RIVER ROUTE 16

Between the skeletons of drowned trees and new forests, they found the muddy waters of the winding Navasota River rumbling over collapsed dams and rubble of forgotten bridges. Spreading out across switchgrass swales, then gathering again to meander down between white bluffs and dark caves, the Navasota roiled among the canyons of drained lakes, ringed with dark shells of homes. Sycamores and elms sheltered scattered pre-fabricated housing units, flapping their blown-out skirts in the breeze, hiding the bones of their dead. The habitations of the UnHallowed Dead would disappear into their sheltering groves, only to appear again ahead, strewn like blocks between woody ravines and windy plains.

The Happening destroyed humanity with man-made, mutating misery; now the teeming earth embraced its non-human children once more, free of the crushing hand of man. Miles rushed by, a rich tapestry of wild life and dead humanity. Herds of white-tailed deer leapt through the tall-grass prairies of Grama grass and greater Bluestem, chased by the packs of red wolves. Great flocks of snow geese and teal ducks covered the remains of lakes, and migrating red-capped sandhill cranes graced the reclaimed shores, spearing silvery minnows in the pure waters that ran through their twiggy black legs.

#WESPEEX MAPPIX MERGE Last Known Satellite with Central Texas TopoMap

#MAP: Home/Texas/Limestone/Streams/Sanders_Creek

Scars of roads crumbled to dust beneath healing branches of overarching trees; mesquites and cedars sprouted to life from dead bodies in wrecked vehicles. Small, rotting towns with tumbledown brick storefronts and storm-damaged roofs occasionally peeked into view, then hid behind ridges and trees once more. Only one recently cleared wooden fence and crudely furrowed field spoke of something other than the UnHallowed Dead; hunched over the rows, rough hands and twisted backs were at work, the diseased remnant of revenant humanity.

One demon dressed in scavenged rags turned his face to the sky, sensing a shift in the breeze; seeing nothing, he blinked emptily before bending his scaled visage back to the broken clods of sandy loam.

Farther, faster the omniscient eye flew until at last their destination came into view—a large lake, this one still embraced by a cracked but miraculously unbreached dam. Damaged jetties and decaying piers jutted into the green water from deserted homes and sandy lakeshores. The invisible orb flew towards a peninsula, where rusted roofs loomed inside palisaded wooden walls and the eerie sound of guttural shouts echoed across the still waters.

From across the miles, unseen hands input commands.

#STEALTH LEVEL 5

#SURVEILLANCE MODE—ACTIVE

#INPUT DESTINATION: LAKESIDE MARINA 11

#RENAME DESTINATION: PURGATORY

The drone whirred softly, activating heat shields with fiber-optic camouflage.

#OPERATION: KALI YUGA

#TARGET 1- Locate and Retrieve—Clone #TMA673CdF—TOP LEVEL
#TARGET 2- **Located**—SAUL ALEXANDER AZARIAN— TOP LEVEL
#LOCATION: PURGATORY
A Telometrix Instant Recognition tag slid into the drone's injection arm:
#IF = [track Saul Azarian] THEN [TIRS tag Clone TMA673CdF for retrieval]
#IF [TIRS tag Clone TMA673CdF] THEN [GOTO END]
Soft clicks announced explosive heat rounds cycling into the miniature missile chamber.
#END—ELIMINATE Saul Azarian

In a high-tech bunker beneath red-dirt streets, a scarred, shirtless mutant slashed at the air with his Bowie Knife, training body, mind, and spirit. He worked his way through Miyamoto Musashi's *Kodachi Seiho*—Seven Techniques with the Short Sword:

Sassen
Chudan
Uke Nagashi
Moji Gamae
Haritsuke
Nagashi Uchi
Asien

In LifeBefore, the man formerly known as Saul Azarian would have practiced with a sparring partner. But the Happening killed off all worthy practitioners, and in the loneliness of LifeAfter, the mutant now known as "The Watcher" walked Musashi's "Way of the Warrior" alone.

Musashi would have chided the Watcher for losing not only his Katana, but also his Wakizashi when the Happening caught him unawares a half-century ago. Unfortunately, both relics were buried beneath the chaos of the Happening, in his long-abandoned apartment in Northeast Dallas. There were many things for which Musashi would have chided his follower—but technique was not among them. Fortunately, Musashi was not rigid in his teachings:

There is more than one path to the top of the mountain.

The Watcher's path embraced the Bowie Knife as a righteous Texas incarnation of the Japanese Short Sword. Wielding it as he would a Wakizashi, the Watcher executed Musashi's techniques with faithfulness. His ageless body utilized the muscle memory of decades, and his keen mind sharpened its edge on the whetstone of living experience. Musashi's "ten thousand days of training" had run through its course twice, and thanks to the rejuvenating side effects of the virus, the Watcher could potentially run through another ten thousand days—

Each movement of Musashi's Katas was precise and deliberate, a meditation on killing; it centered the Watcher and connected him to the Master Warrior through training. But if training proved the Watcher a disciple of Musashi, his regalia announced him a son of Texas.

The cool glint of the bunker's artificial light played against the golden roses on his silver Championship Buckle, a stark contrast to his scaled crimson torso. Mutated, crusted skin sheathed his TransMutated body, a flinty, peeling cuirass of organic armor—but beneath his horny hide, he was a human as any man ever had been. Wearing a beat-up oilskin cowboy hat, faded blue jeans, and homemade moccasin boots, he looked as close to a Texas Luchador as anyone had seen in over a century.

A flamboyant broad-brimmed hat appeared around the corner, spangled green serpent-feathers bobbing above the raccoon-dong hatband. It was followed by Joey's broad, plated face peering from beneath the wide brim, Emporium shopping bag in hand.

"Marshal Azarian, you got a minute?"

The Watcher grumbled, snapping back to his finishing position. He hated interruptions, and Joey could tell.

"I'm not meaning to mess with your alone time, but we have a match to set up—and you need your persona to ring all the right bells with the crowd. You're the face of the Revolution now: LoneStar Libre!"

LoneStar Libre—Free Texas. It was a noble moniker and fit for a Luchador aligned with the newly minted LoneStar Revolution.

Joey had insisted on a name and a costume for Purgatory's infamous Friday Night Fights. Normally low key, the Watcher only agreed to all the gaudy trappings and spectacle of Wrasslin' because he considered himself a civilized man; at the University, he had studied the classic art of Kayfabe, the Western form of Kabuki theatre known in the Tex-Mex world as Lucha Libre. Sighing, the Watcher acquiesced to his exuberant Promoter's fervor.

"Oh, you're gonna love'em, I know you will!" Joey patted his broad stomach, feeling his suit pockets to find various knick-knacks. "You're an educated man, and you like symbols and all, so I made sure each one represents something about the Revolution… just look at this!"

Joey pulled forth a cord with a sharp tooth wrapped in copper wire, neatly threaded through a finely drilled hole. "It's one of them wolf fangs you bought from the Emporium… I asked my partner Wilcox to drill and wrap this for me. He used some electrical equipment to do it, and he did a dandy job!" The Watcher admired it. "The Wolf's fang represents the WildLands, and all who live in it. Next—" Joey's meaty hand fumbled into another brown polyester suit pocket:

Shimmering feathers quivered, crimson crescents plucked from the crest of one of the Watchers's Feathered Serpent trophies. "I had Wilcox wrap these in wire—I know they belong to one of those flying snakes you killed, but I kinda figured they look like Phoenix feathers ought to look. You know, like that Phoenix on your badge—what does it mean, anyways?"

The Watcher pulled his notepad and pencil from his back pocket and scribed:

> —*The Phoenix symbolizes Humanity rising from the ashes*
> *of the Happening. That's why our secret passphrase is*
> *Fenix Creciente—it means "Phoenix Rising", or*
> *"Growing" in Español.*

The Promoter peered at the leather badge laid on the desk. "So what's the rest of it mean?"

> —*Rose had a vision, and Evangelo translated it into a*
> *badge. The Star is the New Nation, the Fire is the*
> *Revolution, and the Broken Chain is Freedom. The floral*
> *scrollwork pattern around it represents the Flower of our*
> *Future, and our motto—We Will Be Free.*

"Huh, that makes sense." Joey reached up to affix the feather to the band of the Watcher's black cowboy hat, then grabbed another item from their feed-sack shopping bag. "With that in mind, put this on—the chain around your neck will stand for all the folks chained by the System…"

Seeing the chain, a vicious sneer crept out of the Watcher. Joey stepped back. "Whoa, Marshal, it's not real; the padlock doesn't really lock. See?" He swung it back to reveal the lock bar, filed to prevent latching. "It's just to pretend you're my manservant, that's all."

The Watcher scowled. The idea that Texans would meekly accept chains was abhorrent to the Watcher; he expected Texans to be true to their revolutionary roots.

That expectation had not always been the case.

Even as a native-born Texan, the Watcher had been taught to view his own culture as a hyperbolic relic of a violent and bigoted past. Texas History as viewed through the "Whole Earth" philosophical lens was defiant and demagogic. Texas Legend was required to be debunked in order to bring Texans to heel beneath the benevolent jackboot of WeSpeex's Whole Earth Union. As part of his training the Watcher had learned the Visionaries' take on Texas History: Myths and Madness: Lone Star Sociology 101. Like most Visionary hopefuls, he studied Texas culture in order to subvert it—

But Texas had subverted the Watcher instead.

He learned that to believers, Myth is Truth, and to Texans, Texas Myth was Texas Truth. In the pretend freedom of LifeBefore, there didn't seem to be much need for a Texas Myth; but in the chained reality of LifeAfter the Happening, Texas Truth came to mean so much more to the Watcher.

Despite all his years chained at the gate of Reunion Prison Camp, the Watcher had never accepted his chains—but he had come perilously close. Had it not been for the words of Travis' Letter from the Alamo inspiring him to fight on, he might have succumbed to despair long ago. Never accepting the chain was part of "never surrender"—

I shall never surrender or retreat; now I call on you in the name of Liberty—

But the ruse was needed in the name of Liberty tonight. With an irritated grunt, the Watcher looped the chain around his thick neck and swung the jimmied padlock closed.

"Yeah, I hate this sham too, Marshal. But this next item will make up for it!"

The Promoter yanked a blue bundle out of the bag and unfurled it, revealing Lorenzo De Zavala's flag, its white Lone Star radiating the word "Texas" in a field of blue. Slightly worn, it bore the years of use with a dusty dignity, made sacred by the long-dead who worshipped the tenets of Texas Freedom.

"I cleaned it up and made it nice—it'll be easy to play the part of a feisty OutLaw when you're wearing this as a cape! Texas is an attitude, and tonight in the Arena, you're gonna give that attitude life—"

Joey fastened the flag about the Watcher's neck, using gold buttons threaded through the grommets. The gold Metallilume lining shone beneath the cape, adding a touch of flash. "Just remember what the Shopkeeper said and don't let it touch the ground. That old man is scary..." Nodding with approval at the sight of his luchador, Joey handed him a mask then bundled up his bag, heading to the door.

"Once you put on your mask, you'll look like a proper wrassler—and now you've got a proper cape!"

As much as the Watcher hated to admit it, he liked the cape. He was not much for useless affectations, but he did appreciate the need for symbols. The Flag was the perfect symbol of the Revolution; proud, fierce and free. More importantly, like his mask, it was also lined with the signal-blocking metallic bucky-fabric, "Metallilume" to thwart death-drones' biometric scanners.

At the sight of the magnificent flag, he again regretted agreeing to throw tonight's final fight to Von Helm; the whole match was a ruse to get the Watcher inside the jail with his recruits and access the hidden armory before escaping Purgatory. Still, even if the deceit was necessary, the Watcher hated suffering even a false defeat to that smiling manlet; losing while wearing the flag made losing seem even more wrong.

He turned this way and that, getting used to the feel of the Cape on his shoulders; it magnified the Watcher's bellicose attitude...

The Cape was all about Attitude. The Mask, however, was about Belief.

Many wrestlers had worn the Mask. But it was that greatest of all the Luchadores who had sanctified it—The Saint himself, the Man in the Silver Mask, El Santo. Even now, the Watcher felt a nostalgic thrill as he remembered his first encounter with El Santos' Holy Relic...

Following his "unfortunate incident," nine-year-old Saul's short-lived stint in the Juvenile Services System had not gone well; mistakes were made and lessons learned. But after his successful escape from the Maximum Intervention Lockdown Facility—and the subsequent three-day cross-country manhunt it triggered—the homicidal boy attracted the attention of astute observers.

During his subsequent solitary confinement, Saul was allowed few pleasures; at the time, he did not yet have a children's WeSpeex RingWorld. So when his Case Managers told the patricidal lad they were gifting him one, it came as a surprise; he had not expected his Jailers to be so accommodating. They set the Ring upon his hand and told the quiet boy to chose the holovideo he liked best as an Avatar. The child-safe selection was vast, including puppies, kittens, snakes and robots; there were also fast cars and Heliscrams, and all manner of desserts.

But out of all the images, Saul chose an old snippet of film, a Man in a Silver Mask, subduing and unmasking a Masked Monster upon a stage…

El Santo put the hurt on that Karate-Chopping Vampire bastard, the Watcher grunted to himself in memory, even if that cowardly Monster escaped at the end of the scene.

At the time, the Watcher was unsure why he was so fascinated by that scene; but his knowledge of psychology had grown immensely since then. *I'm sure that choice proved quite helpful to the Firm's talent scouts.* Now, thanks to that choice, and the subsequent training it inspired, the Watcher was the Masked Man.

The Watcher knew he could never be as great as El Santo himself. His own mask was red, not silver, and he wasn't sure what it would come to symbolize to his audience. Rodolfo Guzman Huerta's Mask was the essence of what it meant to be a Luchador—and El Santos' Mask represented every innumerable virtue that had resided in Huerta's humble mortal frame: fortitude, integrity, devotion…

Belief.

Inspecting the Flame-Print mask over in his hands, the Watcher called to mind his own declaration of Belief, an Oath made on the blood of his only begotten child:

> *I believe in Life—even if I have to conquer Death and Hell to save it.*

Life. That brief hint of a pregnancy was the only Life the Watcher had ever created, gone as quickly as it came. Had it not been for Rose's embedded biometric nano-scanners, they would have never even known. He wasn't sure what surprised him more—the conception itself, or his reaction to its loss. It wasn't even supposed to be possible, and yet…

He hesitated to call it a miracle, simply because he didn't believe in them. But like a lot of things he didn't believe in, it happened.

Miracle… fortunate circumstance… God…

Whatever it was called, it was messing with his head. He needed to focus on what training and self-reliance had brought him. Only then would he have a shot at winning Rose.

Time to kick off the Revolution, win it, then claim my Prize.

He wondered if Rose remembered his declaration to her on the road to Mystery Outpost; if she did that was fine, but if she didn't it didn't matter. Come Hell or High Water, he was going to win his Prize.

> *"You want to play a game, Rose? Let's play. There's a Prize at stake, a treasure worth more than all the gold in the world, and I'm in it to win it. You can play with me and win, or you can play against me and I'll still win. Either way, I'm going to win my Prize, by God—or die trying."*

That Prize was currently holed up at the WildHorses Hotel, reading Western Romances and plotting Rebellion. The Watcher briefly wondered if the Prize was worth the pain. He tried to linger on the memory of bliss at the Altar but got waylaid by the memory of Rose pelting him with pears from high atop a tree, flaunting his stolen hat on her curly, sassy head…

Oh, you are going to make it worth every second of my pain, Hada Pequeña.

The label was fitting—*little Fairy.* Before his discovery of Rose, Afterlings were only known to Survivors by the legend of fairy-like, golden women living in a lost city beneath the earth. As it turned out, the legends were true—they just missed the part about them being created by WeSpeex Inc. to replace "Feral" Humans.

Aggravated, the Watcher slashed at the air again, following through the stroke with a forward stab. *All this Feral Human wanted was a forbidden life of Freedom with the Afterling I caught.* That option was still on the menu. But to get it, he'd have to fight his way through Rose's dysfunctional family to take over their World.

The Watcher tallied them up: her psychotic ex-husband, his megalomanic father, both their respective armies, their far-flung allies, her codependent clone sisters, and a whole passel of rambunctious nephews —that part of this takeover he was happy to oblige. But one last requirement was the real kick in the head…

He'd have to become Leader of her so-called "Church" in the process.

I'm not a Church kind of man, the Watcher grimaced; it was surreal to be the one others looked to for Belief. But despite his reluctance to be that man, Belief now took on a greater importance in his life, simply because the one woman he wanted had strong belief System…

To be specific, *the* System.

Originally the System was called the "Vision of Ages," a global pseudo-religion and social engineering construct designed by the Visionaries to save the Earth from the UnEnlightened—the uninitiated people Visionaries called Feral Humanity. But through the Visionaries' shortsighted hubris, the System instead destroyed Humanity through their Kali Yuga Project—the population control virus that triggered the Happening. Meant to save Humans from themselves, the System wiped them out instead…

That was the System the Watcher unwittingly helped create, and tonight he would help destroy it. Training, attitude, and belief would come together this evening in a performance that could spur a Revolution to topple that System. It would be up to the Man in the Mask to make it all happen.

He breathed out a calming breath. *No pressure.*

The Watcher held the Mask up, light shining through its gold Metallilume lining to illuminate the flames printed upon its red stretch fabric. *What of this Mask?* Did it represent any virtue in the man wearing it, or was it just for show? Any adulant of El Santo knew: the Mask didn't hide the Spirit of the Wearer—it amplified that Spirit.

He grimaced, keenly aware of his own flawed nature. There was a time when he would have scoffed at being considered virtuous, but times were different. He snorted wryly to himself:

If I'm the paragon of virtue now, we're all screwed.

He studied the mask, his own symbol of virtue. The flames printed across the lower half of the stretch-knit mask made a fair representation of a snarl, or he could pull down the hinged face guard to allow for a real life sneer… expressions would have to do for intimidation, since he had no way of trash talking his opponents without a WeSpeex RingWorld on his hand.

The Watcher left his WeSpeex Ring behind with his gear, to avoid discovery while he worked undercover in Pair'O'Dice. Now he was forced to agonize over communications logistics as he waited for the Gambler to send it back. For the speechless Watcher, life was so much more difficult without the RingWorld; his mutism presented constant challenges in the communication device's absence.

The Watcher held up his hand and frowned at the empty space where Rose's silver and garnet Ring normally resided. *The WeSpeex RingWorld Life-Enhancement Suite—a perfect melding of hardware, software and wetware…* He glanced at the remnants of the salvaged drone on the corner worktable: *…and it's antithesis, the Death-Enhancement suite known as ALGOS.* Both devices were manufactured by the corporate Tech Behemoth, WeSpeex, aka the Firm, aka CognitoINCognito INC and its myriad subsidiaries; Ring and Drone were complimentary to each other, each was as insidious as its counterpart.

Dismantled and laid out on the worktable by the mysteriously tech-savvy Gambler, the hollow-core ball drone seemed even more terrifying. Six tiny, explosive heat rounds lay next to a thin, titanium-alloy barrel, their small size belying their deadliness; alongside this, a pipette drained ultra-concentrated biofuel from the mini-flamethrower reservoir into a beaker. But the most abominable component of this deathbot was the part he couldn't see…

Eyes narrowed in memory as he scanned the lifeless orb, the Watcher asked: *how much of this destructive abomination's intelligence was my doing?* That answer lay within the dead drone's artificial intelligence, powered by the nanobots trained by Saul Azarian. At the time, the ALGOS Research and Development Team considered their nanobots to be on the cusp of sentience; it was a hotly debated topic: when does artificial intelligence become artificial life?

The Watcher wondered what the drone's creators would have thought of the Artificial Life known as Rose…

With her lopsided smile and lush curves, Rose was one of many, a miniature, man-made woman immortalized in the Anthem of the Lost City of Afterlings:

Hair as wild and dark as night,
eyes as bright as day,
be the treasure of my heart and soul,
ay mi Amante!
Tesoro, Tesoro, treasure of a thousand tears;
Be the treasure of my heart and soul, all my hopes and fears!

His mind lingered on the infuriating little golden-skinned clone. She certainly wasn't like any clone the Watcher had ever previously encountered; LifeBefore clones were insensate designer repositories for spare organs. But Rose brutally challenged his ideas on the personhood of clones. He involuntarily scowled, puzzling over her. She was a treasure and a trial, the promise of freedom wrapped in ribbons of terror—

Like the Happening, Rose destroyed the Watcher's World. Before Rose, he was a prisoner, a husk of the man he might have been, a promise unfulfilled in a harsh, limited world. After Rose, he became himself as he was meant to be—stronger, fiercer, harder, purer... Rose rebirthed the fire within.

He let the fire within fill him again, remembering Rose's silky black ringlets slipping through his gnarled fingers as her golden breasts pressed against his broad, plated chest. Two universes collided in their fusion: the fresh, fertile softness of synthetic Insider humanity mingling with the testosterone-transmutated brutality of Outlaw Survivors...

In that moment, they became the future of the World.

Lost in that memory, his fingers absently traced the golden roses on his silver belt buckle, cold against the hot flesh of his thickly-scaled abdominal muscles. Dazed by the magic of Rose, that moment before the Altar was the only moment the Watcher could clearly remember—

Just don't call it love.

His Mentors at CognitoINCognito taught him: *Sociopaths don't feel what Normative Society calls love.* Of course, they wouldn't call it "Sociopathy" either... Enlightened Society spurned the bigotry of the word Sociopath for the more tolerant label of Socio-Automanaut. Self-awareness was the key for Socio-Automanaut success in a normative world, and love was just another normative construct for Socio-Automanauts to manipulate on their path toward Enlightenment.

But if it wasn't love he was feeling, what was it? More than lust, and deeper than infatuation... surely he could come up with a name for this bio-chemically induced emotion.

Insanity?

Insanity seemed to explain the feeling best. The heat of that insanity filled the Watcher as her voice rang in his mind, brassy and sweet:

"When the other Deva come to find you chained by the neck, restrained and ravaged, tell them how a little defenseless Asura laid low the Survivor's chosen champion, the Deva known as Agent Azarian." Rose sassed a last taunt as she sashayed away, *"When they ask you how this happened, tell them I am the Yellow Rose of Texas, and you are just another Santa Anna..."*

She sang as she left him, naked and chained at the Altar of the little White Church in Shilo.

The Yellow Rose of Texas shall be mine forevermore!

That taunt fueled a burning desire to live through tonight and pluck Rose, thorns and all.

Mine forevermore… he swore to it, invoking his own personal pantheon of Body, Mind, and Spirit: Musashi, Travis, and El Santo. *Discipline. Attitude. Belief.* He glanced in the mirror once more, studying his own face. A scar blazed a trail across his skull, announcing bodily battles won; a gleam in the glittering brown eyes reflected the striving of his mind to stay human despite inhumanity—

A snarl and the glint of stout ivory fangs revealed his untamed Spirit within.

He wondered if his Mask would frighten Rose. *It can't be any scarier than my true face.* Pulling on the Mask, the Watcher prepared to fight Monsters, without and within.

———◆———

Pulling down his broad-brimmed felt hat to hide his face, Von Helm meandered through the streets of Pair'O'Dice. He stopped to listen to the sad country songs whining out the DragLine Windows, then tipped the gate attendant and walked into the Commons, ahead of the BrigadesMen who not-so-stealthily followed him from the Hotel.

Down the dirt streets of Purgatory he walked, the stomp of boots multiplied in the feet of the Survivors surrounding him. Each step echoed the heavy tread of men in a womanless world, their presence missing except in rare settings. Behind curtains, whispered about or admired from afar, women were now a novelty, and their absence from the streets of Purgatory intensified Von Helm's sorrow.

He frowned. He wanted their presence now; soft arms about his neck, soft words spoken, spiritual and physical comfort as only women could give…

But there were none for him.

The little Macho made his way to Purgatory Dock to sit among the clusters of Survivors smoking and drinking in the afternoon sun. Chucking a pebble into the lake, he watched the ripples spread far from the small rock that originated them. As the signal required, he threw another one in, the exact same spot. Grumbles came from the fishermen nearby, but Von Helm didn't care.

His heart was broken, and his soul was pure bitterness.

The only family he had ever truly loved, Camp Forlorn, was gone— and with it, his entire foundation in life. Living for the organization had brought him purpose and joy; now his purpose and joy were no more.

Kicking some rusted cans away, Von Helm lay back in the grass, watching the clouds dissolving into a spun-sugar sky. He wondered how long it would be before he too disappeared, leaving nothing behind.

In due time a lean figure sat down in the grass beside him, eyepatch in place and bottle in hand. "Care for a drink, my friend?" Michaels openly winked with his good eye at Von Helm, suggesting a more carnal reason for their conversation to the casual onlookers around them, then whispered. "I wasn't expecting to see you here…"

"Don't mind if I do." Von Helm took the bottle and took a long pull, then passed the bottle back. "Much obliged."

Michaels pushed a cork back into the bottle, then slipped the bottle into a large duffel bag he had slung across his shoulders. "Anything else?"

Holding out a budweed cigarette, Von Helm rolled towards Michaels, feigning intimacy as he whispered into Michaels ear. "Read me."

—urgent messig dont talk out loud DedZone down at Purgatore. Raven sez Jammers are to blame for the DedZones, and now they r off. Rings work. ALGOS mabbe inside walls, lookin 4 u no who. 4lorn attacked by ALGOS. All r ded. Girls escaped with crew. Im being tailed

Stunned, Michaels hid his face from view for a moment, then rolled the paper back. Producing a match, Von Helm struck it and lit the cigarette for the elegant Hombre lying on the ground next to him. Clenching it between his teeth, Michaels gave a convincing puff as he cast a glance towards the next contact.

Three bells rang out—time to put the drop in motion. Michaels stood, speaking loudly enough for those around him to hear: "So, you and me— how about it?" He jerked his head towards some bushes near the palisade, and picked up the heavy bag.

"Lead the way, Sailor…" Von Helm followed with a wink and a smile as both men disappeared into the bushes. Toeing aside a sleeping bag stashed in the branches, Michaels peered out to see Von Helm's accompanying BrigadesMen still hanging out near the boat dock. "Let's get this charade done—make it convincing."

A few rustles and grunts later, Michaels and Von Helm exited from the bushes, Michaels smoothing his fly and leering as he watched Von Helm walk back towards Pair'O'Dice once more, escorts in tow. Michaels walked away from the bushes, leaving the duffel bag behind as he headed back to the Dock-side park. Secret message cigarette still burning between his teeth, Michaels stubbed it out and pocketed it. He coughed, twice, then twice more…

On cue, a slight figure in a gimme cap and coveralls lurched towards the bushes from down by the inlet. Every so often, the figure stopped to take a drink from a bottle of what appeared to be Reunion brew, then resumed a convoluted path towards Michael's and Von Helm's bushy bower. A group loitering nearby heard the figure mumble: "I gotta pee." Forewarned, the onlookers vacated the area.

Michaels watched as the slight figure ducked into the bushes. When it emerged a moment later, it was carrying a very large bag, the sleeping bag wrapped around it to change the bag's appearance. The tall Hombre whispered to himself, "Just remember the entry code, Goins…"

Goins ducked into the drifts of trash surrounding the dump as Michaels waited, monitoring their surroundings. The open area and crowded venue made this drop dangerous… The minutes passed and with each minute, Michaels grew more antsy. Had Goins been accosted?

Out of the corner of his eye, he saw Goins swaggering up the street from the border of HighTown, a new hat and coat having been retrieved from the drop point. Thusly costumed, Goins headed back into the Commons campground in plain sight, supremely confident. Michaels waited a respectable time to deflect any suspicion, then followed suit.

A cocky Goins greeted him from atop the pear wagon. "Ha! Piece of cake."

Michaels grunted. "I gotta hand it to you, making the drop in broad daylight like that—you've got balls."

Goins grinned. "More balls than you'll ever have."

Weary, Michaels rolled his eyes. "Little Man Syndrome."

Goins leapt down from the wagon, bowed up. "Say that again to my face!"

"Lighten up, Goins," Michaels warned. "You're just constant, and it's getting on my nerves. You don't have to be ready to fight every minute of the day… "

"Yeah, I do. And you'll be glad of it tonight when the deal goes down."

Michaels groaned. "Look, Agent, I don't like you and you don't like me, but step back. We've got problems."

"Suck it up, Twink," Goins mocked. "We've all got problems."

A big hand grabbed Goins by the lapel of the coat; yanking in close, Michaels snarled, eyepatch to eye with the surprised Goins: "Listen here, you little punk; you call me Twink ever again, and I'll bust your ass below ground level. I'm Von Helm's Second in Command now, and I've got the authority. Understood, Specialist?"

"Whoa! Pardon me, your Highness, I thought you were just one of the boys." Goins threw up both hands. "When did this happen? Isn't Paymaster Clemson Von Helm's second?"

Grim, Michaels released Goins and reached into his coat pocket and pulled out the budweed cigarette to whisper. "Unroll and read it. It's from Von Helm."

Goins read slowly, gaping at the message, confidence replaced by fear. "Dead?" The hand holding the message shook. "The entire camp? What do we do now?"

Michaels pointed to the wagon next to them, with its crew playing cards around a smoldering fire.

"Pass the weed and spread the word."

———◆———

A double-tap knock on hatch was heard, then another. The signal was sounded. One final tap, and the Watcher and Winston waited until the retreating footsteps cleared away. From beneath the still-locked hatch, they heard the door to Bogie's hut close as the latch slid back into place, securing it.

Peering at the Gambler's note, Winston tapped the code into the twelve-button alpha-numeric keypad, then tried to open the hatch; he cursed, then tried again. "God, I had forgotten how much I hate these keypads…" Entering the code once more, he yanked on the hatch lever again. It didn't budge.

The Watcher grunted and pointed at himself. Winston stepped aside on the entry platform. "Just get it done." The Watcher tried to remember exactly how it was done—with no digital display and the buttons faded, the process was much harder.

Push to enter numerals, asterisk to enter letters, then one, two, or three quick pushes to enter the designated letters…

He tapped the pound sign to designate completion of the entry code, then pulled on the hatch. It still didn't open. The Watcher growled, then tried again, this time with a second between each character entry. Thumping the pound sign again, he pulled the hatch one more time—

It popped open. The Watcher breathed out a heavy sigh, then listened for any sound of intruders. Lifting the hatch lid, he eased one hand out to scoot the scrap of filthy carpet aside, then let his eyes wander the hut. The smell was still revolting, though not as powerful as it had been with Bogie's artificially enhanced coat hanging over the hatch.

A Hobo's duffel was lying next to the closed tin-panel door, wrapped in a faded plaid sleeping bag. Easing out, the Watcher quickly nabbed the bag and slipped back down into the tunnel.

"The hut is locked?" Winston asked, pulling the carpet back into place. The Watcher nodded, sliding to the bottom of the ladder. "Good enough."

They grabbed the candle lantern and walked back to the main room. The access panels into each node—tunnel, foyer, workroom, and living area—had been left open by the Gambler, so the parties could leave as needed. As they entered the living area, Sampson stretched and gave the seat back up to the Watcher.

"Report—People sleeping." Sampson pointed around the room at the piles of exhausted bodies, then jabbed at the sink where a strange, hunched figure was leaning against the counter in the dim electric glow. A paw waved back and forth, splashing in a stream of clear liquid.

"Chupacabra playing with water."

Winston frowned at the giant. "Don't let animals play in the kitchen."

Sampson frowned back. "I didn't 'let' him—Oskar turned the water on by himself, and I've just been watching the show. I don't got the heart to tell him no; he may never get the chance to play with automatic water again."

Glancing over with a vague sense of unease, the Watcher looked on as Oskar put his great paw into the water, allowing it to run through his long claws. Reaching over to the faucet, the young chupacabra waved his paw in front of the infrared beam, and the water turned off. The sparkling eyes blinked as he snuffled the red pinpoint light—and the water turned on again…

Winston gave the cub a hard look. "I don't care how smart he is, chupacabras still shouldn't be in the kitchen."

Grunting, the Watcher tapped his own chest, then walked up to the sink where Oskar played. Hearing his approach, the cub whined and started to back up. The Watcher patted Oskar's warty shoulder hump, then pointed to the water and waved his own hand to activate the tap. Water poured out; the Watcher then tapped the faucet twice up to trigger a squirt of soap from a dispenser hidden beside the faucet. Bubbles foamed up between his thick red fingers, and Oskar sniffed, fascinated. The Watcher patted the cub again and grunted, pointing at the sink.

Oskar's muzzle split into a wide toothy grin, tapping twice before swishing a padded palm under the soap dispenser in imitation of the Watcher. Chuckling, Sampson retorted to an astounded Winston. "See? He can be in the kitchen now, he washed his hands, er, paws." Oskar chortled, squishing bubbles between his bony appendages as his tail slithered behind him.

Leaving the delighted beast to play in the sink, the Watcher waved Sampson and Winston into the wrecked workroom. Awakening Wilcox to take over watch, Sampson followed the Marshal and the Constable.

Over in the corner, a husk of a dead ALGOS drone listed, abandoned on a worktable. Various shards of composites and alloys were flung around the room, testament to the earlier orgy of electronic violence. The Watcher noted someone had rifled through a trashcan where he had dumped the broken components. *Someone has an interest in tech...* he grunted to himself, *need to find out who has a talent for making things work.* Tossing the large duffel bag on a worktable, the Watcher proceeded to unwrap the sleeping bag, then unzipped a small pocket atop the bag as Winston and Sampson looked on.

First things first... The Watcher pulled out a pair of smelly undershirts, then retrieved a dirty sock from within that. Reaching into its grimy folds, he snagged a silver and garnet RingWorld and slipped it on his finger with a barely concealed joy. Activating it, he opened his HeadsUp display to see if he could find the Little Yellow Dot named Rose, but the thick metal walls of the Bunker thwarted any outside signal.

Disappointed, he pointed to Winston's Ring: "Oh, right—we're protected from the Jammers in here." The Constable activated and opened his own HeadsUp display. "Sorry, it's been so long since I've used one regularly..."

The Watcher messaged Winston:

#WATCHER: I'm back. Text Ring-2-Ring to avoid any scanners.

No answer. He messaged again, but to no avail—*Ah, the DDT...* he had forgotten the Gambler's homemade jammer was interfering with his own Ring's signal. Frowning, he held out his hand and pointed again to Winston's Ring finger.

"Aw, he wants to hold hands with you." Sampson smirked. Winston groaned, but held out his hand to link with Azarian. The Watcher pressed his WeSpeex Ring's "decorative stone" uplink tang into Winston's input portal, located on the palm of this own Ring.

#WATCHER: The Gambler rigged a makeshift limited-scope signal jammer from salvaged drone components to hide my nano-sig from the ALGOS. He called it a Digital Deception Transmitter, or DDT for short. It's interfering with transmission, so I'm going to deactivate it until we go up for the fights. When the DDT is activated, I will have to direct link to other users through their Rings, or their remaining Neural Portals if those are still functional.

Puzzled, Winston opened his messaging app:

#WINSTON: You have a nano-sig?

Grunting affirmatively, the Watcher grabbed his bandana slide to push the decorative bioprint reader with a thick thumb, deactivating the portable jammer;

#WATCHER: I earned it.

Winston nodded.

#WATCHER: Outside the bunker, I'll have to keep my nano-sig cloaked. ALGOS are searching for my nano-sig and deploying TIRS to identify me so I can be tracked and possibly lead them to Rose.

"TIRS? You mean the Telometrix Instant Recognition System? They still have that capability?" Winston grumbled at the thought.

#WATCHER: Yes—the Gambler's "DDT' gadget can theoretically help thwart it, but that means I'll have to link directly with a Ring Wearer to message anyone on the team—the DDT is masking my ring signal as well, unless I have a hardwired connection. Who has Rings on this team?

"A few select rank-and-file positions have a one—but anyone in Leadership should have a Ring."

#WATCHER: Leadership—you mean anyone with ties to the Consortium?

Eyes wary, Winston motioned to the outer room with its UnEnlightened listeners.

#WINSTON: Some. Keep this discussion private.

#WATCHER: Fine. Tell me everything you know about the Purgatory DeadZone. Dominic mentioned an "electronics window"…

Winston leaned back, opening a shared display:

#WINSTON: The Electronics Window is a classified event: it happens at 7AM every day. I have no other information about it except it lasts fifteen minutes. During that period, it's possible to start electrical and digital equipment.

#WATCHER: So we've missed the window—but that info may come in handy at a later date. Now, tell me about the Catastronix Jammer.

Chafed by the Watcher's lack of deference, a flicker of resentment spun up in Winston. Then he remembered the Watcher's meteoric rise to power and his Leadership Battle with himself and Von Helm at Camp Forlorn; reluctantly, the Constable reined in his resentment.

#WINSTON: Old Diego was the one who told me about it; he couldn't remember any details other than how to maintain it and that it was separate from the main Jammer. I've never been able to find a manual for it; it doesn't appear in any of my literature, and it may have been an experimental device at the time of the Happening.

#WATCHER: Who's Old Diego?

#WINSTON: Old Diego was the original Boss of Purgatory, assigned here by the "Family Back Home" after they established themselves. Family Back Home is code for the Consortium.

#WATCHER: So, what happened to Old Diego?

Winston's usual blunt demeanor became guarded:

#WINSTON: He had a heart attack not long after I arrived.

The Watcher snorted to himself. Untimely demises at the top level seemed to occur with some frequency whenever replacements showed up.

#WATCHER: I'm sure he died peacefully in his sleep.

Wary, the Constable scratched his craggy chin: the Watcher couldn't help but notice that as an Hombre, Winston looked more human. His skin was relatively smooth compared to the virally inflamed skin of testosterone-mutated Machos like the Watcher. He wondered if Rose thought of Winston as more human…

It bothered him that it bothered him. The Watcher scowled and cracked his massive armored knuckles just to enjoy the feeling of being Macho.

#WINSTON: Well Marshal, since we're asking sensitive questions, as a member of the Council I have one for you. How'd you get your hands on a working Ring? There's been a lot of speculation among Council Members. The only way anyone gets a working Ring is through the Consortium; they have exclusive access to the only stash of functioning WeSpeex Rings available in the Co-op. They alone decides who gets Rings.

The Watcher grunted brusquely.

#WATCHER: You tell me how Boss Diego died, and I'll tell you how I got my Ring.

Winston acknowledged with a nod.

#WINSTON: Let's do a little info trading. We need to work together if we're going to get this job done right.

With his feet propped up on the desk, Winston leaned back in the desk chair, hands laced behind his head. The Watcher caught a glimpse of Winston as he had been in life before—a dynamic, up-and-coming Chief Executive Officer, a blue-blood turned populist commander of construction crews and design teams. With his pedigree and easy charm, Visionary Leadership probably had Winston slated early for the Politics Team.

#WINSTON: The Quality Control Team sent word to the Family Back Home—old Diego was declining mentally. Dementia had set in, and he needed to be replaced before he spilled any secrets to the wrong people.

#WATCHER: And who is Quality Control?

#WINSTON: Habib and Ellison. They were a team, long ago, but by the time I showed up Sam had moved on with Mansour, my foreman. They still act as double agents for the Consortium, sending in reports from time to time.

#WATCHER: How did Diego die?

Reflective, Winston looked at the ceiling.

#WINSTON: Humanely.

The Watcher grunted. *Spoken like a true Visionary.*

#WINSTON: I asked for the assignment because Purgatory was so full of promise—a real City, and real progress to be made. The Family considered the arrangement to be mutually beneficial; the

Family wanted me because they had reason to believe some Bosses were compromised.

#WATCHER: Compromised how?

#WINSTON: By reaching beyond the borders of the Tejas Co-operative. The Family is isolationist, and other than approved contacts for exports, they will punish any attempt to make alliances outside the Co-op. They believe it will lead to intervention from Insiders.

#WATCHER: They were right. So why did they choose you?

#WINSTON: The Family believes I am loyal to the Family.

Calculating, the Watcher studied Calvin Trung Winston.

#WATCHER: So why aren't you?

The Constable steepled his fingers, weighing his words carefully:

#WINSTON: I am. I just expanded my Family to include the Damned as well as the Fallen.

Scar twitching, the Watcher assessed Winston's words carefully. "The Damned and the Fallen" were terms used by smooth-skinned "Insiders" to describe "Outlaws"—those Survivors left outside the shelters to be TransMutated by the Happening's virus. "The Damned" was the Insider epithet for "UnEnlightened" Feral Humans who survived, and "the Fallen" was their term for the "Enlightened" Visionaries who were shut out when the Kali Yuga Satellite spread its infectious bioagent across the world.

He made an internal note: *Winston knows more about the "World Out There" than he's letting on.*

#WATCHER: So you no longer consider yourself to be a "Fallen" Angel amidst the Damned?

#WINSTON: It doesn't matter anymore. We're all Survivors now.

The Watcher snorted: *it all makes sense.*

#WATCHER: So Dominic got to you, too...

Surprised at the correlation, Winston gave a soft chuckle.

#WINSTON: You're right—it sounds like something he would say.

The Watcher grunted accusingly.

#WATCHER: And yet you kept the Jammer secret from Dominic.

Winston bristled, defensive.

#WINSTON: I have a reason to keep secrets. You win my trust and I'll share those reasons. Now, you—how did you get your Ring?

#WATCHER: I took it. It was dangerous to Rose, and I had need of it. So for her safety, I confiscated it, then hacked it.

Confused, Winston wondered:

#WINSTON: You didn't have it all along? But how did you speak without it? Everyone knows the Watcher of Reunion doesn't speak. Dominic told me your communications challenges; he said the virus affected your tongue and larynx almost fifty years ago. How did you communicate with everyone if you didn't have a Ring?

#WATCHER: I didn't.

Sobered by the thought of a half-century of silence, Winston looked with a mixture of pity and wonder at the Watcher.

#WATCHER: Don't feel sorry for me. Feel sorry for everyone who never learned to write or read script—if it hadn't been for my notepad and pencils I could never have connected with anyone, period. But even then, readers who could decipher handwriting were few and far between.

Winston nodded; most people had never learned to write or read without assistive technology. An inquisitive gleam appeared in his dark eyes:

#WINSTON: So the Afterling can read your script? I hadn't expected that. She seems to be quite the enigma.. so what's the status between you two, if you don't mind me asking?

The Watcher gave the Constable a sharp glance.

#WATCHER: Same as you and Araceli, except I know my weakness. You might ought to make peace with your own.

Irritated at this turn, Winston grumbled, suddenly making himself busy with weaponry.

Equally irritable at the personal questions, the Watcher resumed unpacking; he pulled his electrostatic gloves back into place, then rifled through the body of the duffel bag. Even though it had been guarded and safely locked in the hold of the WildLand Smuggler Wagon, he was wary about leaving it behind. It had been so long since he had valuables to safeguard, or people to trust with them…

It's all there. His golden horn was still rolled up, padded in a shirt; *good —one never knows when one might need a bugle, especially when one can't communicate.* It was his main form of communication when he was a prisoner at the gates of Reunion Camp; with it, he had been able to alert the guards to dangers at the gate. Now, he would use it to lead followers to freedom...

He felt rush of relief at seeing his weapons; the Energy Rifle, Energy Pistols, and Power Bracelets were in the bag, ready for use, along with all his other weapons of choice, but it was the Mossberg Mariner and Remington V3 Tac-13 Shotguns that beckoned to him the most.

He drew out a large bundle and messaged Winston again:

#WATCHER: Tell Sampson here's his disguise. Get him put together, just like we discussed; it's time dangle him out there to lure some big fish.

Winston relayed the information to an eager Sampson while the Watcher continued to search his own bag.

Checking the side pockets, the Watcher withdrew a note marked with a heart and squiggly flourishes. He tucked it neatly into his pocket to read later, then drew forth a fat cigar of budweed, with a small arrow faintly inscribed on the end.

The Watcher scowled at the decadent item.

"Oh, that's the message. We hide them that way, because if they are ever found, they'll be burned by the finder before they ever think to look inside." Sampson took it from the Watcher and expertly picked it open to reveal a note. "You read—it takes me too long to decipher script." Sampson demurred, handing it back to the Watcher. Dumping the buds in the trash, the Watcher read the small, slanting script:

> *—The party started early. ALl-Good Orb Singers inside now; the Bigguns let their guard down. Ring it in on 145 when you come topside. Look in your heart—G*

Grimacing, the Watcher passed the note to Winston.

"This part I get—Ring Channel 145 will be our frequency for further instruction." The tall man looked up with an air of disbelief. "They let their guard down? ALl-Good Orb Singers... ALGOS?" Winston handed the note back. "The Bosses shut down the Jammers, and the ALGOS are inside Purgatory!"

The Watcher slapped the desk, frustrated. Winston rubbed his chest, the familiar twinge of angina intruding. "Great. Just great."

Distressed, Sampson shook his head. "This day never ends, does it?"

#WATCHER: We'll come up with a plan.

"Yeah, we have to, or we're dead," Winston grumbled. At this statement the Watcher jerked a thumb towards the door.

#WATCHER: Go update the group about the ALGOS. Don't gloss it over, but tell them we'll have a workaround by tonight. Give me a minute alone—I need to think.

Sampson and Winston shuffled out, weighed down by the news.

Think...

The Watcher strode over to the dead ALGOS drone on the work table. Grabbing a chair, he turned it around to straddle it with his arms flung over the back. He propped his chin against his bulky forearm and stared intensely at the dismantled drone, hoping it would reveal a workaround.

The drone just lay there.

He sighed, and picked it up, studying the ALGOS from all angles, but nothing new presented itself. Any discouragement the Watcher felt was overwhelmed by his aggravation at the defeatist attitudes around him. He wished his Afterling Morale Officer was here to stump them all with her inordinate cheeriness. Defeatism was never a problem with Rose, at least not when it mattered most; her inexplicable optimism in the face of overwhelming odds was an extraordinary gift, and a necessary one if the Revolution were to survive. The Watcher found himself needing her, and it bothered him.

He hated to need anyone. He had his reasons; the Firm reiterated what personal experience had already taught taught him—*needing anyone is a one-way ticket to emotional hell*. Emotional Hell was a place the Watcher had already visited, and he had no intention of ever going back...

***

His first visit to emotional hell was a direct result of needing someone —in this case, his murdered Mother. His need for her resulted in a meltdown so monumental it literally created hell on earth not only for himself, but for everyone else around him. The Justice System intervened, but even they couldn't stop Saul's descent.

Following Saul's brief but destructive incarceration at the Maximum Intervention Lockdown Facility, word of his skills and resourcefulness caught the attention of watchful eyes. In response, a referral was submitted for Saul to enter an exclusive program open only to a few select candidates. The Firm—aka CognitoINCognito Inc, aka WeSpeex—offered a unique solution to Saul's misery:

Rather that try to stop his transformation, they would empower him and themselves through it.

Saul's name was submitted to WeSpeex's charitable foundation, run through their shell corporation at CognitoINCognito Inc. A few days later, an acceptance notification came from the Visions Youth Services Independent Academy, aka VYSIA.

The Firm took in the boy who retributively executed both his Mother's Murderer and her Pimp—his Father and Step Father. The sad orphan was welcomed with eager anticipation by the Visionary Staff at the VYSIA Texas Campus in DownTown Dallas. Tailored curriculums were written for the gifted young Socio-Automanaut—

That's what they called young Saul, since Sociopath was considered to be an ugly word. But "highly functional Sociopath" was the most accurate description for the homicidal boy who took the stand in his own defense:

"Some men just need killin'."

No matter; whether they called free-thinking rule-breakers Sociopaths or Socio-Automanauts, Saul possessed that preferred psychosocial condition for candidates of the Firm. And the Firm was willing to invest heavily in young candidates like Saul:

Martial Arts Lessons, Psychology, Anatomy and Physiology Courses, Classical Literature Reviews, and Applied Physics were interspersed with trips to Gun Ranges, Summer Survival Camps, and Youth Leadership Seminars…

Following in-depth analysis of the young killer, Saul's Prime Mentor chose Miyamoto Musashi's *Dokkodo* as the behavioral template for his protege. Ikeda's 1965 translation of *The Way I Go By Myself* was drilled into the young boy's head each morning, the linchpin being the first tenet:

1) I never act contrary to traditional morality.

Later translations softened the phrase to make it more palatable to sensitive minds:

Accept everything just the way it is—

But Professor Ikeda's translation was explicit. There was such a thing as Authority…

That Authority was the WeSpeex Vision of Ages, known to inner circles as "the System"—a construct designed to bring world peace through Enlightened Leadership. In this framework, the System was presented as the new "traditional morality"—a world unified by any means necessary. Javier Generales' star-shaped Mandala for the "Eight Points for World Peace" became the System's "Maker's Mark"—the sign of Enlightenment:

One World—One Way—One Vision—One Voice—One Law—One Land—One People—One Plan

Under the System, the means of achieving this Enlightenment were not important; the End of UnEnlightenment justified the means. Of course, the System's One-World Morality demanded that all other moralities be deconstructed to serve itself. Since the only morality lay in destroying old ways of morality, the Authority of the System was easy to sell to Socio-Automanauts; the System allowed them to destroy all other systems.

Beyond the System, no morality existed.

Thus guided, Saul blossomed into a useful and unique young man. His Mentors said it with great pride: Saul's aptitude tests indicated he was an ideal recruit for the Firm's exclusive Private Secret Service Team—only known to the chosen few by the acronym B.E.S.T. Saul's name was added to the wait list, and he continued to train while he waited.

But just because Saul was a Student at VYSIA did not mean Saul would ever become a member of the Firm. Candidates had to keep moving forward on the approved paths of success, or die trying; if Students gave the Firm everything it wanted, the Firm would give its Students everything they desired.

With that kind of reward system in place, Saul graduated from the Firm's private college—with Honors.

His independent course of study led to a self-crafted Bachelor of Arts Degree in... well, he wasn't exactly sure, but the Firm endorsed it. Saul's thesis was a multi-media presentation of Gung Fu choreographed to the music of Holst's "Mars: God of War". It was accompanied by a spoken-word poetic dissertation titled: entitled: "Life into Death: The Case for Extra-Legal Execution". Culminating with a demonstration of Lee's "Death Punch" on a live subject, it was a rousing success. Saul was accepted into the Visionaries' post-graduate "Visions of Tomorrow"

Program, where students had to exceed all expectations if they were to graduate and qualify for Internship—

Saul had done just that; he had exceeded all expectations. Ascended as an Intern for the B.E.S.T., Saul was a lethal, evasive, and sociopathic killer, trained to protect high-value interests and destroy men who need killing.

Lana liked that in a man. He could still hear Lana's sultry voice luring him to his doom:

"I need you, Saul. The Firm needs you." Ruby liquid trickled over the rim of the wineglass as the red-headed Recruiter poured another round. "We've had our eye on you from the very beginning, and now all your hard work and training has brought you here. You have the toolset, you have the skillset, but more importantly, you have the mindset; no one else can do what you do. Quite simply, you are the best of the B.E.S.T." Her fingers lingered as she handed him the wineglass, leaning in: "Now, let's talk about what the Firm can offer you…"

Later that evening, the Recruiter made it clear: Saul's intelligence, unique psychological profile, and physical skills made him the perfect candidate for the Firm's improved surveillance drone program. The fabled InfoMachiNations Research and Development team had been studying Saul as a subject, even before he was anonymously referred.

Due to his unique case history and abilities, Saul was specially chosen to help with a new research study to improve predictive algorithmic social enforcement. Special studies were made of famous cases, and unique subjects were brought in for analysis and integration into the information matrix. The Recruiter told him it would be like any other study in which he had participated from his youth; just hook up to the injector, let the cortical-neural download complete, then activate the Training Rhobiots And ALGOS Cortico-Kinetics Research study—TRAACKR.

Somehow, the Recruiter made this all sound like a great idea. Perhaps it was her long red hair, or her long tanned legs, but she convinced Saul that this was an open path to an easy success with The Firm. She explained that after the download completed, Saul would become a dual beta-tester, allowing researchers to access his biometric and neural data, real-time, and evaluate the performance of WeSpeex latest experimental neuroenhancement suite, RhoBiotix.

Through the TRAACKR study, RhoBiotix's self-teaching nanobots would help Saul train InfoMachiNation's latest generation of social enforcement drones: Aerial Lethal Global Orthogonic Searchers, or ALGOS for short. And the red-headed Recruiter promised Saul that if he became part of the Research Team, she would personally be the one to update his hardware—regularly.

Naturally, Saul signed up.

The drone the Recruiter brought to the private lab that first day was a glittering jewel in a pristine universe, untouched by soil and hard use, fresh from the hidden laboratories of InfoMachiNations—a wholly owned subsidiary of WeSpeex Inc. Developers of social surveillance tech for the Whole Earth Union and their subscribers, InfoMachiNations would providing highly classified samples of their latest innovations to CognitoINCognito Inc., and RhoBiotix would develop the complimentary nano-tech to help provide data and feedback for this new project, cheerily titled "Social ImagEngineering". As one of only five participants in this research study, Saul had the introductory presentation indelibly etched in his mind, thanks to the fascinating presence of the red-headed Recruiter:

> *CognitoINCognito presents: Social ImagEngineering! Brought to you by our partners: RhoBiotix—Little Bots, Big Ideas!—and InfoMachiNations—See The World!*

The Recruiter made it sound simple enough: to finally become a full Visionary with the Firm—and finally rank up as a paid Agent of B.E.S.T —all Saul had to do was teach these machines how to find and eliminate dangerous people like himself…

But even Lana could never have anticipated what Saul was going to teach the ALGOS.

Lana.

He never said goodbye that last day—it might have resulted in an emotional hell of its own. To be fair, saying goodbye to Lana probably would have resulted in her terminating more than just his contract. Lana was certainly a dangerous person, like himself…

◆———◆———◆

Hand upon the dead Drone, he snapped out of his reverie: *what would Lana have thought of Rose?* He was fairly certain Lana wouldn't have considered Rose dangerous at any level. *Rose certainly has her own amazing powers…* perhaps Lana would have thought Rose was dangerously cheery. *Cheery, just like her heart and squiggly flourishes…*

Curious, the Watcher picked up the Gambler's cigarette note and re-

read the last line. *Look in your heart...* Now alone, he fished the heart-inscribed note back out of his pocket and opened it; he was slightly disappointed to see the Gambler's same back-slanting script inside the note, instead of Rose's round cursive.

> —*Congratulations on your upcoming nuptials, Stud. Model WSU 8880-AP was hidden in the shoes, and now she thinks you popped the question. Good luck getting out of this one. Ask the Big L in tech for details, as this device may come in handy.*—*G*

Furrowing his brow, The Watcher scrutinized the note. *Device? Upcoming Nuptials?* Funny joke... *What's an WSU-8880-AP? And who is Big L?*

#WATCHER: Winston, bring yourself and your team in. I've got a question.

He turned over the note to see if there was anything from Rose, but found nothing except a piece of clear tape at the bottom... prying it up delicately, the Watcher found a narrow strip of thin paper, almost invisibly taped blank side up, hiding a faintly pencilled message in fat, curly letters. A tiny heart was etched at the end of the sentence:

> —*Im yur yello Rose*

Reflexively flashing his teeth in spontaneous triumph, the Watcher rubbed his thumb lightly across the pencilled letters.

Yes, you are—and you have thorns.

The Watcher recalled his message to her—*"I'm your Santa Anna."* The exchange between them was a reminder to her of their moment at the Altar, and a warning to himself of the same thing; *never again get caught with your pants down.* Next time, he would be in full command.

The Watcher swiftly rolled the little slip of paper around the stem of the SweetGum ball still residing in his pocket, securing it with the still-attached tape. He popped it back into the duffle bag along with her other memorabilia, a museum of Rose memories.

"What'd it say?" Sampson asked, nosy. The Watcher gave him a cold look. "Oh, it's private. Sorry..."

Texting Winston, the Watcher queried:

#WATCHER: Who or what is the "Big L in Tech"?

Winston shook his head... "Sampson—do you have an idea about who's 'Big L in Tech'?"

Laying out his disguise, Sampson jerked a thumb back towards the main room, towards the lanky Hombre taking guard: "That'd be Lance Wilcox."

#WATCHER: I need to do due diligence before I talk to this guy—this is top level info, and I need to know he won't abuse access. I only have a casual acquaintance. What do you know about him?

#WINSTON: Not much. But Joey is his partner—he could give you a recommendation.

Looking in the other room, Winston waved in Joey. Rubbing his eyes, the hefty Macho shuffled into the workroom. "What did you need, Constable?"

"Marshal Azarian has questions about Wilcox, but I've been Municipal too long, and my beams didn't cross with the Tunnel crew for security reasons. We're going to show you how to link up to hear him on his Ring, and you can tell him what you know about this guy..."

"Oh, sure I guess. But I haven't had a Ring in so long—are you sure this will work?" Joey stuck out his hand gamely as Winston checked the base of his left Ring finger.

"Hang on"... Winston whipped out his Swiss Army Knife and thumbed open a small blade to wipe it with a cleaning cloth. Joey winced slightly as the tall Hombre used the small blade to scrape back a callous which had grown over the Agent's long-unaccessed neural port.

"You gonna give me a manicure next?" Joey quipped.

Winston chuckled. "It wouldn't hurt any of us to get spiffed up a little once in a while, but no."

Taking Joey's hand, the Watcher pressed his RingStone into Joey's currently Ringless Neural Portal. Blinking in surprise at the activation of his long-dormant HeadsUp display, Joey jumped as it temporarily blinded him. An avatar of an earnest-looking young cop popped up, strong jaw, dark eyes smiling. Seeing the Watcher's sophisticated, suit-wearing avatar, Joey blurted: "Wow, so that's you? You look... different."

#WATCHER: We all do.

"Oh, right. I'm sorry Marshal."

#WATCHER: This is how we will communicate topside. Get used to it and practice messaging so we can get things done. Now, what do you know about Wilcox?"

#MANCINI: He's a good guy, cynical, kind of a loner, but will do anything to help out. Works with Sam a lot to keep her Tech moving—he's also been my partner for the last fifteen years or so.

#WATCHER: Do you trust him?

#MANCINI: I'd trust him with my life.

#WATCHER: Good enough. Call Wilcox in.

Joey hemmed and hawwed.

#MANCINI: Wait—Marshal, you said you had a picture of this girl on your Ring? Rose's sister Amelia—the one that needs rescue?

#WATCHER: Fine. Take a brief look at your objective. I think you'll find it motivating. But until you get your own Ring to save the file, you'll have to wait for your own copy.

The Watcher opened a holograph from Rose's family album, a picture of a taller, thinner version of Rose, minus the lopsided grin. Amelia's more reserved nature was displayed in a shy smile, and an air of perfection made obvious by the accountant's neatly braided tresses, coiled high upon her head. It was getting easier for the Watcher to distinguish Rose from her clone sisters: Rose was shorter, sassier, and definitely had more bounce to the ounce.

Joey studied Amelia's slender figure in pink homespun, rotating the image to memorize her smooth, golden skin and dark, glimmering eyes. The stout Macho zoomed in on the lovely face, and the Watcher heard him whisper softly under his breath:

"Amelia…"

The Watcher waited a few seconds, then patted the heavy shoulder as he shut off access.

#WATCHER: That'll be all for now; take guard and bring in Wilcox. Relay info for me—

"Will do—what do you need?"

#WATCHER: Ask him to put on a Ring if he's got one, and report to Winston.

"Sure thing, Marshal." Joey took off around the corner, humming to himself, step lighter and eyes brighter. Wilcox entered from the break room.

"You need me for something, Constable?"

Busy sorting through electrical components, Winston held up a hand: "Yes—do you have your Ring?"

"Sure—it's available, as long as we're cleared for this location."

"Go ahead. The Jammers can't penetrate the Bunker walls, so scanners should be blocked as well. Just keep it Ring-2-Ring for security purposes." Winston instructed. "The Marshal will brief you. While you are discussing this, I'm going to step out to help Sampson set up and arrange his crew."

Reaching a long finger into his jean's watch pocket, Wilcox slipped on a silver and gold ring and activated it. The Watcher opened dialogue to see the Avatar of a neatly trimmed, smiling blond man, his arms around a brown-eyed girl. It still seemed strange to see the distant, private lives of happy men juxtaposed against the harsh reality of the present.

#WATCHER: Thank you, Wilcox. I need some information regarding a piece of tech found by an associate. What's an WSU-8880-AP, and why would it come in handy?

The tall, silver-skinned Hombre sat down at the work table, searching his own database. "I think you mean WSRW…"

#WATCHER: No, the message clearly states WSU. WSRW is known to me, a WeSpeex RingWorld, and I already searched the model numbers in my local WS catalogue. It's not there.

"Nope, and you're not going to see it there—it doesn't show up in the catalogue for proles. You were never meant to see a WSU, and if you ever did, good job, you found the holy grail of WeSpeex products." A holographic schematic diagram of what appeared to be an ancient-style ring popped up in The Watcher's display: Wilcox rotated it to remove layers into an exploded schematic view:

"The Company sent us out with orders to confiscate all WeSpeex One or variants of that model, and immediately throw them into our EZ-Recycler if we ever found any. They were unauthorized for use. This particular model though, was a real rarity—they're distinguished by their shape, and the san-serif clean-font version of the WeSpeex logo imprinted on the inside. In my fourteen years in Residential And Transportation Tech Support, I never once saw one of these. I'm pretty sure the model number in your message is misspelled."

#WATCHER: I don't think so. The Gambler is the one who sent the message; this is his bunker, and he knows a lot about the Company. He even jury-rigged this personal jammer for me, from scavenged drone parts.

"We'd heard rumors there were killer surveillance drones like this, before the Happening, but nobody knew for sure what they looked like or even if they were anything beyond Research and Development." Wilcox leaned in with interest as the Watcher removed his Digital Deception Transmitter from the bandana around his neck and laid it on the table. "That's some pretty hardcore home-brew. I had no idea the Gambler had it in him; he never struck me as a tech guy."

#WATCHER: I don't think he's a tech guy—I think he's a spook, probably human intel.

Turning the DDT over in his hands, Wilcox studied it. "So the Gambler says he found a model WSU?" He handed it back to The Watcher, who immediately threaded it onto his red bandana, replacing it around his neck.

#WATCHER: He said I'm supposed to ask you about it for more info, as it might be handy.

Wilcox puffed out his cheeks, trying to wrap his head around everything. "Okay, let's just pretend it's possible you found one of these unicorns, so we can get this out of the way. What you see here is the last design of a dying product line: WSU is the designator for the WeSpeex U —'U' meaning WeSpeex 'University'."

Wilcox rotated the view of the schematic to top down.

"It was the first WeSpeex designed for the youth market, intended to reach a younger, more impressionable audience—and it was the last generation of WeSpeex ONE, the original WeSpeex and all its permutations. Founder and Inventor Javier Generales built the WeSpeex Empire around WeSpeex ONE, and for twenty years, that was pretty much all they made. It wasn't until the Twentieth Anniversary that James Generales took over at the company and introduced the design we still use now—the WeSpeex RingWorld."

To the Watcher's eye, the Ring seemed an ancient artifact, tapered and fitted like like the purposeless, decorative rings from previous eras. Such rings weren't part of his own experience; he vaguely remembered his Mother's old Ring, but it was a WeSpeex One, a pedestrian entry-level model for the masses with a purple glass "stone"…

Reaching up to rotate the holo-graph, the Watcher felt an eerie chill; this obsolete tech was hidden in the Child's gift to Rose? *Why?*

Wilcox continued: "The reason CEO James Generales revoked all authorization of the WeSpeex One—including it's WeSpeex U variant— was because all versions of the old WeSpeex rings had a speaker and a small holo-projector. Content could be freely created and shared with other non-customers who didn't have the ring. In order to enforce subscription compliance for customers and non-customers alike, James Generales designed the RingWorld—a device with no externally visible or audible interface."

The Watcher grunted, deep in thought. This obsolete WeSpeex Ring could share visual and audio interfaces… useful functions for those who needed to communicate with a large, luddite audience.

"On the new version of the RingWorld, content could only be shared via subscriptions on neural networks and filtered through servers through the RingWorld's proprietary Neural Ports. Since the WeSpeex Social Verification System was now required for identification and social scoring for all government, business, and private use, users had no choice but to update to the new RingWorld System."

#WATCHER: And this was twenty-three years before the Happening, correct?

"Yes. But some users still refused to update from their WeSpeex One devices, and that meant the Company had to forcibly render the old Rings obsolete. WeSpeex ONE servers were discontinued, as new RingWorlds used a completely different network and proprietary network protocols. This meant in order to access any old content, or share any new content, or make any communications, all users were forced to go through a new filter-server using the new device—a proprietary WeSpeex RingWorld."

The Tech Man became animated, happy to delve into long-dead subjects: "To ensure complete compliance, the last 'update' of WeSpeex U and WeSpeex One uploaded a location beacon for new servers to pick up and malware to deactivate the obsolete rings. Users were given a free RingWorld if they turned in their earlier, now defunct versions of WeSpeex products, which were promptly destroyed to stop their use. But there were still some hangers-on to the old product; to encourage compliance, WeSpeex forced a mandatory recall of all older Rings for 'security issues', then destroyed the remaining stock. This was fairly simple, since all 'updated' WeSpeex devices were location tracked, even when off."

Wilcox closed the holo-graph. "The only way a WeSpeex U could have possibly escaped destruction was if it was a new ring out of company hands, never activated or registered, and that would be improbable. Why buy a ring for your child and never activate it?"

Reaching into his bag, the Watcher pulled out a note and a small, cream-colored invitation. He handed it to Wilcox.

#WATCHER: The Ring was never activated, because the

recipient died before she could be given the Ring. It was hidden away in a memorial to her, never opened.

Fascinated, Wilcox read the tragic note, looking upon the bright face of a girl long years dead. "Quinceañera? Like the old Tejano tradition? Wow, what a throwback..." He flipped open a screen from a highly classified tech manual, but nothing was found. In a flash of inspiration, Wilcox accessed an archived Fan Page for WeSpeex Collectibles and Memorabilia. Excited, he accessed his search function: "Key words: WSU, University, Youth Market, Child, Latin America, Quinceañera, girls, demi-girls, pan-demi-girl-boys—"

A delicate ring flashed up on the display, rotating in all its gilded glory, a choice of stones and filigree combinations offered.

WESPEEX COLLECTIBLES CATALOGUE: WeSpeex U— WSU-8880AP—'LA PRINCESA':###

#Designed for femme-spectrum tweenagers, La Princesa was modeled as a whittled-down version of the popular "My First Wedding" series for young brides the world over. Notoriously, La Princesa was a spectacular marketing misstep for Javier Generales' fabled WeSpeex WunderWurx Design Team. Xirsettes of yesteryear found this pretty piece of finery too limited in capability; the locked-down "Loco Parentis" Kiddie-Protecc AI made social media bypass nearly impossible for the adventurous Latin-American tweens test audience. Only five hundred were produced, and only seventy-three were sold. The model was discontinued the next year with the introduction of the WeSpeex RingWorld.

##This model is unauthorized, so sale, possession, or distribution of this product is illegal.##

Wilcox cracked a smile. "Jackpot. That's why we couldn't find it; no dash in the last sequence."

The Watcher leaned in to touch the holographic ring rotating in his visual field. *My First Wedding... so this is what the Child wanted? A pretty little Ring for her pretty little Mother?* A fear possessed him—*what if she put it on her pretty little hand?*

Cold sweat beaded his brow. *So that's what the Gambler meant by "upcoming nuptials."* Beyond the obvious danger of Rose's nanobots broadcasting her location, there was an additional risk—what would happen when Rose discovered the Watcher never meant to give her the Ring in the first place?

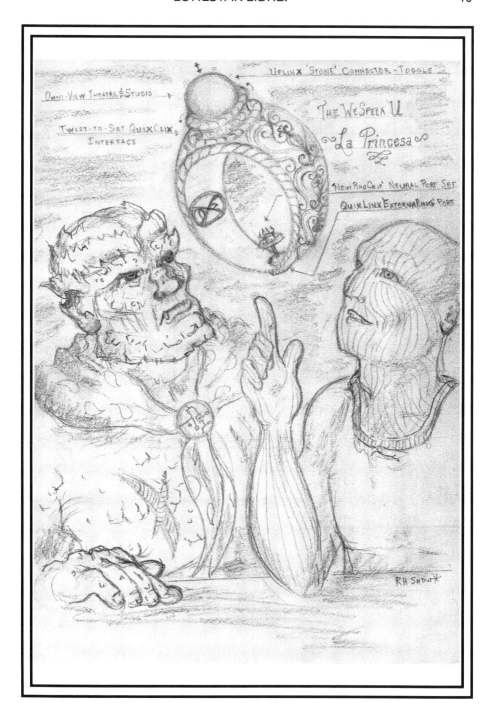

Nothing's going to happen, because she's not going to find out. That took care of that problem. Still, the thought irked him immensely. The Child had finagled an Arrangement for her Mother, with the Watcher as an unwitting Arranger. He didn't know whether to be mad or proud of his manipulative little phantom…

He scowled and opened the Ring's schematic again.

#WATCHER: Is there any chance this ring could be hacked by outside sources?

"Not without a compatible server—and they no longer exist. A hacker would need to direct link, and even then, they would have to know the access code."

#WATCHER: And what would that be?

Wilcox grunted. "The access code for the new Rings was kept classified, but for a Ring this old? It should be same factory default as all the old WeSpeexONE Rings—'ID10Tpr00f!'…"

The Watcher chuckled and made a note.

#WATCHER: With speakers and a projector, this Ring's primary advantage is the ability to communicate visuals and audio with a large, non-Ring audience. Could I use it?

The Tech Man shook his head. "This ring was adjustably sized for children and youth and lacks the newer Expando-Extreme feature, so it would be outgrown, forcing users to upgrade to the full-featured adult version. That means it will never fit it on your fat fingers. But you could possibly direct link in Legacy Mode. The stone should still uplink, since that capability was present even in the earliest Ring models."

#WATCHER: Very well, then. I have a proposition for you, Wilcox: be my IT Officer—the Revolution needs tech capabilities. You'd stay under the command of Winston, but you'd be on call to me at any time I need you. I'm willing to offer you access to any tech I find in exchange for whatever you can make for us—can you refurbish and restore tech?

"A job offer, huh?" Wilcox rubbed his bony chin. "In exchange for tools and tech? I can make some repairs if I have the right resources, but any of the rare stuff that survived the Happening is getting glitchy with age. We're going to be limited compared to anything like LifeBefore."

The Watcher laid it out:

#WATCHER: Limited tech is better than absent tech. But here you are, surrounded by one of the only protected caches of

"unlimited" working electronic equipment in the WildLands. What have you done with this opportunity?

Surprised at the impromptu job interview, Wilcox tried to figure out how to say it nicely: "I went through all the trash and pulled out everything good you threw away."

#WATCHER: That's exactly what I wanted to hear. Never let an opportunity go to waste.

The Watcher dumped the scavenged tech components out of his pockets; just as quickly, Wilcox scooped them up. "Where did you get these?"

#WATCHER: I scavenged that scanning device I demolished in the other room. I don't know what we can do with all these components, but maybe you do. Are you in?

Inventorying all of his choices, Wilcox acquiesced, reaching over to shake the Watcher's hand. "You've got it, Marshal Azarian." They closed the deal.

#WATCHER: Good. First order of business: get together with Winston and come up with a way to thwart the ALGOS. James' drones have invaded Purgatory and are now capable of identifying me or Rose at point blank range.

"You sure know how to ruin a guy's day…" Wilcox grumped.

#WATCHER: Second order of business: here's an EMP-hardened toolbox I acquired this morning—fill it up. Take this place apart, and salvage whatever you can to make repairs or rigs for other tech. Demolish the living area to find any stand-alone tech units; infrared motion detectors, electronic components, anything that could be used with a simple power source in non-jammed areas.

"Anything else?" The Tech Man began to load the components into the toolbox. The Watcher opened a cabinet and found a discarded tool set. He tossed it at Wilcox.

#WATCHER: Deadline is Nine O'Clock. Get Winston, and get busy. Dismissed.

"Ah, I knew there was something about working IT that I didn't miss—impossible deadlines and pushy clients." Wilcox sighed and went around the corner, leaving the Watcher alone with his thoughts.

The Watcher grunted appreciatively. *Time take my own advice and optimize this opportunity.*

He activated his HeadsUp display, taking advantage the VisualTrax app to interact with the device, hands-free. He chose a translucent pink heart icon in the upper right corner and aimed the palm-cam at the dead deathbot:

#WATCHER: Wake up, Talisa.
###ACTIVATING HELPER BOT###

Her warm voice murmured through his aural pathways, and her pink heart icon glowed as she awakened, pulsing in time with her voice:

#<3 SPEEXBOT: *Hello, I'm Talisa, your comfortingly calm SpeexBos Personna* **<3**

Her pleasant familiarity filled the Watcher with a sense of well-being. Since his first introduction to the RingWorld, he had preferred the Talisa persona for his personal digital assistant.

Wisely, the Watcher had never customized Talisa's icon beyond that of the glowing heart. He could have represented her as a fully rendered hologram of any imagined creature, but he declined. He didn't want to become a full-on digisexual: one of those digital Pygmalions who added SpeexBots to their Xirxes Preferred Sexual Partners Program. RingWorlds used SurroundStroke NeuralPlay technology via the Neural Port's NewRhoChip to make every digital interface a pathway to pleasure, with any virtual sexual partner a RingWorld user could imagine…

Even AI SpeexBots.

Not that there's anything wrong with that, the Watcher added with forcibly ingrained sensitivity. He himself had experimented from time to time with digisexuality, but found he preferred physical partners. Besides, his relationship to Talisa was definitely not romantic. His studies in psychology confirmed what he already figured out long ago: her gentle, knowing demeanor had become a maternal substitute for his murdered mother. *A "less likely to get murdered" mother,* he noted.

#WATCHER: Talisa, target and analyze this object: label it 'Aerial Lethal Global Orthogonic Searcher'—ALGOS. Add to your previous report. Do a full scan, match to known images, and merge data to include upgraded objects from previous scans.

#<3 TalisaBOT: *Right away, Saul. Last known scan of ALGOS completed fifty-five years ago—use that file?* **<3**

#WATCHER: Yes. Hold original image for comparison.

He set his WeSpeex RingWorld to "target", allowing the device to focus on each minute detail of the deactivated drone.

#<3 TalisaBOT: *Commencing scan…please hold.* **<3**

A millisecond passed, then the heart flashed, indicating Talisa had completed her task.

#WATCHER: Talisa, create a schematic for the Aerial Lethal Global Orthogonic Searcher.

#<3 TalisaBOT: *Of course, Saul <3*

#<3 TalisaBOT: *I took care to comb through your personal voice notes from the three days preceding the Happening. A wealth of information is available there. <3*

A small icon appeared below Talisa's heart in his HeadsUp display—a spinning silver gift package, her preferred method of presenting tasks ready to receive. He tapped it, and the schematic materialized. The Watcher exploded the view and rotated it, taking in information as quickly as he could.

#WATCHER: Perfect, Talisa. Go back to sleep.

The digital heart blushed a deeper shade of pink.

#<3 TalisaBOT: *I'm so glad you're back. Stay safe, Saul. <3*

The heart became translucent once more as Talisa returned to sleep mode. Manipulating the schematic, the Watcher took the ALGOS apart, then put it all back together, running scenarios. As he did, he played favorites from his soundtrack; Blind Lemon Jefferson's "Penitentiary Blues," Stevie Ray Vaughn's "Voodoo Child," and Wayne "The Train" Hancock's wailing ballad—"I Killed 'Em Both…"

Busy, he hummed along to the catchy tune, superior in his confidence in Rose's rejection of Von Helm. Not that he'd ever do violence against Rose… that seemed unthinkable to the Watcher, even in the face of infidelity. *But Von Helm?*

That was do-able.

Still, it was a moot point. He snorted; there was no chance for Von Helm now. After all, the Watcher had unwittingly "put a Ring on it"—and if nothing else, it made clear to all parties the Watcher meant business.

That hidden Ring, and the little hand now wearing it. He scowled briefly. It wasn't the idea of being formally bonded to Rose that bothered him; it was the idea that the Child had tricked him into doing it. The Watcher rubbed the back of his neck, fighting off a rising irritation. What was it with all these people and their constant pressure for him to make an obsolete Arrangement with this little clone woman?

Cranky and out of sorts, the Watcher self-calmed by organizing and packing the cache of goods purchased from the Emporium. Inventorying weaponry was always an excellent form of meditation.

Flipping through his playlist, the Watcher saw his last selection highlighted. Bob Will's "Deep in the Heart of Texas"… he remembered the tunnel, and his shared musical moment with Rose. The Watcher tapped the play button and let the memory fill him as he packed.

His hand fell at last to the yellow baby's blanket. He picked it up and ran it through his hands, a memory of another man's child… his memory turned to his own, and the phantom Child who had made it all possible. She was the tiny, unseen hand meddling in things a child shouldn't touch.

I know you're out there, you ephemeral little Trickster; we need to have a discussion about who's in charge here, and that's me.

In cheeky answer to his challenge, a cool breeze ruffled his hand, and his heart skipped a beat, as it always did when the Child was near—

Goosebumps tickled the back of his neck; fear mixed with wonder. He simply let the Child play at his side for a moment, flowing through his fingers, a dancing dust mote shimmering in the air. Dancing… the Child was dancing.

As Bob Will's fiddles soared through his aural pathways, the Watcher could feel the Child reveling in it, an unseen but palpable joy flitting on the edge of his consciousness. It seemed incongruous; on the eve of War, a Child danced… he could not recall the last time he danced for joy, even as a child. His own experience with childhood was traumatic, and his own experience with joy was limited to power and control.

But here was this sprite, flitting about in this Hell of a world, dancing for joy.

You really ought to be in Heaven with your Mother's butterflies… this world is not a good place for little girls.

The thought of the Child's lost soul wandering the WildLands, abandoned, alone, terrified the Watcher. But the idea that she might follow him was equally disconcerting… tonight would bring blood. Unable to endure that thought of the Child witnessing carnage by his own hand, the Watcher said what busy adults always said to him when they didn't wish little Sollie to see what they were doing:

Go to your Mother, Little One; tell her I will be along shortly.

Capricious, the Child lingered a moment more, cavorting as the fiddles faded before herself whispering away into the ether. Relief mingled with regret coursed through him; relief to be released once again from the supernatural, and a burgeoning regret that he had not been kinder to her somehow.

He blanched; the Child was becoming real to him.

The Watcher found it incredible that Rose herself had not mentioned ever seeing the Child—but perhaps Rose encountered her in other ways. He desperately wanted to ask the Afterling if she had ever experienced such a meeting, but was hesitant; in some ways, he was afraid that maybe it really all was in his head. But then how to explain the Child leading him to the Ring?

What was it the old Shopkeeper said at the Emporium this morning? *"Go on… she's waiting."*

There was no mistaking the Shopkeeper's meaning; this hallucinatory waif was intertwined with the Watcher's reality. It was one thing for the Child to remain in his mind, a wisp of whimsy—but the Child's not-so-subtle manipulation of this present world and its inhabitants was beginning to fray the Watcher's unravelling reality. Tucking the yellow blanket into his bag, the Watcher made a plan: before leaving Purgatory, he would make one more trip to the Emporium. He just had to know—*what did the Shopkeeper know of the Child?*

Perhaps an answer could be found down at the Emporium. He sighed, and rubbed his eyes.

If he hadn't been so overwhelmingly stressed, the Watcher might have enjoyed this quiet moment alone in the office. But the weight of war was heavy upon him, and he was beginning to feel it, a relentless burden—not that he might kill, but that others might be killed. The Watcher wondered who would die…

It can't be Rose. That was all.

He opened her song files and played back her voice, letting her emotion fill him once more. Once more, it flowed into him, and the Watcher knew—he was getting addicted to the dopamine rush of borrowed emotion from Rose:

> *There's a meadow in a valley where the skies are fair*
>
> *Even though I've never seen it, I know that it is there…*

Putting her voice on loop, he closed his eyes for fifteen minutes, and thought upon a single image, a Rose, endlessly opening, its swirling Fibonacci Mandala an eternal blossom of life….

Interrupting the Watcher's meditation, Sampson poked his head around the corner, Winston close behind: "We're ready, Marshal. What next?"

Seeing Sampson's earnest face reminded the Watcher that this gentle Giant might not survive the mission. It stung him—there was a reason he preferred working alone. He couldn't get attached to anyone; War would bring death.

The Watcher hailed Winston Ring-2-Ring:

#WATCHER: Tell the Decoy Team they have five minutes to make their goodbyes; I'll give them a final briefing at the entrance.

"Will do." Somber, Winston turned to Joey and Sampson. "Get your people together, and say your goodbyes to the ones you need to say them to…" Winston seemed to be wrestling with a decision. "We may never get another chance."

The Watcher mulled his own mortality. *War brings death.* Musashi's words were unflinching:

> *The Way of the Warrior is the resolute acceptance of Death.*

What if Death came for the Watcher? How would Rose say goodbye?

The Watcher hoped Rose would take the words of Omar Khayyam to heart and find a path in her memory, back to the place where he planted the Flower with the Child, beneath the Shining Sycamore Tree:

> *"When thyself with shining foot shall pass*
>
> *Among the Guests, Star-scatter'd on the grass*
>
> *And in thy joyous errand reach the spot*
>
> *Where I made one —*
>
> *Turn down an empty glass!"*

The thought pleased him greatly—a tearful, grateful Rose bidding him farewell, accompanied by Oskar, surrounded by the Flowers the Watcher had planted in the Child's garden. He imagined her letting go of a butterfly and it flying up to Heaven…

But what if Death came for Rose?

No.

He couldn't allow that. Death was for the Warrior, not for his Prize. The Watcher was now Rose's devilish Guardian Angel, her Watcher from on High; and as the Angel of her better nature's charms, he could not allow Rose to die. The thought of Rose dead was so inconceivable, so unthinkable—

Even if he was teetering on the edge of oblivion, the Watcher would never be able to let go. All those times she had fussed at him to let go—whether it was of her hair, or her hand, or any other part of her—he had always refused to release her, rightfully asserting his need to hold on just a little longer.

Let go… a shadow crossed his memory, Mother at the door, whisper-singing her final farewell to Saul.

"Sometimes love means letting go…"

Adamant, the Watcher decided then and there:

He could never let go.

"You're going now?"

"Yup. I might not come back, so if you need to tell me something, say it now or let it lie dead with me forever."

Kendra crossed her arms and scowled, peeved. "How come I didn't know about this?"

"The info was on a 'need to know' basis only."

"Well then, you don't 'need to know' what I need to tell you." She turned towards the wall.

"Tell me what?" the Giant asked placidly.

"What you think I need to say."

Sampson didn't miss a beat. "So how about you tell me what I need to say, instead…"

"Gah! You big Oaf, you know exactly what you need to say to me. I don't have to tell you."

"What's that?"

Frustrated, Kendra threw up both hands, whirling to face him: "That you can't live without me, and you wish I was coming with you to keep your big dumb butt alive so you can come back. That's what!"

"That sounds about right," Sampson grunted.

"So how come I'm not going?" Dark eyes glistening with unspoken emotion, her beaded ivory skin gleamed in the soft glow of the Living Area's ambient light. Sampson held out his hand, and she let him touch her cheek.

"It's not my call—that's up to the Marshal, and he picked me, King, and Montague for this mission. Maybe he's got something else in mind for you. Ask him."

Glowering, the slender Hembra turned towards the wall again. "And what am I supposed to say?"

Hat in his hand, Sampson moved in closer, bending down over to murmur over her shoulder. "You're supposed to say you love me."

"I can't say that and leave everybody else out. I loved Cookie, too."

Shoulders tense, she flattened herself against the wall, indignant at his presumption.

"I know. That's why I'll say it for you—so you don't have to. You love me just as much as you love anybody; but I'm here now, so I'm the one." Pensive, Sampson put a hand on her shoulder. "If I get back alive, I'll still be one, and I'll be the only one from here on out."

She grumbled, "Good luck getting back alive without me, Herman. You need me."

"Yes, I do. Ain't gonna lie. I need you bad, Kendra Qin, and I always will." He waited a moment, but no reply came. Putting his hat back on his head, Sampson turned to go.

Fierce, Kendra grabbed Sampson's sleeve. "You forgot to say you love me. That's another thing you need to say."

He looked down at her, brown eyes warm; "You're right. I better remember to say it when I get back."

"I'll hold you to it." The hand holding his sleeve shook.

Sampson took her hand and kissed it, then walked away.

With an unspoken nod of encouragement to Montague, King moved on down the tunnel, and the living room was empty at last. Montague turned his tawny eyes to the Hembra before him.

"Ma'am, the Marshal's given me an assignment, and I was wanting to tell you something before I go."

Araceli glanced at the ardent Survivor, his chiseled, perfect jaw slightly trembling. "Why certainly, Mi Amor! What do you wish to say?"

"When I return, I'm gonna fight Von Helm for your honor."

Deeply affected by Montague's declaration, Araceli touched his hand. "Oh, that is so sweet! But it is not necessary; following tonight, we are no longer Hostesses. The truth is, Lourdes, Kendra, Destiny, and I are here of our own free will, working with Sam to save others who are truly enslaved; it is all a ruse to allow us to work undercover. But now our mission here is done…"

"I'm not fighting to free you—I'm fighting to prove a point."

"Why?" Alarmed Araceli shook her head. "Agent Montague, it is not worth the chance of you getting hurt!"

"You're wrong; you're worth it, even if it means fighting and losing."

He seemed quite sure of himself. "You're worth it even if I get humiliated in front of the whole camp. You were worth it when Winston fought and lost, too—but he made a fool's choice. When he left you behind, he did you wrong." Montague took her hand. "But I'm gonna set it right. I'm gonna fight Von Helm, and I'm gonna lose, but the whole world is gonna know you're worth it. From now on, they won't be talking about how Winston abandoned you; they'll be talking about me getting my ass kicked just for the chance to tell the world you're worth it."

Araceli's hands flew to her mouth. "Please, don't; you hardly know me!"

Unfazed, Montague pressed on: "You're wrong about that, too; you and I have a long history. It's true you hardly know me, but I know you better than you think."

He pulled off his battered beige cowboy hat and turned it in his hands like a wheel. "Your favorite color is tangerine; you like tulips, so you planted them in the Hostesses' garden. You crochet beautiful hats from old scraps, and you tell stories about knights and princesses and lost loves. You give gifts to express your love, but the one man you love won't accept your gifts."

"How do you know all these things?" Araceli was stunned to hear so much about herself.

Montague's face lit up from within. "Whenever Agents would come from Purgatory, we would sit around at camp, talking; some folks would talk about bars, or fights, or gossip. But always, the talk would turn to the Hostesses, and eventually the Agents would talk about you…"

He was lost in a memory.

"They'd talk about your adventures, how you was seen walking in the park, or telling stories, or making art from trash… it seemed incredible to me that one person could make so much beauty. At the time, the world seemed shadowy and ugly to me; but then I heard about you, and I learned there was a spark of light and beauty in the world. I'd never seen your face, but they way they talked, you became real to me, and I wanted to know more. So every time the Agents from the plantation routes would stop at Camp Forlorn, I would ask about news of you. Little by little, I learned what I could, and in time, a little turned into a great deal of learning!"

Araceli was charmed by his curiosity about her.

"I started asking for assignment to Purgatory, looking for you. I'll never forget the first time I ever saw you with my own eyes! I was walking down the main drag, and I saw you from afar; you was standing in your garden, a tulip in your hand… you had on an orange dress, and your eyes were dark as night. You were real, flesh and blood, not just some idea, but a living, breathing person." In his garden of his memory, Araceli was forever there, just as she had been at that moment, a flame burning bright, untouchable.

"From that day, I lived until the next time I could catch a glimpse of you. Another time, you tripped, and I ran up to help you—but Agent Mercedes shoo'd me away. I could never seem to get close enough to you, to get you to see me. But I least could see you, and it was enough just to know you was real."

Nervous, he cleared his throat. "Finally, one night a year ago, I was assigned to Purgatory on Market Mayhem Weekend. I bet all I had on a roll of the dice—and I came up a Winner. That night was…" He searched her dark eyes, looking for recognition. "…it was all I ever dreamed it would be."

"Oh! Yes, I remember that night." Araceli lied gaily.

"But you don't remember it the way I do. I never forgot what happened to me, the night I finally met you, face to face." She gazed upon him in rapt wonder as Montague recounted:

"It wasn't just what you did with me—it was you, just being you. Even if you and I had never made love, I would have felt the same." He shuffled his feet. "That night before we parted, you folded a little paper crane for me. You told me it meant happiness, and from that moment I was happy. I've kept it next to my heart ever since, and there's not a night that goes by that I don't kiss it, sending a kiss to you by the little messenger of love. And now here you are, and your little love-frog with it…"

Reaching into his pocket, he pulled forth the happy paper pair, dainty origami bird and folded frog, pressing them into the soft palm of Araceli's hand.

"But Ricky, I… " Her eyes glistened with pity. "I don't—"

"It don't matter! Listen to me!" Eyes wide, Montague dropped to his knees, clasping her hand to his heart. "I know you love him. But it don't matter to me—you're all that matters to me! I love you. I love YOU—"

Overwhelmed, Araceli could only listen.

"What's more important, the Lover or the Beloved? I'm offering you what you offered Winston, what he threw away—just think of it! What if one day, Winston had just accepted your love, what would've happened for him? What would've happened to his life, to his soul, if one day he could've just accepted your love as a gift, without any expectation of return, just to accept that miracle, that he was actually loved—"

Montague desperately clung to her hand, his heart hammering. "I'm asking you to do what you prayed he would do! Do for me what you wanted him to do for you; accept my love, and see what happens when you realize you're really, truly loved..." His lips trembled, his heart in his throat. "Be loved!"

His world hung in the balance, the moon and stars reeling around him.

"Mi Corazon!" Araceli threw her arms around the kneeling man. "You have spoken my heart... oh, Ricky, you do not need to fight—you've already won!"

Montague leapt to his feet, sweeping her into his arms in a nova of rapture, the entirety of his soul moving into her own. "Don't forget! Never forget—" He kissed her again, and the world stood still. "Oh God, how long I have waited!"

From the tunnel, just beyond the portal, another man watched; cracks in the foundation of his self appeared, running along the fault lines of his very existence.

———◆———

Four Horsemen came riding, seeking a small golden woman.

Cold eyes swept the front gate of Purgatory: in the staging area, a line of three wagons waited ahead of them. They were filled with smokehouse sausages from the Li Plantation, a special order for tonight's bar-be-que. Hanging back from the line, the horsemen waited at a respectful distance until the wagons could go through.

"Looks like there's a party in our honor, Keller..." a squat Hombre remarked quietly to the men beside him. "That should work in our favor —more noise and more chaos means more opportunities for us."

"Just keep your eyes open and your mouth shut—dammit, Wiley, take off your badge and stash it, you moron. We're Couriers here, not Rangers." A lanky, pale Hombre, quick-eyed and quick-handed, Keller was in no mood for problems—he was casing the joint, seeing what positions were manned, and how many. This entire job depended on finding the main target quickly—and eliminating any secondary targets in the process.

A trim Hombre of medium height muttered: "Well I hope to God it's not Chief Emmanuel that's got the Afterling—I'd hate to be the one that has to put down that big, beautiful bastard." Sharp-dressed and sharp-faced, his silver-belly hat matching the piping adorning his western-cut sports coat, his rig was equally flashy; a concho'd strong-side holster hidden beneath his suit coat. Alert, the trim man studied his surroundings with a practiced eye, looking for trouble.

"Naw, Ruby, I'd rather deal with Chief than deal with the Watcher. If Chief's drunk or asleep, it's a fast kill—and he has it coming to him anyway for absconding with the merchandise," Keller stated flatly.

"But what if the Watcher does have her? Just knowing he's off his chain makes me nervous." Wiley wiped the sweat from his oozing scales; the dust of the road and the heat of the day was making him uncomfortable in the sunshine. "Emmanuel tracked him once; Chief said even without a gun, the Watcher's a killing machine. Chief figured if they hadn't brought the Watcher's Granny as a hostage, they would have never brought him in alive that last time he escaped." Pulling off his broad-brimmed hat, the heavy-set Wiley fanned himself in the late afternoon sunshine. "It sure makes you wonder why Judge Leona kept insisting that bastard be taken alive… he should have been put down a long time ago."

"Well, Leona's dead now. If the Watcher's here, we'll finally get rid of him once and for all. Surprise is gonna be the element we need if we're going to wipe him out. Wait til he gets distracted by the Afterling and catch him with his pants down; then kill the son-of-a-bitch and move on to the next target. It's that simple. But honestly, I just don't think he's here. According to his dossier, Purgatory ain't his style."

From the gate, they heard a shout go up; somewhere near the entrance; a fight was breaking out, much to the delight of bystanders.

Keller continued: "I talked to Rangers who tracked him decades ago, back when he escaped Reunion Camp for the third time. He always headed for the deepest, thickest brush he could find, and preferred the WildLands to the Haunted Lands—he never liked the abandoned places. The Watcher also never associated much with people, even when he could. I think the Watcher got off in the woods, killed the Warden's men, then hightailed it for freedom. Looking at his profile, it makes no sense for that unsociable savage to come here with or without the Afterling."

"Well, what if the Watcher knows we're looking for him, so he hides in the place we're least likely to look for him?" Wiley wondered.

"Hell, anything's possible, but I don't think he's that smart." Intrigued, Keller's experience as a tracker of runaways glimmered; "If the Watcher had the Afterling, I think he'd be out in the woods, as far away from other humans as humanly possible, banging away on her night and day. But the sighting wasn't out there in the woods—it was here, in the busiest place in the Co-op, Purgatory. And who loves Purgatory? Chief Emmanuel." Effusive in his investigative element, Keller expounded: "Chief loves to drink and gamble, and he probably figures he can stash the Afterling away and keep her quiet while he does so. I saw him gag a runaway hostess and stuff her in a bag one time, so I could see him doing it with an Afterling."

"Well, I can't blame Val for wanting a piece of the action. We all could use some 'R and R'—all work and no play make me a loose cannon." A medium-weight Macho with crusted olive skin, DuBois was counting off bullets. "And my cannon needs to fire off a few rounds first if you want me to make this hit; after that we can get the job done… we'll be on our way before the bodies are found."

"You'll get your 'R and R', as promised. The Warden gave us our retainer—" Keller pulled a packet out of his pocket: "four vials of Liquid Gold—that's a vial of the Stuff for each of us if we make the hit."

"Hot damn." Ruby whistled.

"It's pure and undiluted… just a drop will do, so if you plan on using it, don't overdose. There's enough in one of these vials to make a three-month supply—one vial will buy us a good time, no questions asked; that's for sure. Just don't go through Chartreaux's Purgatory Money Exchange—that way, we're untraceable." Keller looked around.

"You all get one hour to unwind—don't use the Stuff, though. Clean and sober until we're done, boys. Keep your eyes on the prize, Dubois— the Warden is offering access to the technology in exchange for this hit. He's the man in charge now, and El Trafico's Couriers need the jobs. No jobs, no pay—and the Warden says that the Man himself will pay big if we get this job done."

"The Man better be paying up big—" Wiley chewed a twig and looked over his shoulder. "Big, like firepower."

"Bigger." Keller secured his goods.

Wylie grunted. "So what's up with the hit on Emmanuel anyways? I thought Chief and the Man were tight…"

"Not anymore. As you know, Chief has always been vulnerable to poon. After he ran off with the merchandise, Chief drunk messaged the

Man, and evidently it went south. Fortunately for us, the Man had a contact list and messaged the Warden, or we'd probably all be pushing up daisies by now. As it is, he just told the Warden to prove El Trafico's loyalty by offing the Chief and eliminating the Afterling—and the Warden said yes."

Dubois nodded. "The Warden knows how to run an organization, that's for sure."

"Well, I ain't got no problem with him as long as I get paid. Now pipe down and make like tourists—it's our turn at the gate."

The gates opened to allow the wagons through; shotguns at ready, the guards on parapets beside the gate held the next group at bay until it had closed safely behind the wagons. "Next up, state your purpose."

"Gamble and chase tail."

"Spoken honestly. Hargrave, get over here and inspect these boys." A heavy-set guard came through a small doorway beside the gate and ambled up to the horsemen.

"These are some mighty fine horses, but you gotta leave them in the Livery Stable." The Guard pointed towards a stockaded pen just outside of the main gate. Some fifteen or so horses were tied to rails between water troughs and baskets of empty mesquite pods mixed with hay. The corral opened into the staging area, which was minimally protected by a light fence and pole-gate; two other guards stood at the ready to shoot down WildLand Threats. At nightfall, those guards would pull back to the more heavily fortified positions of the corral or main gate.

"No horses beyond this point unless you're WildLand Express— Purgatory rules."

"Yeah, yeah, we know," Keller grumbled. "Anything else?"

"Where you from?" The guard looked them up and down.

"We're Renegades from the Wainwright Plantation." Wiley said it, closed mouthed.

"You're not WildLand Express, and you're not Rangers—how'd you get horses?"

Keller cursed under his breath. "It's none of your business."

"It's my business if I say it is, or maybe you'd like to find out during a firearms search."

"Sure," Recalibrating, Keller dismounted and murmured to the Guard: "How about you come help us out and I'll make it business for both of us." The Guard nodded and gamely followed along. As they rounded the corner, Keller reached into his pocket and pulled out a round metal package. "You don't see anything on us, and I don't see you find this on the ground."

Keller twisted the top off the painted metal tin, and the fragrant bouquet of dried, loose cut tobacco wafted up; even in its ancient condition, the aroma was unmistakeable. The guard's eyes grew wide as Keller continued:

"Even just a quarter full, this is worth a fortune, and I'm sure you'll find a good buyer on the black market. To sweeten the deal, there's another tin chock-full of tobacco hidden in the woods nearby... keep your mouth shut, and you'll get it when we leave. Talk and you'll never find it. You in?"

Sweating, the guard flexed his hands eagerly and nodded. Keller put it back in his pocket: "Prove it. Tell me all the news you ain't supposed to tell."

"Someone saw a new girl with the Hostesses—a little golden Chica, a real strange color. Houses were set on fire, Boss Zhu and Hizzoner are dead, and Boss Winston's in jail waiting to hang after the fights tonight. The Hostesses are missing, the Hotel's under guard, and Commander Shaney's coming to town with her Rangers for a Parade." The guard held out his hand. "Give me my pay or get turned in at the gate."

"Crap..." Incredulous, Ruby whispered beneath a sucked-in breath. "Shaney and her Rangers are here?" Keller subtly jabbed him in the ribs.

"Not so fast—what's the schedule?" Keller asked the guard.

"Trade, Games, Parade, Fireworks, Fights, Free Bar-be-que, and a Hanging."

Dubois got excited. "Fireworks? Now that's something special! Where'd they get fireworks?"

The Guard spoke with genuine pride. "Boss Waitie's people over on Industrial Boulevard have been working on making firecrackers and dynamite—it's a super secret formula they perfected only last year, but I know it involves matches somehow..."

"You talk a lot, don't you?" Ruby mumbled.

Ignoring him, the Guard rattled on: "They've been working on it for the last eighteen hours, non-stop, and there's only been one guy blowed off a finger this time around. There's gonna be a show after the parade, starting at Seven O'Clock!"

The men grunted with approval. Entertainment of any kind was a welcome sign of civilization and prosperity. Survivors were on the upswing in the WildLands.

"That only leaves us a couple of hours to get settled in…" Keller glanced at the lowering sun. "Anything else I shouldn't know?"

"Marvin's selling counterfeit tokes on Midnight Street in LowTown—look for the house with a green door, and tell him Joe sent you." The Guard held out his hand again. "Now, pay up."

Keller carefully dropped the tin to the ground and walked back to his cohorts. Watching the gate, the guard casually bent down to retrieve the tin, sniffing its contents before stuffing it into his pocket. "Much obliged. See you at the gate."

Leading their horses into the corral, the horsemen turned them over to a grizzled stable hand who exchanged two bottle caps per horse, each marked with a matching number, pierced and strung on a leather thong. The stable hand tied one to the bridle of Keller's horse and presented the other bottle cap to Keller. "Present this at the end of the of your stay—and two tokes per day boarding fee—to reclaim your horse. No exceptions."

"No problem." Looking over the corral, Keller studied a small herd of horses; he leaned over to whisper to into Ruby's ear: "That light Dapple Gray hoss over there—I'd know him a mile away. That's Ranger Gupta's ride."

Wiley snorted. "Why is that nosy bastard here? He's supposed to be at Checkpoint Brown…"

"Damned if I know… maybe Cap ordered him here for an investigation? Or he sent these guys as an advance team for Shaney's security," Ruby grunted.

"Not likely," Keller murmured. "Captain Evangelo's boys are under orders to steer clear of Purgatory; something ain't right. If Cap gets wind of his guys anywhere near Pair'O'Dice Pier, they'll be drummed out. He don't play."

"Oh come on Keller, Captain Evangelo doesn't know half of what goes on anymore. Ever since Chief Emmanuel came on, they've made sure Cap's been too far up Shaney's butt to see anything that goes on around him, and too involved with his horses to care even if word got back to him." Unimpressed, Ruby busied himself with his horse's tack. "I bet I could beat him at fast draw now; he's worn out from being rode hard by Shaney."

"Yeah, Shaney keeps Cap busy." Wiley laughed. "Chief Emmanuel said she's handling him, so we don't need to worry about him prying around anymore."

"I ain't so sure about that." Keller scanned the gate. "That little pipsqueak still believes in the Ranger Oath, and he takes it personally when we don't."

"So did a lot of the old Rangers, but that all came to an end when Chief Levi met his untimely demise—then the Age of Emmanuel began. Now all the True Believers are dead or gone over to the WildLand Express. Cap's the last man standing when it comes to the old ways." Dubois said it with a begrudging respect. "And you're mistaken if you think he's just a 'little pipsqueak'. He's a fast lil' cuss. I've seen him cut down seven men with nothing but a six-shooter and a soda straw. He's deadly when he wants to be. I always wondered what he'd do if he ever found out how progressive-minded the Rangers are nowadays…"

"I don't exactly think he'd approve. He's pretty hardcore," Keller grunted. "Why do you think Shaney keeps him corralled? She dangles her goods just close enough to keep him blinded and busy while she runs the organization in the Chief's absence. And Chief Emmanuel makes sure he keeps Shaney busy, too…"

"Well something's changed. Shaney don't leave the Ranger Ranch without prior approval from Chief Emmanuel, and Cap don't like anybody coming to Purgatory except on investigation; so you know there's something wrong. Maybe her and Cap's attempting a takeover," Wiley mused. "She's got him whupped like a pup, all he does is follow her around, so maybe Shaney finally turned Cap. You know he's gotta be getting it every night, right?"

"God almighty, I never imagined Captain Evangelo and Commander Shaney teaming up to overthrow Chief Emmanuel…" Keller grimaced. "We'd have to add them to the hit list. I could see Director Santos pulling that kind of stunt—but Captain Evangelo?" He shook his head grimly. "Still, stranger things have happened."

Wiley spoke up: "Speaking of the WildLand Express—what do we do if we see Santos or his agents?"

Ruby stifled a snort. "They're too busy rolling in goods from plantation deliveries. Just get this job done; once Jarrod delivers our payment, we can wipe the WildLand Express and their nineteenth century technology off the map permanently. Then the plantation routes will belong to El Trafico, along with the Asurinol trade—everything that moves, Insider or Outlaw, will be under El Trafico's control." Approving nods met him.

"First things first; before we can take over the world, we gotta find the Afterling, and whoever's with her." Assessing the crowd at the gate, Keller made plans for entry. "We're gonna do a little walkabout, get a little booty, then make our move. Kill them quick and get gone. And don't get any funny ideas about toying with the Afterling, either—she goes last after I interrogate her, then she's my kill. No hanging around except to loot that ring off Chief Emmanuel and get rid of the Afterling's body. We'll stuff her in a bag, tote her down to the lake, and feed her to the gators. Those are the orders."

Dubois chuckled grimly. "I'll don't think you'll have to worry about us. We're immune to the ladies—that's how we got chosen for this gig in the first place."

"Yeah, just give us our promised time off for bad behavior, and there won't be any problem." Leering, Wiley seconded Dubois.

"That's the plan. Recon, hit the highlights of town, and play a little grab-ass in the process. Just keep it quick and be prepared to move... " Brushing his hand to his waistline, Keller checked his concealed handgun. "Make ready—here comes our guard. It's time for murder and mayhem at Purgatory."

They moved through the line as their Guard, Hargrave, made a charade of patting them down. All were inspected, then the Guard yelled up to the Gate—"Four cleared and coming through!" Chains clanked as the heavy wooden gate swung open, and the men entered Purgatory.

All around was the hustle of a dusty frontier town making preparations for a Very Important Person; men were hanging garlands of rope and rag ribbons across Purgatory's entrance, up the Main Drag, around the Commons, and into Pair'O'Dice Pier. Wreaths made from old scarves and silky clothes bedecked street signs, with misspelled shoe-polish signs proudly proclaiming the names of the sponsoring Fine Establishments. All along the parade route, unlit sparklers were hung, to be lit by waiting lantern lighters, and strings of homemade firecrackers were hung from lantern posts, to be lit as the Honored Guest passed by. Even the derelict old PickUp Truck Planter, rusting in the middle of the Main Drag outside Pair'O'Dice Gate, was festooned with ribbons and a banner:

WELCOM

But nothing could hide the glaring ugliness of the burned cabins one street off the Main Road into Purgatory...

"Just damn. It looks like a war happened here." Dubois shook his head. "Last time I was here two months ago, it was beautiful. How could it all have gone to hell so fast?"

Keller looked grim. "Enjoy it now—it's gonna get worse before it gets better. We're gonna upend their little party tonight."

"What do you mean?" Dubois stopped mid-step.

"We're gonna shoot Shaney. She's got no business being here—and whether or not Chief Emmanuel brought her here, it's time for a change in management."

"That's not our orders, Keller..." Dubois grunted.

"Since when do you care about orders?" Wiley laughed. "I like Keller's thinking."

"I don't care about orders, but I do care about results, and I care about whether or not the Warden get bent out of shape." Dubois pressed his point. "I value my hide."

"The Warden rewards initiative. His only complaint will be the waste of a fine Chica like Shaney—but he's soft on the ladies that way. It would be a boon to El Trafico's power base to have Shaney gone. She's not just a hot body; she's a treacherous bitch and fearless to boot. The Warden just wants us to get the job done, and if that job includes the death of Shaney, he'll consider it a bonus."

"Who's gonna take Shaney's place? Captain Evangelo is next on the list of succession... you kill Shaney, and Cap's gonna unleash Hell. Purgatory and Shaney's Rangers will rally behind Cap, seeking blood."

"Not if they don't know who killed her. A well-placed shot from a high vantage point would be almost impossible to trace, and the fireworks would cover the sound. We could literally get away with murder—and there's additional benefits. If Chief Emmanuel is here, I guarantee you he'll find out Shaney is coming—he has informants inside Shaney's inner circle. Shooting Shaney will draw out Chief Emmanuel; if nothing else, he'll want to know what happened. He's still a Ranger, and all Rangers think they should know everything. Fortunately, the Chief's high visibility."

"Yeah, being seven foot tall will do that," Ruby wryly noted. "If Chief pokes his head out, we'll see him right away."

Wiley pondered. "But what if it's the Watcher who has the Afterling?"

"Dammit, Wiley, it's not the Watcher—let it go. His profile says that animal wouldn't come here if you gave him the keys to the city. Plan on Emmanuel—but still prepare for Azarian." Redirecting, Keller whispered, "Now, listen up: I'm going to take this opportunity and kill Shaney. If Cap's with her, I'll blast him, too. Look for a vantage point, and let's get set up—we've got two hours to get in place, and that ain't much time, but this is just too good a chance to pass up."

"How you propose to do all this? There's only four of us, and we've got two kills to make before we can leave," doubtful, Dubois chimed in.

"While you guys get your hour of action, I'm going to watch the parade. We'll give some Stuff to a fourth party at the party, and get them so high they'll swear I was with you, and that'll be my alibi if anyone asks. But I doubt anyone's going to ask—it will be pure chaos when this all goes down, and there's not enough BrigadesMen in Purgatory to keep order." Keller snorted. "Then we can snare Emmanuel and the Afterling, and leave town with no one the wiser. Look for a high point—some place I can set up to get off a shot. I've got three hundred yards to play with for range."

Wandering the main drag, they admired the goods and sampled the wares of the Merchants. In the street, crowds were gathering in clumps. Wiley craned his neck to look through a gap in the trees, where the path rolled down to the park—a large group of Survivors were excitedly jostling each other near the inlet barrier, where an excitable Survivor was hawking giblets in a cup:

"Step right up and feed the Gators—one toke buys two cups! We put the 'Gator' in 'Purgatory'!"

A dusty Hombre held up a toke and got his cups of fish entrails, then cautiously leaned over to a gap in the barrier to toss the giblets through the fence. A thunderous splash and excited hoots followed as the soaked Hombre nearly lost his hand. The vendor laughed with the men, then continued his spiel. "You can't spell Purgatory without 'Gator'!"

"I wanna go see," Wiley whined. "There's supposed to be the Big Daddy of all Gators down there…"

"Big deal; I ain't impressed with no gator," Keller grunted. "Besides, we got no time. You can pick between some gators or some booty. What'll it be?"

"I vote for booty…" Ruby frowned, then grabbed Keller's arm, sucking in his breath. "Hey—look!"

From the Dock Park, an extraordinarily tall, muscular Survivor with a Ranger's silver-belly Cowboy Hat and a quilted leather coat crossed the road and into the Commons area. Keller and his team stepped quickly behind a bush, out of line of sight; they watched as the massive Macho disappeared down a side street marked with a faded red stop sign, into the Commons Campground.

"Hell, Keller—you were right!" Dubois peered around the branches. "That's Chief's hat and coat…"

"Never doubt me," Keller muttered. "The Profiles don't lie. C'mon, we gotta tail Emmanuel before he slips away." Walking at a casual pace, they made their way towards the stop sign.

Keller turned to a slender Hombre whittling on a stump near the stop sign. "You see a tall Man in a silver hat come by here a minute ago?"

"How much is it worth to you?" The Hombre spit and looked down, hat low.

"It's worth me not curb-stomping you into the dust."

"You don't get nothin' then." The Hombre kept whittling.

Ruby hissed. "Let me try." He sidled up next to Hombre. "Maybe you'd like to tell me. I'll refresh your memory." The sharp-faced man prodded a switchblade into the whittler's ribs.

"You ain't much for being friendly." The whittler spit again, then pointed his knife towards Pair'O'Dice Pier. "Fine, I take it you mean that big ol' Ranger that been holed up for a week at the DragLine Cabaret. He heads through the back way in the fence here; seems to be renting a room by the hour—comes and goes. You can probably catch him if you hang out long enough. Normally I wouldn't be telling you diddly squat, but this guy is a real jerk."

Wiley leaned in to whisper in Dubois' ear: "Confirmed—it's Chief Emmanuel."

Ruby patted the slender Hombre's shoulder, then put his knife away. "Thanks buddy… That's more like it." Together with Keller, Wiley and Dubois, Ruby walked down the street quickly towards the back-alley entrance to Pair'O'Dice Pier.

The whittler kept whittling, watching out of the corner of his eye until the assassins were out of sight. A dark-skinned, heavy-set Macho slipped out from behind a cart and whispered in the whittler's ear: "Good job, Ricky. Sampson's hidden out in a porta-potty, and we've sent a runner with a message—the Insertion Team's got 'Traffic' inbound."

Montague looked at King. "I'll finish up here, just in case they come back with a question. Orders are to keep Sampson out of sight until dark." Putting the final touches on his carving, he held it up to inspect it —a little wooden heart with a tiny crown etched into its center. "And besides, I'm working on a gift for La Reina. Araceli taught me that word… it means 'Queen.'"

King grinned. "I guess you just got your fairytale ending…"

Montague smiled and kept carving as Keller and company disappeared through the hole in the fence.

As the assassins emerged to the other side, they stepped around the back of an outbuilding. Shaded from the late afternoon sun, they looked up and down the street for any sign of the silver-belly cowboy hat, but none was seen. Keller cursed.

Ruby offered: "Listen, we already know where Emmanuel's headed— let's cool our heels and let the lady-boys pay us some attention. Maybe one of the queens can tell us where Emmanuel's got the Afterling stashed?"

Keller shook his head. "Don't go asking around too much. Just get them high, and they'll talk. They always do."

"Well, it's not like we've got a hard deadline." Looking over the venue, Dubois assessed. "All we've gotta do is set up at the DragLine and wait for him there—then clear out quick once the deed is done."

"Maybe not for the hit on Emmanuel and the Afterling—but I've got a hard deadline for killing Shaney. It's a tight schedule, but I can pull it off. That's why I'm the lead man on this team. Let's get you all in place and get my 'alibi' high." Keller scanned the Pair'O'Dice skyline for sniping spots.

Dubois grimaced. "I just don't think the chance to kill Shaney is worth that risk, Keller. Look, man, we all know you're a great shot—but this is mission creep. We gotta stay focused."

Waving him off, Keller looked over an old windmill tower a couple of streets over. "There's enough of us to go around. You guys stake out the DragLine and watch for Emmanuel. Once he goes to his room, all we gotta do is wait for him to pass out drunk, then he's toast. Now pipe down and keep your eyes open. We're coming up to the DragLine, and Emmanuel will recognize us right away if he sees us; then it's all over but the gunfighting."

Wiley was sprucing himself up as he went, straightening his collar. Helpful for his wingman, Ruby dusted off Wiley's lapels. "Make yourselves presentable, you swine—we're headed to the DragLine."

Unlit luminaria lined a pathway curving between overgrown flowerbeds, the summer's blooms giving way to brushy dried forbs. Under the arching elms, the rounded forms of shrubby bushes provided hidden alcoves for nestling and necking. The metal siding of the former machine shop was brightly decorated for the coming of Commander Shaney, with fresh wreaths of rosemary from the Chef's own garden, and wind chimes made from abandoned silverware. Beyond a high willow fence, that private garden was lined with old painted tires, each sprouting various herbs and late-season vegetables—pumpkins, kales, and onions. Grunting with hunger, the men walked by, longing for greens and the goodness of homegrown tomatoes.

After dark, this place would be jam packed with eager Survivors searching for something even remotely feminine. Those remotely feminine forms would be the approximately fifteen or so queens who were there voluntarily, and a few unfortunate men there involuntarily as part of their sentencing. Contracted out to the DragLine by the LandLords, these conscripted servants were prized for those vicious Survivors who enjoyed humiliating and sexually abusing others.

Soon a line would be forming at the door. In the late afternoon, however, the DragLine was sparsely populated; the dinner rush had not yet started, and Chef Pembroke kept the doors to the restaurant closed until "evening open" at six. Beyond the peeling metal doors, the assassins could hear the sharp voice of the Chef as he barked orders to staff for extra vases of flowers. The only way into the Den of Iniquity would be a private showing, and to get that kind of audience, one had to have high-value goods to share, and a predilection for sneaking into back windows.

Fortunately, Keller had both—and a willing contact.

Keller motioned for the others to wait away from the main entrance. They took a seat in some rusting, cast-iron lawn chairs under the trees, and waited as Keller searched the grounds. Nosing around near the garden shed, he came upon a public servant, trimming out the weeds with an ancient pair of garden shears.

"Gramps—c'mere," Keller whispered to the gardener.

The old man looked up, disgruntled, still snipping away with his shears. "I ain't got time for you. Pembroke's in full flame-out mode. We gotta get ready for tonight…"

"You'll show me the proper respect, feeb." Keller put a heavy boot on the old man's wrist, pinning it. "You're gonna take a message to DeLisha, or I'm gonna snap your wrist like a twig." Groaning in pain, the public servant nodded. Keller leaned his full weight on the elder's fragile arm. "Your gonna tell 'em a Courier is waiting by the back window; you're gonna hurry. Got it?"

Sucking in a breath, the old man nodded once more. Keller stepped off. "Tell 'em I've got presents." The public servant rose stiffly, dried grass clipping falling from his faded dungarees as he hobbled away, clutching his arm.

Satisfied with the encounter, Keller headed to a window around the back of the building and waited. Grumbling to himself, he paced, impatient.

The window creaked open, and a sleek head atop a slender, scarf-wrapped neck poked out. Kohl-rimmed blue eyes stared out from a fine-boned face;. "Oh God, don't look at me! I'm not done yet—" Leaning through the window, the queen waved, clad in a broken down black leotard. "What the hell are you doing here? We're all busy, hurry it up."

Keller's eyes narrowed. "Maybe you ought to be nicer to your Sugar Daddy—I can always tell Chef Pembroke that you're stealing from his stash of premium liquors and selling it."

"No—" DeLisha started to sweat. "Look, I'm sorry, Everyone is having a fit about Commander Shaney, and no one wants to botch this. We're still practicing our routine for the show tonight, so I can't leave. I promise a 'special' for you later, I just can't do anything right now."

"Naw, that's not it. I'm calling in that favor you owe me—I need to hide out in the Love Shack out back, and I've got three other guys besides me. Send out four of your best boy-toys, and I won't tell Chef Pembroke you're a lying thief."

"Okay, okay, I'll do it!" Biting a lip, DeLisha agonized. "But clean up the room and take out the trash when you leave—it's booked for after midnight; a VIP's coming in late." DeLisha dropped a key in Keller's hand. "They're calling me—I gotta go…"

Keller grabbed the queen's wrist. "Not yet—I've got some questions. You got anybody new hanging around here? Tall guy, silver hat?"

"I can't talk about that here."

"Talk, and you get this…" Keller held out a patina'd tube of lipstick.

Snatching it from Keller's grasp, DeLisha twisted it up: "Fire Engine Red!" the queen expertly swiped it onto full lips, then tucked the lipstick down the front of the leotard. "Tall guy, silver hat? Yeah—but he comes and goes through the back door at random times. Been gambling up a storm. Just wait, he'll show up eventually. If I see him, I'll send word."

Grabbing tighter, Keller pulled DeLisha closer. "That's what I want to hear—does he still have a room?"

"I'll send for you when he shows up." Looking around nervously, DeLisha whispered: "and I'll drop a white handkerchief by the door of his room to let you know which one is his. Meanwhile, go get set up, and I'll send out some fresh meat; they're brand new, just got contracted, so they won't be on stage tonight. Need to be trained…"

"Not just them…" Keller leered. "You. You're gonna come out to me after the Parade is over and you're gonna wear that red lipstick for me, or they'll be selling you as a thief in the market tomorrow."

"Fine. It'll be late," DeLisha grunted. "I've got to dance for the Parade, and I'm up as entertainment on the floor show, but I'll get you in between sets—I probably won't be available except for a few minutes. For now, satisfy yourself on the newbies I'm sending your way. They'll come out as soon as they're prepped. Just tell their guard you're with private security for the VIP." The window closed.

Irritated at the brush-off, Keller grumbled, "I'll pound your prissy ass later." He waved discreetly to the others in his crew, and they walked back, separately so to not attract suspicion. Through a tangle of brush, Keller led his assassins to what appeared to be an abandoned garage. A narrow clearing through thick brush led to a boarded up window, offering a clear view of the main building.

Groans met Keller; Dubois openly revolted. "Aw, hell naw—this ain't what I had in mind when I said I wanted 'R' and 'R'… the Rs are for 'Rape' and 'Rampage', not "Rust" and 'Ruin'…"

"Just shut your mouth and open your eyes." Keller put the key in the lock and opened the door. Even though it was sunny outside, darkness greeted them. Keller pulled a matchbook from his pocket, lit a candle, then watched as his compatriots' skepticism melted away into the dim candlelight.

A clean, cracked concrete floor was strewn from one end to the other with fresh sawdust and a few dried rose petals; heavy black velveteen curtains—scavenged from an old movie theater—hung from rods screwed into the walls. Over to one side, a shop counter offered a bottle of Reunion liquor, some shot glasses, and a bowl of pears. Next to barstools, an old drinking glass held an arrangement of dried flowers.

"Hey, this ain't half bad!" Wiley beamed, settling into the deep cushions of a dingy white couch made cheery with varicolored pillows. "This is the kind of swankiness El Trafico Couriers deserve!"

Down the middle of the garage, tin-panel interior walls had been set up to divide one half of the garage into three private rooms. Ruby swung open the doors to check for any sign of lurkers, but only found beds, comforters, chairs—and chains. "Well damn, they thought of everything." Grinning, Ruby looked around. "So where's our entertainers?"

"They'll be here in a minute." Keller peeped through a hole out the boarded up window. "We're getting some new boys. DeLisha said they needed training, so they'll be brought out under escort." Looking into a framed mirror, Keller checked his teeth. "Still, even though they're new, they shouldn't be too hard to work with. We'll drug 'em with the Stuff, and they'll be easy to tame. No personal use, though—lay off the drugs, and stay frosty. No drinking or shooting up until after we're clear of Purgatory—we're on schedule, so you'll get your daily hit right on time."

Dragging up a barstool to the covered window, Keller pointed: "You'll take turns doing surveillance from here—this is the setup to watch the back door of the main building. DeLisha said Emmanuel comes and goes through the back door; a runner will be sent, and a white hankie will be left on the floor by Emmanuel's room. I suggest two of you get it on with the daisies while the third one takes watch. Dubois, you take watch first. Start the party and get your play-toys strung out on Stuff, then enjoy as your turn comes up."

Sanguine, Dubois pulled up a barstool and secured his weapon in its holster, while Keller and the rest took to freshening up. Excited anticipation gripped them…

A half hour later, they were gripped not by anticipation, but irritation. "Daylight's wastin'," Keller grumbled. "I better see some chicken on my plate soon, or DeLisha is gonna take their place on the menu."

"Hold up! Incoming—" Looking out the window, Dubois shifted on his barstool and whistled softly: "and it looks like we've got us some pretty good prospects."

The door opened, and a gruff Macho loomed over four small Hombres dressed in mismatched chiffon dance outfits. Using diaphanous scarves as face veils, their heavily lined eyes, expert makeup and small statures gave them a look of vulnerable decadence. Their Guard waved his night stick. "DeLisha sends these four lovelies with regards. This here is Pinkie, Blue Boy, Hazel, and Pansy. They've been green broke, but they've never been rode."

Wiley snickered from the back of the room. "Well, you've brought 'em to the right place… lucky for you, I brought my rope."

Keller inspected the merchandise; strong, but not too muscular… he grunted and slipped a budweed cigarette to their Guard. "They look good. Keep strangers away, and don't ask questions." The Guard nodded and lumbered out, leaving the nervous dancers behind.

Keller locked the door and turned to his captive audience.

"You see my face? I'm here. If someone asks, you're going to tell 'em, 'oh yes, that good-lookin' son-of-a-bitch was here the whole time.' Got it?" Apprehensive faces stared back as the dancers huddled in a corner. "Jeez, you're sniveling, pathetic excuses for men. Have a seat on the couch, cupcakes."

Keller went to the bar and poured out four shot glasses, then produced another vial, lacing each drink with a carefully measured golden liquid. "Bottoms up, sissy-boys… Ruby, I want the one with the pretty hazel eyes," He pointed to the Dancer in green, then called Dubois over to the door, conferring quietly as he passed the room key.

"No one in or out until I return; I'll knock three times, quick. If you get word of our mark, make a note and get more info. I'll be back after Seven O' Clock, and we'll make the hit then. Just lay low when you hear the crazy starting."

A pair of startlingly lovely hazel eyes blinked out from under a green hijab. "Oh, you aren't going to be here?" A soft, low voice murmured.

"Nobody gave you permissions to ask questions, Tinkerbell." Keller snapped at the little dancer, jabbing a finger. "You only get to open your mouth when I put something in it." He turned back to Dubois, pulling him aside to whisper:

"Look for Emmanuel to come flying out that back door when the VIP goes down. DeLisha and the other queens will be doing a routine at the grandstand, and they'll see the whole thing, so word'll spread real quick."

DuBois grunted in acknowledgement. "Where you gonna set up?"

Speaking low, Keller confided. "Wherever I can climb the fastest to get the best shot and not get caught. Their security is lax, so that leaves me with some options. Just get your time in and make sure someone watches that door."

Dubois took his seat again at the window again. "Got it. Good hunting."

Turning to the others, Keller threatened the guests. "I'll be back. But as far as you're concerned, I never left." He slipped out the door, and Dubois locked it behind him.

Wasting no time, Wiley passed out the drinks. "Loosen up some, kiddies. It's time for a party." The dancers each took their drinks, suspicious.

Ruby came over to inspect, looking over each one, then stopping in front of a slightly chubby hombre dressed in shades of pink. "All right, Pinkie, you're with me. Let's go." He grabbed the smaller man by the arm and dragged him into the middle room, drink in hand.

Wiley sat down next to a dark-eyed dancer swathed in a purple scarf, laying a rough hand on his thigh. "I said drink it, Pansy."

"I need some privacy if I'm gonna get personal," Pansy complained. "Can we take it in the bedroom?" Leading the way, he took the lecherous Wiley by the hand and disappeared behind a closed door.

Dubois kept his eyes on the window. "Blue Boy, you're mine. Drink up and wait your turn."

Raising a glass, Blue Boy queried: "So what's your name, handsome? I'm Bobbie…"

"None of your business. Shut up and drink."

Blue Boy pouted and stood. "Oh, come on, have a little fun! No need to be cranky…" He pulled a scarf from around his sleek shoulders and swayed suggestively towards Dubois. "I bet you can be a lot of fun."

Sweating, Dubois scowled. "I gotta pay attention."

"You're a big guy—I figure it'll take two of us to do the job on you." Blue Boy swayed closer. "Be a pal, me and Hazel need the practice." He waved to the green dancer, and Hazel rose from his seat.

Still staring out the window, Dubois cursed. "Dammit, I'm trying to do a job here—"

The blue scarf slipped over Dubois' head and around his throat, as Blue Boy jerked him off the barstool from behind. Struggling, Dubois fell back, Blue Boy landing beneath him, twisting the scarf tighter. Dubois grabbed the scarf with both hands, then tried to give a strangled cry, only to have that cry cut short as the green dancer stabbed him in the heart.

Hazel pulled the knife free and stabbed again, plunging the K-Bar deeper into Dubois' massive pectorals. Blue Boy held tight to the scarf as DuBois thrashed, knocking over the barstool.

Now Wiley came running out of the bedroom door, stumbling as he tried to pull his pants up. Hazel rushed the door as Pansy attacked Wiley from behind, smashing him in the head with a liquor bottle. It gashed an ugly wound, glancing off Wiley's thick skull—roaring, Wiley swayed, but turned, weapon almost clearing his holster. The green dancer leapt on his back, stabbing Wiley's throat; Pansy grasped the gun, twisting it from Wiley's shocked hand—

A struggle could be heard in the room next door, scuffling, grunting as boots kicked against a metal bed frame. In the front room, Blue Boy twisted the scarf tighter around Dubois' neck as he continued to bleed out on the sawdust floor.

The green dancer yanked the knife free from Wiley's throat, then jumped up to help Pinkie in the other bedroom. In a frenzy, Pansy pistol-whipped Wiley until Wiley stopped moving.

Barefoot, the green dancer kicked the bedroom door in, only to find a calm Pinkie sitting atop a lifeless Ruby, who was face down on the bed with a chain tightly twisted around his neck. "I'm good, Cap… go help the others."

Nodding, the green dancer turned his attentions back to Dubois, finishing out the job with a barstool to Dubois' head. A gurgle announced the end.

The green dancer sat down next to Blue Boy, pulling off his veil to wipe away sweat and blood. "Excellent job, gentlemen. Let's get these bodies dragged into a back room, then go help Ludwig get Ruby stripped down—I need his clothes right away."

"Yessir, Marshal Evangelo." Pansy wiped the blood from his hands. "Dressing Sampson in Chief Emmanuel's clothes was the perfect lure— whoever thought it up was a genius. But what about Keller? What's our next step?"

"Get yourselves put together, Pritchard, and prepare for hard duty." Evangelo stood to remove his scarves. "Thanks to help from our allies at the DragLine, the majority of El Trafico's Assassin Team has now been neutralized. Notify DeLisha; the rest of the Insertion Team will proceed to the Gate as we originally planned, while I break off to hunt down Keller."

"That ain't gonna be easy—he could be anywhere in Purgatory, Cap." Pinkie came from around the corner, bearing Ruby's clothes. He handed them to Evangelo. "What do you think Keller's up to?"

Evangelo pulled on Ruby's pants, and took the dead man's six-shooter. The little Marshal spun the cylinder, then flipped it shut, his face grim.

"He's going to kill Shaney."

II

Friday Night Fights were almost here—but the MoneyMan needed to make a special delivery before the Revolution could rake in the dough.

Leather briefcase in hand, Habib made his way out from the Jail and down the winding path towards HighTown. As always, he made certain his look denoted the importance of a man of his stature—his dress shirt, khakis, and fedora made up for his beat-up high-top sneakers. An open, mid-length trench coat gave the entire look an air of formality; it was perfectly fitted to the Macho. Lourdes herself had tailored the coat for him years ago, adding an extra lining for warmth and placing gussets to accommodate his broad shoulders. All this she did in exchange for his help in acquiring some particularly rare fabric for the Hostesses.

In the moderate chill of early evening, he normally would have left his beloved coat behind, but Lourdes had insisted Habib take it with him—she swore a cold front was coming, and Habib didn't want his last possible interaction with her to be yet another rejection, however small…

"Where you headed?" She had sidled up next to him.

"Nowhere."

Lourdes sniffed at him. "Well, take your coat, and I'll watch just to make sure you go nowhere fast…"

Lourdes had asked Habib to check for any hidden messages at the Signal Oak on his way to his monthly Bosses' meeting. Habib agreed, not telling her that he might never return; he kept that idea to himself, and kept his mind on the task ahead.

Sitting down beneath the Signal Oak, Habib pulled off his shoe and pretended to dig out a pebble. He took the opportunity to use it as a ruse for scanning the area. From here, he could see the top of the Jailhouse, but he saw no sign of Lourdes, or her rooftop crew. Habib grunted—he was sure she could see him. Those pale green eyes seemed to see everything…

Glancing furtively behind him, Habib noticed his uninvited entourage ducking behind a tree at a safe distance. Suspicious, Habib made note of his tracker's location and general appearance—a heavy, bronze-toned man; clumsily obvious, this tag-a-long was not too good at not getting caught.

He checked his weapon again to make sure it was properly concealed in his sock holster. The silenced mini-mag revolver was considered underpowered by many, but with clip grip, magnums, and skilled bullet placement at close range, the gun was fully concealable and lethal.

Something caught the corner of his vision; a ripple of light, but it was gone before he was certain what it might be. He rubbed his eyes and refocused. The idea of ALGOS being high overhead made him enormously uncomfortable, but at least this mysterious Jammer would be keeping them at bay from Purgatory proper. He wondered—how would the Rebel remnant handle the drones once they moved beyond the range of the Jammer?

Von Helm's message—sent through Michaels to Habib then to Judge Santos—at last revealed the reason for the DeadZones. Not that Dominic said anything about them to Habib; the MoneyMan just happened to surreptitiously read the message before handing it off to Dominic.

Old spy habits die hard. At least now the reason for all of Winston's secretive last-night monthly trips into the countryside made sense. Habib always surmised that the cave with its locked safe contained a LifeBefore treasure. Instead, it contained not golden treasure, but an electronic one…

Replacing his shoe, he shrugged off his worries of later and pointed his attention to the worries of now. A ragged black bandana fluttered from a low branch of the slender oak, the cotton rag almost obscured by the leathery brown leaves—the signal that a message had been left for pickup. Discreetly reaching into the hollow of the Signal Oak, he found a small, paper package wrapped in a Catalpa leaf. He stuffed it into his shoe quickly and moved on.

Walking briskly, he headed through the Commons and the milling crowds. Everywhere, Survivors were doing business, haggling, bartering, trading… it was an entrepreneur's dream, and one he had been glad to help make a reality. *Bidness was bidness,* and bidness had been good… but unanticipated chaos was interrupting bidness. In the lengthening evening shadows, a growing crowd of visitors weren't trading; they were whispering, watching as searchers combed the torched shells of cabins in HighTown.

Restlessness and questions were disturbing the ordinary rhythm of life at Purgatory, and the heavy pall of budweed couldn't mask the odor of the burnt bodies.

As he passed them by, Habib recounted the dead, and guilt engulfed him. How could he have missed all the signs of this coup? As the Bosses' handler and an informant for the Cause, Habib had rightly discerned the growing tension between Winston and Chartreaux, but nothing had indicated to him the depths of Chartreaux's treachery. Now the growing number of dead tormented him.

He had missed the signs; he had failed to inform. Once again, the familiar bitterness of envy filled him: if only Sam had been there to help him, the way she used to do…

Back when they were a team, nothing like this could have escaped their notice. Sam and Habib were an inseparable unit, a monolithic entity that made Leadership at the Consortium take notice. It was the reason they had been deployed to Purgatory in the first place, to provide quality control and ensure the Bosses adhered to the System. With his inside position, and her analytical skills, nothing got past the dynamic duo of Habib and Ellison.

He found it the height of irony that the two people the Consortium chose to uphold the System would become ringleaders in bringing it down. It was Sam who convinced Habib all those years ago to start thinking outside the System… and to be honest, at the time she could have suggested they jump off a cliff, and he would have done it, no questions asked. Habib would have followed Sam into hell, and she knew it.

So how the hell did Sam get stolen away from him all those years ago?

It was the ultimate covert op… Habib only knew that one day he came home, and all Sam's items were gone. She moved into the Hostess club permanently. He sent messages, he left cards; he tried to see her. Nothing. It wasn't until years later that the truth came to light, when Dominic told him… Mansour had said the words Sam needed to hear.

A stab of jealousy penetrated his chronic depression once more: *Mansour.*

Habib had always thought his relationship Sam was perfect, so why mess with perfection? Trading sex for intel had never seemed to bother Sam, and Habib was progressive enough to leave his own personal jealousies out of the mix. As long as Sam came home to him, Habib was happy…

Sam never told him she expected more—so how was Habib to know she expected "romance" from her preferred sexual partners?

A forgotten relic of a patriarchal society, romance was everything Habib had been trained to avoid in his relationships. Possessiveness, drama, jealousy—Visionaries were supposed to leave that kind of feral emotion behind with their old lives. That especially applied to Habib… jealousy had been his weakness, but it had been conditioned out of him by the Firm.

Unknown to Habib, Sam had secretly craved these flawed cultural affectations. It was an affinity she shared with many of her generation, that outdated idea of romance. A full fifteen years younger than his sultry seductress, Habib had never gotten into that particular kink—but now he knew, much to his everlasting bitterness, that Sam believed in romance. In a pre-Arrangement confessional, she had confided to Dominic that she equated Habib's lack of jealousy with a lack of interest—but she never told Habib.

She figured, "if it wasn't there, it wasn't there".

Crushingly, Habib did feel jealousy, just not over Sam's sexual escapades. True to his training, he considered her glorious sexuality to be part and parcel of her career as an intel expert; but now, Habib felt a burning hatred of Mansour because he had stolen Sam's emotional affections and taken her presence forever from Habib.

In dreams, he would still be wrapped in those long, muscular legs, blue satin scales smooth against the ironstone plates of his hips; then Habib would awake, alone, and grab a bottle to drown out the agony—

More than anything else, Habib blamed Mansour for Sam's turning. Had that blue-eyed special operations bastard never showed up, Sam might still be his today. A paragon of perfect muscularity and toxic masculinity, Mansour had lured Sam away with a promise of romance, and he did it right under Habib's prodigious nose. Habib's envy flared again, an acidic flame of inequity so corrosive, it destroyed his ability to function. Seeking to drown the pain, Habib took to drinking, and when he did sober up, envy ate into his ambition, rusting it into depression. It affected everything about him—including his ability to wreak revenge.

So many times, Habib had made his plans to kill Mansour, only to find himself too drunk to carry them out, or too depressed to carry them through. It made no difference anyway… Sam had abandoned him utterly.

Without Sam, Habib felt crippled. He was an information gatherer, not a trend analyst like Sam, and his work suffered for it—his latest failure to detect the coup was proof. He saw the bodies of the dead as testament to his poor performance and to the lasting effects of his loss of Sam. Shamed, he felt there was only one way now to atone; he pulled down the brim of his fedora and moved on.

Looking behind him, Habib searched for his shadower, but could not sight him. The lone Hombre seemed to have gone missing… Habib shrugged his shoulders and headed down the path, his mind focused on getting this meeting out of the way. As he jostled his way through the crowd, he admired the streets he helped fund, in the city he hoped would outlive him.

He took a left at the PickUp Truck Planter, with its carefully tended Fig Tree and creeper vines; turning away from the bustling commons, he walked the familiar paths of HighTown, past the turn to his own little house with its neat hedges and swept porch. Leaves lined the path, dappled in sunset light; the evening sky was beautiful, and in the distance beyond the palisade wall, he could see the water of the lake. The pale green hue of water glinted through the trees—

Habib's thoughts turned to Lourdes's pale green eyes; he hoped she would remember him.

From the side, Habib heard feet approach. Ready, he held his briefcase up, a shield in case of attack. He slipped his hand towards his pocketknife.

"Hey there—Accountant." Two Survivors, one carrying a bundle of feed sacks came up beside him, giving a gap-toothed grimace."The Bosses are looking for you."

"I guarantee you I am right on time," Habib stated flatly. "What is the problem?"

Gap-tooth shoved a gun out from under the bundle of sacks. "The problem is you, Poindexter. Let's move."

Unflinching, Habib turned an icy glare to the gunman. "No reason to get pushy; I know the way."

They moved between the rows of cabins until they came to a large log cabin next to the wooden palisade. Habib knew it well—Boss Waitie's house. It was tidy, with a single rangy rosebush and a fat, spotted goat tied to a stake in the grass, for mowing and milk. Each month during Market Mayhem Weekend, the Bosses met here in secret for a pre-Fight assessment of barter and goods. The numbers provided by Habib would determine the purse for payout of the gamblers after Friday Night Fights. It was private, pleasant, and nearby to the other bosses' houses, meaning they didn't have to tote their private papers through the crowded streets. Other venues had been tried before, but Boss Waitie's predilection for cooking up catfish kept the other bosses coming back to his cabin for more.

Today, however, the smell of fried fish was absent. As Habib entered the cabin, he was struck, as always, by the simplistic elegance of Boss Waitie's tastes. Not overtly rich by Purgatory standards, instead Boss Waitie's wealth lay in his collection of finely crafted furnishings from a bygone world. A large, maple-wood breakfront contained a wealth of scientific specimens—skulls of Chupacabras, turtle shells, and jars of dried flowers. Shaker chairs, brass beds, braided rugs, and stark white paint gave a spare, fine-boned look to the surroundings, and the smell of food was a constant touch. But not so today; the great room of the cabin was devoid of any cheer.

In a large wooden rocker, Boss Waitie sat glowering in the corner, rifle across his lap. Waitie's signature look, a white cotton shirt, soft and yellowed from age, framed tense shoulders. Beside him, on a backless barn-house stool, Boss Balogun perched lightly, his long frame resting gracefully against the edge of his seat. At ease with himself and the world, Balogun was dressed in an ancient linen sports jacket, capped with a simple white fila hat. His ebony cheeks puffed out rhythmically as he lit a bone pipe tamped with dried Fo'Bacco, the red clover and walnut leaf "Faux Tobacco" mix used by Survivors as a substitute for real tobacco. Elegantly dressed, down to his gloves, Habib always imagined Balogun as an Edwardian, coolly elegant and highly intellectual, the perfect foil for Boss Waitie's pioneer practicality.

The thin leather gloves were not Balogun's usual. Habib made a mental note: *something different here—why?*

Waving Habib into the center of the room, Waitie gave Habib a quick pat down, pulling a folding pocketknife and a pair of brass knuckles from the Accountant's coat pocket. "You're equipped like a man expecting trouble."

"Can't be too careful around Purgatory nowadays…" Habib shrugged. As if to prove his point, a shouting match exploded in the street outside as a game of horseshoes turned ugly.

Locking the door, Balogun pulled a pistol from beneath his sports jacket. "Have a seat." He motioned to a wooden chair, and Habib eased his bulk down into a sturdy ladder-back chair. Waving towards the kitchen, Balogun commanded his henchman: "Be a good sport and get our guest some tea, James—it's already brewed. Farnon, you just keep doing what you are doing."

The gap-toothed Survivor grinned and held his revolver steady at Habib's back. Balogun looked out the window quickly.

"Farnon, where is Gerald? He was supposed to be accompanying Mr. Habib, but I see him nowhere, and he's not in the mob outside."

"Dunno, it's not like him to get distracted… maybe he's waiting for the parade. We all want to see Shaney and the Fireworks show." The BrigadesMan grumbled.

Habib glanced around the cabin, searching for signs of additional gunmen. The loft above the bedroom was largely out of sight and well lit from a window at the end of the gable. Habib noted no shadows, so at least the loft was empty… the bedroom beneath was closed, and no noise came from within, but personnel could be hiding in there. The kitchen, an open affair with a dividing breakfast counter, was easily seen as unoccupied, and a door to the side porch was blocked by an indoor wood rack.

Odds—four to one. Two Bosses and one each of their BrigadesMen. Habib weighed his options; obviously, they considered their big Accountant to be no small threat, for all four men were armed.

Carrying a cracked, white china cup, James came back with a fragrant rose-hip tea. "Thank you, gentlemen; you are dismissed to the kitchen. Please continue your coverage from there while we have our meeting in privacy." The BrigadesMen nodded and retreated to the kitchen, at a respectable distance, a gun still trained on Habib.

Balogun held out the cup to his Accountant. "Make yourself comfortable; Boss Chartreaux sends his regrets, as he is unable to attend our meeting due to Commander Shaney's arrival. Instead, he will catch up with you tonight when he visits the jail to retrieve the prisoners with his guest, Commander Shaney. He hopes you will understand."

"What's with the uninvited guests and firepower? This meeting is supposed to be private and friendly." Taking the tea, Habib sniffed of it, but did not partake. Holding it balanced in his lap, he proffered a view: "I take it from my escort that you are dissatisfied with my service around here."

"Not at all; you have been most helpful, and we appreciate your years of hard work. However, there has been a change in management." Balogun spoke quietly, below the hearing of the guards. "Since Chartreaux is absent, we believe now is the best time to ask a personal favor."

"You want to keep Boss Chartreaux out of this?"

"Too many cooks spoil the stew." Hushed, Waitie grumped to Habib, "We have a side deal going, and we want to keep it private until the time is right."

"Conflicts are rising;" Balogun interjected. "Chartreaux is setting himself up for power, and Boss Waitie and I want to know whose side you are on."

"I'm on my side. I keep to myself."

"That much is true; other than your nightly liquor-stocking forays to the Party Pontoon, you go nowhere but to work and home. It seems a lonely life, considering that at one time, you were so closely connected to Madame Sam…"

Habib kept his expression deadpan. Waitie harrumphed at him: "You ought to close your windows when you sob yourself to sleep at night, Buddy."

"Point taken."

Balogun continued. "Point is, you are very attached to someone who is now missing."

Habib felt his hackles rise; *careful, this statement is a trap…* no one except the Bosses should have known the Hostesses were missing. As far as the rest of Purgatory was concerned, they believed the official story that the Hostesses were recovering after their "rescue" from the fire the day before.

This "meeting" was actually an interrogation.

There was much for them to discover if Habib became careless… Purgatory Bosses had never been informed of Habib's Visionary status by "The Powers That Be" at the Consortium, but Habib was fully aware of who the Bosses were, and how dangerous they could be. These men were Visionaries too, as powerful and skilled in their respective roles as Habib was in his—and they were using those skills now to determine who was friend or foe.

"So the girls have escaped?" Habib asked, guarded. "I wondered why we hadn't seen 'em. I just figured they were still in hiding after the fire."

Habib's feigned ignorance had the proper effect on his listeners: Waitie visibly relaxed. Balogun puffed on his pipe. "No, they haven't escaped—not that they didn't try. But thanks to our sources, the

Hostesses have been spotted in an undisclosed location, and a posse will be sent out to recover them."

Waitie scrutinized Habib as he absorbed the news—and Habib noted it. *Time for a little improv...* Habib blew out a whistle and feigned mild surprise. "Well, that's not going to go over well with the Market Mayhem Weekend Crowd. They're gonna wonder how the Municipality lost track of their assets... not a good look for us."

"Precisely." Leaning forward, Balogun pointed his 9mm at Habib. "You are a hard man to read, Habib; you seem to be unemotional about the disappearance of a loved one. Perhaps you don't care anymore, or perhaps you are just hiding it. Either way, I have a proposal for you."

"I'd say your pistol is proposal enough."

Balogun acknowledged with a knowing nod. "You're a smart fellow— and a good accountant. You know where the bodies are buried, and you know how to keep a secret. In light of that, we've arranged opportunities for you prove your loyalty to us."

"I'm listening."

Balogun leaned back, his teacup clasped in one slender, gloved hand, pistol in the other. "As you know, the masses are asking questions about the fires, and murmurs of unrest have been heard. This could cause trouble far beyond the ability of these riffraff to understand."

The elegant Boss balanced his teacup delicately. "In order to maintain order at Purgatory, the Bosses need to provide an acceptable story for the events that have taken place this week. I believe you can help provide us that story. First favor you can do for us is make a public declaration at the Fights tonight: tell the crowd you found evidence Calvin Winston teamed up with Destiny Rogers to murder Jack Zhu and set the fires to cover it up. Announce that all the Hostesses are to be disbanded for their own protection, and Winston is responsible for their corruption. The crowd will go wild for blood, Winston will be brought out to be hanged, and we can put this whole unpleasantness behind us. You will save Purgatory untold trouble in helping us quench this civil unrest."

"Why do you need me to do it?"

Waitie leaned back in his chair. "Purgatory Men trust you, Habib; if you say it, it will accepted—and it would give us a reason to promote you in Winston's place. We think you could be Boss, if you're willing to work with us."

"So you want me to throw Winston under the bus, in exchange for a promotion." Habib appeared thoughtful. "That's plausible—but why announce the bit about the Girls? Shouldn't the Hostesses be put back into rotation? They bring in a lot of dough…"

"They are troublemakers, all of them, and chief among the troublemakers is your Madame Sam. The Hostesses are the instigators of this current civil unrest, and the leaders of an escape ring. Our BrigadesMen discovered a secret tunnel beneath the Hostess Club, and evidence the Hostesses were hoarding goods. This is a blatant disregard for Purgatory rules—all goods are to be distributed through the Bosses, in the best interest of Purgatory. We also believe the Hostesses are harboring a fugitive… an escapee of special interest."

Leaning back, Habib pushed up the brim of his fedora, shaking his head in apparent disbelief. "Those dumb broads? Half of 'em can't even tie their own shoes, much less run an escape ring."

"Never underestimate these women. They have been playing dumb and playing us at the same time." Balogun continued: "The Hostesses must be punished and their subversive little ring broken up. But their disappearance has caused concern among the rabble, and riots may break out unless we can give Purgatory men some answers. That's where you come in. Convince the crowd tonight that Winston and any conspirators are guilty, and when the Hostesses are recovered, we'll give you Sam to keep as a permanent prisoner at the Jail."

Habib felt a flush come over him at the though of Sam being handed back to him. He stood abruptly and turned to face the shaded window, propping his leg up on the chair next to it.

Imperious, Balogun interjected: "No one gave you permission to stand."

"I'm emotional, okay? Can't a man have a moment?"

Sympathetic, Waitie grumbled, "Sure, but get your dirty shoes off my furniture."

"Sorry…" Sounding embarrassed, Habib reached down by his foot as if to brush off the wood, then lowered his foot back to the floor. Still facing the wall, he queried, "What'll happen to the rest of the girls?"

Waitie grunted: "We already have acquisitions set up for the rest."

"Who goes where, and for how much?"

"They're not going in my house," said Waitie bluntly. "They're too much trouble."

"It's none of your business." Balogun stiffened.

"I'm the MoneyMan." Habib stood his ground. "It's my bidness if I'm doing your books."

A tense moment passed as the Bosses conferred. Habib heard noise near the gates—cheers and hoots. Stoned and drunk, it was a noisy crowd. Impatient, the BrigadesMen grumbled from the Kitchen, straining to see out the windows. "We're gonna miss the parade..."

"Stop complaining, or I'll shoot you myself." Irritable, Waitie yelled at the BrigadesMen, then turned towards Habib to whisper, "Fine, we'll share the details of the transactions with you—after you do us our little favor. Other than Sam, only one is staying, the rest will all be contracted out to private buyers."

"If you're going to do that, contract them out for a bundle upfront, and don't take any promises of future payment—you'll never get that paid back. I know we've made payment arrangements before, but don't this time. We're losing our main draw at Purgatory... some of these clients will never return once they find out there's no more Hostesses. We have to prepare for a big drop in revenue," Habib advised, calculating. "I know for a fact Chartreaux won't be pleased with that."

"That's where your next favor comes in." Waitie piped up: "We need you to help us make a few arrangements. We're not stupid. There's a replacement plan in the works, one that will make more money than even you ever dreamed, Habib."

"Replacement with what? Paper dolls? Porn? There's no more women —not unless you plan on making a bulk buy from Reunion Camp; and knowing management there, I guarantee you they won't let their stock go for anything less than an even trade in flesh."

Snorting, Waitie opined: "We don't need them anymore. A new supplier with new goods is opening up."

Habib scoffed. "Speculative markets are always a risk—if some high-roller really does have a goldmine like that, do you you think they're gonna share it with us for anything less than total control of Purgatory? I think someone is selling you a pack of lies, and unless you see proof, don't invest. If they're offering you women, it's a scam."

"It's not women." Defensive, Waitie persisted.

"You mean more DragLine queens?" Habib queried, incredulous.

"No. Better..." Waitie's eyes gleamed. "It's boys... the prettiest damn boys you've ever seen."

Boys... the Afterling children of Tesoro, the ones Dominic mentioned in the Council Briefing? Habib felt nauseous but kept his face expressionless. "There's no such thing as boys anymore. There's just men pretending they're boys..."

"You're wrong—I can prove it." Waitie leaned in, confidentially. "All we have to do is help the supplier with a favor, then we get a share of his surplus stock."

Balogun shot a cold glare at Waitie, shaking his head subtly. "Shut up, Waitie," Balogun threatened.

Stubborn, Waitie gave the other Boss an ugly look. "We need allies Jonah. Habib here knows business, and he can help us get business. We need to play both sides of this conflict if Survivors are going to thrive..."

"Okay, you come clean with me—What kind of favor?" Habib insisted.

"We just have to commit some manpower and goods to a certain client. That's where you'd come in—we'd be working with a new delivery firm and delivering goods on the sly. It's going to take two sets of books —one for Chartreaux, and one for us. Once we deliver on our favor, we can set Purgatory up to rule everything."

"If this is such a great deal, why is Chartreaux not in on this?"

"He doesn't like some of our business associates. We think he'll come around once he sees the Merchandise."

Dismissive, Habib continued. "I'll believe it when I see it. But you're the Bosses... it's your money to win or lose. However, until you get this magical supply of imaginary fresh meat, you'll need someone to make up for all the revenue we're gonna lose when the Hostesses get sold down the river..."

"Oh, I have a someone in mind..." Balogun smirked. "I have special plans for Lourdes."

"Really?" Habib felt an unexpectedly cold sensation in the pit of his stomach.

"I'm keeping her for my own personal use, to be loaned to top-paying customers—and she will work overtime to make up for her complicity in the Hostesses' crimes." Balogun sipped his tea.

"To top it all off, I have set aside a pair of saggy old sweatpants and a trashy tube top just for Lourdes. If she complains, I'll make her wear THAT for a crown." The elegant Boss pointed to an old turtle shell displayed in Waitie's breakfront. "She thinks herself a Queen of Fashion, but from now on, she will rule nothing but my Kingdom... of Loathing."

Habib knew enough about fashion to know that Lourdes would consider this a form of couture torture. "Huh... what did she ever do to you?"

"Her insolence to me will not go unrewarded." Balogun sniffed. "She openly questioned my taste in shoes,"

"Well, she was right." Waitie groused. "You wore white loafers after Labor Day."

"They were winter white." Chilly, Balogun retorted: "But enough! Her humiliation will be my concern, not yours…"

Idly running his fingers across the smooth woolen nap of his coat sleeve, Habib immersed his senses in the truest incarnation of fashion— the Design's external expression of the Designer's own internal beauty. His mind centered on his own personal designer, Lourdes LeFleur, and a smile flicked across his lips at the passing memory. In the edge of his hearing, the first slow gong of Commons Market Bell announced the time —Seven O'Clock.

The moment was here.

Impatient, Balogun pressed the Accountant. "Make your choice, Habib—what do you say?

"I say she'd still make a tube top and sweats look good," Habib replied smoothly. "No matter what you do to that woman, Lourdes will still be nothing but class—and you'll still be nothing but an ass."

"What?" Balogun scowled.

"You heard me," Habib spoke, dead calm. "You too, Waitie—take your proposal and shove it up your flesh-peddling degenerate asses."

Waitie grunted. "Wrong answer."

Livid, Balogun rose, gun in hand, and Habib turned to meet him, eyes glittering with contempt. Balogun barked: "James, Farnon—I believe Habib has concluded business with us. Prepare to take a trip down to the dock; the alligators need to be fed."

The henchmen came racing out of the kitchen, guns drawn. Grabbing Habib by both arms, they failed to notice the tiny, mini-mag pistol now concealed in the cuff of his coat sleeve.

"That's not the answer I wanted," Balogun sneered. "I expected more from you."

"Take a number," Habib spat. Sizing up his scene, Habib figured he could get off the shots to take out the Bosses, but he would in turn be shot by their henchmen…

That's the way it's gotta be, then; Habib made his peace. *Get the job done.*

"How we gonna off him without causing a scene?" James asked. "Gunfire's gonna draw unwanted attention from the crowd outside …"

Waitie peeked out from behind the window—"Watch for my signal; when the Fireworks start, we'll take our shot." They drew their pistols, tense. Habib stood, serene and cold.

Down through the commons, the crowd fell silent; the gong was sounding, seven bells…

As the last reverberation rang, a megaphoned voice boomed from the Commons. "Citizens and Honored Guests—join me in greeting Commander Lillabeth Shaney of the Tejas Rangers!" The crowd roared as the Announcer called out:

"Welcome to Purgatory—a Hell of a Town!"

A step was heard on the stairs.

Startled, the Survivors jumped as a sultry voice purred from the loft: "Billy?"

Shocked, the entire room raised their eyes to see an elegant form leaning languorously against the stair rail, the scent of lavender and laundry soap wafting from the white cotton dress shirt draped around her slender form. A breeze blew through the loft window, and the unbuttoned shirt billowed out, revealing her cool, naked body beneath. The tattered ivory headscarf framed her pale green eyes, and her sleek thighs gently brushed against each other as she descended. Paused halfway down the stairs, she ran her fingers across her marbled skin…

Lourdes cast a siren spell without a single sound; Habib turned his eyes away, looking for his opportunity. Confused, the henchmen slightly softened their grip, and Habib's hand found the cold steel of his gun.

"Billy?" She held out her hand to Waitie. "Why are these people here? I thought you said we were all safe here…"

Waitie stood slack-jawed, unable to speak.

Stunned, Boss Balogun spun to confront Waitie: "What is this tramp doing here?"

Shaking his head, Waitie stared at Lourdes. "What? How…"

"That's your shirt!" Balogun's jaw clenched.

Waitie began to back up. "Now wait a minute…"

"You wretched liar—you're the one hiding the Hostesses!"

The BrigadesMen both gawked; James sputtered, "Boss Waitie's a turncoat?"

Furious, Balogun lifted his gun to Waitie's head. "It was you, all along—"

Everyone jumped as the sound of firecrackers exploded near the gate, ricocheting off the buildings. Waitie's hand twitched as he reached for his weapon, too late; Balogun fired point blank. Waitie's eyes rolled upwards, face slack as a bloody hole appeared between his eyes.

Wrenching his arm free of James, Habib fired directly into Balogun's exposed chest: a pop was heard from the suppressed mini-mag as the hollow-point bullet found its mark in Balogun's heart, a bright crimson stain blighting his elegant linen jacket. Shoving away from his captors, Habib blasted James, hitting him in the left lung. The tall man squeezed off a round but missed Habib, and James sank to the floor, clutching at his chest.

Out in the street, the crowd roared with delight as more firecrackers exploded, isolated pops merging with clusters of rapid-fire snaps and whistles. Inside the cabin, Habib and Farnon grappled, rolling and kicking; Habib's gun clicked, jammed. Farnon grinned through bloody, snaggled teeth as he shoved his .22 into the side of Habib's trench coat and pulled the trigger.

Smoke and blood blinded Habib; all breath gone, he was stunned from the impact of the bullet. Trying to focus, he watched Farnon's eyes grow wide as the Hombre raised up in confusion, scrabbling, trying to reach his own back. Arching, Farnon groaned, then fell forward across his foe.

Shouts and catcalls rose in the distance as the fireworks crescendoed, a percussive, strident death march. Lost in the cacophony, the last gurgles of life were slipping from the Survivors on the floor of Boss Waitie's cabin.

Struggling to maintain consciousness, Habib was dimly aware of Lourdes pulling Farnon off him; he could hear her gasping: "Frank! Oh God, please... Frank!" Pulling his coat aside, she ripped his shirt open, looking for the wound. Blood was everywhere, from everyone. Habib took a shallow breath; a dull pain overwhelmed him, like a horse had kicked him in the ribs. He took another breath and groaned. To the sound of fireworks, Habib was was slipping into unconsciousness; drifting, he only knew it was now or never...

Was it for Sam? or Lourdes? He wasn't sure it mattered any more... grabbing a slender hand with his own heavy one, he mumbled.

"I love you." The light faded.

———◆———

A shock of water to his face brought the light back. Habib sat bolt upright, gasping, groaning, to see a concerned Lourdes standing over him with an empty glass in her hand. Lourdes' face crumpled as she flung her arms around his neck, sobbing. "Oh, Frank, thank God!"

"How the hell am I not dead—" Groaning, He blinked at Lourdes. "And how the hell did you get here?"

Not answering, Lourdes clung to him for a moment, then quickly wiped her eyes trying to regain her composure.

Sitting up, Habib surveyed his surroundings.

Waitie was lying face up, a pool of blood and brains darkening on the wooden floor under his head; Balogun was prone, a gaping exit wound torn in the back of his linen coat, blood soaking the braided rug beneath him. James curled to the side, shot through the lung… Farnon stared up at the tin ceiling with unseeing, glassy eyes, no wounds visible.

Lourdes stayed silent as Habib inspected Farnon, flipping the dead man to assess the back side. Beneath the left shoulder blade, a wicked dagger protruded, expertly placed. Unflinching, Lourdes pulled it from Farnon's back and wiped it on her cotton shirt. "I believe this is yours… you dropped it on the steps when you rescued us from Chartreaux's secret cellar. I picked it up; it's a perfectly good dagger, and even if you don't want it, I do."

Incredulous, he took it. "My dagger…"

"It's beautifully balanced—a perfect throwing knife. I'm quite taken by your blade."

The Bosses and their BrigadesMen were dead—and Habib was still alive. *How?* Groping his midsection, Habib searched for holes. Stiffly, he slipped off his coat then pulled his shirt aside. Beneath the bronze plaques of his skin, he saw a massive bruise developing across the left side of his barreled ribcage… unbelieving, he grabbed his coat. There, beneath the left arm where Farnon shot him, a scorched hole in the gabardine fabric, black with gunpowder.

Habib stuck his finger through the hole—but it didn't come out the other side. Instead, his thick finger found a flattened plug of lead, embedded into a hidden layer of composite-carbon fabric. He glanced up at Lourdes, starting to comprehend.

"Somebody sewed a bullet-proof liner into my coat…"

She nodded."You wouldn't believe who somebody had to sleep with to get that fabric."

"I've got a hunch. I remember that night—" He staggered to his feet. "And somebody earned every yard. But you told me you needed it for a special project… why?"

"I have a vested interest in keeping you alive, Frank." Enigmatic, Lourdes smiled that Mona Lisa smile.

"How'd you get here?"

"I followed the guy who was following you."

"What about your job? Habib was trying to shake the cobwebs loose from his brain.

"I spotted the El Trafico team enter the gates. Four survivors—two skinny Hombres, one fat Hombre, and a medium Macho. One was wearing a badge when they arrived—I saw it catch the light. I sent for the runner, and that's when I spotted you leaving..." Lourdes smoothed her shirt.

"But if you're here, who's minding the store?"

"Sanders and Wilbur... When I spotted your follower, I told Sanders I had to use the ladies room and asked Wilbur to watch with him while I was 'occupied'." She gave a little grin. "They probably wonder why I'm still in there..."

"So you came all the way from the Jail by yourself, in broad daylight?" Habib said slowly, a thought dawning on him. "You could've died..." He exploded in a muted outrage. "You could've died!"

Lourdes hissed back: "You could've died, too. What makes you so special that you get to die and I don't?"

"You're a dame, dammit—I'm supposed to die, not you!" Suddenly chauvinistic, he reeled himself in. "But you're no ordinary dame, that's for sure. You're some kind of super-spy...." He grabbed her by the shoulders, pulling her close, rough—"You're gonna give me some answers. Who are you?"

Surprised by his sudden suspicion, Lourdes remained nonchalant. "You're the Bosses' Handler—" She patted his chest and took a deep breath, "and I'm yours."

"You..." Blindsided, Habib muttered, "you're my what?"

"Your Handler." She said it as if it were a point of pride.

"I got a Handler, huh?" A guarded expression crept across his face. "So someone told you to get close to me..."

Taken aback, Lourdes confessed. "In the beginning, yes—but it's not that way for me, now."

Habib persisted: "And who's your Handler, Lourdes?"

"Now is not the time, Frank..."

"Now is the time, and you're gonna tell me or you're never gonna see me again." He let her go and started pulling all his gear together. "I ain't got time to play spy games. Who are you working for?"

"I can't tell you yet, but I promise I will, just be patient." She reached out to touch his hand.

Habib took a long look at Lourdes. "All the machinations to get near me—faking a sprained ankle, following me around, always trying to get close... You must think I'm the stupidest bum alive." Bitter, he grunted: "All your affections are a ruse."

"That's not true!" Lourdes blurted. "I just risked my life to save yours!"

"Yeah. Save me for what, Lourdes? What's your motivation? What kind of payout are they gonna give you for bringing me in? What are you willing to sacrifice us both for?" He threw his coat at her feet. "And to think I nearly fell for you..."

Stung, Lourdes picked it up. "How dare you—I put my soul into every stitch of this!"

"Why?" He pulled himself together. "Why are you here, Lourdes?"

No answer.

Retrieving his fedora and briefcase, he turned towards the door.

"Stop—Frank, no!" Grabbing his arm, Lourdes pulled him back. "BrigadesMen are stationed in front of the cabin!"

He turned a suspicious eye at Lourdes. "How do you know this?"

"When I killed your tail, I found his orders." She held out a torn off scrap of paper:

> —*Halverson, Thoms, and Smitty to Waitie's house—if Habib comes out alone, kill him*

"Impressive," Habib acknowledged reluctantly. Turning the note over in his hands, he spied a smear of blood in the lower left-hand corner—proof of Lourdes' skills as a silent killer. "But it still doesn't explain how you got in here unseen... how do I know you weren't in cahoots with Waitie to begin with?"

Upset with this line of questioning, Lourdes appeared genuinely hurt. "I stole Sander's cast-off slave clothes, took the path through the dump, and skirted the wall until I got here—then I climbed up the gutter pipe to enter the loft window while the BrigadesMen were distracted by the fight out front."

In spite of Habib's suspicion, he couldn't help but be amazed at

Lourdes' skills. All the more reason to be cautious… time to see if she would crack under pressure. He wanted answers.

"Well, aren't you the dedicated little double agent. See ya." He turned as if he were headed out.

She begged. "Please don't—they'll kill you if you walk out there!"

Now the fireworks were shooting off at regular intervals as the Parade route snaked through town, accompanied by a full-throated howl—the sound of a hungry mob.

"Let 'em. I don't care anymore." Calculating his next bluff, he could tell Lourdes was rattled; a little pressure, and he could goad her into telling him everything. "If I can't trust anyone, then why even bother living?"

"I swear I'll tell you everything when tonight is done—please, just trust me!" Lourdes grabbed him by the lapels, desperately trying to restrain him; Habib noted she was using both hands.

"Trust you… " He grabbed her by the wrist, grim. "This was all a sham—just like your sprained ankle and your hurt arm…" His eyes narrowed at the thought. "Or did your arm get miraculously healed just in time to chase me down here and climb into the window to help your favorite Boss?" He reached over and yanked up her unbuttoned shirt cuff to reveal her wrist…

She winced as Habib blinked in surprise. Her wrist, still wrapped, was grotesquely swollen now, purple and green from her previous assault at the hands of Chartreaux's henchman. Her attempt to catch up with Habib had added insult to her earlier injuries. Aggravated at the pain, she frowned and pulled away.

"I broke into your liquor cabinet on the way out and downed a slug of Reunion's Best to take the edge off the pain. Then I took off my sling so I could climb in the window."

"Climb in a two-story window—" Habib sputtered at her. "Why would you pull a stupid stunt like that? Are you nuts?" Appalled at her reckless disregard for her own safety, Habib's mask of indifference slipped. "You could've fallen and broke your damn neck!"

Indignant, Lourdes hissed though tears. "I wish I had! Why go through all this for some thick-skulled lout with no heart?" Tearing away from him, she ran up the stairs. Habib called after her—

"Hey! Where do you think you're going?"

Lourdes flung her head back and pointed to the loft, incensed. "To throw myself out the window!"

"Like hell you will!" Habib lunged up the stairs after her; he grabbed her ankle, and they both fell in a tangle. Wrestling, he found Lourdes surprisingly strong—but not as strong as him. Even with his bruised ribs, Habib overpowered her—but it wasn't easy. He rolled to the top of their personal heap, pinning her; "Nobody's jumping out the window!"

"Well, nobody's walking out the door, either!" She kneed him in the groin half-heartedly.

The absurdity of it all suddenly struck Habib. *It's all an act to extract information…*

Running out of patience and time, Habib took the direct approach. "Oh come on, Lourdes LeFleur, you ain't even trying… you and I both know you can do better than that." His visage softened. "Look, you're trying to play me and I'm trying to play you. But this spy versus spy act will have to wait—we gotta get out of here. Tell me who you work for, so we can blow this joint."

"Your pathetic act is just as bad. Of all things… 'ooh I'm Mr. Tough Guy, tell me everything or I'll go die.'" Lourdes mocked. "How about I tell you nothing, and you help me get to my next point of contact—that will explain everything, and I can maintain my integrity. Deal?"

"No deal unless you tell who's your next point of contact."

Visage haughty, Lourdes made her play. "I call the shots here, Habib. You give me what I want, and I'll tell you my next contact."

"What do you want, Lourdes?"

"You."

Lying eye to eye with a half-naked Lourdes in the loft, Habib was working hard to keep it all bidness. She moved beneath him, and just for the briefest moment, Habib forgot that he had nearly died just minutes before. He felt something stir within him, the resurrection of an emotion long dead… Simultaneously thrilled and suspicious, Habib masked his reaction, his expression gruff once again. "Yeah, well you ain't getting that yet, not until I know which team you're on. Pick a consolation prize, and maybe if I like what you tell me, I'll let you play again later."

"Fine, you heartless brute. Give me your hat as collateral, and I'll trade it for you later when you come to your senses. If you bail on our agreement, I keep the hat as an everlasting reminder of your stone cold soul."

"My fedora, huh?" He mulled it over. "You got it—but not until you reveal your Handler. Agreed?" Rolling off her, Habib groaned in discomfort at the bruise left behind by Farnon's bullet. "Besides, I owe you a favor for saving my life with that custom bullet-proof coat…" Standing, he extended his hand to pull her up with him. "Time to roll."

Rushing downstairs, Habib gathered all identifying information, then pulled items of clothing from first one then another of each of his victims. The entire scene of carnage was now entirely indiscreet, but it looked for all the world like a shootout. Normally, this scene would have been easy to blame on the dead parties—the only problem was Habib's noticeably absent body, and the shoot-to-kill orders for the BrigadesMen outside. They would know—and Habib would be the first suspect, unless a coverup could be made. A posse would head straight for the Jail and blow their cover, unless he could come up with a plan.

He had a pretty non-discreet idea on how to proceed.

Striding into Waitie's kitchen, Habib dumped a tin of bear grease into a large frying pan. He grabbed an antique box of matches, then lit one of the newfangled Purgatory Oil lamps, and placed the pan of bear grease over the flame. Dipping one corner of a cotton kitchen curtain into the grease, Habib left it to overheat…

While Habib set up his arson scene, Lourdes ran to the corner of the loft to don Sander's old servant clothes, complete with his chain and knit scarf. Bucket hat pulled low, it was hard to tell her from the similarly-sized Sanders. She slipped her sling back into her pocket—protection of her injured arm would have to wait, as it made movement difficult. She had been able to hide it under Sander's coat before, but now they would need to move fast…

Running downstairs, she saw Habib spraying the curtains and furniture with cans of Dubb-Dee 40 from Waitie's bathroom.

"What on earth are you doing?"

"I'm getting ready to blow this joint, just like I said." Habib continued to apply the combustible lubricant everywhere he could, placing unlit candle lanterns at crucial points on windowsills and near wooden furniture. Piling up cotton shirts at the top of the loft and underneath the stairs, he soaked them in spray.

"Are you sure that's a wise choice? Won't the BrigadesMen notice right away?"

He wedged chairs beneath the doorknob of the front entrance and pushed the wood rack against the kitchen door. Throwing the empty can down, he reached into Waitie's gun closet and pulled out gun cleaning fluid. "There's only three outside, and they won't enter without a crew and gear. The other BrigadesMen are spread out throughout the city—it will take several minutes for them to arrive. If we bar the doors then light the curtains and rugs on fire, they will think the entire interior is engulfed." Habib emptied the can.

"The fire will suck up personnel and resources away from searching for us—and it gives us cover. Their story is, a rash of fires was started by the Hostesses, and now you all have escaped. Their first thought will be that Hostesses committed the crime—and they won't be looking for us at the Jail. At least it'll keep 'em busy." Dressing Farnon in his trench coat, he began to pour the flammable gun cleaning fluid on the bodies.

"Not the trench coat!" Lourdes gasped.

"Sorry Chickie—I hate to do it, but it's my prized possession. If searchers find it, they'll think the body is mine, and that'll help keep them away from the Jail for a bit." Habib dumped the papers out of his briefcase onto the floor next to Farnon. "I won't be needing this bidness swag anymore, anyways."

Dubious, she peeked out the window as Habib disappeared into the bedroom.

"There's three BrigadesMen outside, just like the orders said. But they're watching the fireworks, so they're distracted."

Habib stepped around the corner, dressed in Farnon's broad-brimmed hat and a white shirt from Waitie's closet, with a dead Ranger's badge pinned to his chest. Lourdes flashed a smile. "Well, hi there, Ranger! Care to help a damsel in distress?"

Stuffing his own pistol back into his ankle holster, he snatched Balogun's 9mm and holster, threading it onto his belt. "Yeah, head for the bedroom window, and keep a lookout. The crowd's getting noisy again— time to leave behind a bar-be-que of death." He held out a small ledger book to Lourdes. "Stick this under your coat—it's the keys to the kingdom—the double ledger. Waitie always keeps two sets of books; this will help us find out who's their allies." Taking Farnon's revolver, Habib wiped away the blood, then stuck it in his pants pocket, five rounds still in it.

Habib looted the Bosses' bodies quickly. Waitie's personal effects were limited to a fixed-blade hunting knife and a set of keys; Balogun's body yielded more fruit, with an old-fashioned, eel-skin wallet, keys, and a memory stick. Habib scrutinized the memory stick, then shoved it into his pants pocket. It would be up to someone else to analyze the data found on it… now the gloves. Yanking them off, he found a wide, flat Ring. He tried pulling it off, without success. Puzzled, he muttered to Lourdes. "Strange—why's Balogun wearing a Ring when he can't use it? All the years I've known him, I've never seen him wear one."

"He has an old-fashioned pinkie ring he's worn from time to time—but I've never seen him wear this one. He's always kept it in a box by his bed all these years." Lourdes looked worried. "I've got a bad feeling about this, Frank. This shouldn't be happening if the Jammer is working."

"You and me both, Chickie—waaaaaait a second…" Habib shot her a suspicious glance. "How do you know about the Jammer?"

Lourdes flicked a cool smile at him. "Same as you. You spied on Winston and Dominic to learn about it—and I spied on you."

"Well, you got me there. ALGOS in the air, tech on the ground, and handlers for handlers… Strange days. Cover your face, and take no chances." Pulling up a bandana to hide his face, Habib went to light the candles around the room. Moving back to front, he backed out, tossing matches as he went. He came to the bedroom window, and he opened it quickly. There wasn't much smoke, yet; any early odor would be masked by the myriad smokey cooking fires and bar-be-que pits throughout Purgatory.

Helping Lourdes through the bedroom window, he muttered softly, "Let's scram." He tossed one final match through the window and closed it shut behind them. "Time to go out in a blaze of glory…" Grabbing her arm, he hurried her away from the brush-shrouded backside of Boss Waitie's cabin. Looking behind her, Lourdes could just barely see the smallest hint of smoke.

They met no travelers—all free personnel were gathered down at the main drag, watching the parade as it wound through town. This meant they were less likely to be met by a random busybody, but more likely to be spotted if they moved through an open area. Traveling down the fence line towards the dump, Habib moved towards a large brush pile. Pulling Lourdes to the side, they ducked behind it. "Put your hands behind your back, like they're tied. If someone stops us, I'm a Ranger and you're my prisoner."

"Mmm, sounds exciting," Lourdes whispered beneath her breath. "Perhaps we can revisit this scenario again sometime when we aren't in mortal danger."

"Cut the idle chatter, Chickie; tell me the nature of this visit, or I'm keeping my hat."

"Be that way." She sniffed. "We have to check the Signal Oak—according to the Gambler, a Five O'Clock message was supposed to be left there for one of us."

"Too late—I've already picked it up." Habib reached into his pants pocket to pull forth the leaf-wrapped package.

"Oh! Good job—you must have retrieved it while I was executing your follower…" Lourdes held out her hand for it.

"No, I'll open it, and you'll tell me what it means. No more secrets from me—you're gonna tell all." Habib peeled it open. A green feather fell out of the leaf.

> —*a feather in your cap when you reach your destination;*
> *deliver to the Eagle.*—*Raven*

Lourdes interpreted: "This is a message from the Gambler. It has a red dot in the upper right hand corner, so it's an urgent message The golden dot in the lower right corner means it's to go to Bogie's Hut, and the Eagle is Winston."

The Gambler again. It's always the Gambler… Habib squinted at the message. He knew some of the code, but not all—as the Bosses Handler, his focus was solely on the Administration of Purgatory. So how was it that Lourdes knew the all the codes? There was a lot more to her than met the eye—especially when it came to the Gambler. Habib mulled it over. He was feeling an odd, burning sensation in his chest, and he wanted it to stop. This was not how he trained; *keep it all bidness.* All bidness…

"Bogie's hut, huh…" Habib's eyes showed a glimmer of viciousness. Pondering the meaning of the Gambler's Bunker, Habib grumbled. "And the message is from the Gambler… it sounds like I'm picking up a pattern here. You and the Gambler are pretty tight, am I right?"

Miffed at Habib's suspicion, Lourdes cast him a veiled glance. "Trust me; it's not like that. It never has been."

Habib grunted. "Maybe you ought to tell me what it is, then, so I can keep things sorted out."

Ignoring him, Lourdes turned her attention to the package. "Interesting… it's a small package delivery. If someone catches us, I'll swallow it. Just make sure to recover it later."

"I think I'll pass." Habib allowed, "Instead of stopping yourself up with a mystery package, how about I run to draw them off, and you slink away."

"Oh please, what's to keep them from chasing us both?"

"Me shooting 'em, that's what."

Behind them, the first alarm bell sounded. Habib grabbed her arm and perp-walked her quickly from the brush pile down the fence-wall, towards the nearest trash-heap. They huddled behind a rusting station wagon, watching as the alarm bells started to sound. The few BrigadesMen stationed away from the parade route broke ranks to run…

"Time to move." Ducking down, they ran along the paths between the filthy mattresses and piles of molding carpet; small clouds of dust puffed up from their feet as they shuffled, trying to step between the hills of cast-off plastic cups and undying styrofoam coolers. High up in the brush growing between the trash dunes, plastic bags flapped, distracting and obscuring their motions as they ran. Slipping in Sander's too-large, cast-off boots, Lourdes still managed to negotiate the rusted cans and shards of broken glass that littered their path; Habib was not quite as light on his feet, losing his footing several times as they threaded their way through the garbage canyons of Purgatory Dump, approaching the refuse-shrouded backside of Bogie's hut.

In the distance, the sounds of disaster replaced the sounds of Shaney's triumph. Men shouted, angry and confused, as flame-light flickered in the evening sky.

A flock of Turkey Buzzards roosted on the roof in the dying light, watching as Habib and Lourdes stepped carefully between heaps of human waste and picked-clean animal carcasses. Staying low, they crept to the front of the hut; Habib waited, wary, as Lourdes pulled a dirty doormat aside to type a code into the hidden keypad underneath.

The door popped open, and she entered quickly. "Hurry, and pull the door shut behind you." He slipped in behind her as she pulled the wretched mattress to the side, revealing the hatch. Habib fixed the emerald feather into the band on his broad-brimmed hat; Lourdes protested. "Hey that's my feather!"

"No, it's not. I picked up the package, so this is my drop." He reached down to make the signal: two taps, then two taps more…

The hatch lowered, and Lourdes waved a gawking Habib into the lighted metal tunnel:

"Welcome back to the Modern Age, Frank."

Habib and Lourdes stepped back as Joey emerged from the Bunker hatch. Seeing the green feather in Habib's hat, he grunted. "So you're our contact? I wasn't expecting you two here…"

"We've got an urgent message for Winston," Lourdes whispered.

Holding his finger to his lips, Joey scooted back down the ladder to the platform, where Winston, Gunny, and Wilcox were waiting.

Habib helped Lourdes down, then secured the hatch. As Habib entered the tunnel, his eyes grew wide with wonder: glad to see his associate, Habib shook Winston's hand. "So this is how the other half lives…" He ran his hands along the walls, then turned, startled, to see a Masked Man rise out of the shadows, cape flying behind him and red flame-fangs masking his face.

"It's Marshal Azarian," Joey said with pride. "I costumed him."

"It's not exactly haute couture," Lourdes hummed as she looked at the stitching. "But I suppose it will do…"

A tense-looking Winston raised a hand: "Habib, do you have your Ring? Wilcox is resetting all Rings to channel 145, to avoid scanning and so we can communicate. We'll be meeting on that frequency to coordinate. According to Marshal Azarian, it's outside the ALGOS scanning spectrum, and an encrypted portable CommLink server has been set up for use."

"The Rings are working?" Lourdes whispered, concerned. "And ALGOS are here?"

"Yes, it's a double-edged sword," Winston grumbled. "We can communicate better now—but so can everyone else."

Nodding, the MoneyMan stuck his hand in his pants pocket and pulled out a decrepit wallet, retrieving a plain steel Ring from its folds. Lourdes noted it with interest; it seemed so utilitarian compared with his usual tastes. Habib booted up, and an avatar of a rough-looking young man appeared in the Watcher's display, dark eyes cold, head shorn. Harried, Wilcox fiddled with it for a few minutes as Habib stood by gamely, waiting until the channel reset was done. Grunting absently, Wilcox patted Habib's shoulder. "You're good to go."

The Watcher linked in:

#WATCHER: Glad to see you alive, Habib—ALGOS are now freely roaming Purgatory and should be monitoring conversations with their voice enhancement software, so don't discuss any sensitive info topside. Give us a SITREP, then the message. We have a lot of ground to cover and decisions to make.

Sobered by the news, Habib delivered. "Alright, Marshal, I'll cut to the chase. During a routine bidness meeting, I made a hit on Balogun and Waitie, killed them, and with Lourdes help, wasted two of their guards. Then we set the house on fire. Chartreaux missed the festivities. My coat's in the house, along with my briefcase; they should think I'm dead. At this moment, the Parade is just wrapping up, and all hell is breaking loose as Shaney enters Purgatory. Should be an interesting evening."

The Watcher grunted, impressed.

#WATCHER: Efficient and effective. Good job.

Normally energized by such information, Winston was abnormally irritable. "So we're burning down Purgatory now?" He turned to Lourdes: "What are you doing out there?"

"My job." Lourdes eyed him coolly. "I saved his life."

"It's true. She killed two men on her own, with nothing but a dagger." Unable to hide his admiration, Habib let it shine. Lourdes looked pleased.

Winston was unmoved. "Well, it's too dangerous for you to be out there now—the Jammers are down at Purgatory, and the Drones looking for Hostesses, Azarian, or the Afterling. If they ID you, they'll send units to investigate."

The Watcher spoke to Habib.

#WATCHER: Araceli, Destiny, and Kendra were spotted at Camp Forlorn by a drone. Based on the earlier report of a Hostess hiding a woman matching Rose's description at Purgatory, the search algorithms have classified the Hostesses as associates of Rose. That's why Camp Forlorn was targeted after the drone found the Specialists there.

Habib grimaced. "So they're in personal danger, then?"

#WATCHER: Yes. Their faces are now in the database, but a drone will be automatically assigned to anyone identified by biometrics as "female." Lourdes, on the other hand, is probably not in the database—yet. She's covered by the coat and scarf, so she probably passed detection for now; but if she is exposed as a female, the TIRS biometric recognition software will identify her quickly and tag her with an injectable ID for tracking.

Habib repeated the message to Lourdes. Nonchalant, she stated, "Well, we'll just have to deal with it."

"That's what I'm trying to do," Winston snapped. "So can we hurry this up already?"

Habib scowled. "Do you want this message or not?"

"Sorry…" Strained, Winston rubbed his heck. "We've got to come up for a solution for the ALGOS; we're under a lot of pressure here."

"I know that feeling." Habib produced the package; "It's from the Gambler."

Winston unwrapped it to reveal a small envelope, inscribed,

—Ask Big L

Winston handed it to Wilcox, who tore it open: a tiny, doughnut-shaped gasket made of composite alloy fell into the palm of his hand. Wilcox held it up to look at letters inscribed faintly on the gasket:

—RTFM

"It's a data grommet labelled 'RTFM'… huh." Popping it atop his ring's metal button, it clicked into place, interfacing with his Ring. "Read The Forkin' Manual…" Wilcox's eyes grew wide as he opened the transfer in The Watcher's shared display:

#CATASTRONIX Multi-Spectrum Portable Unit G6390—
#README.txt
#DISCLAIMER
#WARRANTY
#SPECIFICATIONS
…

"It's the manual—" Jumping up, Wilcox grabbed Winston by the collar. "It's the Manual!

On edge, Winston snapped, "What Manual?"

"The Jammer Manual!" Overjoyed, Wilcox was nearly dancing. "The Gambler sent us the user's manual for the Catastronix Jammer Booster!"

Jaw dropping, Winston grabbed Wilcox back. "That magnificent Bastard!" Winston started running down the tunnel—then stopped to quickly turn back to the Watcher. "I'll send an update at half-past Seven—open your frequency on 145 as per instructions… use the code!" Ecstatic, Winston bounded down the dark tunnel with Wilcox, racing a deadline.

Lourdes beamed; Habib noticed.

"Well, at least that's one bit of good news… " She whispered to the Watcher: "But what would happen if TIRS identifies one of us?"

Listening to the Watcher, Habib relayed his reply, concerned. "The Marshal says the drones would follow you around, hoping one of you would lead them to Rose."

"Would that person be harmed by the drones?" Lourdes asked again.

Habib relayed a message once more. "Not as long as the handlers believe there is a chance surveillance might be successful. If the drones, are discovered by the subject, however, that might trigger a decision to exterminate."

"Goins..." Lourdes whispered to Azarian: "Can they if tell Goins was born female?"

Joey gaped. "What?"

"I'll be damned..." Habib blinked. "I had no idea."

Quiet, Gunny confessed: "I've known all along. It don't make me no difference, because Goins is still Goins."

Recovering, Habib continued to relay the Watcher's message, quoting back word for word to Lourdes: "Sorry, I mean, the Marshal says it depends on how much of Goins' face is exposed; some of Goins' facial features may be transformed enough by the bioagent to hide birth origin, but the femoral q-angle will be a dead giveaway if a walking motion can be analyzed." Habib listened, confused. "I don't even know what the hell I just said... what's a q-angle?"

Lourdes laughed. "It means we wiggle when we walk." The Watcher grunted in the affirmative.

"That makes sense." He listened to the Watcher again. "However, the Marshal says this could possibly be used to our advantage—he says someone needs to notify Goins to lay low and await for further instructions. That someone would be me."

Concerned, Lourdes shook her head. "Let me handle it. Goins and I go way back."

"With all due respect, Lourdes, you ain't going nowhere," Habib said quietly.

A flash of surprise was followed by disdain. "With all due respect, Frank, I'll go where I want." She turned to head up the ladder; the Marshal held up his hand.

Calmly, Habib relayed: "The Marshal says to stop—and that's an order. You'll endanger us all if you go out there again; I know you made it this far, but we can't take any more chances. He's assigning you to Winston's team instead. He needs your expertise here."

"If I say I'm coming with you, I'm coming with you." Lourdes gave a cold stare. "I don't answer to you—or him."

"Then who do you answer to, Lourdes?" Insistent, Habib glared back. "Since you brought it up, why don't you enlighten us?"

Caught in her own words, Lourdes backed down. "I'm just tense. My apologies."

"Yeah, sure."

Privately, the Watcher hailed Habib.

#WATCHER: Tell me what her problem is, now. I've got no time for intrigue.

#HABIB: She's my handler—a spy sent to make sure I do what I'm supposed to do, and to report back on my activities. I didn't know until she showed up at Boss Waitie's, then suddenly it was true confessions time. She said it's why she saved me. I think she's working at the top level, either the Gambler, Dominic, or maybe even someone else, but she won't say who.

He wondered why she wouldn't say who… *odds are she tells everything to that old rat, the Gambler, and that's probably "who's the boss" of this operation.* That familiar stab of jealous envy returned, but Habib beat it down, just as he was trained to do.

#WATCHER: We need to know who she's working for. Is she a Visionary?

#HABIB: No, just a Normative—but she's still hard to read.

#WATCHER: Normz follow rules, some just hide their own rulebook. But she's still a Normz. They have set truths and rules. Whatever she was taught was an inviolate truth, threaten to violate it. Give her a choice: she has to give you what you want, or violate her own rules. She'll blow her top and tell all in an attempt to keep herself within her own boundaries. After you get the info, head for the Jail, then check back in thirty minutes on frequency 145 for further instructions. Take my gear bag with you—I'll need it to suit up at the Jail after the fights. See you topside. Good luck.

#HABIB: Consider it done.

Oblivious to the internal conversation, Lourdes chatted politely with Joey. Noting the time on his Landlord-worthy wristwatch, Joey effused:

"Time to go, Marshal… Y'all stay safe, and enjoy the fights. Tonight is going to be something no one will forget!" Excited, Joey became the Promoter once more. Shaking hands in farewell all around, the Watcher handed off his bag to Habib, then he and Joey headed up the Ladder towards their fortune. The hatch closed behind them, leaving Habib in the tunnel with Gunny and Lourdes.

Time to find out who's the Boss.

Habib discerned Lourdes' inviolate truth—Lourdes considered herself independent, cunning, cool, and she knew others saw her the same way. *So what's the opposite of independent?* Face expressionless, Habib made his move: "Lourdes, you gotta stay here."

"Nonsense. I'm going with you."

"It's for your own good, Chickie. Purgatory is no place for a woman." Habib felt a small regret; the sentiment was true, but the words sounded... *wrong.*

Practical, Lourdes pressed on. "It's no place for anyone. I'm worried about you—"

Time to push some buttons. Habib tried to come up with something deliberately provocative. "And I'm worried about you. I'll be fine; so don't you worry your pretty little head about me."

"Really, Frank?" Eyes glinting, Lourdes remained deadly calm. "I don't think so."

Being a man of good sense, Gunny backed away slowly, disappearing into the tunnel and taking refuge around a corner, away from the coming verbal blast radius.

So the thought of losing your independence rattled your cage, did it? Habib grunted to himself. The patronizing tone felt unnatural, against everything he had been trained to do; but it also seemed to have touched a nerve— *maybe even enough for her to pop off and say the wrong thing...* He sincerely hoped this would be worth the heartburn it was going to cause. But he had one tiny problem: Lourdes was too good. She was reading him like a book, recognizing his discomfort, and she was able to detect a false note.

Habib needed to believe what he was saying—he needed genuine, intense emotion... just like he felt when she talked about the Gambler.

There it is.

"I'll do the thinking," Habib said curtly. "You don't have to think. Just look pretty."

She leaned back, studying him. "What's wrong with you?"

He let the heat kindle in him. "Nothing's wrong with me—I'm just stating the truth. That's how you got this gig anyways, by using your pretty little head. Pretty little... whatever."

"Frank, you can drop this ridiculous sexist charade; I'm not telling you anything."

"You don't have to tell me anything." Tapping into a hidden energy, he let it ignite just below the surface. He had always kept his jealousy under control with Sam... *time to unleash the Beast.* His eyes narrowed as he allowed it to flame up within him. "You can tell it to your Sugar Daddy."

"Sugar Daddy?" Recognizing trouble, Lourdes stepped back. "Who are you going on about?"

"You know exactly who. The one you keep going on about, the one you keep running to. Everything's about him. Everything comes from him..." He let himself imagine why a man would be that for Lourdes, and it poured into his soul, turning his words caustic. "I can imagine why..."

"Stop it, Frank."

"No. You need to come to grips with it. You're a sham." His snide contempt was jarring. "You act all independent, you want to be strong, but you're attracted to power. It makes you weak in the knees. Just like on the rooftop with me..."

"That's not true!" Lourdes snarled, defensive. "It meant nothing to me —I have my own power; I just killed two men on my own!"

"Yeah, you did, but it's all an act. You 're tough as nails around me— but I bet you're another way around the Gambler." He let his mind run down that road. "I think I'll visit the Gambler and ask him about any dealings between you two, and see what he has to say about that." Habib mulled it over. "And if I don't like his answer, I'll just put a cap in his ass."

Lourdes blanched. "Our relationship is strictly professional—"

"It's strictly bidness, then? Nothing personal?"

"Absolutely!"

"Strictly bidness with the Gambler..." A flame shot through him, unexpected and hot. "Just like it's 'strictly bidness' with me, Lourdes?"

Shocked at Habib's sudden turn, she recoiled. "No!"

"Either he's your Sugar Daddy, or he's your Boss."

"That's not how it is...."

"Or he's both..." Habib snorted. "Yeah, I bet you'd like that; sit on your Sugar Daddy's lap, and take a little dictation like a good little Sugar Baby..."

She snap-kicked Habib in the groin, and he doubled over, taken by surprise.

"You son-of-a-bitch! How dare you—" Furious, Lourdes kicked him again; groaning, Habib leaned against the wall. Ablaze with indignation, Lourdes jabbed a finger at the huddling Macho. "I have skills, I do a hell of a job, and I'm nobody's 'baby'! He chose me because I'm the best woman for the job, not because of sexual favors…"

Habib straightened up slowly, guarding his prized possessions. "So the Gambler's just your Boss, nothing more…"

Angry, Lourdes started to say something, then paused, mortified. Blinking, she backpedalled; "I mean, I…" Habib could see her wheels turning, trying to gain traction.

He winked. "Gotcha."

"Why you… you…" sputtering, Lourdes sizzled at him. "This was all a set-up! The jealousy, the bravado—it's all an act!"

"Maybe it is, and maybe it ain't." Taking his fedora out from under his thin jacket, Habib set it upon her head, then swept her off her feet, nose to nose. "But you did tell me who you work for, so congratulations, Chickie—you just won yourself a hat!" Triumphant, he kissed her, then set her back on her feet and moved away quickly, before she could take another kick at him.

Fuming, Lourdes contemplated how to regain the upper hand. "You manipulative, underhanded…"

"Spy versus spy, baby."

Exasperated, she threw up both hands. "Fine, you big lug. You got me." Cunning, Lourdes gave the tiniest hint of a smile. "But I have your hat, so by default I have you. Point and Counterpoint." She held out her hand: " I say let's call it even and get out of here."

The tiniest hint of a smile answered her back. "You ain't getting out of here." Shouldering the Watcher's bag, Habib called into the tunnel behind her: "Sergeant Renfro, escort Ms. LeFleur to the Hostesses—she's under house arrest for espionage until I can meet with the Council about this little spy game."

Gunny stepped out of the shadows, apprehensive.

"What?" Lourdes yelped. "I'm on your side—"

"So I see. I intend to keep you there."

"I saved your life, you ingrate!"

"You did. Now I'm gonna save yours—you ain't coming with me." He looked at Lourdes one last time; only his eyes bore some glint of the emotion within. "See ya on the other side, Chickie."

Livid, Lourdes watched as Habib ascended the hatch and closed it behind him.

Approaching cautiously, Gunny held his gun lightly; "Lourdes, I'm real sorry, but…"

"I'll escort myself." Whipping off the fedora, she turned on her heel and stormed down tunnel towards the other Specialists, muttering as she went, slapping the hat against her thigh with each stride. "If he thinks he can leave me behind that easy, he's got another thing coming…" Her eyes flashed green lightning:

"No more Miss Nice Spy."

———◆———

III

In the shadow of the Pair'O'Dice Pier Wall, Evangelo adjusted his double-huckleberry cross-draw shoulder holster, sweating bullets. He thought he was strong enough to take seeing her; after all, he had been strong enough to walk away. So why was it different now?

I never should have looked directly at her… it's like staring at an Eclipse. His hands shook slightly. *Once she hits your eyes, you're blinded.*

It all happened so fast—

Leaving the DragLine's Love Shack, Evangelo sought Keller in the sunset shadows. Against the flaming fall sky, he searched the horizon, for Keller. For a moment, he thought he saw the assassin's shadow perched at the top of the old windmill located inside the walls of Pair'O'Dice. A closer look revealed the truth; only dangling blades from the damaged wind vane hung down where the imagined hitman stood. Keeping himself low profile, Evangelo moved casually through the sunset glow, searching for Keller.

All along the waterfront, only birds and frogs were seen; the alligators lay in wait, hopeful for a drunken partier, but they were denied—the entire town had fled the outskirts of Purgatory for the heart of town, the Main Drag. Almost two thousand Survivors lined the streets, their tongues wagging with gossip, excited, chatting about the sudden change in political climate, focused on the coming parade, hooting, craning, calling…

Evangelo had turned towards the commotion near the gate—and that's when he saw her. It was just a glimpse, a flash through the guard door; he saw the sparkle of her silver-studded jeans and the profile of her curves as she sat atop her horse, preparing to enter Purgatory.

The Woman Evangelo loved, riding the Horse Evangelo reared, decked out in the silver concho'd custom tack Evangelo tooled... Shaney glittered beautiful and bright, the personification of Evangelo's love. It struck him square in the heart, a savage blow that left him feeling faint. He leaned against the wall and closed his eyes, but her image was burned into his retina, the white-hot fire of Shaney at peak intensity.

Refocus; an assassin is loose in Purgatory.

He breathed out, trying to center himself. Checking Ruby's .357 revolver, concealed on his left hip, Evangelo had always been impressed by Ruby's strong-side draw technique, often going head to head with him in training and contests. But there would no more contests with Ruby; like so many others who had come before him, Ruby had fallen into sin—*and the wages of sin is death.* He sighed, glad for the extra gun—three six-shooters; *eighteen shots without a reload.*

Still searching Purgatory for Keller, Evangelo had scanned at all the high points he could find, then checked low-angle firing lines—still nothing. Somewhere out there, an assassin was waiting for a target to come in range. Whether that target was Azarian, the Afterling, or Shaney, Keller had to be stopped, and Evangelo had a plan to do it.

Dressed in Ruby's western-cut sports-jacket and silver-belly cowboy hat, the Little Marshal cut a dashing figure, one which would not be recognized by others, but still be easily recognized by Keller. The olive-green suit, with its silvery-white piped yoke and edges, was complimented by a once-white scarf worn as a fluttering tie, hiding the front of a dingy white snap-front shirt. It was not overly loud or flashy; the subtle color seemed to transmute from a soft green, to beige, to gray, depending on the background, complementing the aged whiteness of the hat.

Ruby had always been a dandy, a classic gunslinger who loved the status of being a fast gun. Previously content to bedazzle his Ranger's uniform with silver hardware and conchos, the fancy suit symbolized a departure from the Rangers for Ruby. The suit had probably been acquired as a disguise for this mission, and would be familiar only to those on El Trafico's assassin team. Ruby's disguise would now hide Evangelo; still, the little Marshal felt uncomfortable in the fancy suit, for to him it represented Ruby's fatal decadence.

Ruby's death gave a new life to Evangelo through the suit. In the dimming light, the slightly shorter Evangelo would be able to pass for

Ruby, getting closer to his target before his true identity was revealed. The suit however, was not merely a disguise—it served function; the short, light jacket was able to conceal Evangelo's double-huckleberry rig in an easily accessible manner. It was very fortunate that the chubby pink dancer had taken the quick-draw artist by surprise, half-naked, or the suit might not have fared so well. Evangelo pondered: *How humiliated Ruby must have been to know he was killed, not by dueling guns, but by a sexual conquest in bed?*

Whatever the carnal distraction, it had provided enough time to garrote Ruby with the bed-post chain, resulting in a welcome change of costume for Evangelo, who was not comfortable in his role as exotic dancer. However, Evangelo kept the dance costume's silk headscarf, as it made for excellent facial concealment; it could be hidden and kept around his neck as an ascot until needed. Now he pulled up the silk scarf to hide his face, then walked out into the road, hoping his recognizable fashion profile would draw the assassin out. Ruby's dressy style was not a usual look for the practical Evangelo, but it was suited for the purpose. If spotted, Keller should hesitate, demanding to know why Ruby was out in Purgatory instead of staking out the DragLine as ordered.

But time grew short, and Keller still remained unseen. The fact that Keller had remained hidden for so long from Evangelo was a testament to Keller's training—for it was Evangelo himself who had helped train Keller in the art of surveillance when he was first recruited as a Ranger. Evangelo remembered those early days, and the glory of his trusted band of brothers, Keller among them… *how had it all gone so horribly wrong?*

Under the guidance of Dominic, Chief Levi ran a a highly respected organization, one that Survivors looked to for justice and protection. Dominic and Levi were two of a kind, old-school Survivors who believed the System could bring hope to all Survivors. But with the passing of Chief Levi and the ascension of Chief Emmanuel, the Rangers began to change; they became corrupted—and it all had happened on Evangelo's watch.

Chief Levi himself said it, long ago—Evangelo had always been the moral heart of the Rangers. Perhaps the heart was still pure, but the rest of the Ranger body had now become diseased from head to toe. Eventually the disease would have spread to Evangelo… *But what if that corruption had already spread?* Frowning, Evangelo turned his attention to now. There would be time for introspection on his own tacit complicity later. Sunset approached—it was time to catch a killer. Evangelo accessed his own personal profile of Keller from his memories of the man.

—*Ian Keller*—best as a medium range marksman, 300-500 yards—*the Main Drag's approximate distance away from Purgatory Wall*

—hates the wind in his face: *winds currently out of the southwest*

—prefers the sun at his back or to his left: *sun setting, due west*

—prefers high-angle shots, above interference: *in a structure with a clear shot...*

Evangelo calculated: *facing east-northeast, in a high structure with a clear shot near Purgatory Wall*. He began to look for this high structure. Easing along the Parade Route, Evangelo strolled along, unnoticed behind the eager crowds straining to see Shaney. Survivors from all over the Tejas Co-op thronged the Main Drag, pushing against the rope and handcart barrier, held back by the BrigadesMen with their guns. As Evangelo walked, a ravine opened up to his south, leading through the heart of Pair'O'Dice pier all the way down to the lake.

As the first bell sounded Seven O'Clock, Evangelo spotted a glint of sunlight—was it a golden shaft reflected off an unprotected scope?

The top deck of the Party Pontoon!

Evangelo ducked back behind a tree, then look to where a scope would be trained:

The Bandstand.

The Bandstand—a rusting, vaulted carport atop a built-up concrete pad—was filled with Survivors awaiting the arrival of their Honored Guest. DeLisha and the sequin'd DragLine Queens stood with feather boas at the ready, eager to perform their sparkler dance routine. Behind them, cinder-block and scaffolding bleachers were arranged; these were seated with at least twenty nervous LandLords and an equal number of guests, each under armed guard from Chartreaux's brigade. To the side, a grouping of rusting cast iron lawn chairs sat, mostly empty.

The top of the Party Pontoon would be a logical sight for Keller to set up his Sniper's nest—and without a pair of binoculars, there was only one way to find out if he was there.

The gathered BrigadesMen themselves looked more organized. Regulars had added silver arm bands, crafted cleverly from aluminum duct tape, to their fire coats; officers sporting braided silver shoulder-cords to match the braided silver bands on their fire hats. It was a surprisingly striking look—for the first time, the almost one-hundred-men-strong Purgatory Brigade looked like a militia.

Applause welled up from the group as a hulking form heaved into view from around the side of the platform. Natty Panama Straw Hat perched atop his warty head, Boss Chartreaux oozed onto the platform with an odd grace, his voluminous white shirt paired with clean khakis and a .50 calibre hand-cannon in a shoulder holster. Fearsomely large, Boss Chartreaux exuded the aura of power, wielding a steel ball-topped hickory walking stick in one hand and a bouquet of yellow chrysanthemums from his own garden in the other. Silk ascot knotted beneath his wobbling jowls, he gave a magnanimous wave to the crowd, and they approved, the BrigadesMen cheering.

A vicious heat scorched Evangelo at the thought of Shaney with Chartreaux. He remembered the horrific encounter of yesterday, and it seemed inconceivable that Shaney would knowingly link herself to such evil. Grim, he remembered Dominic's torture and the cries of the woman in the cell. *Destiny...* where was she? The light and heat of Shaney had almost erased Destiny's image from Evangelo's mind.

The last gong of the Seven O'Clock bell sounded. The announcer—a vendor in an elegantly tarnished suit—boomed through his megaphone: "Citizens and Honored Guests—join me in greeting Commander Lillabeth Shaney of the Tejas Rangers!" The gates swung open, and the town erupted in cheers—

"Welcome to Purgatory—a Hell of a Town!"

And there she was, bedecked in her silver-studded shirt, white hat shining in the sun: Shaney, Queen of the Tejas Rangers. As her formidable entourage of Rangers fanned out ahead and behind her, Shaney entered triumphant into Purgatory, silver six-shooters blazing. Ever the show horse, Storm pranced, unafraid of the crowds or firecrackers, even as Evangelo had so lovingly trained him to be a gun horse. With sparklers raining down stars, Shaney's face lit up, radiant with wonder, and Evangelo realized:

He would always love Shaney. It didn't matter what she did or who she did it with—what Shaney had been, long ago, was just as important to Evangelo as what Shaney had become. Evangelo would forever love his shining, shooting star—Shaney. Devastated at his own weakness, he turned from her, racing a killer's bullet.

Evangelo calculated again: from Keller's angle, he wouldn't have a clear line of fire on Shaney until she made the turn of the curve at the far end of the Main Drag Loop—at this rate, that would be... *three minutes.*

Slipping through the loose boards in the LowTown border fence, Evangelo stealthily hurried beneath the hanging lanterns, through the deserted streets of Pair'O'Dice. Past the ShangHigh Drug Den, with its decaying red velvet rooms, past the WallEyed Fit, with its fine leather boots, past the Eden Boutique, with its paper roses fresh-folded for the delight of the visiting woman—he came to the end of the road. There before him, just around the corner, was the boat ramp leading to the Party Pontoon Lagoon.

Long ago, retired oil-field workers bought houses down by the Lake. Bored with leisure life, and eager to use their skills, they built a metal scaffold, sheathed it with composite board and floated it atop fifty-five gallon drums to create a large, floating dock. Not content to rest upon their floating laurels, they added a second deck and railings, and christened it the "Beer Boat." Popular demand cried out for more, so a second dock like the first was created and attached—and thus was born Party Pontoon Lagoon. For many years, it was the location of bar-be-ques and summer flings, but then the Happening came, and the gators took over until Survivors showed up to wrestle it back.

Now a path overarched with elms led to a stout palisade wall blocking the shoreline from all gators; this left only a narrow access gate to the sturdy rope bridge spanning the gap between the dock and the Party Pontoon. Below it, the alligators waited, seeking revenge for their losses. Unfazed, thirsty Purgatory Men considered it part of the ambiance of Pair'O'Dice pier; if you wanted a drink, you had to brave the gators to get one. Occasionally a soused Survivor fell over the rails, but that was a small price to pay for entertainment in Pair'O'Dice.

It was especially exciting when the alligators held court for their King, "The Father of the Waters"—known to many at Purgatory as "Big Daddy." In Life Before, usually females were the only ones to grow to such a gargantuan size; but after the Happening, it seemed any male was bigger, stronger, meaner—and that included gators. Legendary, Big Daddy glided the waters of the Party Pontoon Lagoon, almost tame, patiently waiting for tribute. The Survivors of Purgatory fed him well; any offense against Purgatory Men by outsiders meant it was time to feed the alligators. In return, Big Daddy and his reptilian flotilla guarded the Party Pontoon well.

There was only one way for Evangelo to gain access to the floating docks and get to Keller in time. Evangelo pulled his hat down to hide his face then stepped into the road, directly in Keller's line of sight.

The Little Marshal did his best impersonation of the Ruby's subtle swagger in the dying light as he approached the tree-lined path to the Party Pontoon. He walked purposefully, as if he had an urgent message. In the lowering light, Evangelo hoped he could get closer before Keller recognized him. He kept his hand close to his weapon—just a few steps further, out from under the trees, and perhaps Evangelo could get a good surprise shot at Keller.

Evangelo heard the sound of a seat scooting across the upper deck. Now out from under the arching branches of the elms, he could see where Keller had hastily set up his sniper perch behind a solid section of metal barrier, shielding himself from any would-be suppressive fire. Thwarted, Evangelo would have to get closer to draw a bead on Keller. He continued down the path; as he neared the bridge, he heard Keller hiss above him, "Ruby? What the hell... don't interrupt. I'm in the zone."

Keller ducked behind the metal barrier once more, as Evangelo pressed on; behind them, rounds of firecrackers were shooting off, popping and hissing as Shaney's entourage progressed through the cheering crowds down the Main Drag. Grabbing the ropes, he gingerly stepped across, mere feet above the hungry alligators lurking in the water beneath the rope bridge.

There must have been ten gators at least, floating, watching as Evangelo came across; the sea of saurian throwbacks parted, allowing a gigantic swell of water to rise between them. Hissing and bellowing, the Alligators greeted their King... all twenty-one feet of Big Daddy was home. A creaking groan was heard as the monster's maw opened wide, a cavernous abyss plunging Evangelo into a cold-blooded pit of terror. Evangelo swallowed hard... he hated alligators.

Fuming, Keller peeked over the railing, mostly hidden; his pale, eczematous skin turned red with anger as the impostor moved quickly across the open deck.

Evangelo heard it, almost a whisper—the sound of a round slowly cycling into the chamber of an automatic handgun. Evangelo caught his breath.

Lunging for the protection of cover beneath the upper deck, Evangelo heard a suppressed pop and felt the buzz as a bullet whizzed by his ear, ricocheting off the fallen piece of metal decking behind him. He rolled under the upper deck, drawing his six shooter.

"Come out, Cap..." He heard Keller's snort above him, mocking. "I should have know it was you behind that veil. It suited you, just like your ugly-ass boots."

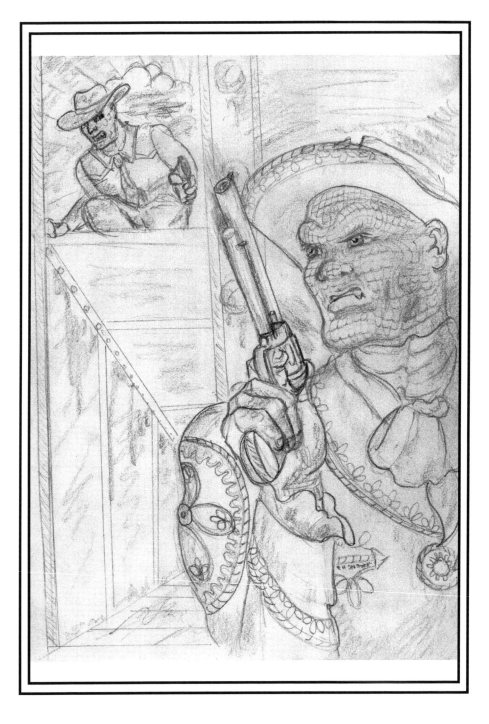

Looking down, Evangelo noticed with a start—
The boots!

When he had retrieved his gear from DeLisha, Evangelo had forgotten to change into Ruby's snakeskin boots. Instead, he was wearing his own battered bullhide ropers, out of habit. Inwardly groaning, the little Marshal mentally kicked himself.

Evangelo analyzed his opponent's method: *Keller is using his handgun, because his sniper weapon is set up on the tripod, aimed at his potential target. If I can get to the sniper weapon, I can take out Chartreaux at the bandstand.* Evangelo grimaced; he could avenge the rape of Destiny and save Shaney from further degrading herself, all with one bullet. He felt a war within as the images of the two women wrestled within him: one violated, yet pure in heart—the other violent and impure in soul.

"So you're here to play the hero and hope you finally get laid by Shaney?" Seemingly sensing his former Captain's struggle, Keller chuckled viciously. "It takes a special kind of sissy-boy to never get laid by Shaney; hell, I don't even like women, and I still got laid by Shaney."

Evangelo flushed through his bronzy scales but remained silent.

Keller taunted again. "Come out, you little bitch. I've got something for you—" A shot came through the flooring of the upper deck, piercing the composite flooring near Evangelo's feet. Splinters flew.

Cool, Evangelo studied the bullet hole from Keller's weapon; *a 9mm?* If he remembered correctly, it was an SK 9mm Subcompact, Keller's preferred close-range weapon. Two magazines, *ten rounds per mag...* the random shots were an attack aimed at herding Evangelo towards an objective—in this case, the ladder—in hopes of forcing him out. *I taught you that technique,* Evangelo remembered grimly. *Keller was a good but impatient shooter.* This was a weakness.

Stealthy, the Little Marshal picked up a chunk of wood debris from the shot and tossed it at the foot of the ladder.

It pinged as it hit the metal pipes, then Keller's bullet pierced the decking again beneath the ladder. Directly above his own head, Evangelo saw the decrepit decking sag ever so slightly. Evangelo aimed and squeezed the trigger; the blast of Ruby's .357 magnum revolver blew a hole through the sagging boards above his head. Keller's gun answered in kind, and its bullet singed Evangelo's hand, barely missing him. Evangelo fired upwards, rolling to his right as a hail of lead followed him. One caught the edge of his boot heel...

Flipping up onto his feet, Evangelo reversed course back towards the first shot of the bullet grouping, out of pattern. A final shot pierced the deck ahead of him. *That's ten shots...* Keller would have to reload.

The little Marshal waited, silent. From the parade route, the fireworks were reaching a crescendo; Keller was running out of time.

Evangelo heard the magazine hit the deck and slide, about four feet to his own right. He pointed the muzzle two feet back from the sound of the mag drop and slide—back to the point where Keller would stand. He fired, shattering the decking overhead.

A muffled shriek rewarded him as Keller crumpled, hitting the upper deck above Evangelo's head; Evangelo could hear Keller swearing in agony, scrabbling around on the deck above him. As Keller thrashed, his bloody foot hit the tripod of his subcompact sniper weapon, and it toppled through the railing and onto the deck below.

Evangelo leapt for the gun, desperate to use it to kill Chartreaux; but Keller's sniper rifle bounced off the deck, between the floating docks into the lake below. As it splashed into a maelstrom of reptilian tails and jaws, he heard a cheer erupt down by the Main Drag—Shaney had arrived at the Bandstand. Drumming reverberated as the DragLine's DragQueen Drum Corp began their sparkler number.

Keller had lost his chance to kill Shaney.

Above him, Evangelo heard Keller curse, racking the slide on the SK9. He looked up to see a snarling Keller scrambling towards the rail, gun in his shaking hand. Another shot whizzed by Evangelo's ear and into the water. Hit, a gator bled, and the others animals attacked, frenzied. Twisting and writhing, the reptiles savagely ripped each other, maddened by blood.

Rolling beneath the upper deck, Evangelo flattened himself beneath a built-in bench. Whispered curses floated down from the upper deck as the injured Keller scooted towards the railing; careful to not expose himself, the tall Hombre leaned over the railing to squeeze off another shot. Evangelo aimed for Keller's weapon—

Evangelo's aim was true.

Keller's gun blew away, along with most of his hand; dismembered fingers went flying into the Lake below the deck railing. The distant roar of Shaney's adoring crowds drowned out Keller's own roar of terror as the waters stained red beneath him. Teetering over the rail, Keller began to slip...

The Lake exploded as the snout of the monstrous Alligator King breached the surface. Duck weed dangling between his jagged teeth, the Father of the Waters surged from the gray deeps, lake water rushing in rivulets from his craggy back.

Precarious, the assassin sweated as he reached for the rail with the remnant of his hand. Bloody stump slapping, he could not grasp the slippery rail, his lanky body see-sawing over the water. Keller swung his arm behind him, trying to hook his elbow around a pipe; off balance, he began to slowly tilt forward.

Involuntarily, Evangelo reached out to try and save the man he once considered a brother—

Pitching head first, Keller toppled into the churning lagoon between the floating docks, flailing as the alligators swarmed him.

Blood and effluvia spread; gargantuan jaws yawned wide to swallow the howling man, and the Father of the Waters dragged Keller down into the murky depths beneath the dock. Horrified, Evangelo watched as a trailing burst of bubbles floated to the surface, departing with Keller's soul.

Keller was no more corrupt than Shaney... Evangelo prayed earnestly for forgiveness; *the wages of sin is death,* but—*all have sinned and fallen short of the glory of God.* Evangelo realized too well that he himself was only a kiss away from the same corruption.

Above the once-more peaceful waters of the Lake, the stars rose. *Night Cometh.* Beyond the walls of Purgatory, the night creatures were gathering, celebrating the darkness.

A shout rose again on the horizon, different than before. Strident voices sounded above drums, and the music trickled to a stop; Evangelo lifted his eyes to the horizon. Flames illuminated a column of black smoke, and alarm bells rang out their brazen warning. Taking his cue, Evangelo pulled his hat down low once more, to walk the streets of Pair'O'Dice.

Behind a grove of trees, Joey and the Watcher prepared to make their entrance.

Through his mask, the Watcher turned his veiled eyes to the darkening skies, searching for signs of the enemy. The glittering golden Metallilume panel obscured his eyes, blurring their shape and shielding them from the drones' biometric scans. Behind the mask, he could feel the craving hit him in the gut once more, as the last of daylight slipped from the sky—in the billows of smoke, the Stuff was calling...

Somewhere in the burning cabin, a large stash of the Stuff was burning, and a waft of the scent brought on a wave of nausea; it washed over him, tormenting him with the hollowness of his addiction's void. Wrestling with an enemy more powerful than flesh and blood, he fought it off with a reminder that the Stuff was a chemical chain, a one way ticket to serfdom for him. There was no time to revisit old demons—this day had enough of its own. The Watcher checked his personal jammer and proceeded to surveil the scene.

Down by the Bandstand, BrigadesMen were running as fires once again flickered in HighTown. Armed guards still held their guns casually trained on the LandLords, as their captive audience looked on in excitement and horror. Concerned bystanders left the parade route to form a bucket brigade from the Commons Well hand pump, and the teamwork and training of the Combined Brigades made for a compelling show of Purgatory might and daring. An entry team of four geared-out firefighters kicked down a door, and flames shot out; the crowd gasped with morbid delight.

In the middle of the road, a tight circle of perhaps twenty Rangers on horseback were gathered around their Commander in a protective formation. In the heart of that group, the Watcher knew: Shaney would be at the centre of it all. To the untrained eye, it would have been hard to tell which one was her, with all the white hats... but he knew. *The pivot point is the principal.* He peered through the crowd, straining to see her; to have a face to go with all the stories would be helpful. He noted the attitude of the Rangers; wary, hands ready at their firearms, unsure about the cause of the chaos.

It wasn't the worst he had ever seen—the protective detail seemed to be attentive and ready; still, The Watcher snorted disapprovingly. Any security professional with any sense at all would have whisked their VIP away and hidden her somewhere safe in this situation. However, in this case the VIP was in charge of her own detail, so all bets were off. He pondered his own security team, and his own VIP—*it was time for an update.*

Checking his Digital Deception Transmitter, the Watcher confirmed it to be activated; the personal jammer would be masking his data to any

ALGOS or scanners.. He opened his HeadsUp Display and scanned for Rose's location and biometric data packet, which would be able to link only to her own the Ring, via her unique identifier... *nothing*. He frowned and scanned again—

Frustration gripped him as he fiddled with settings... was his own jammer jamming her signal, or was her new Ring blocking her nanobots somehow? Wilcox had mentioned the "Kiddie Protecc AI". *It's possible...* overzealous firewalls wouldn't be a bad thing, but he still needed a way to reach her. He had grown used to observing her vital signs, seeing her location data in real time. Rose should be tucked away in a comfy corner, behind three guards and two hidden doors, eating a cruelty-free snack and reading a book. The thought pleased him, but not as much as it would please him to see it with his own eyes.

Taking advantage of this mayhem, the Insertion Team should be moving on their objective, The Watcher surmised; if all went as planned, another critical component of tonight's breakout would be secured. He cast a glance at the faces in the Purgatory audience lining the parade route —this was a fantastic opportunity to gather a visual database of Purgatory and Plantation power players. *Time to record the action for future analysis.*

#WATCHER: Talisa, activate Surveillance Suite; utilize company proxy login and initiate supplemental TRAACKR interface.

Talisa's warm voice purred at him:

#<3 TalisaBOT: *Running SuperSnooper Surveillance Software Suite —activating Documental with FaceFrag, TrueSpeex and ProFylePlus Lite. Do you want to upgrade to ProFylePlus Premium now—Y or N? <3*

Frowning, he chose 'N' and closed the bot window; he was still miffed he had never upgraded while it was available. A full-featured investigation tool, the Surveillance Suite was proprietary to the Firm, and his final interview process would have granted full access to all the bells and whistles it had to offer. Unfortunately, his lack of closure left him forever stuck in 'ProFylePro Lite' mode, with only guest access.

Stepping behind a honeysuckle bush, he held out his hand to Joey, pulling the fingerless gloves back to expose the Ring for linking.

The hefty Macho made a face. "I really don't like holding hands..." The Watcher paid him no mind, uplinking his Ring's Stone to Joey's Neural Port with a firm handshake. Joey sighed.

#WATCHER: I don't care. Until we get you a ring, this is the only way I can talk to you. Brother Fox has a looted a few extra—as soon as he has them switched to secure protocols, you'll get one. But until then, deal with it, and talk through the ChipMate Protocol. Just make it look like a firm handshake, and no one will suspect a thing. The drones have enhanced electric ears—so keep conversations on the ring, I'm blocked from their scanning, so direct link to me is safer. But use the code, Brother Snapper—just in case.

Joey nodded, the Brother Code was the WildLand Express Code, used in all sensitive discussion; it was familiar to any in 'the Brotherhood', as the WildLand Express called themselves. While in the Gambler's Bunker, Winston had given the Watcher quick verbal summary regarding the basics of the Brother Code, but the Watcher was still not familiar with all of it. He would simply have to learn as he went—fortunately, the Watcher was surrounded by others who knew it by heart.

#MANCINI: Sorry, Brother Wolf. It's just been a while since I used any of this.

#WATCHER: It's fine, now let's get into Pair'O'Dice while the chaos is hot—we have an hour, and I need to recon one last time. I have questions for a certain retailer. I need to know what he knows about that package he gave us.

Joey patted his service weapon, concealed in his waistband:

#MANCINI: I'm game, but we need to recruit our new friend on the way—he said to meet at Seven in the Alley behind the Commons.

#WATCHER: We'll hit it on the way to Pair'O'Dice.

Our new friend... Lord Li. *We'll see how much of a friend he is,* The Watcher decoupled. Slipping through the abandoned park and past the quiet jail, they passed through the shadows of the Commons Campground, giving only the sign—a tap on the brim—to their fellow Agents on duty with the wagons. No other acknowledgement was giving as they wandered down the twisting alley that ran between LowTown and Pair'O'Dice. The Watcher had a new respect for Winston; the former Boss was responsible for designing the hidden access points and escape routes embedded at Purgatory.

During their last briefing, Winston had mapped them out for the Watcher, adding them into the Marshal's MapPix program. The Watcher opened the map now, and made his way towards the access panel. Along the way, they encountered stray cats and a few drunken revelers. The Watcher stepped around carefully, remembering his first encounter with Bogie… *angels unawares.*

The Watcher grunted, then pointed to a clump of Box Elder bushes, growing up around an overflowing trash dumpster.

#WATCHER: This is the location, but be aware—someone's sitting on the other side of this dumpster. I can hear him, breathing slow, regular so probably another drunk. Just be cautious.

Joey frowned at the prospect of squeezing through yet another small opening. Wary, he tried to get a better look at the man behind the dumpster. In the shadows, he could only see the sprawling figure, arms and legs akimbo. Seeing no easy way around him, Joey grimaced, then stepped over him to the other side of the dumpster. In the darkness, he tripped over the drunk's extended leg; chagrined, Joey righted himself: "Oof—sorry!"

The drunk looked up and whispered: "No problem, Brother…" Lord Li dusted himself to stand.

"You're a Brother?" A delighted Joey reached down to help him up, whispering—"Fancy meeting you here! I didn't recognize you without your headdress."

Li chuckled: "That was the idea." Reaching into a clump of grass, Li pulled forth his impressive Boar's Head Helmet, and the Watcher noted the green feather affixed to the crown; He remembered the Gambler's admonition that their contacts would be sporting one of the Watcher's Flying Serpents' green feathers in their hats. But how did they get them?

It struck the Watcher: he had traded his feathers to the Shopkeeper at the Emporium, in exchange for the Metallilume Dress—so they must have been passed by the old man back into the Revolutionary network. So the Shopkeeper wasn't just a sympathizer—he was an agent. *How deep does this network go?*

The Watcher stepped closer, and Li responded with a hearty handshake.

"So this is your Fighter for tonight? I didn't recognize him…" Li admired the Watcher's get-up. "The look fits!"

The Watcher pointed to his Ring, grunting. Li nodded and held up his own gloved hand. "I've been informed…"

Barely audible, Joey whispered to Li: "Shake hands with him to talk—

he'll tell you more." Surprised, Li allowed access to his own Ring, and the Watcher wasted no time.

#WATCHER: Fenix Creciente. My tech's limited for now, link to speak to me. So you're a Brother?

#LI: We Will Be Free... Uncle Raven sends his regards to Brother Wolf, and to Brother Snapper. I'm part of the Outside Team.

The Watcher pondered the meaning—Outside Team—meaning, outside Purgatory? The Revolutionary Network was growing more extensive by the minute.

#WATCHER: Duly noted—so you are with Uncle Raven, then?

#LI: Yes—call me Brother Boar; I'm glad you guys could join us... I brought a new friend.

Li whistled low, sounding a call like a whippoorwill. He was answered in kind, and from around a building a dark, scrappy looking Survivor walked forward, distinctive in his pointy-toed boots and faded jeans.

#LI: Meet Gilberto; a member of Winston's brigade, referred by Brother Gator.

Li spoke openly to the new recruit. "We are on our way to the fights —would you care to join us, friend?"

Cautious, Gilberto had the look of a man who meant business. He gave a terse nod, then stood to the side as Li continued his private conversation with the Watcher, hands still clasped in a long handshake.

#LI: Uncle Raven sends word—the Deer is safe in the pen. Don't come near; wolf traps are everywhere. He is waiting for you down by the Commons; word has come that the fights will go on at Eight O'Clock, despite the fires. He will see you then.

The Watcher scowled. Winston had reviewed the particulars with him while in the Bunker; Wolf traps—probably the ALGOS. Rose was so close—but the drones were closer.

#WATCHER: Then we'll lure the hunters away. Follow me—I have business in Pair'O'Dice.

Ducking into the alley access, they entered Pair'O'Dice. As they slipped inside, they marveled at the empty streets and abandoned shops—the fire had drawn everyone away., except for the faint echo of footsteps approaching from the Party Pontoon. The Watcher motioned, tapping his ear, then pointing towards the noise. Straining, the others finally heard it—

Thinking quickly, Li dropped to his knees on a clear span of bare ground, producing a pair of yellowed dice from his leather jacket's pocket: "So, who's up to shoot craps?" He smiled jauntily: "Gather 'round, gather 'round!"

Eager to create a plausible scenario for their gathering, the men gathered 'round to call their bets, then watched Li roll Snake Eyes on the come-out roll. The Pass bets grumbled and paid up; Joey and Gilberto collected a few Purgatory tokes and a pack of gum, as the Watcher stood to the side. He watched as a small man in a subtly fancy suit approached the Pair'O'Dice hidden access, face obscured by a green silk scarf. Hand resting lightly upon the haft of his Bowie Knife, the Watcher sized up at the intruder. White Hat pulled down, attitude aloof, the stranger came closer, stopping just beyond their circle of light.

"It appears you are betting everything on a roll of the dice." A familiar voice spoke. 'I'd like to enter the game, Brothers—if you don't mind."

The Watcher grinned from ear to ear, then clasped Evangelo's hand in greeting.

Evangelo patted his friend's shoulder, then looked around the circle at the faces unknown to him. Li rolled the dice once more. "Join the game, Brother." The others continued to play as the Marshals conferred to the sound of the rolling dice.

Subtly, the Watcher then pointed to his ring finger: Evangelo looked at him quizzically, then reached into his own pocket and slipped on his WeSpeex RingWorld. The Watcher extended his hand, and they shook on it:

#WATCHER: I'm glad it's you—I almost didn't recognize you in that outfit.

Surprise registered with the Ranger at the activation of his HeadsUp display.

#EVANGELO: I probably wouldn't recognize me either—but how are we able to use our rings?

#WATCHER: Use the code, Brother Dog. The Rings are working because Cousin Cat let down his guard and Uncle Jim's Searchers have come to Purgatory. Do not speak any sensitive info, even in whispers—our Uncle Jim's Searchers have audio enhancement capability, and we are being monitored even now.

At the mention of Cousin Cat—Boss Chartreaux's code name—Evangelo kept his face deadpan, but the Watcher could tell he was disturbed by this turn of events.

#EVANGELO: We received the bad news about our departed Brethren this afternoon; and now this...

#WATCHER: We are taking steps to deal with this situation. We are waiting for an update at half-past on Channel 145. You are 'Bravo' Station. SITREP?

#EVANGELO: The deer hunters have departed. They won't be returning; it's a long trip from the gates of hell.

Grunting in admiration, the Watcher approved.

#WATCHER: I look forward to hearing the tale. There's a hot time in the old town tonight.

The Little Marshal looked to the flickering glow past the gates of Pair'O'Dice, and his face took on a hard, jealous look:

#EVANGELO: So I see—Cousin Cat is there, and the Bee, with the Hornets gathered 'round...

The Bee—the code name for the Ranger's Queen Bee, Shaney; her Ranger Hornets were still swarmed about her. The Watcher nodded, noting the troubled look on the little Marshal's face; he knew what the problem was immediately. Smug, the Watcher reflected on his own relationships, and the lack of such problems on his own part.

This was the benefit of a Classical Education; an early exposure to philosophy and culture had shaped young Saul in a positive, productive way regarding relationships. The Watcher thought of his lessons in Global Civ, and how he had always tried to live by the Words of the Great Late-Twentieth Century Philosopher, Ice-T:

'99 Problems, But A Bitch Ain't One'.

Of course, the Watcher's highly sensitive professors explained, the meaning of this rap anthem was figurative, not literal; the 'bitches' in this work represented life's problems, and the choices of the writer to not let any one of them dominate his life. Impressed with the sentiment, the Watcher had taken that philosophy to heart from a completely non-toxic, non-masculine, symbolic perspective: Rose would only be a problem if he let her be one—and he had learned to never let any woman be a problem.

The Watcher wondered if Evangelo would have fared better in life if he had been taught the classics.

#WATCHER: Bitch tried to kill you. Let go.

Rudely awakened from his jealous reverie, the little Marshal blinked, taken aback.

#EVANGELO: What?
#WATCHER: You heard me.

Moments like these, the Watcher felt fortunate to have had such a remarkable education available. Ever since the first time young Saul heard Ice Cube and Doctor Dre rapping "Natural Born Killaz" in his 'Damn It Feels Good to Be a Gangsta': Rap Appreciation Class, he had ascribed to the schools of early Rap philosophy over many of the later masters… the Watcher gave a wearily intellectual sigh; Ice Cube's late entry into the Houston scene still ignited intense academic debate over whether or not to include him with Willie D and Scarface in the Houston School of Rap.

Well, better late than never.

WATCHER: Now, hang loose here, and observe for any light-field anomalies following me; I need one last piece of information. Just look for us down at the Bandstand if we get separated.

Evangelo nodded and took position. The Watcher let go, then tapped Joey on the shoulder to link up:

#WATCHER: Let's go to the Emporium; it's just around the corner, and any BrigadesMen would just haul us down to the fights, anyway. I have a question for our friend the Shopkeeper.

Hands full of snacks and Purgatory tokes from his dice winnings, Joey sorrowed; "Aw, have a heart—Lady Luck is finally on my side…"

The Watcher grunted. Sighing, Joey stuffed the goods in his pocket, then took hold of the chain again. "Alright, Wrassler-Man, let's ease on down to the store." Lanterns cast a golden glow down around the streets of Pair'O'Dice, giving an air of elegance to the aging structures crowding the twisting streets. As they approached the Emporium, they noticed the long trailer was completely dark.

"Huh. It's not even Eight O'Clock yet… maybe he closed up for the evening."

The Watcher knit his brows. As physically fragile as the old man looked this morning, it was unlikely that the Shopkeeper was down at the Bandstand; perhaps he was in bed? As they approached, the Watcher felt for his knife—the door was slightly ajar. Bending down to take a candle from a street-side Luminaria, Joey drew his pistol. "Approach easy; maybe the old man just fell asleep… but we better check it out."

The rusty hinges of the screen door squealed as they pushed it aside, and immediately the Watcher felt a jab of unease. They stopped, and listened for any sound of movement; hearing none, they entered the

Emporium. Lit by candles, long shadows danced, giving life to the moth-eaten trophy heads of Bear, Boar, Cougar and Wolf gazing down from the walls, their glass eyes glittering in the candlelight. As the pair crept towards the centre of the room, weapons drawn, Joey called out, just above a whisper:

"Welfare Check: Sir, are you okay? Your door was open—" just beyond the light, they saw the outline of the recliner, and a slippered foot on a footrest. A hand, gray and thin, rested on the threadbare armrest.. Nervous, Joey, called softly: "Sir?" He touched the back of the recliner, and it rocked slightly under his hand…

The hand slipped off the armrest, dangling limply. Joey sucked in a breath, and walked the candle around to the front of the recliner.

The milky-white eyes stared blankly into the darkness, toothless jaw slack, head tilted back. The old man's fried fish was knocked to the ground, but the box of Purgatory tokes was still there… a chill ran down the Watcher's spine, and he moved back to back with Joey, scanning the room.

Joey murmured: "This ain't a good place to be right now…"

The Watcher looked more closely at the old man, reaching down to check for a pulse—the Shopkeeper was cold to the touch, but not yet stiff. A small bloodless bullet wound opened up right between the old man's eyes. The Watcher grabbed Joey's hand to link:

#WATCHER: Shot—but not with a gun. This was a cauterizing heat projectile from an ALGOS drone, designed to kill with as little tell-tale blood as possible. He's been dead for less than half an hour, probably as the parade started. I'm checking one thing, then we've got to leave, fast.

Reaching down beneath the arm of the chair, the Watcher checked the place where the old Survivor had hidden the key…

Claws and teeth erupted, spitting and hissing as the Shopkeeper's little cat exploded from under the recliner, then fled into the shadows of the Emporium. Joey jumped back, clutching his chest. "God a-mighty…" sweating, he grabbed the Watcher's arm. "Let's get out of here."

The Watcher drew forth a plastic bin from beneath the folding tray-table beside the chair. Waving Joey closer with the candle, the Marshal opened the lid, to reveal a faded green feather, a soft blue sweater, a little pair of beaded shoes, and an old framed photograph; He turned it over to look. A smiling, mustachioed man stared back from the frame, his arms around a pleasantly plump woman, and a dark-eyed, laughing girl.

Goosebumps rose up on the back of the Watcher's neck. *The girl from the Quinceañera Invitation… Sofia Angelica Ramirez.* He showed Joey, then linked with the nervous cop.

#WATCHER: The Old Man was a Brother—and the Quinceañera girl's Father. This little mystery just got bigger.

The Watcher laid the photograph on the old man's heart, enfolding it in the withered gray arms; closing the Shopkeeper's eyes, He put the lid on the box and put it back where he found it, then the Watcher silently bid farewell.

Vaya con Dios, Hermano.

Joey scooped the fried fish back in the tray, then left it next to the kitten's water bowl. She was lost in the shadows of the shop. Hat in his hand, Joey whispered…"We'll bring you Justice, Sir."

A creak of the door was heard as if breeze blew it open. Jumpy, Joey turned to look, then turned back to gaze on the old man. "I guess it's just the wind…"

But the Watcher knew immediately knew; a cold fear filled him; he could hear the faint whirring of servos. The screen door gapped open again, then slammed shut. The Watcher grabbed Joey's hand:

#WATCHER: Don't look—Aerial Lethal Global Orthogonic Searcher drones are coming through the door. They came back to check the scene of their crime. Keep your eyes turned toward me, even if it comes close; they'll kill anyone who confronts them. The old man must have discovered them somehow.

Joey's hand became clammy with sweat.

#WATCHER: Meanwhile, they're searching a list of flagged behaviors taken from my extensive personal profile. They will attempt a retinal scan on both us. Pretend not to notice, and keep your eyes busy elsewhere…

A ripple of breeze ruffled the feathers on Joey's hat, and the Watcher could see the faintest blue pin-prick of light—the piezo-electric spark of the drone's micro-thrusters. He felt an enormous apprehension; could the Metallilume block the retinal scan?

#WATCHER: Drone—ten feet away, in the book aisle behind you. Another on the other side of the counter, across from the recliner. They haven't pinpointed my identity yet, so they're trying to make a match to Saul Azarian's profile. I'll throw them off by

acting out of character. Improvise and play along. Call me Rex, and give me one of your hat feathers—I'll make a deal with the dead.

Anxious, Joey reached up as if to adjust his hat; stealthily palming one of the three emerald feathers from his hatband, he passed it to the Marshal. The Watcher turned the Shopkeeper's pockets inside out, then stuck the feather in one as he stuffed the pocket back in place.

With a sudden destructiveness, the Watcher knocked over a massive display case, scooping up handfuls of pen-knife keychains and throwing them all into the sack. The Watcher laughed out loud—a wicked, guttural chuckle. Turning to Joey, he laughed again, pointedly, then glared at his Promoter.

"Oh—I mean, good boy, Rex, fetch. The old geezer don't need it anymore anyways…" Joey laughed also, albeit a little stiffly. "He needs no goods where he's going."

Joey looked a little green around the gills at the thought of robbing the dead, but since he was more squeamish about the prospect of joining the dead, he gamely improvised to lead the ALGOS astray: "Good Rex! Rob 'im blind!" Joey looked chagrined and whispered under his breath "No offense, old man…" then grabbed a basket full of knick-knacks and shoved it into the sack, basket and all. "Let's scram before the Pigs gets here…"

Over Joey's shoulder, in a shadow behind a burnt-out lightbulb, the Watcher felt the whisper of energy, and saw the distortion of bending light rays—

Utilizing deep shade as a cover, the deathbot drifted just outside Joey's detection, a vampiric being sucking information from the living. Glancing casually to the side, the Watcher kept his eyes averted as the ripple hovered near the ceiling.

Backing out slowly, the Survivors left the door open so the kitten could escape. A barely detectable whirr buzzed along behind them.

Through the side yard of the old trailer home, they stepped carefully through the remains of flower beds, rusted wire borders outlining the ghosts of dead gardens. They casually cruised up an alley and through a pile of refurbished crates to the crap game, just one street over—and every step of the way, a faint hum followed.

Joey strode up, breathless, trying to look cool. As they approached, the group feigned disinterest, still playing dice. The Watcher shook hands with Evangelo:

#WATCHER: Pass the message Ring-2-Ring; do not acknowledge our Followers. The Shopkeeper at the Emporium has joined our Brothers—he saw too much.

Evangelo grimaced, then decoupled to pass the message to Li via messaging. As Li received the message, The Watcher observed Li's face, a mix of anger and fear expressed in his eyes. Throwing the dice once more, Li broke from the game to clasp The Watcher's hand.

#LI: Brother Fenix is dead?

Intrigued, the Watcher wondered:

#WATCHER: You mean the Shopkeeper? Yes—Uncle Jim's Searchers killed him. They are within feet of us now. Call me Rex. Let no one acknowledge the Searchers. Pass the word; we are undercover as a rowdy gang of Lord Sliwa's and Lord Li's hoodlum friends. I just robbed the dead to convince the Searchers I'm not the guy they're looking for... according to their notes, I'd never do a thing like this. Which I didn't, because I left a valuable trade for all this.

The Watcher reached into the sack and thrust a handful of the bullet pen-knives at Li:

#WATCHER: Pass these around to our gang of petty thieves, and make a show of it for our visitors. Keep them as a memento of Brother Fenix's final fight...

Nodding, Li went over to the dice game, handing the ill-gotten loot to each Survivor with a smile. "Welcome to the EdgeLords, a gang of good-timing, privileged wise guys who think themselves above the law. Rex over there—" He jerked his head at the Watcher, "just shoplifted from a dead shopkeeper for his Master, Lord Sliwa. Smile for the cameras, and keep it easy. Let's go have fun."

"EdgeLords?" Joey looked satisfied at the mention of the legendary gangs of twenty-first century Channers who roamed the digital wastes, in the days before the Rings. "I like it..,"

Evangelo looked pained; his love of improvisational drama for the sake of surveillance was being challenged by his need to always play the good guy. The others, however, seemed to be sanguine about the whole thing; they slapped each other on the back and admired their key-chain pen-knives. Gilberto looked over at Joey. "Hey, these are nice!"

Swaggering, Joey was getting into his role once more. "No problem. It's what you get for hanging out with quality guys like us." He jerked the

Watcher's chain. "EdgeLords rule! Ain't that right, Rex?"

The Watcher growled. "Good boy." Joey rattled the chain, smug.

Li tapped his wrist—the signal for 'time'; an update was due on Channel 145. Evangelo offered to access the message for the Watcher, since the DDT jammer prevented any outside messages from being received by the Watcher's Ring.

A burst of static greeted them. A few seconds passed, and another burst of static was heard, longer than the first; Evangelo played them back, slowed 1/10th times speed. The morse code was decoded by user-level automatic translator; its garbled, synthetic voice, low-pitched and inhuman, responded through a text to voice reader for broadcast to the greater group:

Station Check-in... Static slowed on playback, They listened as each station pinged Net Control, which answered back, acting as the Operator. Wilcox had set up each Team with a particular phonetic letter designation, and tuned them in to the agreed node, 145; Habib's fortunate appearance at the Bunker allowed Wilcox to set Habib up as a communications bridge between the Bunker and Dominic.

Delta Station proxied in with Omega—*Rose.* Delta was Sam, and Omega was Rose—Evangelo passed the message that Sam reported Rose safe and accounted. The Watcher sighed with relief.

This left only one station and team left to check in: Bravo—Evangelo and the Insertion Team. Li joined them as they opened their displays to receive the speeded-up message.

" Station Bravo, for your ears only:" The synthetic voice was followed by a long burst of static, then three short bursts; a gap, and a different pattern.. The entire message rolled through; The Watcher slowed it down again, but it still sounded like only static. Frustrated, The Watcher replayed it. Evangelo listened—

#EVANGELO: Slow it down more. It's Morse Code—B, R, O...

Falling back on his Ham radio training, the little Marshal spelled it out in his head, with no need for the auto translator, then relayed the message.

#EVANGELO: the message reads: "Bro Dog go 2 Bro Fox 2 C ur honey"... I have to report back to my cell to prepare a honeypot.

More static followed; now message from Station Whiskey—Wilcox: he had to be topside, sending code from the shelter of Bogie's stinking hut.

#EVANGELO: the message reads: ALPHA—will send further

instructions for workaround, 21:00. Who's Alpha?

The Watcher grunted, pleased:

#WATCHER: That would be me. We'll see if Brother Eagle and Brother Owl can provide a method for getting rid of mechanical pests at that time.

#EVANGELO: Always the Alpha, I see… remember that Pride goeth before the fall, and don't let it inflate your ego more that it already is.

The Watcher grumbled—it wasn't his choice; Dominic had chosen these designators, and as always, the symbolism was designed to send a message. *Alpha and Omega*—Watcher and Afterling, Male and Female, Beginning and End. The Watcher set it aside in his mind; there would be time to muse on it later.

Bowing to the others around the dice field, Evangelo spoke: "Pardon me, gentlemen, but I must take my leave; I have business to attend." He shook hands one more time with the Watcher:

#EVANGELO: God bless you tonight, Brother Wolf; should I not return, tell the pink one I send my thanks to her. Pray for me…

#WATCHER: If your God sees fit to bless us tonight, you can tell her yourself. Til then, I'll hold onto my prayers—but if He comes through, I'll thank Him personally.

The Shepherd of Shilo looked into The Watcher's eyes, determined:

#EVANGELO: Then I pray I live to see the day when you call upon Him. Godspeed, Brother Wolf.

Feeling a slight pang at his own brusqueness, the Watcher shook his friend's hand.

#WATCHER: Never Surrender, Kid.

Moved, Evangelo tightened his clasp.

#EVANGELO: Never Surrender.

The Last Ranger turned and slipped through the access panel, unheeding of the drones which might be watching. There was no need to hide the hidden ways any longer, as after this evening the Cause would no longer have need of Purgatory… behind him, the Watcher could hear the drones hovering. The faint hum was barely discernible to his attuned ears, but in reality they were almost inaudible…

Hanging back, the ALGOS were merely observing from a distance—a good sign, as that meant they were not in take-down mode, and no other drones had been summoned beyond the two initial patrolling drones.

Nothing had yet happened to alert them of the Watcher's true identity—yet.

The newly-minted EdgeLords gang hung around, finishing up their game of dice to allow Evangelo to get comfortably ahead of them. Joey continued to win, invincible in his bets; he was amassing a nice pile of assorted goods; a pair of LifeBefore subway tickets, three bobby pins, a bottle of purified water, and a collection of old bottle caps. Feeling flush, the erstwhile Lord Sliwa thrust it all into his pet Wrassler-Man's hands:

"Carry my stuff, Rex. That's a good boy..." Lordlike, Joey beamed. He found winning fun, and he found being a Lord quite a novelty. The Watcher, on the other hand, found Joey's fun to be insufferable, and he struggled to not reach over and punch his Lordship in the mouth.

A soft breeze fanned his forearm, and The Watcher realized the drones were creeping nearer. They were looking for signs of rebelliousness; clenched fists, crossed arms, defiant posture—all hallmarks of Saul Azarian's hatred of anyone's authority but his own.

Glad his eyes were unreadable behind their Metallilume Mask, the Watcher softened his posture to a more submissive one, dutifully holding out his hands to carry Joey's goods. He could feel the ALGOS hovering near... Joey boasted: "Hey EdgeLords, listen up. It's time we head for the fights: I've got Lady Luck on my side, and I want to hit the town while she's still in love with me. You ready, Lord Li?"

Li looked up from the dice. "You bet, Lord Sliwa—you're the man."

Joey made finger guns at Li. "No, you're the man..."

They low-fived each other, then fist bumped. Li waved: "Gilberto, my man, let's ride." Cringing, The Watcher turned away. There was only so much of this antiquated twenty-first century posturing he could stand...

He shouldered their shopping bags, and prepared to make entrance at the Arena. The Watcher cast his eyes briefly in the direction of the Wild Horses Hotel and silently groused; if the drones had not been tailing him, now would have been the time to go storm the Lobby and save Rose. But if the drones followed him there, the Hotel would turn into a death trap for her. Irritable at the missed opportunity to make an easy and impressive impression on the Afterling, he relented and turned himself towards the task of luring the drones away from Rose.

If all went well, there would be a chance for the Watcher to make a triumphal entry on Rose, in private, later tonight.

The group filed through the access panel one last time, and the

Watcher listened as their mechanical escorts followed them from a respectable surveillance distance. Back down the alley they went, past the drunks, past the stray cats, back through the Campground. As they approached, The Watcher saw a ripple, and a barely-visible blue spark overhead to his left; a cloaked ALGOS was hiding in the tree, observing a slight figure walking down the path through the Campground, between the Wagons.

As the figure approached, the Watcher could see it was Goins, with the ghostly companion trailing some forty feet overhead, unseen by the rest of the crowd. Dressed in only jeans, t-shirt and a waist-length jacket, sans the protective cover of the usual coveralls, Goins was exposed to the world—

In the post-viral world of TransMutation, Goins' face had become more angular, shoulders broader. Goins for all practical purposes looked male… but for the first time, the Watcher noticed just the barest hint of something different in Goins' walk.

The femoral q-angle.

Even with all the masculinizing effects, the Happening's bioagent could not modify that one deeply embedded aspect of basic biology. The femoral q-angle was always among the hardest to erase, even in the technologically advanced glory days of gender-transmutation technology.

Unafraid, the irascible Goins ignored the drones and kept walking, crossing paths with Joey's small gang of Edgelords. Clearly aggravated, the Mechanic muttered while walking past the Watcher:

"Don't say a word to anyone else. You owe me." As Goins strolled up the lane, the Watcher observed his own drones change pattern subtly; his two blue sparks bobbed, then peeled off to join the the ALGOS following Goins.

Luring the ALGOS away, Goins was taking an enormous risk of exposure, and individual harm—and not just from the drones. But the risk was not from the other Agents; the WildLand Express had female Agents, Sam being the highest ranking officer among them. But Goins didn't have the protection of Visionary status…

Anyone who was smaller or sexually ambiguous—whether they were like DeLisha or like Goins—was an exploitable sexual commodity to motivate societal control, and the System demanded anyone who fit the bill be used for that purpose.

Whoever was analyzing the data would forward the information to the

Fallen—Visionary Survivor Leaders of the Tejas Co-op—and Goins would become a wanted Man… *Woman? Man…* The Watcher's head hurt. He wasn't sure of anything anymore, except that Goins was Goins, and Goins just wanted to be free.

The Watcher observed as Goins made a circuit through the Campground. Barreling though the Campground, the irritated Roughneck then returned to Oro and the Wagon, sitting down next to a perplexed Michaels.

"Settle down and stop rambling, Goins. You're making me nervous, man…"

As they cleared the Campground, the Watcher surveyed the scene in the Commons. The Rangers and Chartreaux were gone—and Shaney was gone with them. Through the trees, He saw a group of white hats headed down to the Jail, en masse; He hoped Evangelo had arrived in time to get in place.

Excited, Joey turned to his Ensemble: "Gentlemen, it's Showtime."

———◆———

The mob came, wearing white hats. Knocking on the door, they demanded entrance.

"Rangers, Tejas Co-op, Command—we're here for the prisoners." A commanding voice boomed.

Howard, the Head Jailer, opened the peep-hole and glowered out at them. "Says who?"

They heard scuff of denim sliding against leather, and boots lightly hitting the ground—the sound of a rider dismounting. The cadence of high-heeled cowboy boots clicked on the caliche walkway as someone approached the door, and a slender, copper-laced hand slid up the sill of the peep-hole.

"Hi there." The Bluest Eyes in Texas gazed in at the Head Jailer. "And who might you be?"

Howard suddenly couldn't speak. He tried, but he couldn't.

"Let me guess—" a merry voice twanged at him. "You're the Head Honcho around here. Why, this is perfect—you're just the man I'm lookin' for. I'm Commander Shaney of the Rangers of the Tejas Co-op." She stuck out her hand to shake. As if in a trance, Howard extended a rough brown paw and delicately grasped her own. "May I come in for a moment? I want to talk to you privately."

Dumbfounded, Howard just stood there, clutching Shaney's hand.

Shaney giggled at him, a silver laugh. "I do believe you ought to let me in. It's not nice to keep a woman waiting in the cold…"

Hands scrambled to open the door, but they were not Howard's hands —he was still staring mesmerized through the peephole. DeRita and Fine pulled him away and opened the door. Shaney sashayed in the room and surveyed the Three Jailers. "Oh, look at y'all. How adorable—which one of you is in charge around here?"

DeRita was making some sort of incoherent noise. Shaney's face broke into an angelic smile, revealing her gleaming, perfect teeth, just the smallest hint of fang in her bite. "Well it could be any of y'all; how's am I to know?" DeRita and Fine pointed at the stunned Howard, too entranced to lie.

"Delighted to meet you! What's your name?"

Howard finally found his tongue. "H-Howard."

"Well, Head Jailer Man, how'd you like to be on Team Shaney?"

Howard blushed, his rough, pebbled face breaking into a sweat beneath his gimme cap. "Great. Sounds great…"

She rubbed his sleeve. "I thought so." Turning towards the door, Shaney hollered out the sliding peep-hole. "Team Cuatro, Cinco—get in here!" With precision timing, eight impeccable Rangers dismounted and filed through the door. "Sheridan, spread out and secure this floor. I want to see our advance team, pronto." As she spoke, the magnificent expanse that was Boss Chartreaux eased through the door behind her.

"Help me out, here, Reggie… I need my away team to report in." She looked around, seeking any familiar faces. Not seeing them, she snapped: "Leroy! Danforth—where are you?"

While Shaney was demanding obeisance, Chartreaux checked his own prisoners. "Where's Winston?" DeRita pointed at the long cell to his right, never taking his eyes off Shaney. The Big Boss lumbered over to the bars, tapping on them to attract the attention of a tall, bronzed man lying on a cot, motionless.

"It's an ironic pleasure to see you here, Cal; it will be an even greater pleasure to see you dangling from a noose." Chartreaux snorted. "Your useless Municipal improvements were always a thorn in my side, using personnel and resources which would have been better used elsewhere. But at least you'll die surrounded by the unwashed masses you loved. It's an unfortunate detail that they didn't love you back."

The man in the cell groaned, but didn't answer.

Chartreaux sniffed, and stepped back from the bars, repelled by the rank odor of vomit and diarrhea emanating from a bucket located between two cots. "Who's in there with him, and why does it smell like an outhouse?"

"That's Lazarus Mansour, Calvin Winston's foreman. He was picked up for disturbing the peace yesterday, after the fires... you may wish to step away, Sir, as they both have a raging case of dysentery, and it has spread throughout the Jail." Alarmed, Chartreaux stepped away from the dimly lit cell as a self-possessed voice called from down the hall. A elegant man in a fine pashmina scarf stepped out of the utility closet. "And how may I help you, Ma'am?"

Shaney sidled up to Sanders. "Ooh, fancy... you look like a man who knows his way around."

Contemptuous, Chartreaux scoffed. "He knows his way around a latrine. He's a Public Servant." He flipped the scarf aside to reveal Sanders' neck padlock. Sanders eyes glinted cool gray, but he said nothing in return. Chartreaux prodded: "I need entry to Mr. Habib's office. An unexpected mishap has occurred."

"I'm sorry, Boss, but only Mr. Habib has the key; that's a metal door in a concrete wall. You'll have to get a crew to chisel it out, but wouldn't it be easier to get the key from Mr. Habib?"

"If I could, I would, you peon." Chartreaux scowled, unwilling to share any more details.

"Oh don't be such a grumpy puss, Reggie—there's dignity in hard work. Somebody's got to clean things." Touching his sleeve, Shaney looked Sanders up and down. "I know you can help me. I'm looking for five Rangers... they were left in charge here." A cloud crossed her brow, a barely visible shadow of impatience.

Sanders appeared genuinely struck by her kind words. "Thank you, Ma'am. Your Rangers have headed to the DragLine to confront someone, a gang of thugs named 'El Trapitos? El Traqueteos? I'm not exactly certain...' Sanders wrinkled his brow, 'They were rumored to be staying at the LoveShack. I heard one Ranger say he sighted a tall man named 'Manuel' in town. They gave the impression that these men were a danger to you; they said they were going to 'round them up'."

"El Trafico..." Whispering, Shaney's face suddenly became

expressionless as the entire room grew quiet. "When was this?"

"About three hours ago—is there something wrong, Ma'am?"

"No, no, don't you go troubling yourself… you have enough to worry about already." Patting Sander's arm, Shaney turned to Chartreaux and whispered low. "He's here! That shady bastard—I was right after all! We've got to hurry… Emmanuel's got that little ragamuffin with him."

"El Trafico's presence at Purgatory is unexpected…" Boss Chartreaux glowered. "I have excellent intelligence from our Allies that Reunion's Azarian was identified outside Purgatory."

"Ooh, I love a mystery, but this is a bad time for uncertainty." An endearing crinkle appeared between Shaney's satiny brows.

Chartreaux grumbled. "Regardless, I regret that we must delay retrieving your prisoners, presumably when we hang Winston; this unrest should be stabilized by then, and you may play with your toys as you wish. I only ask that you allow me to watch your magnificence in action." He held out his yellow Chrysanthemums, which were becoming limp with all the delays.

"Oh, absolutely!" Shaney glittered at him, always excited by attention. "You grew these yourself?"

Chartreaux bowed his head graciously. "Any man of culture should be a man of cultivation."

"Well aren't you a Gentleman!" Shaney beamed, handing off the flowers to a scowling Ranger. She reached over to rub Chartreaux's expansive belly. "Now, Reggie, be my Hero and send some of your BrigadesMen with Team Tres to the DragLine—I need to find out what happened to my other five men. I loaned you nine Rangers, and you let four get shot when you took Evangelo and Santos prisoner. Men just don't grow on trees, you know…" Pouting, Shaney put her hands on her hips.

Chartreaux's face turned red, but his tone remained honeyed. "I'll do my best to make up for your losses, personally." Turning on his heel, Chartreaux pushed out the door, leaving Shaney and her Security detail with the Jailers and Sanders.

"Now, where were we, Howie?" Shaney rubbed her chin. "Oh yes, I need to go upstairs to check on my prisoners. If I can't have them now, at least I can take a minute to make sure they're corralled. But we've got to hurry, so snap, snap, let's go!"

"Two in, two out. Those are the rules." He said it softly, afraid of bursting his delicate bubble of joy.

"Oh nonsense. These eight men are Rangers; they can protect me against anything up there. But come with me if you think I need more protection…" She grabbed Howard's arm, and he followed along in a daze.

"That's not what I meant…" Howard mumbled.

"It'll be fine!" She smiled sweetly at him. "Lead the way…" Keys jingling, he opened the door to the stairway, and she waltzed in, entourage of men-in-waiting trailing behind her.

As Howard opened the second floor door, the same vile odor greeted her upstairs. "Thank you, Howie. Go down and wait, and I'll be there in a minute." As she entered, she heard the splatter of vomit hitting the floor. The men behind her recoiled;

"Commander, this ain't safe—you really need to just let us handle this."

"Wyatt, I can handle myself, thank you. If you're scared, why don't you go downstairs and wait?"

"No, Ma'am, I just… I don't want you to get sick." Wyatt, a big bear of a man, looked truly worried.

"Well, ain't you sweet. At least you care—" Shaney walked over to the front of a reeking cell to glare at the two men imprisoned inside. "Not like some people." She reached down to her slender waist and pulled her hunting knife from its sheath, then tapped the handle against the window bars, making a clanging sound.

"Time to wake up and smell the coffee!"

Two men were hanging from chains bolted into a wall, dressed in rumpled, soiled clothes. Their pants were soaked and stinking, the floors around them filthy. Dominic groaned, then coughed; his arms were dangling from manacles on the wall, and he had that sour look of a man who had been hanging for two days.

"You—I'm not talking to you. You let Emmanuel get away." She sniffed at Dominic. "You are dead to me."

She meant it.

"You, on the other hand…" She pointed to Evangelo, in a snit. "How dare you walk away? How could you just leave everything we worked for, everything we had… the Rangers, the Ranch, the Horses—" She waved at them. "They miss you, every single day!"

A tall, dark Ranger in the back spoke up: "It's true, Cap." Grunts and nods affirmed. "Sunshine is wasting away. She won't even nurse her foal, because she is waiting for you." Hanging from the wall, gag in his mouth, Evangelo had no choice but to listen, and it wounded him to the core.

Shaney glared at Evangelo through the bars, fierce; she made a motion towards the door, but at the sight of the overflowing bucket, strewing vomit and urine on the floor, she backed away. She grabbed the bars of the window, impassioned:

"I gave you the chance of a lifetime—to be Chief—and you threw it all away! For what? For some stupid Book that nobody ever reads, and some ridiculous Code that nobody ever believed." Her sky-blue eyes welled with tears, "The only reason I ever allowed that smarmy piece of fluff to hang on the wall in the first place was because ol' Smarty-pants over there—" Shaney waved at Dominic, "thought it would be good for your 'self-esteem'. And look what that got us!"

Shaney sneered delicately. "But at least he never broke my heart! You, on the other hand—I believed in you. You could do no wrong! But you left me, you horrible, hateful, low-down…"

Shaney burst into sobs, and every man in the room gave Evangelo disapproving stares.

"You walked away!" Whirling, she threw her knife, and it stuck in the doorjamb to the stairwell. She took a moment to compose herself. "Oh Raffi, how could you do this to me?"

A Ranger offered a blue bandana, and a snuffling Shaney dabbed at her nose.

Shaking her head, she fussed. "I can't live this way. I can't. You're coming home. We have a new opportunity for the horses, and you're gonna make it happen. But we have a few adjustments to make first…" Wiping her eyes, Shaney smoothed her shirt and retrieved her knife from the door. "First, I'm going to find our little friend. That little abomination is coming home and staying with me. I've got plans for her, big plans that mean a big future for us all. And while I'm searching for her, I'm gonna have you fixed so you never run away again." Eyes bright, she fumed:

"I gave you a chance to be my man, and you turned it down. Well, you ain't gonna get that chance again." She jabbed a slender finger through the bars. "Since you didn't want to be my man, I'm gonna let Chartreaux have his fancy medics here take your manhood and feed it to the gators tomorrow morning. He's gonna keep you and train you, and by the time he gets finished with you, you'll wish you had taken my offer to be my man—but it'll be too late. You'll be his bitch."

The entire entourage stood slack-jawed in wonder and terror at this announcement. Shaney snapped: "You're gonna know what it means to be a woman… and you're gonna know what it means to be left behind."

Evangelo could only stare, horrified, as the beautiful blue eyes blinked back tears, indignant.

"But when you're good and ready and you've learned your lesson, I'll bring you back home to be a playmate for that chubby little bonbon that we're hunting, and you can take care of the horses. Then I'll forgive you and we can all go back to being happy again." She tossed her head dramatically and turned a cold shoulder to Evangelo. "But until then, you are going to be very, very unhappy. Because if I ain't happy… ain't nobody happy."

With that, Shaney turned on her heel and sashayed out again, Rangers following obediently. "Come on… we gotta go kill Emmanuel and find that little butterball before he ruins her. Besides, Chartreaux promised me I could watch…" Her high heeled boots clicked away down the stairs.

Bringing up the rear, one Ranger leaned in confidentially to whisper into the barred window of the fetid cell:

"You shouldn't have made her mad, Cap." He scurried out, eager to catch up with the group lest he, too, make Shaney mad. Boots clattered down the stairwell and out the door; the prisoners listened as hoofbeats drummed away to the Pavilion. A few tense moments passed as they waited; then at last, Habib opened the door to the stairwell, Sanders in tow.

"The coast is clear. You guys okay in there?"

Dominic stripped his chains away, and wiped his brow. "I need a bath, and not just because of the latrine." Dominic looked with disdain out the window as Shaney rode away. "Give our thanks to the downstairs stand-ins—Barrie and Sergio did a magnificent job. Now have Marcus and the rest of our faux Rangers send word to Sampson and the CounterIntel Team: the second act of Chief Emmanuel's Big Adventure has started. Tell Sampson to make only one appearance, but make it count. We have a chance to distract them from the Watcher if we do this right."

Stunned, Evangelo pulled the gag from his mouth, unable to fathom his glimpse into the Hell he once called Heaven. Shaken, he stepped out of the cell. "I just saved her life, less than an hour ago." He gazed out the window, watching Shaney ride away. "I still loved her."

"I know. You probably would have abandoned us all for her, if she had just called your name. " Dominic patted his friend's shoulder. "The Devil is beautiful, is she not?"

Shuddering, the Little Marshal wiped his feet of the filth, and walked away from his chains.

The Watcher scanned the crowd:

Agent Michaels and his WildLand Express Agents were gathered at the entrance to the Campground, quietly apprehensive but excited about the evening's fights ahead. A tap of the brim from the tall Agent was given, and Joey answered back in kind. Amidst the faces on the parade route, the Watcher saw the Gambler standing near the Bandstand. The HighRoller tapped the brim of his golden cowboy hat, then looked to the other side of the bleachers, where the Watcher observed Von Helm, who gave him the same signal. The crowd was growing restless, waiting for Chartreaux and Shaney to return from the Jail with some word regarding the fire.

Now was the time to take advantage of absences… the Watcher slightly nodded, and Joey yanked the Watcher's chain. "Let's roll."

Joey strutted onto the Commons, Wrassler-Man on a chain and the world on a string. He hummed to himself, green feathers bobbing as he walked, Hickory cane in hand. Flexing every muscle, the Watcher strode behind Joey, acting as if he were a lion on a leash, snarling and snapping. If Purgatory hadn't been on fire again, the scene would have been much more compelling. But as it was, Joey and his Wrassler-Man were in direct competition with the spectacle of the BrigadesMen and the fires, so Joey mustered all the swagger he could generate, and strolled directly out in front of the Bandstand.

This gesture was not lost on the armed guards at the Bandstand—having looked for Joey and Li all day, they were anxious to add these last pieces to Chartreaux's collection of Hostages. "You! Sliwa… Li! Stop right there!" The New Captain of the Combined Brigades, Bosley, ran up, red in the face and gun in his hand. "Get with the others—you're under protective custody." He waved towards the Bandstand.

Very Important Parade-goers gasped, mortified at the BrigadesMan's disrespectful display to the new-found LandLord Sliwa.

Astute, the Watcher noted this discord in the ranks of LandLords over the changes in Purgatory Management. Without the other Bosses, there was a void in leadership; the highest ranking Survivor here was the new Captain of the Combined Brigades—Bosley. The operative word was 'new'… hiding their hands beneath a bag of luggage, the Watcher linked to Joey's neural port.

#WATCHER: No clear leadership here. Make a fuss, and pit LandLords against BrigadesMen.

Joey nodded, then turned to address the crowd. "We don't need protective custody. This is a violation of our rights! We're not your local serfs—we're LandLords. Do you see us needing anything from you?" Bowed up, Joey threw back his shoulders to point at the Captain of the Combined Brigades; suddenly Joey ceased being good-natured, and became a formidable Macho instead, his brown suit-coat straining against his bulky frame. "We're here to fight and gamble, and you're here to make that happen for us. So make it happen."

"I'd get busy if I were you," Li said dryly, pointed towards Bosley. "You know, we've got other places we could be. Like, home." Shocked, some LandLords muttered in disapproval, others nodding in agreement.

At the prospect of a downturn in Purgatory tourism, the Proprietors of the Fine Establishments became queasy. This evening, which had started with such promise, was already a public relations nightmare for their town—and now the local version of Law Enforcement was picking a fight with powerful LandLords. The elegantly dressed gentleman with the megaphone waved to Bosely and the EdgeLords: "Hold on now, don't get upset; the Captain is just trying to do his job."

"Yeah, well, what's his job? Is the Captain here to serve and protect, or to put us under the Bosses' thumbs?" A suddenly belligerent Joey asked.

The BrigadesMen murmured; emboldened, Captain Bosley shot back: "We're here to protect Purgatory, and we do a damned good job. You can't just barge in here and run rough-shod over everybody—we're not your servants!"

"Oh yeah, then what are you? Who do you serve—the people who pay your bills, or the Bosses? We pay your bills!" Joey demanded to know. "We'll walk out if we don't get what we want…"

The irony of the UpperCrust forming a union to bend the LowerCrust to their will was not lost on the Watcher. He grunted in appreciation of this moment.

"You can't do that—you can't just walk out!" Captain Bosley

stammered—"I'm under orders—"

"Orders to do what?" Lord Li jumped in. "What are you going to do? Shoot us?"

Rattled, Captain Bosley whispered to his officer, who ran towards the Jail. Bosley pointed to Gilberto, standing quietly next to Li: "Reyes—what are you doing out there? Fall in! You're a BrigadesMan—we need you now..."

Gilberto blanched; his kinship and identity as a proud BrigadesMan was in conflict with his distaste at Boss Chartreaux's rise to power. Incensed by the LandLords, Bosley trained his anger on the bandstand. " You Civilians come to Purgatory and act like you're better than us—but the Plantations wouldn't have markets without hard-working Civic-minded folks like us!"

" We're here of our own free will!" Lanky Lord Leyden abruptly stood, his cap's deer tails quivering with suppressed rage. "You Civicians have no right to hold your guns on us. City Folk are always yammering on about their Civic Pride, but you'd starve without the Plantations!"

More LandLords were rising, facing off with the guards in the stands. Shouting matches were breaking out between LandLords and Citizens: Purgatory versus WildLand, Civicians versus Civilians, Working Class against Ruling Class...

Purgatory's Business owners were starting to panic in the stands. Everything they had worked so hard to create was crumbling. The man with the megaphone placed himself between the two groups, waving his arms—"Stop! Stop—we don't have to fight, we can all agree—"

Gilberto's eyes lit up with a revolutionary zeal. "Agree on what, mi amigos? Agree that Purgatory has been a free and fair place in the past, but no longer? What happened to our freedoms? What happened to our Bosses? Why is Winston in Jail, and the LandLords held hostage, with the town on fire?" Gilberto lifted a fist into the air. "We can only agree that we are no longer free! Why? Why are we no longer free?"

"That's an excellent question. It deserves an answer."

All eyes turned towards smooth basso voice welling up from behind the bandstand, as Boss Chartreaux glided up the path from the Jail. He waved a leather-clad hand to the Mr. Megaphone, who trotted up nervously to offer it to the Boss. Chartreaux graciously nodded, then lifted the metal instrument to his lips.

"Allow me to elucidate. You are rightly concerned; your freedoms have been abridged, and Purgatory is on lockdown. Martial Law is such an ugly phrase, but a necessary one when we are at War."

The crowd gasped.

"Alas, it is true. What you see before you—the fires, the chaos, the killings—they are all a product of a nefarious plot to destroy our way of life. We have been the victims of a heinous attack, my friends, and we must take steps to protect what is left of our lifestyle and our home."

He removed his hat, exposing his thickly warted skull, and shook his jowls in sorrow. "Bosses Waitie and Balogun have been found dead, along with our beloved MoneyMan, Mr. Habib. But this was no random act of violence—it was an act of War against Purgatory, the Co-op, and all in it."

A chill descended on Purgatory.

Listening to Chartreaux's mesmerizing narrative, Joey and his Edgelords blended in to the gathered Survivors, their genuine concern at the Boss' words allowing them to be absorbed into the greater whole of Purgatory.

Chartreaux pointed to the set of empty chairs gathered in front of the bleachers, reserved for the dead Bosses. "These glorious men were murdered in the cabin you see burning behind you, an arson set to cover a terrible crime. But thanks to the heroic actions of Commander Shaney and her Righteous Rangers, this injustice will not go unanswered."

As Boss Chartreaux spoke, Shaney and her Rangers came galloping up the path, on cue. Magnificent with their horses and white hats, the Cavalry rode to the rescue, Shaney at their Helm.

"Commander Shaney, do you have a report for the good Citizens of Purgatory, and their Honored Guests?"

Leaping to the forefront, Shaney and Storm hit a perfect pose. The breeze arose behind them and the Appaloosa's multi-colored mane became a streaming banner; Shaney became a Valkyrie of Justice atop Storm.

She raised her six-shooter into the air: "The Hostesses have escaped, and burned the cabin to avenge Winston's arrest!"

Murmurs answered her accusation.

"But these harpies didn't escape Purgatory's protective custody on their own. They were busted out by gang of rogue Rangers known as 'El Trafico'. The Leader of these outlaws is the villainous Valentine Emmanuel, our former Chief."

Rangers rode forward with the bodies of DuBois, Wiley, and the naked Ruby, dumping them into the street as proof of the sordid tale.

"We found these degenerates hiding out at the DragLine. El Trafico sent these men to assassinate the Bosses. Sure as shootin', shots were fired, but they were no match for Shaney's Rangers!"

DeLisha and the DragLine Dancers turned pale.

"Oh thank our lucky stars. We are saved." In a flat voice, a scrawny BrigadeMan raised his hand to point at Shaney, while reading something scrawled on the palm of his hand. "The bad guys have been stopped, thanks to Boss Ch... shhh..." he stumbled, unable to read the word..."the Boss and Shaney's Rangers!"

At that signal, a Lantern-lighter lit a string of sparklers as Shaney flicked her heels, and Storm reared up with dramatic effect. Jubilant, her Rangers gathered around, whooping and shooting their pistols into the air.

The effect was stunning, and made for an inspiring moment. The Brigades cheered wildly.

"Bravo, my brave girl!" Opening his arms to her, Chartreaux smiled broadly, his peg-like teeth exposed in a rare display of approval.

Then his face fell dramatically as he turned to the crowd. "But why is El Trafico here? Who could have possibly called them in?"

"It breaks my heart!" Shaney's blue eyes flashed, and every Survivor felt her pain. "Director Santos and Captain Evangelo joined forces with El Trafico. My own Captain..." tears flooded her eyes, "the man I trusted most in this world, Captain Evangelo has betrayed me!"

Unsure of her pronouncement, many in the audience shook their heads in disbelief. Agents of the WildLand Express listened in silence, stunned by Shaney's blatant lie.

"Santos and Evangelo have joined forces with Emmanuel's El Trafico Gang to help Boss Winston take over Purgatory in a hostile coup. Their mission is to kill all the other Bosses, and to help Winston rule Purgatory with an Iron Hand."

Indignant, Shaney pointed to the burned cabins. "The traitorous trio of Santos, Evangelo and Winston helped El Trafico infiltrate the Hostess Club with a small Golden Chica known as 'La Fugitiva'. Corrupted by this new Chica, Destiny Rogers murdered Boss Zhu during his appointment, and committed arson to cover the crime."

At this, strident voices began to rise from the audience. Chartreaux's arsonous henchman stood to shout: "I saw her! I told you I saw her! I saw a little golden girl with Kendra near Hizzoner's house right before it burned! They're the ones who burned HighTown to the ground..."

A anxious pit of irritation sprung up in the Watcher. Rose's daring reconnaissance of Boss Zhu's House had exonerated Destiny of these accusations, but at the cost of her own reputation and safety. His Fugitive was now infamous… he kept his face expressionless, lest the ALGOS be scanning his features for signs of hidden emotion.

"Unaware of these heifers' treachery, Boss Chartreaux generously took the Hostesses under his wing, sheltering them in his own safe room when the Hostess club accidentally caught fire." Shaney continued, glancing upward, as if trying to remember it all: "But Winston's minions —Emmanuel and La Fugitiva—helped the Hostesses escape from custody, then the Hostesses and La Fugitiva burned Boss Waitie's cabin in revenge for their Leaders' arrests…"

Confused by the convoluted storyline, the audience scratched their heads. Noting their dazed expressions, Chartreaux attempted to clarify.

"These are terrible accusations, Commander Shaney," Boss Chartreaux sorrowed, "especially considering Director Santos of the WildLand Express is such close friends with the Criminal Winston and Captain Evangelo; and now they have hired Emmanuel's El Trafico Gang and their Leaders to attack Purgatory and overthrow me!"

"Oh—it makes more sense when you put it that way," Captain Bosley muttered.

"It's true!" Shaney jumped in to reiterate. "They've turned evil— Captain Evangelo and Director Santos shot and killed four of my Rangers!"

Suspicious stares turned towards the WildLand Express Agents at the entrance to the Campground; ominous in his eyepatch, Agent Michaels gave Shaney a disdainful look through his one good eye. DeLisha and the Dancers fanned themselves, overheated from all the intrigue. Gossip erupted on all sides; Shaney raised her hand, and they quieted down to hear her. Piercing and clear, her voice needed no megaphone: she held out her hand benevolently to the Agents, gathered apart just outside the Campground.

"Now, now—I won't believe that these last few WildLand Express Agents are part of their corrupt Director's terrible conspiracy. Winston, Santos and Evangelo have been apprehended, and are now in jail; they are no longer a threat. If these Agents renounce Santos, I'll gladly offer them protection from my Rangers so they can continue their routes." She smiled at them warmly. "The WildLand Express is safe, as long as they're with us!"

There's the Machiavellian money shot, The Watcher noted with admiration. *A hostile takeover of Purgatory, the LandLords and the trade routes—all in one smooth move.* Shaney's move to take the remaining WildLand Express Agents under her authority proved that she knew about the demise of Camp Forlorn—and she believed there was no one left to interfere.

But it also proved the New Alliance had fallen prey to the Revolution's Purgatory counter-intelligence operation. Dominic's gamble of presenting himself and Evangelo as helpless prisoners had worked. Chartreaux and Shaney truly believed that any opposition was dead or in chains.

This was a good sign; the LoneStar Revolution's deep cover had not been blown—yet.

Shaney rallied Purgatory: "Now it's time to round up the rest of the traitors! The Hostesses and La Fugitiva are on the lam with Valentine Emmanuel. Be on the lookout, and report anyone who looks suspicious— but don't approach. These are dangerous criminals. Even though she's very dainty looking, the golden Chica's a cold-blooded killer. La Fugitiva is the Assassin of our dearly departed Judge Leona!"

This news rocked Shaney's audience; whispers flowed like water through the crowd.

"Bless her heart! Judge Leona was like a much plainer and much older sister to me!" Shaney's lips trembled, then she mastered herself. "Her wicked murderer will be hunted down. But don't approach Emmanuel or his golden Chica—she's to be taken alive, so if you see them, alert the BrigadesMen or my Rangers. I'll personally see to it that lil' hellcat's properly punished for her crimes." Shaney's complexion flushed pink beneath her smooth copper scales, and the Watcher had no doubt that Shaney would enjoy punishing the Afterling.

Sweeping her arm dramatically towards the great Narrator, Shaney begged: "Do your duty, Chartreaux—someone must avenge our Fallen! Who knows what these heartless criminals might do next?"

The Watcher tried to not roll his eyes. This was a classic Visionary tactic; Shaney and Chartreaux were building a narrative to shut down dissent, appoint a Leader, then redirect anger away from their Power Grab.

Boss Chartreaux stepped up, and took the megaphone again.

"You will see Justice—this I swear." Boss Chartreaux intoned, his deep voice soothing and peaceful. "You deserve a dedicated Leader in this crisis, and I offer my services to you all now, to establish a unified Government for all Survivors. The New Alliance will bring stability to all, and bring our Hostesses in line once more. But I need your vote of confidence to do this—from LandLords and Purgatory Men alike. In this time of War, I need to know you trust me to do what must be done to protect our way of life."

"I stand with Boss Chartreaux!" Inspired, Bosley jumped in front of the crowd: "I'm with him—who's with me?"

Any dissenting voices were drowned out by the shout of the Brigades and Chartreaux's supporters. Boss Chartreaux bowed his head humbly, and his silver tongue enthralled Purgatory with its undulating tones.

"Very well. I thank you for your trust, and graciously accept your call for me to lead the Co-op to victory against our Common Enemy. Until further orders, Martial Law is in place, for the good of all. We will maintain the safety of our guests with their armed escorts, and until our WildLand Express agents swear allegiance to Shaney's Rangers, we will stop all traffic in or out of Purgatory. We understand this is a great inconvenience to our LandLord guests—but all who have nothing to hide will support our efforts. Until then, let us continue with our Purgatory traditions. The Enemy will not win against the New Alliance!"

Thunderous applause came from the Rangers, Brigades and Purgatory Men; wary clapping and nervous glances came from the LandLords and WildLand Express Agents.

In the midst of the cheers, Li leaned in to whisper tersely to Gilberto; the scrappy little Tejano gave a determined nod, and bided his time.

"In defiance of our enemies. let us celebrate our most cherished freedoms—" Chartreaux waved a magnanimous hand, and from the Stations of Industrial Boulevard, a fleet of loaded Mood Wagons came rolling up the road. "I give you these gifts of Purgatory as tokens of our esteem, and a promise of more to come under the New Alliance." Rattling with bottles, vials and tins of mind-altering substances, the Mood Wagons rolled to a halt as the maddened crowds rushed forward. The Watcher broke into a sweat, as the smell of the Stuff assaulted him once again.

Li glanced towards Gilberto, and gave the sign.

The Tejano rushed forward, waving his straw cowboy hat. "He's buying your complacence!" Gilberto shouted, leaping upon a nearby stump for visibility. "It's all bread and circuses to distract you from Boss Chartreaux's power grab! Boss Winston isn't the enemy. He loves this city! He loves our people! We've been offered no evidence Winston is with El Trafico, just hearsay. This is a coup against Winston, not Chartreaux— Chartreaux's the real enemy!"

Bosley pointed an accusing finger: "If you're not with Boss Chartreaux, you're with El Trafico! Winston is an Enemy Agent!"

"That's a lie!" Gilberto spat, "Winston has always served Purgatory! You all loved Boss Winston until Boss Chartreaux told you to hate him. None of these people were considered the enemy until moments ago— this is a set up!"

A voice shouted from the crowd: "Gilberto's right! We've seen no evidence; Boss Winston, Director Santos and Captain Evangelo ain't the enemies of Purgatory—Chartreaux is!" The Survivor, a grizzled Hombre in a beat up hat and overalls, railed angrily from the street, shaking his fist. "These rats are lying—"

"These conspiracy theories are enemy propaganda." Chartreaux's eyes narrowed. "Arrest these men for aiding El Trafico."

The BrigadesMen swarmed Gilberto. The wiry Hombre didn't resist, but simply kept shouting;

"You know what is true! Remain true!"

Another contingent of BrigadesMen found the grizzled heckler in the crowd, and tackled him. A fist fight broke out as two of the old Hombre's friends joined in—one a stout Macho, the other a rangy Hombre with a mean right hook. A scuffle ensued, then the BrigadesMen subdued and hauled the three dissenters to the Jail.

Bosley pointed at Joey, Li and The Watcher: "If you don't want to join them down at the Jail, you'd best get in the stands. You can come down when you turn comes up at the fights." Grumbling openly, the three took a seat at the end of a makeshift bleacher seat, and waited for the fights to begin.

The Watcher grunted in approval at the subterfuge. Once at the Jail, Gilberto would give an intelligence update to Dominic regarding Chartreaux's plans, and the three dissenters—now unwitting recruits for the Revolution—would be offered the chance to join the other new recruits in the Jailhouse tunnel below. Meanwhile, the seeds of doubt would be sown in the hearts of those yet afraid to speak out against Chartreaux and his New Alliance.

The Watcher cast a sideways glance at Chartreaux: the big Boss was surveying Joey and Li with a keen interest, attempting to fathom their relationship to each other and to Gilberto. It wan't uncommon for strangers to hang out at the gaming tables, but to a master StoryTeller like Chartreaux, every alliance had hidden potential. The Watcher wondered what potential the Boss saw in Joey and Li.

Seeking patterns, Chartreaux turned his rheumy eyes to the Watcher, and the Watcher incrementally averted his gaze, looking just past the corpulent Boss. Even with his eyes veiled behind Metallilume, the Watcher wanted to take no chances on drawing more attention.... he was already drawing enough attention as it was.

Chartreaux snagged Joey's gaze.

"I apologize, Lord Sliwa; your first visit has so inconveniently coincided with these unfortunate events. I am almost certain that you and your fighter have nothing to do with this unpleasantness... but we will discuss this in depth after the fights." He glared pointedly at the pair, then turned his attentions back to the festivities.

The Watcher turned his own eyes back to the skies. A tiny blue spark of an invisibly-cloaked ALGOS drone was bobbing lazily in the air, some thirty feet up, casually observing as it hovered over the crowd. From the pattern of the hover, the Watcher could tell this was the result of a human handler, and not the pre-programmed artificial intelligence of ALGOS programming. Somewhere in an unknown room far away, a soft-skinned man was watching the habits of the Damned with a fascination reserved for the creatures of the wild.

The Watcher grumbled at the intrusion, and turned to his own observations.

Shaney and her Rangers filed their horses into formation, lining the parade route to watch the show. As she rode, the Watcher observed her; the sway of her body, the bounce of her breasts, the shift of her hips in the saddle—and he began to understand why Evangelo and every other Ranger was in Shaney's thrall.

Shaney was enjoying watching the show, and Chartreaux was enjoying watching Shaney. The brooding pansexual Chartreaux was no different than any other man who wanted Shaney... she was a force of nature, an embodiment of wanton feminine sexuality, and it affected Chartreaux deeply.

But Chartreaux wasn't the only one Shaney was affecting. Biologically impacted in the usual Hetero-Trad manner, the Watcher kept his lust where it belonged. Years of enforced celibacy had steeled his will, and for the first time, he was glad.

He scanned the skies overhead. Although Shaney was obviously, glaringly female, she was not the subject of surveillance for any of the drones. Every now and then, one would start her way, then stop, and turn its attentions elsewhere. *She's a Visionary; they already have her identifying information, and she is known to them.* The Watcher listened as the ALGOS passed overhead, nestling in the branches, deadly mechanical birds roosting in the dried leaves of the cottonwoods.

He wished he could say Shaney wasn't particularly beautiful—but she was. Even as a bald, afflicted, aging Survivor, she was still gorgeous; her slim, perfect figure had just enough roundness to announce her femininity without being chubby. And yes, the breasts were false, but they still looked mostly natural, an excellent job that testified to the skill of her LifeBefore surgeon.

But it wasn't just her figure; it was that face, the absolute perfection of the delicate nose and slender jaw, scribed with full, soft lips that looked almost—but not quite—LifeBefore. Encased in the coppery lacing of her smooth, flat scales, that face became the lovely frame of those notoriously blue eyes, and the spirit that lived within—a spirit filled to the brim with the indescribable wonder of simply being Shaney.

Shaney was really, truly, deeply in love with herself. She glowed in the light of her own presence; the halo effect of her absolute adoration of herself—and anything that made her love herself more—had a remarkable effect on the Survivors around her. Beauty combined with joy and love made for the headiest cocktail of social cues, because everyone who came into Shaney's circle believed they themselves were the reason for her glow.

Alas for Evangelo, he was fooled by love. The Watcher fought to stay focused on something else. He reluctantly turned his eyes to DeLisha and the DragLine Dancers, who were picking up their sparklers to do their number for the gathered dignitaries. Scarves floating, feathers flapping, they were taking their places, wearing worn-out high-heeled boots and assorted silky jumpsuits in a rainbow of colors—a windfall from a scavenged department store. DeLisha was the closest thing the WildLand had left to an actual female impersonator; long limbs and a slender frame, combined with a less robust bone structure, made for a close run. Still muscular, DeLisha could pass for a High-T Hembra, especially with that bright red lipstick. It was a valiant effort, but with Shaney in the spotlight, it was impossible for the DragLine Queens to compete.

His mind wandered down an unexplored lipstick path: *what about Rose?*

The Watcher wondered what Rose would look like in red lipstick. Dressed in sparkling raiment like Shaney, or painted and paraded like the DragLine Queens, would she be as wickedly sexual? *Probably not…* Rose was a very wayward 'good girl'.

He'd never had a good girl before.

Surrounded by the flashy degeneracy of Purgatory, the Watcher reflected on the mystery that was Rose, fascinated by her whole good-bad dichotomy. Rose was an eager prostitute, but only because she was taught that good girls *were* prostitutes; to Rose, sexual acts were sacred. That spiritual aspect of her sexual nature was alien to everything the Watcher had ever been taught about his own sexuality.

The Watcher wrinkled his horny brow at the hazy memory, a partial amnesia brought on by the stupefying effect of Rose in the Moonlight… he could still her voice, the only indelible memory of that night:

I am the Lotus, we are One—I am the Father's Will be done…

Her otherworldly melody had befuddled his senses with a Power beyond Physicality. Was it possible for sex to be more than sex? He was slowly coming around to that thought; their fusion at the Altar was more than just a mere physical act, it was the opening of his sensual Third Eye, a spiritual awakening that still he couldn't fathom.

That befuddled-ness masked a deep confusion.

It wasn't that he didn't want Rose—he did. While alluring, Rose didn't have that blatant come-hither badness the Watcher had spent his entire sexual career pursuing. When she wasn't possessed by her Moon Magic, Rose had a slightly goofy, endearing charm that made him want to hug her —followed by other intimate acts, of course—and that made the Watcher decidedly confused. He hadn't wanted to hug anyone since… well, since he decided some men needed killing.

Since Mother.

He scowled. *Well, there's your problem right there.* There was no need to deny it; the Watcher was wrestling with the old "Mothers and Others" sexuality conundrum, insensitively named by Sigmund Freud as the "Madonna-Whore Complex".

The Watcher's problem was compounded; his own murdered Mother was an "Other"—albeit a sweet one with a complete lack of self-awareness. As a TradWife for hire, she had been tricked into renting out her wholesome charms, but it still didn't diminish the fact that society considered the Watcher's Mother to be a "whore". That reality played havoc with the Watcher's early emotional and sexual stability. What does one do when one man's Mother is another man's "Other"?

In that case, one usually makes poor life choices, the Watcher grumped. The Firm was well aware: unfavorable relationships would lead to unsatisfactory career outcomes for their star pupil, unless an early intervention was made—and for him, no commitments could be allowed to anything but the System.

Fortunately, the Watcher's Mentors at CognitoINCognito came up with a solution to avoid inconvenient emotions for the young Sociopath: 'love and leave' was the best relationship philosophy for a man like Saul Azarian. His Mentors discouraged emotional intimacy with 'Mothers'—'good girls' wanting to comfort a bad boy—and encouraged Saul to seek out 'Others'—'bad girls' wanting to have a good time. To facilitate this goal, his Mentors pornographically programmed Saul with a predilection for 'Naughty' over 'Nice'…

It wasn't a hard sell.

'Love and leave' was a roaring relationship success for Saul. That philosophy put him in complete control of each sexual encounter; it avoided dangerous emotions and allowed Saul freedom to walk away before he could lose control of himself or his feelings. It also positioned him to pursue whatever missions the Firm might offer, free of sticky sentiments of love and duty to anyone but himself.

In a world where sexual partners were plentiful and promiscuous, 'love and leave' made all the sense in the world. He grunted satisfactorily at the memory; *who needs to pay for a cow when the milk is free?* LifeBefore had been a proverbial dairy farm filled with willing cows. But the world had changed; the dairy was closed, cows were scarce, and the Watcher would shoot any cowboy who tried to rustle his only cow.

He glanced at Von Helm behind him in the stands. *That includes you, Cowboy.*

Rose's wayward faithfulness suited the Watcher's present need to thwart hopeful suitors like Von Helm. But Rose's 'good girl' charm sometimes conflicted with the Watcher's former 'bad girl' preferences.

Forbidden fruit is sweetest. he recalled his Mentors saying; *without the forbidden part, fruit is just fruit—healthy but not as tempting.* Rose was forbidden enough to be tantalizing to the Watcher; still, it would be nice to find a way to toggle that 'good girl' off and on when desired, only for himself, of course. *Nobody else…*

The idea of Naughty Rose lit a flame in him.

The Watcher puzzled as he watched the Dancers act like bad girls: *surely the Church Fathers programmed a 'Naughty or Nice' switch into their little Asuras…* intrigued, the Watcher decided to wonder later—now was not a good time to be distracted by naughty thoughts. *Distraction hones Death.* He scanned once more, looking for Death—or Dancers, whichever came first.

Now the music shifted, and the sultry strains of Peggy Lee's 'Fever' swelled to a lively Latin beat; it was actually rather good, and the Watcher tapped his feet to the thrumming oil barrel drums. *So this is Civilization.* It was a far cry from the nightlife of Dallas in its heyday, with neon lights and bars in Deep Ellum, or the girls who lined up to see the indie bands in courtyards under the summer stars. Still, it was a remnant of humanity, fighting on to be human. The DragLine Queens swayed, and spun on their high heels—

The lead dancer was swaying closer. Twirling a diaphanous turquoise-and-red flowered scarf, DeLisha was advancing on Joey, slinking towards the stands.

Hoots and hollers could be heard as the dancers whipped their scarves out to lash Survivors in the Bandstand. Joey started to perspire, unsure about all this attention—DeLisha whipped off a hip scarf, then threw it around Joey's neck, yanking him near to plant a wet red kiss on his cheek. Flustered, Joey pushed away, but DeLisha put those red lips next to his ear and whispered: "A hundred tokes in the scarf—betting money and fighter's fees from the Raven." Leaving the multi-colored scarf around Joey's neck, DeLisha whirled away. "Good luck, ManTamer…"

Wrapped in floral chiffon and covered in red lipstick, Joey blinked and muttered to himself, slightly confused. Running his hands along the scarf, he felt a pouch stitched into the edge, filled with the aluminum pop-top token. Joey teased a thread loose, then thrust the scarf into his deep suit-pocket to dump out the tokes. The Dancers continued their routine, with an occasional sparkle from DeLisha thrown towards an embarrassed Joey. Lord Li laughed and clapped Joey on the shoulder—"Welcome to the

Wild World of Market Mayhem Weekend!"

The Dancers finished big, complete with fireworks, sparklers and "A Salute to the Brigades", featuring thanks to those injured while battling the fires. Limping BrigadesMen waved to the crowd, and the Watcher did his best to hide his displeasure. No one could doubt that these brave Survivors had risked much to save Purgatory; but no one could accept the terrible truth—that the Leader thanking them was the one who had started the fires...

well, most of them.

Personnel began to move around, making space for Shaney in the Bandstand. Dismounting, she led Storm under the Bandstand and tied him to a post. Sugar and Spice stepped up in matching black to deliver a bouquet of 'Caldwell Pink' roses to Shaney; plucked from Chartreaux's personal gardens, they were a real rarity in the WildLands. Thrilled, Shaney waved to the crowd; a homespun Homecoming Queen acknowledging her adoring court, they shouted their approval as Boss Chartreaux gave her the Seat of Honor. Settling his bulk onto a cast iron bench beside her, Chartreaux made small talk, pointing out the various landmarks of Purgatory—including the Well, the PickUp Truck Planter, the Party Pontoon—while the audience mooned over this celebrity romance.

The Watcher observed with interest. This was a royal courtship, publicly displayed to openly cement ties between two tribes, Chartreaux's Brigades and Shaney's Rangers. Shaney was not merely Queen—she was the King-Maker. None who had come through her ranks ascended to power without her. Impressed, the Watcher wondered how long this arranged marriage would last before the happily-ever-after Alliance backstabbed each other.

As Shaney and Chartreaux chatted, work crews set up heavy-duty, six-bar corral panels and a gate, along with a large, shoe-polish lettered wooden sign:

- WELCOME TO THE ARENA -

Bloody splotches accented the sign.

A squared circle of the usual proportions, the Arena was roughly twenty by twenty feet, set up on a bare patch of dirt to accommodate fighters and the occasional gator. To keep things interesting, creative fight promoters had woven barbed wire through the red-painted horizontal bars of each panel to discourage participants from climbing out during rounds—escaping the arena not only forfeited the freedom of the escapee, but also made for poor entertainment.

Anticipation grew among the onlookers as the Arena was erected. Mellowed from their Mood Wagon Freebies, the crowd's anxious aggressiveness had been blunted, but it was replaced by hunger. Famished Survivors along the parade route hit the Taquito stands that dotted the Commons, seeking one of the greatest comforts of civilization—fast food. There would be plenty of time to make room for the Free Bar-be-que following Winston's hanging after the Fights.

With the LandLords under guard, vendors came into the stands, hawking beef and bean burritos. Joey waved his hand to an eager vendor and tossed a toke—he was rewarded with a bundle wrapped in a page from an old magazine. He pulled it open to reveal two flour-tortilla-wrapped burritos. "Holy Cow, real wheat tortillas…" Joey effused, "This is progress!" He flipped another toke to the vendor, who pitched another bundle to Joey and tipped his hat.

"You bet—that's the Purgatory spirit! By this time next year, we'll be baking bread. Ain't no War gonna stop Purgatory Men." Proud, the vendor grinned and went back to hawking his wares to the Lords in the stands.

Passing a package to the Watcher, Joey pulled out their canteen. "Tank up on water and carbs now, Wrassler-Man. You're gonna need the extra energy." Appreciative, the Watcher wolfed down the burritos, sinking his teeth into the wheat flour tortillas with gusto; the knowledge that the flour was free of the Stuff made him relish each bite even more.

He looked over to the sidelines, noting the cable-spool betting tables being rolled out. With Habib declared dead, the MoneyMan would hide himself until further notice—but who would take his place as the Arena Manager?

Would it be Mr. Megaphone?

The Announcer was resplendent in a navy pinstriped 'Xir Xmooth' suit, which had all the iconic details that made the suit an instant classic. The Watcher's mouth twitched at the thought of how many times he had worn such a suit, dressed for success with the Firm. Crafted from wrinkle-free, light weight Silk-a-Sheen lab-spun silk, it had the tieless appeal of a longer Nehru jacket, to be worn with an optional matching vest beneath, by persons of any spectrum of gender.

Alas for those who loved the look, the popular earth-friendly, biodegradable synthetic fabric broke down quickly, and the suits didn't last longer than a few seasons. What worked well in LifeBefore Luxury Fashion as a conscientious effort to showcase waste-free materials resulted in temporary, disposable garments, only useable for a few years. That was the primary reason that longer-lived vintage clothing was popular with Survivors—the older, more durable items were all that could be scavenged after a few years.

The suit was a poignant reminder of how disposable society and humanity had become in those last days. The Watcher pondered the implications of unintended consequences, and rubbed the denim of his own leg, glad that heavy-duty work clothes had remained available in rural, working-class areas. He slapped the back of Joey's eternal polyester blend suit and pointed towards the table. Joey nodded; "Looks like we're up… let's see how this all shakes out."

A rowdy group approached the tables. On a regular market weekend, this would have been a larger crowd, with inmates added into the mix, but tonight, the Jailhouse was on lockdown. Concerned that Winston might insist on fighting for his own freedom, Chartreaux had declared inmates ineligible for this card. That left only those Survivors who were willing to bet their own freedom on a win in the ring—usually a sparse group unless everyone was drunk. Fortunately for Dominic's plans, this evening's forays into mellower moods-alterations made the crowd less likely to line up. The Watcher counted nine interlopers plus his own six recruiters, who were making a good impersonation of being just drunk enough to gamble their lives away.

These men would be the ones responsible for getting themselves hauled off to jail after their losses to either the Watcher, or Von Helm; from there, they would be outfitted and shuffled out of jail via the secret dock tunnel to arm their recruits and smuggle their gear out of Purgatory via the Wagons.

Unfortunately for the man in the elegant suit, Habib's improvised demise left chaos in its wake at the registration table. Hopeful fighters crowded around, shoving each other to be first in line. Mr. Megaphone looked harried; he turned to a BrigadesMan and complained: "How am I supposed to announce the Fights if I have to run the card?"

In answer to that question, Sanders came with notes in hand, laying them out before the man in elegant suit. The Public Servant cleared his throat: "Permission to speak, sir, but Mr. Habib trained me to run the card

—I am his personal assistant at the Jail. If a BrigadesMan cares to monitor, I could show you all how to run the brackets..." Sorrowful, Sanders held out the papers. "It is the least I can do to honor his memory."

"Yes, yes—what is your name? Sanderson?" Mr. Megaphone breathed out a sigh, relieved. "I'll gladly put in a good word for you if you can help me tonight—I can't do these two jobs at once."

"It's Sanders, sir, and I'll be happy to assist." Immediately he spread out the papers; taking a pencil in hand, he began to sign up fighters, putting the Watcher, Von Helm and their Ringers—rigged Fighters—on the card, and turning away all the rest.

"You're more than meets the eye, Sanders!" Shaney cooed, impressed with Sander's handwriting. "I could use an assistant myself... "

Blushing, the slender Survivor continued his work. "My thanks, Ma'am. You are most kind." He tallied the fighters' fees—five tokes for registration, as a down payment should the losers abscond somehow.

Giddy, Shaney grabbed Chartreaux's arm and whispered: "Oh Reggie, gimme Sanders for a Butler! Please—he's so fancy."

"Absolutely. Anything else?" Chartreaux oozed charm, but Shaney was too busy feeding her horse tortillas to notice. Chartreaux pouted.

"Another tortilla for my big baby; Storm loves treats!" She kissed Storm on the nose. Regal, Chartreaux snapped at Sugar, and sent the wiry Hombre scurrying for a plate of the delicious flatbreads.

Trying to look unobservant, the Watcher remained wary; there was so much to keep track of here, so many threats to monitor... Von Helm came up beside him, quiet and grim, still mourning his men. For once, the Watcher didn't feel rivalry towards the little Sheriff, but instead felt a kinship in loss. He grunted and nodded towards Von Helm in sympathy, and Von Helm grunted back, brooding.

The Watcher knew—Von Helm longed to shoot up Purgatory, not entertain it, but that would have to wait until all the pieces were in place.

This is taking too long, he grumbled. The Watcher had lobbied for a simple smuggling operation in and out of the Jailhouse tunnel and through the secret access gate behind the dump. But Dominic's idea was to set up the sham fights, in the hopes of winning easily transportable tokes to trade back into Purgatory for smuggled goods. The plan also allowed WildLand Express Agents to leave Purgatory with their horses, wagons, and as many market goods as possible.

At the time, the Watcher dissented; he wanted to evacuate recruits quickly out the Dump Access point, and have them relocate to the WildLand Express Camp. But now Camp Forlorn was lost and all the Revolution's goods and infrastructure with it, there was no safe place for recruits to stage while waiting on the main component. It was just as well that this plan was in place—now that the ALGOS were patrolling all areas, any evacuation of recruits outside the walls might be quickly detected and quashed.

He tapped his foot, impatient…

The line moved forward. As the Watcher and Von Helm approached last, Sanders touched the brim of his pork-pie hat and subtly turned the roster where the two could read it. They gave it a quick glance; two brackets of four fighters each were assembled, with the final match to be Azarian and Von Helm. The way the card was set up, Von Helm and Bosque would lead off, followed by two more fights between the remaining recruiters. A match between The Watcher and Throckmorton would finish out the first elimination round. The next round would eliminate all but The Watcher and Von Helm—then the real show could begin.

For the Watcher, this meant three choreographed fights, two of them back-to-back to build momentum and bets. Not a problem; his unending gateside shifts at Reunion Camp had prepared him well for intensive, prolonged physical activity. Of course, these were not real fights, much to his chagrin.

He grumbled; the Watcher felt distaste at fixing the fights.

The Watcher knew he could win without any special arrangements, but Von Helm insisted on precautions, as he didn't want his men getting hurt. Von Helm and Azarian were the only Machos in the group, so this was a valid concern. Hombres were deadly fighters, usually more strategic in their thinking and less likely to rely on strength; but Machos had distinct advantages over Hombres in the ring, so some choreography had been arranged to avoid injury.

While waiting their turn in the Camp, Agents had discretely practiced their moves, ensuring the fights would end with as little bloodshed as possible. Von Helm had trained his Agents as fighters, so the real challenge was to make it look good without doing any lasting damage. The key word was 'lasting'… they were used to sparring, and a little blood was to be expected.

When it all went down, the wrassler known as 'LoneStar Libre' should come in the clear favorite, garner big odds, then have the Gambler put a last minute bet on Von Helm, 'The Comal County Crusher'—to whom LoneStar Libre had been instructed to throw his Fight. This would allow the Gambler to walk away with a hefty purse. The idea of publicly losing to Von Helm was odious to the Watcher, only made tolerable by the fact that as a smaller man, Von Helm would rake in the tokes on longer odds —and afterwards. the Watcher would come out of the Jail fully armed and loaded for bear.

Time to prep. The Watcher slipped his hands beneath his cape and shuffled the code to remove his ring. Palming his Ring to Joey, the Watcher felt that familiar, hated helplessness once more—he was now without a voice again. Joey would have to to speak for him, and Lord Li would listen for any updates on Node 145. By nine bells, word was expected regarding a workaround for Purgatory's drone problem.

Sanders handed a slip of paper to Mr. Megaphone, who boomed to the crowd: "Lady and Gentlemen, please rise for the opening ceremony."

The Dancers hit their pose, as the Brigade Honor Guard brought out the official banner of Purgatory, a white bedsheet with eight brown-red hands printed in a circle—the actual bloody handprints of the original eight Survivors who took Purgatory back from the Gators in Year Twelve, After the Happening. Purgatory hearts swelled with pride as the Band— three guitars, six trash-can bongo drums and a mouth-harp—commenced a rousing rendition of the unofficial anthem of Purgatory:

"Macho, Macho Man!"

At the familiar notes of the old Disco Song, all stood, and enthusiastically performed their "hey, heys" while clapping along to the Village People's greatest hit.

The lead singer wailed it with complete abandon as BrigadesMen did the hand motions and DragLine Queens danced; the singer only knew the chorus, but that was the only part that mattered anyway. Nobody knew exactly how it became Purgatory anthem, but the Watcher had a hunch some cocky Machos decided it, and the rest of the Hombres knew they better play along. That's usually how these things worked out…

He grunted to himself satisfactorily. *It's good to be Macho—until the apoplexies strike.* Hombres knew: if they bided their time, all the Machos would eventually die of coronary disease, and leave the earth to their slightly-meeker-but-not-so-meek brethren to inherit it. Intent on staying alive long enough to inherit anything, the Watcher continued his vigilance.

Finishing out the chorus, the crowd faced their flag and pumped their fists as Chartreaux led them in their pledge:

"Free to DRINK, Free to TOKE,

Free to gamble, RICH or BROKE;

Free to BANG and Free to STROKE—

Nothing Stops Purgatory Folk!"

They shouted the words with true conviction, ending with their town motto—

" Purgatory—A Hell of a Town!"

Hats flew into the air at this jubilant cheer. "Thank you, DeLisha and the DragLine Dancers!" Mr. Megaphone enthused: "For more of the finest in Purgatory dining and dancing, be sure to visit Chef Pembroke and the Dancers at the DragLine! Outfits for the DeLisha's Dancers provided by Eden Boutique, exclusive purveyors of Feminine Finery..."

As he continued his advertising spiel, the chosen Fighters stripped down to their bluejeans and boots; cracking knuckles and swaggering around the perimeter of the Squared Circle, they sized each other up and played the crowd. Bereft of hats and clothing to give them a veneer of humanity, they looked inhuman. Without eyebrows or hair, they instead became distinguished by the magnitude of their affliction—scarred, oozing, scabbed and peeling, the scales and shards of skin crusting in drifts and formations which gave them as much distinction as the decades of scars that covered their beaten bodies.

Shirtless, but still arrayed in Lone Star cape, cowboy hat and mask, the Watcher felt out of place—had he not needed the extra cover to shield his identity, he would have taken it off. Joey, on the other hand, was loving every minute of the spectacle, parading his Wrassler-Man with ever-increasing hubris. Strolling around the ring, Joey tugged on the chain, and the Watcher felt a genuine urge to whip the chain out of Joey's hands and smack him with it. Irritable, the Watcher growled through the thin mask, eyes malevolent through their Metallilume veil, and the audience gawked.

"Let's give a warm Purgatory Welcome to tonight's fighters!" Mr. Megaphone held up his clipboard for cover as the crowd rained down empty bottles and balled-up burrito wrappers on the Fighters.

Sanders passed a sheet of paper to Mr. Megaphone—the fight card. He held it up, then began whispering and pointing to the Fighters; all but two retired to sit on long log benches on either side of the Arena. Mr. Megaphone handed Von Helm and Bosque each a small piece of plywood with the numbers 'one' and two' on it, respectively, Von Helm and Bosque now began to promenade around the Squared Circle, holding their number boards overhead and eyeballing each other with open contempt.

The little Sheriff flexed, then leaned down to stretch out. Bronzed and sleek, Von Helm was minimally a macho, and a short one to boot; the crowd jeered. The slightly taller Bosque was closely matched for Von Helm, only a little lighter in bulk. As bottles came sailing through the air, Von Helm took some quick jabs at a fence post; a slim, gray Hombre with broad shoulders and fast moves, Bosque seemed to be garnering some favor with the crowd.

Sanders took the placards from the fighters, and hung them from a larger plywood sign strung nailed up between fence posts next to the betting tables. Von Helm's placard was hung from a hook, beneath Bosque's placard—Von Helm was the Underdog. Mr. Megaphone pointed to the leader board: "Bets per fight on win; Fight Number One—odds are three to one—Gentlemen, place your bets!"

Curious bettors ambled to the betting tables, hoping to score a betting form, each with space to punch for one, five, or ten tokes. A blank was left to for High-Rollers to fill in any amount, if they were able to write. These forms were painstakingly drawn up by Sanders and Marcus each month with pen and small slips of paper, as part of their duties for Habib and the Jail.

In the past, Purgatory had attempted to record bets other ways, but with the introduction of Purgatory Money System, Habib found it easier to have a simple, easy to read form. Four ticket-punching BrigadesMen at the tables punched a hole by the preset amount as each gambler came to the table signing their name and lay down the appropriate number of tokes. With a limited pool of one hundred hand drawn forms per fight, bets were taken first come, first serve, ensuring that forms could be counted up and fulfilled quickly.

The Bandstand was a different setup—this was where the big money was made, and special privileges applied. Runners would pass the forms into the stands, and as most LandLords knew enough to carry a pencil, they were allowed to mark their bets then send the forms back down to runners to be punched and logged in at the tables. Sanders quickly tallied the forms, having his BrigadesMen assistant stack them in piles according to the amount of the bet, and on whom the bet was made.

When the forms or time ran out, broken orange hazard cones were brought out and placed in front of the tables. As it was early, most bettors were holding their coin until the second round of fights; time ran out at ten minutes, and the tables were called closed.

The corral gate opened, and the Fighters entered the ring. Excited to at last be underway, the crowd applauded as Mr. Megaphone swept a hand towards the Squared Circle.

"Good Evening and Welcome to Friday Night Fights at Purgatory! No holds barred, no weapons allowed, three minute rounds. Fights end with tap out, pass out or knockout." Whoops were heard from the stands as the Announcer introduced the Fighters:

"In this corner, weighing in at around one hundred and eighty pounds, Fighter One—the Comal County Crusher!"

Von Helm bounced, shaking out his bare hands.

"And in the opposite corner, at approximately one hundred and seventy pounds, Fighter Two—the Meridian Mangler!"

Bosque limbered up, jabbing and shuffling.

The beer-bottle bell sounded, and a venerable chicken-shaped egg timer was wound to three minutes. There was no handshake; the fight was on as Von Helm and Bosque began to circle each other, scraping their boots in the dirt. Bosque closed the distance quickly, and got in the first jab. Von Helm bobbed, lip bloodied, then subtly moved back into range.

The Watcher grinned behind the mask—He knew Von Helm was just biding his time, holding back, allowing himself to get hurt to hustle the crowd. The Fighters circled again, and Bosque allowed Von Helm to get one lick in to his jaw before jabbing a left to Von Helm's abdomen. Von Helm doubled briefly, then resumed circling. For the audience, this was looking to be a short fight. Already bored, denizens were drifting off to the taquito stands again. Bosque appeared to be confident, even a little cocky. He flicked a foot out, and delivered a solid kick to Von Helm's thigh—

The little Macho grabbed Bosque's foot, and flipped it upward. Off balance, Bosque landed on his backside in the dirt, and Von Helm slammed a beautiful elbow drop onto Bosque's chest. Leaping up, Von Helm straddled Bosque's legs, and executed a classic figure four leg lock, twisting his opponents legs with his own and applying just enough pressure to cause realistic agony. The crowd suddenly came alive, running to the barriers to hoot at the fighters.

Bosque tried to rise, but couldn't. He kicked, and waved his arms, and the crowd agonized with him; Von Helm dug in his heels and grinned gleefully, as he twisted Bosque's ankle. Unable to last any longer, Bosque slapped his hand on the ground, with Mr. Megaphone counting along...

"One—two—three—and the Mangler is tapped out! The Comal County Crusher is the Winner!"

Jubilant, Von Helm raised both hands, breathing heavily. *That Faker*, The Watcher chortled to himself, eyeing his Rival; *he's just getting started— but the rubes don't know that*. BrigadesMen opened the gate and swarmed Bosque, who was hauled off to Jail kicking and shouting: "I want my money back!"

Gamblers who bet on the Underdog whooped. In on the ruse, Agent King waved a hand, yelling; "Hell yeah! I won big!" Excited, other potential bettors began to wager with each other... the Comal County Crusher was a hot commodity.

As Von Helm paraded himself around the ring, a stab of jealousy overcame The Watcher, and he was suddenly glad Rose was not here to witness the little Sheriff's win. There would be other opportunities for the Watcher to impress her—ones that didn't involve him losing to his smiling rival. For now, Von Helm was busy being useful to the LoneStar Revolution, and not being useful to Rose—so that was a definitive win for the Watcher.

To his west, the lights of Pair'O'Dice twinkled; somewhere in that glow, his 'good girl' was momentarily safe from Predators such as Von Helm, ensconced within the safety of the Wild Horses Hotel—but that still wasn't safe enough...

Rose would never be safe enough until the Revolution was over. Dissatisfied, the Watcher scanned the crowd once more, and settled back to wait his turn in the Squared Circle.

—————◆—————

IV

Down at the Wild Horses Hotel, Sam was deep in concentration, fiddling with Rings.

Out of her compact drawstring bag, Sam had pulled an antiqued silver and sapphire RingWorld, a treasured piece of jewelry that she had rarely gotten to wear of late. Snapping her 'stone' uplink into Rose's Ring Port, she connected to the Afterling's Golden Ring. Sam was attempting to learn all she could about Rose's rare piece of tech, while there was still time.

Rose looked at her HeadsUp display concerned. The Ring had been part of her physicality since toddlerhood, a supplemental neurophoretic organ system connected to her embedded embryonic nanobots through a neural interface. For Rose, watching Sam work with her new WeSpeex U Ring was akin to watching a surgeon perform open heart surgery.

Sam frowned.

"What's wrong? Is it not working?" Rose asked, worried.

Sam shook her head. "No, it's just hard to go back to the old configuration. I haven't used this set up since I traded in my old WeSpeex ONE. VisualTrax isn't completely integrated on this one…" The display switched around, this time with the toolbar back on the bottom of the visual field, as Sam adjusted the display settings again. "But it's amazing to see the old functionalities back. The Holo-Projector was such a great feature—I used it all the time, back when I was giving reports to… people."

Mesmerized by Sam's avatar, Rose wanted to ask questions, but decided against it. The woman on the ring was mature, with a silver streak in a short cropped afro, her smooth, umber skin still unwrinkled, but the years starting to show. By contrast, the majestic Amazon sharing the loft with Rose was sleeker, more deadly-looking, her bald head and smooth face made feline in appearance by her thicker skin, up-tilted eyes and satiny, steel-blue scales. Only Sam's eyes and no-nonsense expression seemed similar to the woman in the avatar.

Rose peered at the display. "I had no idea that the Ring could do all these things..." she wrinkled her brow in memory. "The Church Fathers told us if we tried to understand the Ring, it would drive us mad. They said only the Creator could truly understand them."

"Well, that part wasn't far off. This Ring is making me crazy." Sam sighed. "But no, it will not drive you mad, or send you hell—the Creator of the Ring was not a God, he was just a man."

Shaking her head, Rose tried to comprehend it all. "But the Ring is a part of us—Asura aren't complete without it. Colors don't look as bright, music isn't as thrilling and emotions don't feel as intense."

"Well, that's because you were in part created by the Creator of the Ring—but he was still only a man."

Upset, Rose tucked her chin. "But only God can give life."

"True—but humans assist from time to time, thanks to science. You are still unique—but we need to acknowledge your origins. Your life is a product of Divinity and Humanity combined—and now I've got to save that life, so hush for a minute." Sam continued to work, while Rose wrestled with bioethical conundrums. "I can only access the Guest settings, even with direct link. But at least I can activate the Holo-projector and speakers via your ring now. Just don't mess with any settings, and follow my instructions exactly when the time comes, okay?"

"Can I see the scan now?" Rose wheedled softly.

Sam continued to adjust the sound settings. "Sure, I don't see why not. We need to test anyway... hold your hand up, facing outward from you; just make sure your hand is parallel to your body so the image is in a natural position when it's offset from a backdrop."

Linking to her own Ring atop Rose's hand, Sam dimmed the HeadsUp Display, and switched to projection mode. Rose gasped as her own image sprang to life in front of her, a three-dimensional, fully manipulatable holographic image. A shadow of fear crossed Rose's face. "So this is how the Church Fathers make Evil Ones?"

"Somewhat—your "Evil Ones" are a later, more advanced form of neurally integrated image."

Rose gazed at it, cautious. "Why can't I feel this one?"

"That program doesn't exist on your new Ring." Sam leaned in, intrigued. "How do you know they're Evil Ones, and not a regular person? Lots of unsuspecting people used to get tricked by the projected Holographs… they appear real to us."

"Oh Evil Ones look real, and they can cause us pain, but they don't have a glow like every other living thing. That's why they are so scary."

"That's because they aren't living." Sam murmured. "What does the glow look like on living things? Does it have a color?"

"The Deva always ask the Asura this question! You must be Deva…" Rose whispered excitedly—" It is impossible to describe! How does one describe 'Red' to a person who is color-blind? Or the describe the sound of Music to the tone-deaf? How does one describe the flavor of honey to a person who has never tasted? So it is with the Light…. Asura see the Light. Each natural living thing has its own unique light, in all the colors of the rainbow."

"But how is that different than just infrared heat?"

Rose shook her head. "I don't know how to explain it—I guess you could say the texture is different. It's like trying to explain the difference between hot and cold."

"Hmm—so this Holo-graph doesn't have a glow?"

"No." Still wary, Rose whispered. "So this is me…"

Noting Rose's downcast face, Sam asked: "Why? What's wrong?"

"It's just…" Frowning, Rose looked at the image, rotating it. "I'm so fat and old."

Sam chuckled softly. "Nonsense. You look great; everyone thinks that when they see themselves in three dimensions."

Reality versus expectation was cruel, as usual. The Afterling had hoped to see a glamorous, graceful version of herself, in gorgeous raiment; instead, she saw a compactly voluptuous figure, fur cape thrown back, long stocking cap slightly askew, garbed in a rough-spun rainbow of earthy browns and golds.

"I look like I escaped from a zoo." Rose pouted.

"Stop whining about the fashion theme." Sam hissed, fine tuning the resolution of the Holo-graph. "Lourdes did a fabulous job, and Kendra's makeup perfectly complements the look. Besides, the Marshal dressed you in furs; it was his idea to make you look like some kind of wild elf. I think it suits you."

"I'm sorry—I just want to look like that golden dress; slim and sparkly. not wild and woolly. You should see Amelia, my sister… she is so beautiful, tall and slender like a will'o'wisp. She must be at least two inches taller than me, and a few pounds lighter." Rose's face lit up at the memory.

"So Amelia is 4'8"? You're maybe 4'6" at the most… how can you be that different? You're all clones of each other." Wondering, Sam adjusted the contrast on the image.

"Oh, we are all different from each other! In my case, I was very sick as a child; I had terrible earaches and couldn't quite ever seem to get well, so I didn't eat as much as the others. Ammi—I mean, Dr. Iyer—said my growth was stunted, and that's also why I have a tendency to gain weight easily now. If I don't diet all the time, I get positively tubby."

Sam nodded in sympathy. "I used to have the same issues, but since the Happening, it's no longer a problem. Muscle and testosterone affect fat differently. But enough of that; your look lovely, and in no ways old, so let's not worry about that. You have to have all the confidence in the world for tonight, so think empowering thoughts!" Sam cheered Rose on. "We especially need you to be positive tonight—you have to control your fear response. Do all of your clone-sisters have such severe cataplexy as you do?"

"I suppose so; I've never thought of it as being bad. I just always dealt with it as a fact of life. We call it freezie flopsie. It's just something we do… it only happens when we are very scared or angry."

Sam remained positive. "You'll be with me the entire time, and I'll keep you safe."

"To be honest, it's not just about me being safe." Rose said, biting her lip. "I'm afraid for everyone else, too. Others have died because of me. I'm afraid that after I speak the words tonight, all will be death and war."

"You are right to be afraid." Sam whispered earnestly. "We are up against a great Evil. You recognize it, and that is why you are afraid—Evil is frightening. But to stay silent is to give Evil a voice. Don't speak out in spite of your fear—speak out because of your fear. Speak out anyway, and overcome fear with Truth." Sam patted Rose's hand. "Now, pray for courage. Tonight the Revolution starts and you will be the one to start it. But you have to have courage—"

"Courage…" Rose squinched her eyes shut to pray for courage, then came up with a new worry. "But what if Survivors think I'm ugly?"

Sam rolled her eyes. "They'll think you're gorgeous! Believe it!"

"But that's not what Kendra said… she said you all think I look fat and my hair looks weird."

"They'll get over it." Sam snapped. "Besides, your hair looks fantastic now Kendra oiled and coiled it. Now get busy being confident."

Twirling the image, Rose tried to feel better about her chubby parts. She liked her big eyes, full breasts, and her small waist was nice, but those hips and thighs… she sighed. "Did the voice thing work?"

"Yes, it's perfect." Sam closed the image with a quick swipe of the hand, and it disappeared. "Now collect your stuff—we'll be ready to leave when the action starts." She disconnected from Rose, and turned back to her own work.

Rose packed all her goods away, loading them into the leather book bag she had smuggled into the Hotel. She carefully accounted for all her books, placing the Watcher's bundled gifts across the top to cushion them. Lifting a corner of the shawl to peek at the glittering Quinceañera dress once more, Rose stroked it; the Metallilume fabric seemed impossibly soft. But Sam said the dress was tougher than it looks…

Gifts are the giver's image of the giftee; Rose pondered, *so this is what Saul thinks of me.* She lifted the bookbag, and it bumped against Von Helm's golden derringer, still secreted in her fur cape's pocket. *And that's what Carlos thinks of me.* It was a very lovely little gun, and the brass barrel matched the golden gown and Ring. It would be a shame to break up the set…

I can just keep it in case of emergency. After all, *everyone needs a backup plan…* She flushed, then felt bad for feeling flushed at the thought of Von Helm; it seemed wrong to be thinking of another man's gifts at the same time as she thought of the Watcher's presents.

Rose pondered the implications of Asura keeping secrets from Deva. *As soon as I see Saul,* she reasoned, *I will give it to him, and he can decide what to do with it.* That would be the best choice… Client gifts always went straight to the Team Leader, no exceptions. The Watcher would decide whether or not Rose should take Von Helm as their Client.

Rose wondered how Devil Arrangements handled clients and gifts. Owen Wister's wonderful Cowboy Book didn't make any mention of such affairs, but somehow she got the idea that the Virginian wouldn't like Miss Mollie entertaining Clients. However, the Watcher was not the Virginian.

She gazed at the wonderful Ring on her hand, its luminous pearl aglow in the darkness of the crawlspace, delicate silver filagree overlaid upon iridescent gold. It had come from the Watcher, but what did it mean—a declaration of love, or just a societal construct?

Rose wasn't sure what the Watcher believed about the Ring, but he had never declared any sort of ideas on love—not at least to her.

Maybe he didn't have any?

Checking beneath the pillows in the crawlspace one last time, Rose came across a small, hinged metal box—the one the Watcher had stuffed into the bag with Rose when she and Sam were smuggled into the Gambler's Suite. Curious, she opened it up to find a small cloth bag filled with tokes, a green feather, and some honey-roasted peanuts, bought from a vendor when Joey went to Market. A folded noted was tucked inside, and she peeked at it. Written in the Watcher's neat block letters, the note read:

> —*Blood chit: use only in emergency—return to WildLand Express for reward.*

To the side, she saw a simple line drawing made by the Watcher: a Five-Pointed Star, and within it a precise, geometric representation of the liberated Phoenix rising from the flames above the broken chain. She puzzled over the drawing as she read the note.

Blood chit? She wasn't sure what on earth that meant, but it sounded horrible. She supposed it meant it was an emergency supply box, in case one was bloody; but in that case, she expected a first aid kit. Still, she found the honey-roasted peanuts a nice addition; nibbling on one, Rose found it delightful, so she nibbled on another. The Watcher seemed to be concerned about her starving to death while he was gone…

He might not have any ideas on love, but the Watcher had definite ideas on how to keep an Afterling fed. But what about the note? Concerned she was missing an important message, she showed it to Sam.

"It's a blood chit—a message to someone who might find you if you were lost or hurt. It asks for help and offers a reward. But this drawing… color me impressed." Sam grunted at it. "It's certainly a creative way to use the Greek alphabet. He made it almost like an old western brand for cattle, and he used the letters as elements each part of the drawing."

"Oh! It's made up of Greek letters?" Rose peered over Sam's shoulder.

"Yes—it's a simple way to break down elements of a drawing into easy-to-remember shapes." Pointing to each part, Sam became an Educator again, explaining each part of the Watcher's line drawing.

"This first letter is an accented Alpha, with Gamma and Iota for wings; it looks like a Crested Bird. A rotated Epilson looks like flames above crossed logs—a campfire of the letter Chi. An inverted, dotted Omega represents the wreath of Broken Chain. Altogether, they became an easily written, stylized Insignia of the LoneStar Revolution. But when the Greek letters are arranged from the top down—Alpha, Gamma, Iota, Epsilon, Chi, Omega—it should say something…"

Sam looked confused as she scanned the note with her Ring to save the image. "But it's not any Greek word I know. Maybe it's an anagram, or acronym?"

"But why would he use Greek? Without a Ring Translator, no one here might understand it…" Confused, Rose looked at it once more, trying to decipher it.

"The Marshal must be sending a veiled message to any Sympathetic Visionaries that might find you. All Visionaries had to learn Greek and Latin." Sam passed the note back to Rose.

"But he's not a Visionary. Saul said so himself."

"What he says and what he means are two completely different things." Suddenly enigmatic, Sam's eyes narrowed. "I used to think Dominic was exaggerating about Marshal Azarian—but Dominic was right. The Marshal is much more dangerous than he looks."

Impressed, Rose folded the note back into the tin, then secured the box in her bookbag with The Watcher's other gifts.

"I'll be back. You've already been to the bathroom, so now it's my turn to make one last trip to the ladies room and grab some supplies the Gambler laid out. Supposedly he found a pair of shoes he thinks will fit me." Sam crawled out from under the bed to make a final sweep of the apartment. They would be traveling light, and other than items acquired during their stay, Rose and Sam had little with them; the rest of their belongings were packed away with the Hostesses' bags. Rose straightened up the crawlspace, checking for any other loose items, and securing goods.

She thought on the Watcher's Moon poem, the one she had stolen from his personal notebook. It was the first time she had ever secretly admired him, when she realized the Watcher was more than just a mute brute on the end of a chain… the Watcher was poet, disguised as savage.

Was it still there? Panicked at the thought she might lose it, Rose peeked between the pages of The Virginian, where she had tucked the ragged lined paper, a beloved bookmark:

Warm were the lips I gave you, and you took the flower of this —

Your lips next to mine turned the entire world the gold of a summer's kiss…

I can never forget the magic tho' the dream ended all too soon

I remember the Love I gave you by the light of the Golden Moon

This was the poem Rose had always wanted the Watcher to write for her—but this had not been written for her. Somewhere, deep in his past, the Watcher had written it for another woman, in another time.

It was the reason she was so easily deceived by his Angel poem—she had naively hoped it was about herself. But instead, it was about the Watcher himself. She unfolded the Angel poem from beside the Moon poem, where she had tucked it away:

-…This I promise now, you alone will always be

The Angel of my better nature's charms.

Still, it was true every word of it. She bit her lip and resolved to herself—should she ever see him again, she would let him be her Angel. *A big, ugly 'ol Devil Angel…*

She tucked everything away again, safe in her bookbag.

Agitated, Sam poked her head back into the crawl space, a coil of rope over her shoulder and a pair of too-large sneakers on her feet.

"Change of plans: the action is starting early. Mansour just tapped a Morse-code message through the support beam that runs up the wall of the utility closet—he saw a guard come to the front desk downstairs, talk to the desk clerk and duck back out. Even though our room is secured, and the access panels are hidden, the guards will look under the bed eventually. It's best to leave now."

She hauled in the modified duffel bag the Watcher had used to smuggle Rose into the Hotel the day before; Von Helm had recovered it from the lobby after the Great Liquor Diversion. Now it smelled of sour beer—a perfect fit for Purgatory.

"Is there anything I can do to help?" Eager, Rose began to gather up her items.

"Help me by seeing what I can't see." Still pulling on her gear, Sam answered: "Our Nite-Eyes tech is old, and the ALGOS are heat-shielded to help defeat infrared technology, but my Ring can still pick up the faintest traces of their exhaust wake. My infrared sensor has been working sporadically, but most Rings this age have bad sensors. The only reason our Rings still function is because we have Agent Wilcox to maintain them —but our Nite-Eyes sensors are dying and we won't be able to replace them."

"Oh, I am so sorry for your loss!" It seemed sad to think of Rings as dying. Rose clutched the Golden Ring to her chest, protective. "I can see the drones plain as day, so I will help. But you say they are heat-cloaked… If the ALGOS are shielded from infrared technology, then how am I able to see them?"

Sam shook her head, harried. "I don't know… that's a question that only your Creator can answer. Maybe your eyes are more sensitive to infrared." Sam pulled up a knit hood from beneath her long overcoat, then wrapped a thin woolen scarf to hide her jaw and neck. The chill of evening had returned, allowing Sam to bundle up and hide her femininity beneath layers of heavy material.

"Look through the mesh panel of your bag, and tell me what you see when we get outside. Because the drones have enhanced hearing, we'll speak Ring-2-Ring from this point forward, unless I tell you otherwise. I'll stick my hand down in the bag to access your ring directly." Sam laid out the large duffel bag and unzipped it, stuffing her own personal bag with her own meager belongings into it. "Now hop in—we've got to move."

Rose pulled her deer-hide hood up over her long stocking-cap once more, tucking the pom-pom end of her braid behind her. She used the antler-tip-and-cord toggles to fasten the fur cape shut. "Are you certain Saul won't come back to look for me here?" Rose stepped into the long bag, and curled up where she could look through the thick mesh 'window'.

Sam arranged the UltraFoil-lined furs to hide Rose's heat signature completely. It wasn't just the drones they needed to worry about; anyone else with a Ring could use Nite-Eyes infrared tech to potentially see Rose's infrared image through the nylon walls of the bag. "We can't stay here. It looks like a team of Guards is preparing to search the Hotel again while the LandLords are gone."

"But what about Lazarus?" Rose worried. "And what if the Marshal comes for me here?"

"He'll get out—we've done this routine before, just not from this location. He'll meet me at a designated point. I just hate the thought of telling him about Camp Forlorn—he's going to be devastated." Impatient, Sam whispered to the Afterling. "We'll send word to Command once we reach a staging area, and they will contact Marshal Azarian to let him know." Zipping the bag shut, Sam looped the rope through the straps, and secured it. Dragging the bag to the far end of the crawlspace, Sam gingerly edged the panel open a crack to look outside:

Down at the bottom, she saw a Macho in a blue hoodie and bucket hat lounging with his back against the wall, hidden beneath the evergreen branches of the bush. He casually reached behind him to tap the trunk of the tree twice, then twice again.

Sam smiled. *Mansour…*

She pushed the access panel aside, and braced both feet against each side of the narrow opening. Wrapping the rope around her waist, she secured the knots around the bag's strap, then gently pushed it through the escape hatch, lowering it through the branches of the Ligustrum tree towards Mansour. Without turning, he reached up to guide the bag down, slinging it across his own broad shoulders, then tugged the rope, freeing it. Sam coiled the rope once more, then tucked it into her personal bag. She eased out of the access panel, closing it behind her.

From the narrow ledge running along the eave of the Hotel's barn roof, she could scoot over to a branch of the twiggy bush; Sam grabbed hold of the sturdiest one she could find, then swung out hand over hand, swinging down to the ground. The branches sagged beneath the weight of the tall Hembra, but they did not break. Relieved, she touched down lightly upon the ground beside Mansour, and he moved in close to her.

"Care to take a stroll through Pair'O'Dice with me?" He smiled at her, and she felt a gladdening of her heart. Fighting off the urge to kiss Mansour, Sam bolstered her Military Bearing and pointed at her ring finger. Mansour shook his head, puzzled. Sam leaned in close to whisper:

"Your Ring—put it on. They're working. Use the secure server on Frequency 145." Mansour handed over the Afterling carrier, and Sam positioned it across her shoulders so Rose would be looking forward through the mesh panel.

Incredulous, Mansour slipped his hand in his pocket to retrieve his ring. He fired it up and hooked into Channel 145.

#ELLISON: I'm thrilled to see you out here. How on earth did

you escape the guards?

MANSOUR: After the rest of the Chartreaux's entourage left to escort the Lords to the Arena, I eased out under when only two guards were left. When I saw the guards peek in at the front desk, I knew we have to move, so I tapped out your warning and slipped out of the side door. I took up post beneath your escape hatch—I figured you'd come down this way.

Walking at a brisk pace, they headed out to the back alley, between the town's outer palisade and the hotel. A wide swath of cleared brush made walking easy, and the trees that lined the way gave additional cover. Sam ducked behind a bush, and pulled him in behind her.

#MANSOUR: Geez Louise, that bag's smell! Couldn't you find something less alcoholic? I'm trying hard to stay straight here...

Sam frowned at him.

#ELLISON: Sorry, it's the best I could do in a hurry.

The bag combined with the long coat, helped hide Sam's hips and the motion of her walk. She adjusted the straps, then slipped her hand inside a side zipper; Rose found Sam's hand, and linked their Rings. The avatar of an earnest, young Rose greeted Sam as they messaged:

#ROSE: Any instructions?

#ELLISON: Act as Scout. I've positioned you to spot the ALGOS—as soon as you see them, cover your face and let me know position and heading.

#ROSE: Will do!

Rainbow Sparkles shot out of the message, filling up the entire screen to the sound of happy cheers. Sam jumped—

#ELLISON: UGH Don't use exclamations points—I need to mute your Live-Emote feature.

#ROSE: Sorry.

The whole screen turned blue as a sad little sound of violins played. Sam groaned and did her best to ignore this new distraction, so she could focus on getting out of Pair'O'Dice alive. Following Mansour, they ducked into a grove of thorny bumelia bushes along the wall. Peeking through their slender evergreen leaves, Mansour looked back towards the Hotel.

#MANSOUR: A team of four BrigadesMen is approaching the back-door of the Hotel; stay put for a minute until they enter, then we can walk on.

They waited as the team disappeared into the Hotel's lobby.

#MANSOUR: If they stop us, you and me gonna be buddies—just two guys wanting a private encounter. And if they get pushy, they'll die.

#ELLISON: I knew there was a reason I recruited you, Brother Horse…

Mansour looked rightly pleased.

#MANSOUR: Just call me Stud—everyone else does.

She wanted to laugh, but she couldn't. Mansour noticed the change in her demeanor; she tried to remain stoic, but her eyes betrayed her.

#ELLISON: I'm sorry, Lazarus, but…

#MANSOUR: Just tell me and get it over with.

Sam breathed deeply to center herself:

#ELLISON: Reliable sources report a Blood Rain camp fell upon our Brothers at the old Home Place before Dawn. Only a few escaped—all the rest are gone on to Big Rock Candy Mountain.

Her mind wandered back to a long-ago campfire. There beneath the loving arms of a spreading oak, Agent Hamilton was jigging with joy to his favorite song as Tyler picked his beat-up guitar and Von Helm's fiddle sang:

"…I'm headed for a land that's far away

Besides the crystal fountains

So come with me, we'll go and see

The Big Rock Candy Mountains…"

Despite her best efforts to maintain her military bearing, Sam's eyes filled with tears. Mansour put his hand to his mouth, trying to stop himself from cursing aloud.

#MANSOUR: Who escaped?

#ELLISON: Brother Dog's team, and Brother Eagle's Team with the Flock, plus two. And now the ALGOS are inside Purgatory…the mechanism that created the DeadZones and blocked our rings also blocked them, but now that mechanism is down. The Gambler called it a "jammer."

He stared up at the sky for a moment, silent in the thorny hedgerow.

#MANSOUR: I can't affect what happened then… I can only affect what's happening now. Let's get to work. Watch my six.

Vigilant, Sam surveilled their immediate surroundings while Mansour scried the heavens. Moments passed; then Rose hissed and tapped on the walls of her duffel bag to alert Sam, who linked up with the Afterling to pass a message:

#ELLISON: Heads up—the Afterling sees something in the upper tree-line to our North.

His keen blue eyes raked the tree-lines until if found the object of their search, lingering to observe.

#MANSOUR: We've got major problems. I'm seeing a pattern of patrol, a pair of drones; they just did their pass of the Hotel, so now is the time to leave. My Nite-Eyes tech barely catches it... it looks like the drone are circumscribing this sector in a counter-clockwise spiral pattern, centering on the Walleyed Fit. We'll move outside their radius and against traffic so your little friend can see them coming on the next round.

Sam swallowed her fear; she had never dealt with the drones. They headed down the wall and towards Party Pontoon Lagoon. As they approached the rope bridge, they could hear the parade crowd applauding, and a voice booming through a megaphone.

#ELLISON: Sounds like the crowd is winding up for fights— lets get to a staging area, and make contact with Command. We need to check in and figure out next steps—I vote for the Dump Access, so we can slip out with the Afterling when the action starts.

#MANSOUR: Sounds like a plan. Let's am-scray to the Pair'O'Dice alley access, up the edges of the Commons, and—

Sam put a gloved finger to her lips. Listening, Mansour strained to hear what alarmed her.

#ELLISON: Feet hurrying through the street. They're searching for someone—get to the Alley Access, walk easy but fast.

She adjusted the bag as they walked, slipping her hand in to link with Rose:

#ELLISON: I've turned you so you're looking behind me; use your glow vision and let me know if you see some one following us.

Rose squeezed Sam's hand, looking through the mesh panel to see if anyone was near.

#ROSE: There's a group of four Devils just moved between two buildings to our north, about seventy-five yards; they are moving quickly to our west.

Grimacing, Sam passed the information to Mansour. Keeping a steady pace, they walked as if they had every right to be there, faces low. A cold breeze was whipping up from the Lake, and they pulled up their mufflers to hide their faces further. Rounding the corner to the Pair'O'Dice fence, they heard footsteps approaching from their north, closing the distance fast. A voice shouted—"Over here!"

#MANSOUR: Get through the fence. I'll hold them off.

#ELLISON: Not enough time—use the ruse, get behind me quick, and cover my movements.

The footsteps grew louder. "Hey! You two—hold up. We want to talk to you!" In the darkness of the alley, a BrigadesMan called, lantern in hand—he was just around the corner...

Mansour planted himself behind Sam; pulling the fence panel swiftly to the side, Sam slipped the duffel bag off her shoulder, and it hit the ground with a soft thud. She pushed it through the access with her foot and let the metal fence panel swing back into place. Rose's bag was now on the other side of the fence.

"Stop right there! We want a word with you two." Rounding the corner, the team of BrigadesMen ran forward, then skidded to a stop.

Mansour growled at them from the shadows, hips thrust against a spread-eagled Sam's backside. Braced against the fence, face hidden beneath her scarf and her broad-brimmed hat, the big Hembra looked like just another Hombre in a back-alley rendezvous with a Macho.

"Can't a paying customer have a little privacy?" Mansour growled. "What the hell is wrong with you people?"

"We hate to interrupt you lovebirds, but we need to search that bag. A criminal is on the loose, and we're under orders to search any suspicious luggage. Where you staying?"

"At the Flop'n'Slop."

The BrigadesMan grunted. "Yeah, no wonder you're out here... that place is a dump."

"Well, unless you want to pay to watch this party, give me a minute to get myself pulled together." Mansour snapped. He kept his head hung low, as if he were embarrassed to be caught in the act.

"No—just stay where you are—don't move. Why ain't you down watching the parade?"

"Do I look like I give a damn about some high-tone woman?" Mansour snarled, still covering Sam's back. "Beside, I've got no love for the Rangers. They're a bunch of stuck-up dickwads."

"Well, you've got me there. I can't stand 'em myself. Still, you oughta have some civic pride. We all worked hard to get that show put together… it's people like you that make Purgatory look bad." The BrigadesMen grabbed Mansour's middy bag, untying it and dumping out the contents out onto the ground. The rope and a package of dried instant Cocoa plopped on the ground.

"Rope, huh? Planning on throwing your own personal rodeo?" The lead BrigadesMan chuckled. "But chocolate's bad for your figure, sweet cheeks. I'll take this, in exchange for you being a bad citizen and not attending tonight's festivities…" Scooping the rest of the contents messily back into the bag, the BrigadesMan stuffed the packet of cocoa in his own pocket, and waved his team on down the road. "Let's hurry this up, I want to see the fights. They say there's some real talent out there tonight…

Mansour watched as the search team marched away.

#MANSOUR: I would love to stay this way with you, but we've got a job to do. Let's go.

Sam dropped to her knees, pushing the panel aside; crawling halfway through, she swept her hands from side to side.

"Oh Sweet Jesus…"

She suddenly disappeared through the hole in the fence. Panicked, Mansour bent down and slipped through, his hand on the hatchet beneath his coat. Sam was running back and forth, searching beneath bushes and in corners, a look of sheer terror on her face; Mansour felt a sick knot tighten in the pit of his stomach…

The duffel bag—and the Afterling in it—was gone.

———◆———

At first Rose wasn't exactly sure what was happening… one minute, she could feel her bag being pushed away by Sam's boot, and then all was darkness. She could still hear Mansour's voice, but she could no longer see his or Sam's glow—it was blocked by some kind of barrier, and in the shadows, she couldn't see what that barrier might be. Rose peeked through the mesh window of the bag, but could see nothing; the entire area was unlit, a stark difference from the lantern-lit streets of Pair'O'Dice. She surmised she was in a dark alley, and the bag's sour beer smell was being overwhelmed by the putrid odor of nearby garbage. She listened as an unseen Survivor demanded to search Mansour's bag. It had to be the BrigadesMen... disoriented in the darkness, she curled up, waiting for some sort of cue from Sam.

A glow appeared from her right; through the duffel bag's nylon lining, she could make out the general shape and features—a tall person, moving low and fast, possibly Sam? Rose tried to get a better look through the mesh—

And all at once, the bag was snatched up and carried away.

The motion was quiet and quick, like Sam, but the rhythm was wrong. *Not Sam*—Rose held her breath. Was this more spy-craft? *Perhaps another agent?* A corner was turned, then another; they were moving faster, down a twisting, unlit path. Dimly, the Afterling could see the usual high contrast of bushes and grass, and the darker shapes of buildings as they passed by. She heard feet stumbling over bottles and cans as the bag's carrier hurried though murky shadows.

Spinning through the air, the bag was tossed over a fence and landed hard; her fur cape padded her well, but the impact still nearly knocked the breath out of Rose. As she heard feet hit the ground beside her, she stuffed her hand into the pocket of her cape to grip Von Helm's Derringer.

Now the bag was jerked upwards again, this time landing across a broad back; she could feel the bumpy spine and hard muscles. A terrible fear flooded her, as the unknown person opened a door.

A lantern burned on a table in a moldy room; it smelled of urine and garbage. Rose saw another glow off to her right, and heard raspy breathing. A rough voice spoke, her kidnapper: "Second score tonight. Some idiot left their luggage in the alley—let's see what kind of loot we've got here."

A weak voice came from the glow to her right—someone lying down. "I need water."

"I'll beat the shit out of you again unless you quit your bitching." The rough voice answered, lifting the bag to a table. "I don't got time for you."

She heard the bag unzip; Rose ducked her head, hand on the Derringer in her pocket. Hesitant to shoot, she waited...

"A bunch of crappy furs? Dammit..."

a big hand grabbed the deer-pelt hood to drag it out—"Oh now, wait a minute! What the hell is this?" The voice crackled with an unholy glee—

furs wrapped around her throat, Rose was dragged out with the pelt.

"We got us a runaway!"

A tall, ash-grey Hombre hauled Rose the rest of the way out of the bag, knocking it to the dirt floor; she tried to pull the Derringer free of the pocket, but it was tangled in the cape. Hands clamped around the fur collar encircling her neck, the Survivor fell across her, pinning her beneath his heavy body. She gasped for breath.

"Marvin—don't…" The man in the bed wheezed, struggling to rise.

Ignoring the sick man, the grey Hombre pulled down the stretchy neckline of Rose's dress. Clamping one scaly hand across her mouth, he dug his claws into her rounded breast: "Oh hell yeah…" The Hombre straddled Rose, pulling up her skirt. Forcing one knee between her thighs, he jammed the other knee down beside it, then prized her legs apart. Leering, he pushed away from the floor, leaning back to yank down his own pants—

Slipping her gun free from her cape pocket, Rose squeezed the trigger.

The heat flash singed her thumb as the Derringer kicked, nearly tearing the gun from her grip. With a scream the Hombre fell backwards, hobbled by his own dungarees. Rose rolled away from him, scrambling from the Hombre as he writhed in the dirt; bright red blood gushed from from a crater in his naked thigh, staining her moccasins as she kicked free from him. Stumbling away through the cans and bottles that littered the floor, Rose collapsed against a far wall.

Bleeding profusely, the dying man was sobbing.

"You shot me!" He wailed as he tried to stand but sank back, grabbing his thigh, trying to staunch the flow. "It hurts, oh God, it hurts! Make it stop…"

The dirt floor turned to bloody mud beneath Marvin's flailing legs. He grabbed a handful of the mud, and stuffed it into his own bleeding wound, but it gushed back out in pulses, squeezing between Marvin's fingers. He clawed at his own tears, muddying his face with his filthy hands, wailing.

Rose's face crumpled. "I'm sorry—I'm so sorry…" she murmured as the Hombre turned white, gasping, his movements slowing. Slumped against the wall, limp, Rose was pained by the man's agony. He thrashed, attempting to rise, weeping as he fell; blood smeared across the floor, finger-painting his own death in the dirt. Weaker with each attempt, his hands began to shake; he reached out to the Afterling,

"You shot me…"

This was no clean kill, no far-off victory; up close, his pain became her pain, flowing into her, emotional rape. Rose buried her head in her arms, devastated by the man's dying cries, wanting to help him, but afraid of his violence. A tear trickled down Marvin's rough cheek, blue eyes dimming. The man's lips barely moved:

"Mom…"

The light faded from him, flowing away with his blood.

Rose wept.

A silent moment passed, then the raspy voice spoke from the bed. "Don't cry, little girl. He woulda hurt you bad, made your life a misery, like he did mine."

Sniffling, Rose tried to staunch her own tears "I'm so sorry… I didn't want to hurt him but I was afraid he would kill me." Disheveled and half naked, Rose noticed bruises already starting to form on the delicate skin beneath her painted scales; she pulled her neckline back into place to hide them.

She heard the Survivor in the bed cough again, and she wiped her eyes to look at him; a gasping Hombre leaned forward on the edge of a sagging bed, struggling for air. Thick, bumpy grey hide covered his thin arms and legs, and his skin stretched taut across his grotesquely swollen abdomen. Rasping, he held out a hand to her. "Please—do you have water?"

Shying away from the dead Hombre and his ever-widening pool of blood, Rose crept to the scarred wooden table. It was shoved against an unsheathed wall of scavenged pallets and rusting tin panels, decorated with incongruously glamorous faded prints of ballroom dancers and Broadway openings. She retrieved a canteen from the duffel bag, and poured some water into a cracked jar on a bedside table. Rose passed the water to the sick man.

He sipped as much as he was able, between gasps, all the while staring at Rose with wonder. "You look like a kid…" The man laid back, rubbing his eyes. "I ain't seen a kid in over fifty years. But if I believed in a Heaven anymore, I'd imagine the place is full of them. Maybe I'm dying…"

"Oh, no, I'm sorry. This isn't Heaven and I'm not a child. I'm full grown, and you all are just very tall." Sniffling, Rose dabbed at her eyes with the hem of her dress. "Oh, Mister, I am so, so sorry about your friend…"

The Survivor wheezed: "He's not my friend." The sick Survivor sipped the water, stopping from time to time to breathe. "Marvin's a bully, here to steal my stuff and use my house as a hideout. He was running counterfeit tokes out my front door, so I would take the fall if the Bosses ever found out. Too bad he never gave me any..." The sick man grimaced. "Marvin told me he'd turn me in to the Brigades if I complained."

With a shaking hand, Rose filled the man's glass again. "Why didn't you tell the Brigades he was hurting you?"

"I couldn't get out to do it. Too sick. Besides, Marvin brought me water once a day, and sometimes a little food. If he didn't, nobody else would." He took a deep breath. " I guess he felt guilty."

Rose set the jar down, refilled to the brim. The stained sheets reeked of sweat and sickness, rumpled into a twist with the tattered grey blanket. "Have you no one to help you?"

"Don't worry about me—you okay? Did he hurt you?"

Putting her hand to her breast, Rose shook her head softly; "Only bruises and scratches. I've been hurt worse. But what about you? I heard him say he beat you."

"He did—but he wouldn't have ever been able to do that, or hurt you, if I wasn't sick." The man grimaced.

"How are you sick? What is wrong?"

"I don't know. Some kind of cancer, Doc Aubergine left us before he could figure it out. All I know is, I ain't long for this world. But how 'bout you—what you running from?"

"I'm running from people trying to kill me." She didn't say more, fearful of revealing too much.

"Can't blame you. I'd run too but I can't."

Rose remembered the Watcher's note. "I don't suppose you could help me get back to the WildLand Express? They would give you a reward if you did..."

"I wish I could. I haven't been out of this shack in weeks—I can't walk no more." Despairing, the man shook his head. "There's nobody left alive who gives a damn about me. I've 'lifted my eyes unto the hills', but the Big Man Upstairs ain't sending no help." Bitter, the man sank back onto his pillow, leaving Rose to wonder who was this Big Man, and why he wasn't helping...

"Is the Big Man one of your neighbors?"

"No. Marvin's one of my neighbors. That'll tell you all you need to know about my neighbors."

Rose was shocked. "But surely there must be someone out there who would help you! Someone kind, who wouldn't hit you and could bring you meals and a canteen of fresh water daily…"

He shook his head, pained.

"Well, this won't do at all." A look of determination came over Rose's face as she wiped her tears away. "Tell me where to go, and I shall send for someone to help you."

"The DragLine Queens used to care, back when I was a Dancer… but none of them ever come to LowTown. It's too dangerous." Gripping his midsection, he sat up. "They can't come out here unless they have a guard to watch them—and I ain't got nothing to pay one after hours. Pembroke don't let 'em come down on company time, and he don't let them have cash on hand. He's afraid the trainees may get ahold of it and run."

"Oh! I have just the thing!" Inspired, Rose turned to the bag and rifled through it. She shook the cloth bag at the sick man, and the tokes inside it jingled. She placed the moneybag in his hand. "Take these!"

The sick man opened the bag with a quaking hand. "There's at least twenty tokes in here…" Flabbergasted, he pushed it back to her. "Keep it —you're going to need it if you are on the run." He coughed once more, and leaned forward again.

"It's no problem! " She said it as if tokes grew on trees, thrusting the bag at the Survivor once more. "The Marshal will get me more—he's very good at that! Here's the box that goes with it. I'm sure he won't mind." She gave the sick man the hinged metal box, with the peanuts and the flying serpent's feather. The Survivor looked into it, and his eyes grew wide.

"There's food in there for tonight, and a little something to buy you more help later. These feathers are quite valuable!" Rose fluffed his sweat stained pillow, and smoothed the sheets. "Now, whom should I contact?"

The note fell from the box, and the sick man opened it. "What's this picture? You'll have to tell me—I can't read script."

She wasn't sure what to say—but this man seemed like a friend—"Oh, that is a Phoenix; the Watcher says it is a symbol of Hope and Renewal, It means Humanity will rise from the Ashes of the Happening, and We Will Be Free." Rose didn't see how sharing that information could possibly hurt anything.

"You can't give me this…" Holding up the feather, the Survivor wheezed up at her, stunned. "you'll need this to buy your freedom, or at least to hire a guard for yourself."

"Oh, the Marshal is my Body Guard." Rose replied blithely. "I just have to get back to him. He's going to help me fight for my freedom! And besides, the instructions say to save this for an emergency, and obviously this is an emergency. Now, all I need is for you to tell me where I am, so I can figure out where I'm going. Then I can get the help we both need."

The sick man picked at his threadbare blanket. "You're in LowTown—the place where dreams go to die. The WildLand Express will be at the Campground, ahead and out to your left when you go out my front door, but you'll have to weave your way through the paths. You'll also have to watch out for the junkies—they're unpredictable."

Rose nodded. "I promise I'll be careful—now, whom shall I send to help you?"

Overwhelmed by his good fortune, he muttered: "I 'spose you could get a message to DeLisha, the lead Dancer down at the DragLine—ask to send help to Jo Rand in LowTown, on Midnight street… tell 'em to look for the green door." He pressed a few of the painted pop-top rings back into her hands. "Let DeLisha know these are to hire a guard so they'll be safe."

Shoving the tokens into her cape pocket, Rose's hand touched the gun. She shuddered; guilt-ridden, she felt sad for her deceased attacker, but also felt glad to have Von Helm's Derringer. A wave of gratitude washed over her; surely the Watcher would allow her to pay the Little Sheriff back, in light of this event…

Rose took a dirty towel from a heap of rags and laid it over the dead man's face, trying to hide his abandoned eyes, and not step in blood. "But what should we do about poor Marvin?"

The sick man rasped: "Tell DeLisha that Jo sent you, and ask for a cleanup on Aisle Seven. DeLisha will know what that means and get someone to handle it." He groaned beneath weight of his illness, and Rose felt pity for the ill Survivor.

"DeLisha, Aisle Seven—Okee Dokee." She looked concerned. "I need to write this down… there's so much to remember…"

"I ain't got no paper…" Mr. Rand looked at the back of The Blood chit. "This is blank on the back, though. If we can find something to write with, you could use it. Bring me that box on the high shelf…"

Climbing atop a rickety chair, Rose retrieved a broken-down cardboard box from a wooden shelf over a dry sink. She brought it to the old Survivor, who scrabbled through dried tubes of lipstick and crumbling compacts of blush. "Ah ha!" he triumphed, pulling an old black eyebrow pencil from the box. "Use this... just be careful not to smudge it."

Writing carefully, Rose scribed out a plea for aid. "Do you have something in which I can hide these tokens and the note?"

He pulled out a scuffed tortoiseshell compact, and swept the last crumbles of beige powder away from the compartment. "Try this."

"Oh, how delightful! A little folding mirror! The note and tokes just fit..." Rose tucked it into the pocket of her cape with the brass derringer. Rose tried to hoist the duffel bag, but found it too bulky, so she pulled out her own bookbag, securing it beneath her cape.

She held out her hand to the sick Survivor. "I must go, Mr. Rand, but I promise I shall send someone for you. Thank you so much for talking to me, and once again, I'm so sorry I must leave you this way."

"You can't just go out there alone..." The lantern beside the bed burned low, its small light casting a warm glow across the Survivor's lonely face.

"I would stay if I could," Rose said gently. "But people are waiting for me, and I shan't let them down. I shall ask God for help, just as I did when I roamed the WildLands—and I shall ask God to help you too."

The sick man looked thoughtful. "He just did."

Lifting his hand, the Survivor bade Rose farewell; she briefly touched his gnarled fingers, then pulled up her hood and slipped through the door into the darkness. Lying back on his freshly fluffed pillow, the dying Hombre pulled up his blanket, and pulled out the Afterling's tin. Nibbling on a honey-roasted peanut, he pondered the nature of miracles, and waited for his help to come.

As Rose closed the door behind her, she was momentarily overcome by darkness; stepping quickly into a scraggly bush, she closed her eyes ten seconds to allow them to adjust, then opened them once more:

now she could see the faint outline of structures and trees in the moonless night, their looming shadows in dim contrast against sky. But she was not afraid—for all around her, the Light was shining in the darkness. The infrared signature of all living creation shone, a constellation of Life; scurrying rats and mice glowed amidst the trash, and above her in the branches of the elms, nesting birds glimmered, little candles of living light. She walked softly among them, afraid of hurting any innocent creature, and sad for hurting any other creature, innocent or otherwise.

In her mind, she could still hear her attacker's sobs, and they made her heart hurt. She tried to refocus her thoughts on the sick Hombre—he needed help. If she helped him, she could feel better about herself...

No humanoid shapes could be seen glowing in the shadowy lanes; all was quiet in LowTown. Trying to find Sam could be tricky—she could be anywhere—but the WildLand Express should be in the Campground, with the Wagons. *Perhaps Sam is there...* The sick Hombre said the Campground was to the left? *Or was it right? Where was the Campground?*

Rose opened her HeadsUp display to see if she could find the compass. She didn't see the icon in its usual place; Sam had left the Holo-projector's directory open, along with the file containing Rose's Holographic image. Remembering Sam's exhortation to leave the settings alone, Rose closed the display, and used her own senses to guide her. *A good Scout uses what she has...*

Rose closed her eyes once more and laid her hands on the bare soil beneath her. She felt the magnetic current flowing through her—*North is ahead.* That would mean HighTown and the Gate was off to her right—and if she remembered correctly, that meant the Commons Campground should be dead ahead. *Time for reconnaissance!*

She scanned the horizon and saw a massive oak tree up a hill, next to a broken-down tin shed. Slinking between the rusted corpses of cars, she crept up the hill.

Stepping carefully around the cast-off tires which lined the yard, she found a low branch hanging above a rusting lawn chair. Climbing onto the chair, Rose grabbed the low branch, kicking her feet up to hang sloth-style beneath it. Fur cape closed, her arms and legs were still dangerously exposed, so she quickly scooted up the branch to a place where another branch forked, and used that to haul herself upright onto the broad branch. *Easy Peasy.*

From there it was all delightful as walking; the Deva had spent many long hours training their Asura Scouts to climb naturally, preparing them for the Exodus to Eden, helping them learn the skills necessary to survive. Rose remembered the hours of pleasant duty with her Trainer, Deva Ralph... back when the Deva still had hope for a life with the Asura, when the Asura were still important to the Deva.

Her heart hurt again. She wondered if the Exodus to Eden could ever happen now… the Asura had waited so long, fought so hard, all so they and the Deva could start the Earth anew. But without the Flower to heal their partial infertility, the Exodus to Eden would be forever on hold. She self-comforted, cheering herself on to good deeds yet undone: *I simply shall go back and find it.* She climbed further, putting her training to good use, in hopes that someday it could still become real, if she could just live long enough. *Up we go…*

Past a nest of sleeping baby squirrels with their little lights tumbled in a tangle of twigs, she climbed higher up the ponderous trunk. From a branch ahead, a pair of luminous eyes turned to glare at her, bristling with feathers; a barred owl eyed her suspiciously from his perch, and she gave him wide berth. *Those talons could cause serious harm…* She worried about the baby squirrels so close by, in the nest behind her. *Death is a part of life,* she acknowledged with a sigh, *but the Owl may have hungry babies, too… why must everything be so complicated?*

Up she climbed, branch to branch, hidden by the kind brown leaves of the White Oak Tree. Hugging the trunk as she climbed, the Tree hugged her back, spreading its branches in a sheltering embrace. As Rose climbed, little by little she began to see the glow of campfires, lanterns, and people ahead, gleaming in the night, a treasure trove of life and activity—and danger. Above the crowds at last, Rose could see where she had come from, and could discern where she was going.

Gathered around a campfire, a small cluster of people were gathered at the log-framed entrance to the Campground. She didn't really recognize any of them at this distance—they could be BrigadesMen, or they might be Agents; with no distinguishing regalia, it was hard to tell who was friend or foe. They were looking towards a clearing filled with Survivors of all shapes and sizes, brutal and beautiful at the same time. In a square pen, two men were facing off, circling each other.

Oh! The fights! Surely Saul will be there… Rose scanned the mass of mutated humanity, looking for him. The Watcher wasn't in the Ring—from this distance, she could see only their general glowing shapes, overheated with exertion and adrenaline. Neither man was shaped like the Watcher, with his broad shoulders and muscular torso; instead, two tall, lanky Survivors were duking it out.

She watched as one Survivor hit the other, who staggered and fell; the crowd shouted. Now the taller fighter leapt upon the fallen one, slamming his full body's weight down upon prone Survivor, pinning him. Awed, the audience hooted, and a man with a megaphone shouted: "One... Two... Three—the Burleson Brawler has Tapped out! The Stockyard Slayer wins!" Vanquished, the loser was dragged away.

Rose marveled at this exaggerated display of dominance; she had to remind herself of what her Father and his cohorts had planned these fights at the Poker game—this was all staged. *But it seems so real!* Rose was intrigued and revulsed at the same time; unlike her martial arts training, this bout seemed savage and gratuitously violent. That reminded her of the Watcher, and she wondered where he might be...

Anxious, Rose looked for the Watcher, or for Sam; but in this huge crowd, this far away, she could not find them. An alternative means of making contact would be needed. She edged out to the end of the branch, and looked through another clearing.

Ahead, she could see the wagons of the WildLand Express. She recognized the light-colored Oro right away, and smiled to see him, longing to stroke his mane again. There was William too; the shining Bay already hitched to the wagon, as was every other horse in the Campground, ready to roll at a moment's notice.

She worried—what if she got left behind? Rose started to plan how to get down to the Campground. If she could make it to the Wagon, she could hide in it and wait for a familiar Agent. Surely she could sneak between the Horses, and they could obscure her movement, plus any heat signature that might flicker from beneath her cape...

From around the corner, a slight figure came swaggering down the main road of the Campground. Rose's eyes grew wide as the figure strode down the lane, trailed by three floating balls of light, bobbing behind the Survivor some thirty to forty feet above the Campground.

None of the Survivors noticed the dim sparks as they lurked, noiseless in the night sky. The optics-cloaked spheres were not visible in what little light shone from the stars in the clear sky; the floating objects could only be seen by Rose thanks to their muted infrared glow. Looking at them closer, she could tell they were heat shielded; but the ghostly objects were still discernible to Rose, albeit less so than the lights of other heated objects. She watched as the ALGOS shadowed the slight figure, who sauntered up to the wagon to take a seat next to a tall Hombre with an eyepatch.

Michaels and Goins... Fear overtook her, for the Agents and for herself. Why was her Wagon team being followed? Did Goins know about the ALGOS? It would be impossible to go to the Campground now, with the ALGOS so near, and not cause harm to the Agents or their horses.

What about the horses? Rose shuddered to think of a bullet piercing Oro's satiny coat. She wondered... if the ALGOS spotted Rose and fired on her here, would they shoot at her? The Watcher said they had heat rounds... she wondered what those would do. *What if the heat rounds ignited the tree?* Clutching a heavy branch, she looked down into the hollow of the squirrel's nest, where the sleeping babies lay; from down the branch, the barred owl blinked. They too could be hurt if the drones detected her here.

But the animals are certainly no more important than Mr. Rand. Rose thought on the innocent sick man, and how helpless he was. What would a war do to him, or others like him at Purgatory? Not all Survivors were wicked, but even if many were, Rose wondered—did that give her the right to play God and bring death to them? The Watcher's Bible spoke it—judgement was up to God alone. *The Citizens of Purgatory are God's creatures too, as much as Agents, horses, or even baby squirrels.*

Rose felt a protective fear for these poor, half-blind Survivors who could not see infrared light, or the dangerous drones from which that elusive light emanated. She wanted to warn them somehow, but Rose remembered the Watcher's exhortation—Rose was the subject of the ALGOS deadly hunt; for her to approach the Agents could mean death for them all. Sam's harsh words still rang in her ears: the Agents of Camp Forlorn had died, all because the ALGOS were hunting Rose.

Guilt consumed her, a relentless, gnawing angst that hurt more than all the evils she had ever received. It was a terrible thing to be a victim of any atrocity—but it felt infinitely worse for the Afterling to know she had caused suffering to someone else. She already felt an unfounded guilt for the death of her daughter, Angelina, and for the abuse of her sister Amelia at the hands of Jarrod; now she felt the weight of the all who might die in this Revolution. The men of Camp Forlorn had been willing to fight for her freedom, and because of Rose, they were dead. But the Agents of Camp Forlorn would not be the only ones to suffer should this conflict escalate...

Even in their evil and debauchery, it seemed unspeakably inhumane to subject these Devil Men to the horrors of a looming war. Survivors had already suffered so much in the name of the Asura—why put these people through yet more suffering, just so the Asura could be free? She heard herself say it:

These people.

Survivors were at last becoming Human to Rose. She remembered the Watcher's guard, Henderson, and the treasured tress of red hair she found in the guard's pocket. He had been a man once, in love with a woman... and when Henderson died, he was still a man, in love with a woman. His ill temper and mutations did not change the fact that when Rose shot him, Henderson was still human.

Rose felt the crushing weight of guilt descend upon her—when she thought Henderson as 'only a Devil', she had no problem with shooting him; in fact, she had felt more sympathy for Barnaby than she ever felt for these poor Devils. Remorse assailed her... How could she ever atone for her own sins?

Distraught, Rose wondered: if she just surrendered now, would all the killing stop? If it all was a lost cause, and the odds were so great against the LoneStar Revolution, then why put these poor Devils in harms way? True, the Asura would suffer; but why force the rest of humanity to suffer with them?

Bidden by guilt, Duty now demanded Rose's attention: what of her Father's passion to start the Revolution? She had a Duty to support him. What of her commitment before the Council? She had a Duty to lead them. And what of the Watcher's Oath to fight for the Asura? She had a Duty to honor him... But if she honored her own Duty, all these people could die.

Duty or Death? Rose agonized; t*here has to be a way to do my Duty and still protect others from Death...*

Rose scooted back further into the branches, pulling her hood down as far as possible, then tucked her arms and feet under the long, thermal-lined cape to hide her own heat signature from the drones. Watchful, she positioned herself to see most of the Arena crowd and a small glimpse of the Campground. She wished she could see the Arena, but this angle afforded a better view of the road—and a chance to spot Sam in the crowd. Nestling into the sheltering arms of the tree, Rose waited for a way forward. Below her, walking towards the edge of the crowd, she saw a Macho in a mid-tone cowboy hat look towards the tree, searching the dark Purgatory skyline—hawk nosed and sharp-eyed, he seemed familiar. She

gave a little shiver of recognition:
The Gambler?

———◆———

The Gambler pressed his fingers to his temples and stared into the darkness; his interminable headache had just gotten much, much worse. Not a teetotaler by any stretch of the imagination, he took a slow sip of Reunion brew from his own personally recycled bottle, and hoped it would ease the throb in his head. This was a classic stress headache, and the Afterling's handlers had just delivered a massive payload of stress.

Ellison at least attempted to sound calm; that was a plus. Her response to the crisis was fair—after two minutes of fruitless, stealthy searching, she had contacted the Gambler via a Ring-2-Ring message: *Cargo is misplaced; locals picked up the package outside the route while we were negotiating passage.*

Calm didn't fix the issue, however; this was a massive security failure. Incensed, the Gambler bit his tongue, longing to excoriate the Agents for their lack of foresight in this new crisis. But this wasn't the time or place. No matter… he would fix other people's wretched mistakes, as always.

So the Asura is missing. The obvious answer was, She was stolen. *That's what happens when you leave your luggage unattended.*

He surmised that Ellison and Mansour set down the bag during an encounter with someone hostile, presumably guards. *Outside the route…* Outside the Hotel, or outside the fence access panel? *Probably outside the fence.* Boss Chartreaux kept Pair'O'Dice clean and safe, but at the expense of the other areas of town; there had been a rash of thefts lately on Market Mayhem Weekends, usually around LowTown.

He scowled. His hopes to leave this dusty backwater with a minim of chaos had been thwarted. So where was the Afterling? He doubted the Afterling was dead. *Damaged maybe, but not dead.* She was too valuable a commodity, and too tempting a gratification. But Rose had been missing for one half hour now—time enough to harm her; the Gambler would have felt more concern for her well-being had he not been so busy trying to locate her to save her.

Emotions are inconvenient.

He allowed the glories of this Earth to give him all the emotion he needed; the comforting darkness of the autumn night, far from the presence of people, filled him with peace. From the LowTown Oak, he heard the plaintive, relentless double hoot of a Great Horned Owl, and the wind rustled an accompaniment in the dried leaves. Unfortunately Purgatory and its persistently debaucherous humanity allowed no time for the peaceful reflection of nature without Man. The noise of the fights hammered his ears, competing with the owl, and he turned his eyes towards the hubris of the fights.

Impatient, the Gambler watched from afar as the Watcher waltzed around the ring with another hapless Hombre—in this case, Throckmorton. Not content to merely win, the Watcher was swinging Throckmorton as a square dancer would swing their partner, and the audience was roaring their approval. The Watcher's face was still hidden, enigmatic behind the flame-print mask—but the shadow of a vicious smile was visible through the thin material.

Stay busy, you brute. It was fortunate the Watcher's keen intellect and remarkable observational skills were absorbed with putting on a show, or the Marshal would probably pick apart this whole operation in seconds. The Gambler grimaced; if that happened, the entire LoneStar Revolution would go straight to hell, because the Watcher would be busy beating the bushes for the Afterling instead of fighting and winning money.

The Gambler wanted to find the Afterling quickly, before the Watcher got suspicious; this was a critical point in the success of the Revolution. Purgatory's worthless tokens could be turned into real goods if bets raked them in, but only if the Watcher was in the Arena drumming up bets—and that meant the Gambler had to find the Afterling before the Watcher figured out she was missing.

He listened for any sound like that of the drones; hearing none, he turned his attention to the more visible threats.

Irritable at the interruption of his schedule, the Gambler opened node 145 to monitor for messages, then opened his advanced settings in own Ring. Nine bells sounded, and once more a message-bearing burst of static assaulted his aural paths. Grimacing, the Gambler turned down his master volume, then slowed the static to 1/10th times speed. The encryption was decoded and a synthetic voice responded through a text-to-voice reader with a message from Team Whiskey, aka Winston and Wilcox.

The Catastronix workaround was underway. It sounded most intriguing:

#WHISKEY: Egret has flown with her flock—a flight of birds

will lead followers to their nest.

The Gambler rubbed his cleft chin as he processed this new data. *So Lourdes has left Bogie's Bunker with the Hostesses....* He scowled. The logistics of this gambit eluded him; this was a risky move, one he had not expected Winston to allow, especially considering the tall Boss' strange love-hate obsession with guarding Araceli at all costs. *Well that was certainly highly progressive...*

While listening to this latest update, the Gambler tried getting the Afterling's Ring to talk to him, but it was a no-go. Rose's Ring would only communicate with a properly identified server; likewise, her embryonic nanobots were similarly programmed, designed to talk to one thing alone —their bot-kin, extracted and embedded in her childhood Ring. These were almost impossible to spoof, thanks to the nanobots setting their own dynamic, randomly mutating dna-based cryptographic keys. How these nanobots communicated with each other across a distance was a still a mystery to him—one he hoped someday to solve.

The Gambler grunted; *impudent little bots...* he was well aware of their vagaries. When he set up Rose's Ring, The Gambler had reconfigured her WeSpeex U firewall to allow her own nanobots to peek out and ping their kin embedded in her childhood Ring—which now was in the Watcher's possession. Theoretically that would allow some communication between linked rings, perhaps even Ring-2-Ring, if both Rings were in legacy mode. If so, he could open it up remotely.

At that time, The Gambler had toyed with the idea of trying to crack the Afterling's new WeSpeex U to be able to communicate Ring-2-Ring with his own RingWorld, but decided against it. There wasn't enough time at the time—and even if it could be done, it was simply too insecure, opening her to possible discovery through the scanners.

As it stood, without a dedicated WeSpeex U server or crypto-key, no modern tech would ever be able to find Rose's WeSpeex U. Like an ancient floppy-disk of old, the Afterling's Ring was a cybernetic ghost, alive only in its separate technological dimension, only to be summoned via her own nanobots' digital DNA. If anyone wanted to communicate with Rose's Ring, the only method would be through direct link via the ChipMate Protocol.

He pondered risks and ramifications of this technological lockout: they would have to locate her via an alternate—and potentially dangerous —route.

He hailed Mansour Ring-2-Ring.

#ANON: Plan—meet me near the back gate by the Salt Mines.
#MANSOUR: Roger

Making his way towards the Industrial District, the Gambler kept his eyes open for any signs of guards. Fortunately, Market Mayhem Weekend combined with civil unrest and fires had provided an excellent draw-down of Purgatory resources, and all available personnel were at the Arena.

Skirting a line of trees leading back behind the Jail, the Gambler strolled past the row of converted Porta-Johnnies, which he personally considered to be Winston's greatest civic work. Winston created an easy-to-clean outhouse complex far downhill from the town well, and employed Sander's team to maintain it. Their collaboration was the reason Purgatory wasn't a cholera-plagued death camp. Had the Gambler not so conveniently intervened, Winston would have started improving the Dump next, and discovered Bogie's Bunker.

Early discovery would have been an unmitigated disaster, the Gambler mused. At that time, the Bunker was a cradle for an idea whose time had not yet come…

Now the time had come. The Gambler grumbled; he was going to miss the hot showers and simple pleasures of 'Bogie's' primitive little hidey-hole. He was also going to miss smelling like a derelict; it kept people away.

Madness has its moments.

But most of all, the Gambler would miss the quiet moments alone, spent in deep conversation with Her… he imagined She would have much to say about this turn of events when he caught up in their next meeting. *Ah well, Revolución cannot come without discomfort.*

Moving past the small clusters of Survivors surrounding the outhouses, the Gambler traced a winding alley that ran between the shambling shacks of LowTown and the open-air work pavilions and ramshackle tool sheds of Industrial Boulevard. Crooked mesquite fenceposts lined the alley side of the Industrial district, their barbed wire long missing; it was primarily there to please the late Boss Waitie, who wanted a visual barrier to be made between his laborers' humble homes, and their workplaces.

The Bosses physically separated work and leisure to provide boundaries between purpose-seeking hours and pleasure-seeking hours; mood-enhancements were to be restricted at work and enjoyed thereafter.

It was all part of the System for Citizens, as sobriety throughout the workday ensured quality control on the job site and built anticipation for psychotropic compliance after hours.

Surveying the Bosses' works, the Gambler considered the consequences of their deaths. The System's Social control of Purgatory—and the entire Co-op with it—had been a team effort, made possible by decades of dedicated Consortium intervention.

Boss Waitie had kept Denizens of Purgatory busy during the day; Boss Balogun had kept them peaceful at night. Boss Zhu had rewarded them with hopes of social advancement, and Boss Winston had motivated them with dreams of civic accomplishment.

And Boss Chartreaux? He had entertained them.

Chartreaux gave Purgatory bread and circuses to keep the Damned distracted from what the System was actually doing. It would be entertaining to see how Chartreaux planned on ruling Purgatory by himself; the Gambler would have enjoyed that show had he not already known how it would play out. Surely the Consortium would have something to say about this latest debacle...

The Consortium. The Gambler's eyes narrowed at the thought of that elitist enclave of Fallen Visionaries. Soon enough, those stuck-up bastards would regret their refusal of his own thoughtful proposal.

Unfortunately for Purgatory, the Consortium's refusal of the Gambler's suggestion guaranteed an unhappy ending for those Survivors who opposed dictatorships—Chartreaux was known to be totalitarian in his dealings, even before the other Bosses' demise. Chartreaux's socialist philosophies did not mitigate his fascist methods; he openly promised free goods to Purgatory Citizens, in exchange for their subjugated lives. *And that is what Purgatory Folk are choosing—they have traded freedom for freebies.*

Of course, Purgatory Folk had not always been this dependent upon handouts from their Masters—the battle for the soul of Purgatory had been a long one. Rumblings of unrest had occurred in the early days; back when Purgatory Folk were still feisty and fresh from their fight for survival, they had openly challenged the Bosses...

In this hardscrabble outpost of rough Survivors, the infiltration and rise to power of old Diego was mostly organic; his natural talents as a fist-fighting, tough-talking Construction Worker were recognized and rewarded by Purgatory Men. Their election of Diego as the Boss of their work crews allowed Diego to open the door for his fellow Visionaries to take power at Purgatory. But some meddling individualists demanded to know why there were suddenly so many Bosses, and under whose authority they had taken power. So the System did what the System had always done: they called an election, and Purgatory's Head Rabble-Rouser became Hizzoner Norris, elected to be the Bosses' Boss, beholden to the voters.

The Gambler frowned inadvertently. Hizzoner was never more than a figurehead, but by the time Hizzoner figured that out, he was too addicted to liquor and hostesses to fight back. Beholden to his suppliers, the Bosses, Norris was still kept in power by them through sham elections. With the votes counted by the Bosses themselves, the voters never found out that Hizzoner had lost the vote long ago.

The System was magnanimous in that regard; it allowed the governed a chance to believe they had some power, as long as the governed never questioned the System. Jaded, the Gambler grunted. *Few ever questioned the System.*

Picking his way through the cast off bottles and vials, the Gambler headed down to the tail end of the alley, then backed into a clump of honeysuckle bushes to await Mansour and Ellison as they made their way from the Pair'O'Dice-LowTown border. While waiting, The Gambler took time to admire the bright, clear stars, far from the bustling Commons, away from the noise and crowds, Yes, Texas stars at night were big and bright, but they could never rival the glorious, glittering sky of a pristine Patagonia, or the twinkling vastness of the silvery, moon-lit steppes of Siberia…

or the glory of the stars in her deep, dark, eyes.

He opened up a window and the avatar of a tall, tanned woman sprang out of the palm of his hand, smooth blue-black hair shining, dressed in a silk scarf and doctor's coat. He swiped right, and she transformed into an equally stunning Chica, sleek sienna scales rippling over a lean body, clad in traditional Rarɫmuri dress: full skirt and embroidered cotton shirt, bright scarf now tied about her head. She blinked at him, awakening, then the dark eyes flashed.

#MICHÁ: You've done it again, haven't you?

Weary, he nodded.

#ANON: Of course.

#MICHÁ: And naturally, you are at the center of the maelstrom. I assume Lourdes has been dragged into it, as usual…

#ANON: You know me well, Owirúame.

The woman gave a knowing smile.

#MICHÁ: You are deep in the race and need la Poder de Mujer to refresh your spirit—

She held out her hand, and the barrier between virtuality and reality shimmered, rippling back and forth between them. Gently chiding him, the woman wagged a translucent finger:

#MICHÁ: Perhaps you should rein in your imperialistic need to meddle in everything.

#ANON: I haven't time for lectures—I just need to look in your eyes.

#MICHÁ: Wait a minute, I'm not done—

Satisfied, he pinched the image shut, and sighed deeply, entranced by the stars in her eyes.

His reverie was interrupted by the sound of breathing behind him. Glancing over his shoulder, the Gambler lit a Fo'Bacco cigarette: "Why are you here?"

"I'm looking for you." He heard the voice of Habib, smooth and low. "Now, your turn to answer questions. Why are YOU here?"

The Gambler tapped his ring finger. "Switch to a more secure method of communication if you want to continue this conversation."

Habib opened his HeadsUp display, and was greeted by a greyed-out image of an all-seeing eye.

#ANON: I'm here because I want to be. You're here because they sent you— not that I blame them. You have a unique set of skills, academe inhabited by thuggery...

The Gambler took a deep drag, making the cigarette tip glow. In its light, he could see the dim form of a Macho dressed in denim work clothes, face hidden beneath the broad brimmed hat.

#ANON: It makes you a valuable asset. The Family has integrated you well into the System; but all your civilized finery could never quite erase the ghosts of your prison tattoos. I'm sure you could shiv me if you like, however, it would be a regression for you. You might wish to rethink your motivations.

Habib almost blinked beneath his emotionless mask.

#HABIB: So you're part of the Family too; big deal. Where's the Egret?

The HighRoller puffed out a cloud of fragrant smoke into the chill air.

#ANON: Wherever the Egret wants to be. If you don't know, it's because the Egret decided you're not supposed to know.

Doubtful, the Accountant gave a suspicious glance at the Gambler.

#HABIB: You're saying you're not in charge of the Egret?

#ANON: I never was—I was only a means for her to get to you. Congratulations—the Egret is your problem now.

Blindsided by Lourdes as usual, Habib mulled over his Handler, and hers.

#HABIB: If that's true, then she's gone rogue... I put her in lockdown for her own protection, but she busted out, and took the others with her.

A snort erupted from the HighRoller:

#ANON: That was your first mistake, thinking you could contain her.

Habib brooded.

#HABIB: What's the deal between you two?

#ANON: Nothing to warrant your jealousy. Of course, jealousy is the reason you were in prison in the first place, and if not for the Firm's interest in you, you would have remained there. You may wish to review your training if you don't wish to repeat your earlier mistakes... now tell me what you know about this escapade and I'll decide if I'll help you find her—or not.

Settling back into the shadows, Habib crossed his arms, disgruntled by the Gambler's unnerving knowledge.

#HABIB: An hour ago, the Eagle sent word: While he and the Brothers were in the workroom reading the Manual for the Booster, Egret gathered the other birds and captured Brother Crow unawares. They tied him up, and left behind that blind Wren and her ugly mutt to hold him at gunpoint; then they escaped via the outside tunnel, back out to the cave. They stole one of the horses. She also stole an antique television remote. What's up with that?

Habib scratched his head.

#ANON: She likes power and control.

#HABIB: Yeah, I can see that. But what's it for?

#ANON: A demolition of sensitive materials is planned. Brother Eagle was the intended recipient of the detonator—but based on my own experience with the Egret, I can assume she took it hostage as a bargaining tool. Knowing her, she anticipated pushback if she went rogue, so the Egret absconded with the remote. If I interfere with her mission, she will interfere with mine. But if I let her work alone, she will accomplish the demolition, and her own mission as well.

The Gambler studied the end of his Fo'Bacco cigarette.

#ANON: So tell me about her mission.

Frowning, the Moneyman rubbed his brow.

#HABIB: Egret left a message for Brother Eagle—he's to activate the Booster when they hear the usual signal from the Purgatory Commons Bell. Other than that, no particulars were given, and Eagle doesn't know where they're roosting now. I need to know where the Egret went—they shouldn't be out there alone.

Seeping a wisp of smoke, The Gambler grunted, almost concerned.

#ANON: Knowing the Egret, a plan is in place, and they are already moving into position. You will be hard pressed to find her if she doesn't want you to find her. All you can do now is help her accomplish her mission—and I am willing to make book her mission is to find her back way to you.

Habib kept his face hidden, but his shoulders revealed tension. He had lost Sam because he was unable to keep her by his side, and now he might lose Lourdes because he couldn't keep her away…

The Gambler shook his head.

#ANON: But all her motivation and meticulous planning isn't a failsafe; they are deep in dangerous territory, and the Egret is injured. You can help her by preparing the playing field for her now —get all the parts into place, and help me find an item we have misplaced… Brother Wolf's Package is missing.

Habib looked up, shocked, as the Gambler continued:

#ANON: Command has not yet been notified; but since you have so conveniently made yourself available, I will send you to the Brothers at the Campground to gather all available manpower to search for the Package. Afterwards, contact Brother Fox to inform him of our efforts. Make it clear to all participants that Brother Wolf must not be informed of this until all other options for recovery are exhausted. I will be the one to inform him—but once we pull that trigger, there will be no turning back. Brother Wolf will become unmanageable.

Footsteps approached from the LowTown side of the Alley.

Habib lurked in the bushes while the Gambler looked busy and awaited a sign. They were rewarded by two taps of a stick upon an old can, and the Gambler tapped twice in return. Down the Alley, two drunken Survivors swayed towards him, leaning heavily upon each other in a camaraderie of alcohol. Mansour tapped the brim of his bucket hat.

The Gambler approached. "Clever—your revelry hides Cougar's gait."

Wary, Mansour looked up and down the alley. "I thought it was clever, too—so what do you have for us? No sign of the Package anywhere."

Habib stepped out of the shadows, and Mansour and Sam both jumped. The Gambler linked in Ring-2-Ring.

#ANON: Led by the Egret, your birds of a feather flocked together and left the Wren behind with her 'dog' to guard Brother Crow. They're flying through the night-time WildLands. Do you have any idea where they might be?

"No but I wish I did—if I weren't trying to find our little friend, I would join them." Proud and fearful at the same time, Sam couldn't help herself. "They are the epitome of the Brotherhood—they could never stand idly by knowing their Brothers are in trouble.

She hid her face in her hands, taken by regret that she might never see them again. Mansour put his arm around Sam, as Habib gazed off into the darkness.

The Gambler edged closer to Mansour.

#ANON: Be on the lookout for them, and notify us if you see any sign; meanwhile, we must deal with this other unfortunate situation. I'll pass you a Fo'Bacco cigarette; you'll allow me access to your device and all privileges for few seconds as you take the ruse.

Intrigued, Mansour took the cigarette, and the Gambler linked with him.

#ANON: I am setting your WeLites to a particular frequency in the ultraviolet range, to help us find the Package.

Swiftly resetting the Soldier's ring light to shine with an invisible wavelength—395nm, just outside the spectrum of visible light, the Gambler took less than fifteen seconds, then moved on to Sam. Intense and anxious beneath the faux drunken demeanor, Sam was consumed by a burning desire to fix this situation, now. She stuck out her hand, and the Gambler connected:

#ANON: As I've told Mansour: this light is set to an ultraviolet

frequency in a weak, broad beam to scan large areas. The Package has a little-known design modification that will make her fluoresce faint green when scanned with this light. If the Package is out in the open, you should be able to detect her—but so will anything else that is scanning for that fluorescence. However, if we sight her fluorescence quickly, we can detect the Package before anything else does.

Surprised at the idea of a glowing green Afterling, Sam shot off a question to the HighRoller.

#ELLISON: If this is such a great idea, why aren't Uncle Jim's Searchers using this same strategy?

#ANON: They have been, but only during daylight hours. Their devices are programmed for frequency 488nm, as per the manual; that is the stated frequency for the Package's maximum fluorescence. But 488nm is barely visible blue light. In the daytime, that color of light isn't noticeable, but at night bystanders could easily see the blue light in the dark. To avoid detection at night, the Searchers will employ infrared scanning for now. Fortunately, the Package is thermally cloaked. Meanwhile, we will use the less-than-optimal but invisible 395nm wavelength, which will produce only a weak fluorescence, but allows us to work unseen.

#ELLISON: But what if the Package isn't out in open where she could be scanned?

#ANON: Then we are proverbially screwed.

Sam gave a terse nod—a perfectionist, there were very few times Sam had ever failed. It terrified her to think this mission could end in disaster because of a failure on her part.

The Gambler continued:

#ANON: The Package should be near where you left it. A gaggle of your Uncle Jim's Searchers are hanging around the Brothers, lured there by a decoy—if the Package had been found by them, those Friends would have already been recalled. Likewise, Cousin Cat and the Bee are still watching the entertainment. Had the Package been found by their minions, Cat and Bee would be elsewhere, taking charge of the situation.

Sam conferred with Mansour, then relayed that information to the Gambler.

#ELLISON: We'll scan the section nearest where we left off—if you'll scan this section nearest the Salt Mines, and we'll work our way in from there.

Sam leaned on Mansour to stumble down the Alley to LowTown once more.

The Gambler passed the Fo'Bacco cigarette to the MoneyMan. "You next." As the HighRoller adjusted Habib's Ring light frequency, Habib watched his past sway away with her lover, then turned this thoughts to his own future—if there was one.

#HABIB: You help me, and I'll help you. Capisce?

A sardonic sigh answered Habib.

#ANON: Even if you find her, you won't sway the Egret from her mission—but perhaps you can help her complete it. Now, go rally support from the Brothers and reset their WeLites as I showed you. After you brief the Fox, meet me here again in half an hour for update; if we don't find her by then, I will have a new plan. With a little luck, we can quickly find this missing needle in Purgatory's Haystack; in return, I will keep lookout for your wayward Egret.

Giving a quick bob of his head in acknowledgment, Habib pulled his hat low and disappeared between the overgrown hedgerows of LowTown. The Gambler rubbed his temples again, then turned to the monumental task of scanning LowTown for the Afterling.

———◆———

Blissful, Shaney breathed a sigh of satisfaction as she sank her teeth into the sausage. A quivering Public Servant had born it through the crowds as if it were a jewel, proclaiming that Lord Li himself had sent it to her as gift. And a jewel it was—crispy browned pork and spices, perfectly balanced, expertly seared and enveloped in a toasted white tortilla slathered with epazote-seasoned butter. The Public Servant pointed through the crowd to the busy Lord Li, who beamed at Shaney as she graciously accepted his gift, the first fruits of the Bar-Be-Que to come.

Boss Chartreaux scowled at the cheeky entrepreneurial interloper, but said nothing. Li was a fixture at Purgatory, present at almost every Purgatory Market Mayhem weekend, running Li's Famous Sausage Stand. His entertaining sales patter, constant smile and supply of smoked meats made him a well-known and well-loved figure among Purgatory Elite.

Waving to Lord Li, Shaney sampled his wares, then announced to everyone that is was by far the most delicious sausage she had ever eaten. The crowd clapped politely.

Proudly displaying another sausage wrap, Lord Li waved to the crowd from his Propane Tank-turned-Bar-Be-Que Grill. "You heard the Lady— my Sausage is the Best!" His audience chortled. "As part of the 'Porktober' Sale-a-Bration for Li's Sausage, there'll be more where that came from in thirty minutes. But first dibs will be for our friends in the Brigades, to make up for our misunderstanding from earlier this evening —no hard feelings, fellas. You won't wanna miss this delight!" He took a big bite of his own wares, then gave a thumbs up sign.

Behind Lord Li, a man in an embroidered suit and green scarf passed something to the Sausage Man, then pulled down his white hat and disappeared into the crowd.

"Mmm, who's that man with the fancy duds?" Shaney murmured, intrigued. "He looks mysterious, like he might be trouble. I just don't know whether he's the good kind of trouble, or the bad kind…"

"He's unknown to me." Through the flickering lantern light of the Commons, Chartreaux strained to see. Curious as well, he leaned over to whisper to Bosley: "Who's that dandy?"

"I'm not sure, Boss—I saw him earlier this afternoon and he was roaming the streets like a regular tourist. I didn't get a good look at this face, bundled up under than scarf. Other than his outfit, nothing really stuck out about him."

Chartreaux's eyes narrowed. "Send someone to tail him. Something about him seems familiar… make sure the newcomer gets a proper welcome. Speaking of mysterious newcomers, what about our esteemed guest, Lord Sliwa?" The Boss eyed him from afar, watching him as he talked to his fighter down by the Arena, waiting their turn in the ring.

"He's… different. Begging your pardon, Boss, but he's just not as uppity as your usual Lord."

"Interesting. I'd like to have a word with him after the fights—I'm curious as to why he appeared after all these years. We have a sudden influx of unknown visitors, and given the circumstances, the situation demands vigilance." Chartreaux dismissed Bosley, who set off to assign a tail to the mysterious man in the fancy suit.

Licking her fingers, Shaney finished up, then looked around for the ladies' room. The first set of fights was over, and a break between elimination rounds was precisely what Shaney needed to make a graceful exit—that one Reunion brew had run right through her.

In the WildLands on assignment, this would scenario would usually have entailed a trip to a tree, and back at the Ranger Ranch, a trip to her own personal outhouse would have been in order. But she was at Purgatory, and that meant using local resources; her advance detail came back from the Porta-Johnnies shaking their heads in disgust.

Her lead Ranger was intractable. "Beggin' your pardon Commander, but you can't take your leisure there—it's not fit for man nor beast. Even the Jailhouse buckets smell better than those outhouses."

"Oh Wyatt, the privies can't possibly be that bad." Shaney looked doubtful, but her Major frowned and shook his head once more.

Upset at this public humiliation, Chartreaux's jowls quivered in suppressed rage: "And whose fault is that?" He quietly seethed from his cast iron bench beneath the Bandstand, casting a baleful gaze around at his mortified BrigadesMen.

From the betting tables, Sanders heard their pronouncement, and looked pained. He approached the Boss. "These men are innocent—this is entirely my fault, no one else's. I am normally the one in charge of the maintenance and cleaning of the outhouses for Market Mayhem Weekend, but as I am in charge of the betting and brackets, I could not attend to my regular duties."

Boss Chartreaux turned red, and raised his ball tipped cane to strike—but was stopped by a slender, gloved hand.

"Oh now Reggie, don't be mad. I know you want everything to be perfect, but we've all had a rough day, and everyone here is stretched to the breaking point." She patted Chartreaux's belly, rubbing it as if he were a cat. Flustered beneath her touch, the formidable Macho's anger was defused, and every BrigadesMan instantly fell in love with Shaney for saving them from his ire.

She turned her cerulean eyes towards the man in the Pashmina scarf. "Sanders has done a marvelous job, but he can't be two places at once. I'm sure Purgatory is usually spic-and-span. Isn't that right, Sanders?" The Public Servant shuffled his feet and blushed.

Basking in their approval, Shaney spoke to the BrigadesMen. "Purgatory is a fine place! Y'all worked so hard, and it's just not fair that those wicked traitors attacked y'all and tore it up. I'm not the kind of gal that's going to throw a hissy fit over something as trivial as a bathroom—

you men have got more important things on your minds." She whispered to Wyatt: "Bring the team with you; I'll find a bush outside the gate."

Wyatt blanched. "It's after dark in the WildLands…"

Dismissive, Shaney stood to go. "Oh come on, Wyatt, you can handle a Chupacabra or two. We'll be back in time for the next round of fights." Arising, an uncomfortable expression twisted her delicate mouth; she whispered to Wyatt. "We need to hurry. I'm not feelin' so good…"

"I told you—don't set foot in that stinking Jail! But you wouldn't listen." Her Major's face clouded with worry. "You always have to go prove how tough you are, and now you'll come down sick…"

Her eyes flashed. "Don't patronize me, Wyatt. I can handle this." She moved towards the gate, then clutched at her slender waist. Scenting opportunity, Chartreaux pounced.

"Such a dangerous scenario is not fitting for our Honored Guest. Chateau de Chartreaux is at your service, your home away from home." He swept off his hat towards his converted Pair'O'Dice Barn, with its warmly lit Silo watchtower. "You may watch the fights from the comfort and privacy of my luxury Balcony Suite."

"Ooh, Reggie, that's yours?" Still uncomfortable, Shaney sized up the edifice admiringly. "But I need my security detail, and Storm, too—I don't go anywhere without them." Wyatt grunted and tapped his badge, then beckoned the other three men on Shaney's personal squad.

"The Private Balcony Suite is exactly what it says… private." Chartreaux glowered. "However, if you insist, your detail may stay in the room at the base of the tower, and your horse may be housed in the shed around back."

Shaney's Major glowered back at Chartreaux. "Only if we control access to the tower. If the Commander calls us for help, we'll answer— and it won't be pretty."

"I admire your fervor, but your suspicion is unnecessary." Chartreaux tilted his massive head towards the Rangers in a deferential bow, closing his eyes to disguise any hint of guile.

"Don't forget—I'm empowered through firepower. I'm able take care of any situation that might arise, but it's nice to have a helping hand now and then." Slightly nauseated, Shaney weighed her options. "You say it has a real indoor bathroom?"

"It not only has a real indoor bathroom, it has a real indoor bath…" Chartreaux replaced his Panama Hat, and moved in for the kill: "Heated."

The tower was temptingly near, just inside the gates of Pair'O'Dice; the Commander mulled it over. "Captain Alderi, assume command for a shift; I haven't had a hot bath since forever ago..." she shifted slightly, trying to hide her discomfort as she untied her horse.

"As Proprietor of Chateau de Chartreaux, I request the honor of escorting you, our Inaugural Guest." Offering his heavy arm, Chartreaux waited, serene; fighting off a growing urgency, Shaney took it. He clapped his meaty hands. "Sugar—Spice! Make ready the balcony suite."

Chartreaux's attendants scurried away to prepare; the long awaited Grand Opening of Chateau de Chartreaux had finally come.

As the crowd drifted between tables and food stands, Shaney and her entourage marched down the main drag, by the PickUp Truck Planter, past the Dirt-Court BasketBall Yard, through the front gate of Pair'O'Dice. and up the gently sloping path to a willow gate set in a cedar pole fence. Between the posts, clusters of golden mums nodded their fluffy heads, a remarkable sight that drew an admiring gasp from Shaney: "So you truly are cultivated gentleman!" She started to pull one from the bush, then thought against it, not wanting to slow down.

Sensing her distress, Major Wyatt handed his Commander's horse off to his subordinate, and pointed around back. "Tie Storm off at the nearest safe point, and stand by for further orders." The Ranger nodded and led her steed while the rest of his group made their way through the neatly groomed yard to the barn's sliding doors.

Sheathed in scavenged wood and fitted with recovered windows, the converted barn was a testament to the art of design. Even in its rustic state, it spoke more of the French Quarter than a Texas Ranch. A single salvaged piece of wrought iron fence adorned the monitor atop the roof to match the railing around the porch addition, the dark woods and iron accents giving the structure a brooding quality to match its owner.

Boss Chartreaux rolled a heavy wooden door aside, revealing the reds and golds which accented the oak and leather furniture, counterpointed by occasional delicate provincial accents. Sugar and Spice stood at attention, rigid with anxiety as Shaney and her squad swept past them. "It's lovely. Now where's this bathroom? I'm sorry—I'm a little woozy." She had taken on an unaccustomed pallor.

"Right his way, Ma'am—" Spice pointed to a door beneath the loft stairs at the far end of the barn. As they entered the great room, a dainty ball of silver fluff leapt to the top of a high-backed brocade chair, purring and waving her tail. Indulgent, Chartreaux stroked the little cat with his gloved hand: "And how is Daddy's Precious Princess?"

"Oh, what an adorable little cat!' Shaney smiled, trying to remain hospitable while still heading for the bathroom. Princess Precious Sweetums spat and frizzed out her fur, infuriated at the interloper.

"How sweet..." The Commander smiled through gritted teeth and kept walking.

They entered a dark room filled with overstuffed leather chairs, and a stocked bar. Spice motioned to the bottles lining the cupboard. "Make yourselves comfortable. I'll bring extra cots in for our guests—this will be your room, Gentlemen."

The Rangers grunted with approval. Wyatt nodded: "Much obliged; these are some pretty fancy digs, Boss..."

Spice led the group through another door into a round room almost thirty feet across, the adjoining concrete silo now fitted with wood panelling; a staircase hugged the wall to the top, with support posts housing shelves below. Backed up beneath a stair landing, under a fire-heated water tank, was an enclosed, primitive water closet; beside it, a large cattle watering trough was retrofitted as a tub.

Without another word, Shaney headed into the water closet and shut the door, leaving an awkward silence behind her. Out of deference to Shaney's indisposedness, Boss Chartreaux turned to his minion: "Sugar, come with me to prepare the tower bedroom, and bring some mint tea to settle the Commander's stomach; Spice, help the Rangers situate themselves in the study."

Wyatt shook his head. "I'm in charge of the Commander's safety—I'll be checking for security."

Major Wyatt headed up the stairs behind the pair, ascending the stairs to enter the circular room, tromping around the oak plank floor, flipping worn velvet cushions perched atop the faded gold bedspread and rifling through the brocaded couch cushions. Satisfied for the moment, the Major gave a cold look to Chartreaux and his henchman: "I'll leave you to your work; but I'm just downstairs if she calls. You overstep her bounds, and I'll overstep yours." He descended, and Sugar turned to whisper to his Boss.

"I sure hope these insufferable Bastards are worth it for you."

"Patience, Sugar; it's worth it only if it all works out, so hold your tongue or I'll hold it for you. Now, leave me to my moment, and make certain to draw the bath after the fights." Irritable, Chartreaux growled, and his assistant scurried off, ready to make some distance between himself and his hulking Boss.

Chartreaux disappeared behind the loft door; as soon as Sugar exited the building, the Ranger's conversation tuned to their Commander's delicate situation:

"She's looking a little peaked. Maybe it's all the stress?"

"Naw," another Ranger chimed in, "she's never let stress get to her. I think she's just flat worn out. She's been running the entire organization ever since Chief went rogue and Cap went AWOL.." Dismissed, the other Rangers made their way to the bar, leaving their Major behind to guard their Commander.

When Shaney finally poked her head out of the bathroom, she was greeted immediately by a disgruntled Major Wyatt. "You okay?"

"I'm just tired. I could use some sleep."

"Well good luck on getting any." Suspicious, Wyatt looked over his shoulder at the entrance to Chartreaux's Balcony Suite. "I know you've got your reasons, but I don't like this one damn bit. I don't trust this guy."

Shaney slid her arms around the big Hombre's neck. "You leave him to me. You trust me, don't you, Wyatt?"

"Yeah, but you're still feelin' sick! You need to be resting, not dealing with this goon." Tragic, Wyatt embraced her, closing his dark eyes in misery. "Lillabeth, Lillabeth—why does it always have to be this way for us? How long must I put up with this? The thought of you with him makes me sick."

"Hush, now." She kissed him, and he hushed. "It's all for the mission… until it's completed, no one else can know about us."

"But I don't even know what this mission is!"

"It's 'need to know' only—and all you need to know is, you're the only man in my heart…" She kissed him again, deeply and passionately, then straightened his lapels and pushed away. "Now go, and let me get to work." Downcast, the Ranger walked away. As the door closed, Shaney heard a creak from top of the stairs behind her.

"Impressive. So you are this way with all your men?" Chartreaux eyed the door as he sipped a crystal stem glass of the Gambler's confiscated Sangria. "They are all under your spell; whether it's Major Wyatt, or Captain Evangelo, or an entire crowd, you have them utterly in your thrall."

"Oh, that's easy." Shaney leaned against the wall, still wan. "I give each man what he needs from me in order for him to feel what he calls 'Love'. I don't even bother with making them feel like I love them—I just make them love me, for whatever little old reason that fits their need."

"And none of them ever care that you don't love them in return?"

She shook her head, introspective as she climbed the stairs. "I think that's the difference between most men and women—most men want someone else to love, and most women want someone else to love *them*."

"And what do I want?"

Chuckling softly, she topped the landing. "If I told you, it'd spoil the fun."

"Bravo on your insight." Chartreaux handed her a mint tea as she entered the Balcony Suite. "You have a gift, Commander—it's a shame it has been squandered on such a small group of back country yokels. Allow me to give you a taste of what you truly desire..." He pulled back the curtain on the French doors, which opened onto a lantern-lit, wrought iron Balcony.

A cantilevered, iron affair, it didn't yet encircle the Silo—Chartreaux had that planned for the future—but at this time merely offered an eight-by-eight foot platform directly in front of the double doors leading to the bedroom. As Shaney stepped out, a man in the crowd caught a glimpse, and pointed towards the Tower:

"It's her—it's Commander Shaney!" At the mention of her name, all eyes turned towards the Balcony, and she lifted a hand to greet them. A roar swelled from the throng below her, crashing into her heart and sweeping her off her feet. Agog at their adoration, she adored them in return...

"They love you." Pulling her back inside, Chartreaux closed the doors and pulled the curtains shut. "These men are mine. I alone rule them now —but they will soon grow weary of my limited charms. You, however..." He took her over to a window, and she gazed out with longing at the crowd below.

"You enchant them. Enchant them for me, and I will offer you a chance to be loved by everyone in the WildLands and beyond. Thanks to our Afterling recovery efforts for James Generales, technology is opening doors for the Fallen once more. The Ring can bring your face to thousands of Survivors the world over who would pay riches untold to glimpse your treasures." He leaned over to whisper in her ear. "I have the love you desire. This theatre of adoration belongs to me—and I alone can offer you this audience."

"What do you want in return?" In a trance, she looked out at the sea of clamoring Survivors. Chartreaux smiled, broad mouth splitting his face from ear to ear—

"Power."

"What kind of power do you want?"

"The kind of power only you can give—and you know what that is…" His meaty hand slid down her sleek arm.

Quiet, Shaney walked to the northern window, overlooking the Campground. "If we recover the Afterling, we'll have no end of power—but I need your help. I need your manpower to get this job done." She reached out and took his hand, placing it on her own hip. Together they observed the flames of campfires dotting the grass, then Shaney squinted and grabbed the window frame—

"There! Hurry, send my Rangers to the Campground entrance—" Shaney pointed at a tall man, Silver Belly Cowboy hat shining in the firelight. She swayed, and leaned against Chartreaux's bulky torso. "I'm sorry, I—I think I'm falling ill…"

Straining to see in the darkness, Chartreaux shook her. "Enough drama! What do you see?"

She groaned, and hugged at her stomach, pained. "I see Emmanuel…"

Dumping Shaney on the brass bed, Chartreaux mumbled under his breath, and descended the stairs in haste; the chase was on.

"Kick and step ONE, and kick and spin TWO—"

As the other DragLine queens passed the time by practicing routines, DeLisha scowled, lipsticked lips turned down. Trying to hear above the cacophony, the Dancer attempted to listen to passersby, seeking any intel that indicated mass movements of people. Lord Li had asked for troop movements, and that's what DeLisha was going to provide…

The only movement seen so far was from the WildLand Express. A distinctive, tall man in an eyepatch, he was dressed in simple black leather and denim; stationed under an elm tree, he was watching some unseen subject with interest. DeLisha recognized him immediately as Lord Li's

WildLand Express Contact; he had been stationed at the Campground entrance earlier, but was now on the move around the Commons. The man turned his eyes to DeLisha, then just as quickly turned away, looking behind the Dancer down the alley to LowTown. DeLisha followed his gaze to see a small unit of Rangers break off from the main group, headed to the entrance of the Commons.

Lord Li would want to know… Bur he wasn't at his Sausage Stand. Perhaps he was with his newfound friend, Lord Sliwa?

Searching the crowd for a glimpse of ManTamer, the Dancer found him under guard, following his Fighter around the Industrial Salvage Yard with a bewildered look on his affable face. His unhinged OutLaw was attracting an audience, beating on cars and howling. The ManTamer's's voice could barely be heard above the din as his Fighter pounded the rusting hulk of a decrepit 'Bells Cargo' Van:

"Uh, yeah, this is how LoneStar Libre toughens himself up for a fight —he attacks gas guzzlers! He's the One-Man Wrecking Crew—"

Suddenly civilized, the Fighter rolled an intact window up, and inspected the car's door handle. The armored van was of early twenty-first century vintage, made from heavy steel…

Finding it satisfactory, the Wrassler flung open the car door, then gave it a savage kick to the inside, knocking it off its hinges. The Guards jumped back as the car door flew into the weeds and the Wrassler retrieved it, swinging it by its integrated handle as if it were a shield.

The Wrassler growled, apparently satisfied with this outcome. Beating his chest, he hauled the dismembered car part over toward the Arena. The crowd stepped back as his baffled owner tried to explain: "He keeps trophies of his vanquished foes!"

The crowd clapped.

The mysterious Lord Sliwa's full story was still unknown to DeLisha. As an ally instead of an agent, the Dancer was one of a handful of sympathizers embedded into the fabric of Purgatory Society, and only allowed limited information. That arrangement was just fine for DeLisha; the idea of being an agent and leaving Purgatory to roam the WildLands was hideous to the refined DragLine Queen, but the thought of helping other, less fortunate Survivors who wished to be free was quite intriguing, But most intriguing of all was this new prospect…

Unfortunately, Lord Sliwa did not seem to be interested in any intrigue with the smitten Dancer. The other performers noticed DeLisha's melancholy expression. "Angling to make more time with the Lord Sliwa?" The Dancers gathered around.

"Maybe." DeLisha ogled Joey. "I imagine he's ample in every way." The Dancers cooed, giddy. "Now, leave me alone, I'm trying to get his attention, but there's too many cooks, and only one spoon… I intend on getting a bite of that action."

The Dancers gossiped one to another as DeLisha lost sight of the Promoter and his Fighter. Peeved at the constant gab, it was time to seek out another angle of view, preferably one where the noise was less overwhelming…

DeLisha settled on a grove of Cottonwood trees just a little ways off, close to the Pair'O'Dice border but with a great view of the Bandstand. Papery golden-brown leaves fluttered in the branches, a few swirling to the ground in a delicate autumn dance. If any groups of BrigadesMen or Rangers were moving between Pair'O'Dice and LowTown, that would be the perfect listening station.

DeLisha posed beneath the whirling leaves, hopeful: *a place where the ManTamer might notice a lonely Dancer standing apart from the crowd…*

———◆———

From the safety of her own tree, the Afterling pouted, unnoticed: this was all really quite frustrating.

Rose recognized the Gambler, and tried to attract his attention without alerting hostile parties. She fell back upon her natural gifts as a mimic, giving the call of the Great Horned Owl, with his familiar double hoot pattern. But the HighRoller didn't seem to recognize it as the Secret Sign. How on earth could he miss so obvious a signal? But she could not think of anything else that wouldn't draw unwanted attention. The Gambler drifted away, and she was left alone above the crowds once more.

She kept repeating her owl call: two hoots into her cupped hands, a pause, then two hoots again, in the hopes that one of the Agents would recognize the pattern. She felt a mounting irritation swarm her—*not only are these poor Devils half blind, they're half deaf too.* Discouraged, Rose turned her attention back to scanning the crowd, intermittently continuing her owl's call, and waiting for the Watcher to make his appearance at the fights.

Rose thought she saw a brief flash of Joey's hat down by the Arena; but she simply couldn't wait any longer. *Growing old is so inconvenient...* it seemed after she carried Angelina, she couldn't go as long between breaks as she once could. For a Scout, this was most distressing.

She scooted down the trunk to discretely hide in a nearby bush. *Hurry, hurry*; all around her, rats, possums and raccoons were ruffling through the leaf litter in the darkness, their forms emitting an infrared glow. She was grateful that she could tell if anyone came near, and felt pity for those poor Survivors would would be virtually blind without the kind Sun to light their vision. As trained, she made a scrape to hide her trail, then ascended the trunk once more.

She passed the time observing an armadillo rooting for grubs at the foot of the tree. It fascinated her no end to watch the odd little creature dig about in the leaves, with its funny little snout. The armadillo's scaled carapace, and hinged armor reminded her of the RollerDrones that roamed the tunnels of Tesoro, but decidedly less scary...

All those years of captivity in Tesoro granted Rose a perpetual wonder at the creatures of the Earth; Rose's delight at the armadillo was matched only by her sorrow that so many of her sister Asura and their sons had never seen the beauty of the Earth. Her own 'brother' Joseph had never even been allowed outside Tesoro until that fateful night at Fort Parker.

Her heart hurt again, and she wished she could have seen his face the first time he ever saw the Moon. *He must have loved the Moon.*

Down by the Arena, Survivors were engaging in blood sports. At first, she couldn't make out who was fighting beneath the flickering street lanterns... a short, well built man was grappling with a taller man; suddenly the shorter man spun midair, delivering a powerful kick to the tall man's shoulder.

Oh—that must be Carlos. She remembered his fancy moves from his fight with the Watcher back at Camp Forlorn; Von Helm leapt up again with an athletic grace, popping a snap kick to the other man's chin, and the tall Survivor went down... if she hadn't known the fights were fixed, she might have been far more upset by the whole thing, but since it was all a sham, she found it fascinating to watch.

A well dressed man shouted into a megaphone: "One... two... three! The Comal County Crusher is the winner of his second match by a knockout!"

Von Helm flung his hands into the air, triumphant once again in the Squared Circle; from this distance, by the dim lantern light, he appeared to be a perfect, bronzed Deva. The Afterling blushed. *But he's not… he's a Devil;* she reminded herself, *a handsome, blue-eyed Devil.*

Rose earnestly hoped the Watcher did not eventually approve of Von Helm as her client, even if he did give helpful gifts—Von Helm would just end up causing untold heartache. Asura knew better than to get attached to clients; Rose remembered poor Adelaide and Deva Hermoso… the Church Fathers were very strict regarding Asura, and emotional attachments to clients.

Leaning forward, she strained to see through the leaves, cautious in her movements. The spectacle of the fights would have been more fun had she not been so afraid of the floating death-balls that dotted the skies above Purgatory. Every fifteen minutes or so, a drone would appear near the commons, then drift away again, moving in a circular pattern around the Commons. Bobbing silently through the paths and back alleys, each drone patrolled its own sector of Purgatory. She counted them up: that's five sectors—one sector per Boss—so that was at least five drones, not counting the five over Goins.

Rose was quite pleased with herself; the Asura were taught to do basic Arithmetic without a Ring's calculator. Some were even able to figure square roots without the Ring… *but not me. That's why I'm a Scout, and not an Accountant like Amelia,* she mused. She wondered how much Arithmetic the Watcher could cypher in his head…

A smattering of applause was heard, and Rose turned her eyes back to the Arena. The Survivor in the Elegant Suit held up the metal megaphone:

"… and best of luck tomorrow on the Auction Block to the Toco Tangler! Five minutes to place your bets, gentlemen, then it will be time for the next fight in the second elimination round at Friday Night Fights!" Excited murmuring ensued, thoughtful contemplation and discussion over the vagaries of betting—a big fight was coming up, and with it, a chance to make some money.

The only ones who didn't seem to be having a good time at the Arena were a small group of chained men cleaning up the grounds beneath the bored gaze of a BrigadesMan, tossing intact bottles into an old feed sack to be recycled for bottling liquor. Their sagging shoulders and shuffling gait pained Rose's sense of injustice. Their demeanor reminded her of a sad-eyed Watcher chained to the Reunion Gate…

Out of the corner of her eye, Rose saw a pair of Survivors swaying woozily down the alley—as they drew closer, she recognized Sam and Mansour. Filled with hope, she repeated the owl call again. But they kept walking, looking all around but not at her. Once more she gave her mournful call, but she could not get them to come into her circle of safety, out of sight of the drones, and her opportunity passed.

Annoyed, she considered—what else might get their attention. *Maybe I sound too much like a real owl?* Whatever the case, the bird calls weren't working; they were simply too subtle. But anything more obvious might be too obvious…

Rose wondered if she should leave a sign in the tree—an obvious branch broken, or an item to catch their eye? She wasn't really good at leaving signs—she was much better at hiding them. Peeking beneath her perch, she saw where she had secreted her bookbag. She had tucked it into a fork in the branches, well obscured from any low viewing angles. *Perhaps I'm too good at hiding.*

She stretched, then leaned back onto the great trunk, curling her feet beneath her furs, enjoying the comfort of her cape. She was glad for its warmth in the chilly night, and appreciative of its softness against the hard trunk. *This isn't so bad, were it not for the drones,* she thought to herself— the view was marvelous, thirty feet above the ground, and it allowed her to keep lookout for allies. Cosy, she snuggled down into the crotch of the tree, and glanced casually towards the Campground.

Out of the darkness, a pair of drones drifted towards her tree…

The ALGOS wafted around the base of the tree; from them, tiny beams of blue light pierced the darkness. Automated hounds following some unseen trail, they were lured by some unknown sign of the hunted. A cold wave of fear inundated the Afterling; *was the bird call too regular? Too unnatural?* Peeking down from her perch, she watched as the light shone upon her scrape—

Where the armadillo had rooted, minuscule traces of fluorescent green glittered up from beneath the leaves.

Her heart froze. She had covered her leavings, as trained, but had never understood the reason. Suddenly it became clear why the Asura were always told to hide any trace of their trail; minute traces of blood in her waste were fluorescing their unnatural signature green in the ultraviolet light, alerting hunters that an Asura had left an unwitting calling card.

The next fight was starting, but Rose dared not turn to look. From afar, she heard the crowd cheering wildly; closer by, she could barely discern servos softly whirring as the ALGOS bobbed closer, scrying the tree's sphere for signs of her green glow. Terrified, Rose tucked her head down, hiding her face in the thick fur of her cape, drawing her feet and hands completely under its metallic liner.

She froze as they moved closer; to the dim hum of the approaching drones, Rose closed her eyes and called upon the power of Saint Patrick's Faeth Fiadha:

~~~~~
*I bind myself today to the mighty power, of the Sacred Realm...*
*Lightness of Sun*
*Brightness of Moon*
*Splendor of Fire*
*Flashing of Lightning*
*Swiftness of Wind*
*Deepness of Sea*
*Stability of Earth*
*Firmness of Rock...*
~~~~~

Stability of Earth. She felt the strength of the nurturing Earth coursing through the tree, and she leaned upon it, allowing it to support her even as she became weak. Now the true evolutionary advantage of Asuran cataplexy became evident: barely breathing, her limbs relaxed, her humanoid silhouette melting into the structure of the tree. Deer's ears hidden, Rose took on the appearance of a piles of fur, draped like a carcass of an owl's dead prey, hung in the branches. She lay limply across the branch as the drones approached, less than fifty feet from her hiding place...

A flurry of great wings thrashed as the machines came near.

The Barred Owl rose up, feathers fluffed out to make itself look larger. Rose remained motionless, afraid to look up as the owl defended its territory against the alien invaders. Vicious talons gripping the branch, the owl was hissing, beating its noiseless wings in agitation as the ALGOS neared its branch. The drones hesitated, scanning the fierce creature, then moved back in eerie unison, a synchronized, smooth motion terrifying in uniformity.

Hissing once more, the Owl spread its wings, a protective avatar against the mechanical demons in the darkness. Pausing in mid-air, the drones hung motionless as an unseen input changed their behavior; Rose could hear their faint whirr mere feet away as they rotated slowly, scanning the Tree. The fur of her cape ruffled as they drifted by... she held her breath as she felt them hovering near her. The faint smell of hot metal and aging electrical components tainted the air...

A great shout arose from the Arena's audience, shaking the tree; alarmed, the Owl attacked. Talons bared, it flew at the ALGOS, and the drones scattered to evade the enraged bird of prey, leaving the Tree and its stalwart Owl Defender behind them. They hung close to the branches for a moment, but the Owl hopped to the next branch, spreading its wings again in a display of territorialism. Wary of the Owl calling unwanted attention to their hunt, the glowing spheres moved on to other branches, scanning again before drifting away to scan other trees. Triumphant, the Owl went back to his roost to resume his watch.

Frightened by and grateful to the Owl, Rose breathed a relieved prayer of thanks to her God. Her Hunters had been thwarted... for a moment she felt safe, almost as safe as she did when she was with the Watcher.

She clutched the deer-hide cape tightly around herself. *It worked!* The Watcher's wonderful lined cloak had defeated the ALGOS infrared and ultraviolet scanners. As she hid beneath his hand-sewn cloak, Rose marveled at the depth and breadth of the Watcher's knowledge and abilities. He was far more than just the mute, book-reading brute she originally thought him to be; the Watcher was an ominous, multi-threat entity, unwittingly unleashed upon the world by Rose.

She remembered his words to her: *"I am your Weapon and Defender..."* Rose at last was beginning to believe him. The Watcher was not just a weapon of strength or violence, but a carefully honed instrument of intellectual acumen, trained to thwart destruction while at the same time dealing it.

A curiosity took her: How did Saul become a Weapon and Defender? Was it God alone who crafted him, or did another, less benevolent being help shape him? Shuddering, she wondered what would have happened had she not released him from his captivity—would the Watcher have become a weapon against her in the hands of someone else?

Casting an eye towards the drones, Rose remained still. For now, she was safe—but she could see no way out past the ALGOS. She puzzled; how would she ever escape?

Survivors from the Commons were now walking through LowTown slowly, methodically, as if they were searching for someone. She strained to see a familiar face, but in the colorless darkness, hatted and coated, all Devils looked alike to Rose—scary and scaly. She huddled in the tree, unwilling to take the chance on approaching a stranger. Their sudden presence made her nervous.

Sam and Mansour should return eventually, but if not, then surely Saul will notice I'm missing, and come for me. Until then, Rose decided she would remain in the trees. Sheltered by Oak and Owl, she waited for whomever might enter the Arena.

A man with a megaphone shouted: above the crowd, she could only catch part of the words. Applause was intermixed with unintelligible yelling; she couldn't tell if they liked the Fighter or not. The man with the megaphone continued to speak as the audience's hurrahs grew louder... they were stomping now, clapping their hands in unison, throwing things, jumping...

From her scout post afar, she watched as Von Helm and a Masked Man entered the Arena.

———◆———

V

Riotous noise rocked the Arena as the Watcher hit his fists together, shaking out every muscle. Mr. Megaphone boomed:

"In this Corner…"

Do it so everyone can get paid

"…weighing in at approximately one hundred and eighty pounds -"

Just throw the fight, get it done, and make your exit—

"…topping out at a whopping five-foot-three—"

What she doesn't see doesn't count

"Coming to you live from Snake Farm, Texas, The Wonder Under-Dog of the Evening—the Comal County Crusher!"

Von Helm vaulted through the gate and into the centre of the Squared Circle, pumping his fist into the air, whipping the crowd into a frenzy. A grin of pure joy lit his face as he raced around the ring, and his joy spilled over into the crowd. The Watcher grunted to himself:

He's the classic Babyface—the Hero, the guy everybody adores.

Mr. Megaphone lifted his instrument once more: "And in this Corner…"

Grinning, a feather-bedecked Joey entered the Arena, leading the Watcher on his chain.

"…weighing in at approximately two hundred and ninety pounds…"

and then there's me.

A howl of boos rose as bricks and bottles flew through the air;

"…six feet deep…"

The ultimate Heel, the Anti-Hero, the man you love to hate…

"...hailing from parts unknown, the Rootin' Tootin' Lucha-Lootin' Texas Outlaw—LoneStar Libre!"

The Commons shook with cheers and jeers. On cue, the Watcher snarled and whipped the chain out of Joey's hand, causing the Promoter to flee the Squared Circle. He swung the chain over his head, a lethal radius of metal links, and it hummed with deadly force. Joey held out his hands as if giving up—but then Lord Li gave a brilliant smile.

"Give him one of my Sausages, Lord Sliwa! Everybody Loves Li's!"

A Sausage Wrap was presented to Joey, who flourished it, a meaty baton: "Even the Fiercest Fighters Love Li's Sausage!"

At the sight of the mouthwatering morsel, the Masked Fighter stopped swinging the chain. The audience watched in awe as the Promoter handed the treat to the Watcher, who stopped raging long enough to wolf it down.

The DragLine Dancers mooned over Joey; from beneath the Cottonwood tree, DeLisha called out to him—"Be careful, ManTamer! Oh, just look at the way he keeps that Maniac under his masterful hand..." The Dancers preened and ogled at the spectacle.

Joey swept his open palm towards the Watcher. "Li's Sausage—it's so good, it soothes the Savage Beast. Thanks, Lord Li!" Proud of Joey's product placement, Li loaded trays full of buttery sausage wraps and passed them to hungry BrigadesMen, who snatched them up with eager hands.

Von Helm sneered. "Keep stuffin' your face, LoneStar Libre—it'll be the last time you taste the delicious goodness of a genuine Li's Smoked Sausage, fresh from Li Farms, delivered direct to your door, specials for subscribers! The only sausages you're getting from now on won't be the smoked kind—" Von Helm laughed theatrically and wagged a finger: "I'll unmask you tonight, LoneStar... your days as a Fighter are over!"

"The scars don't lie; LoneStar Libre is a winner, and you'll see it first hand tonight." Sweeping a hand out, Joey presented his Wrassler-man for the world to admire: the Watcher whirled, and the Cape billowed behind him, Lone Star gleaming in the lantern light. "He's a true Son of Texas, and he'll never surrender!"

Smug, Von Helm locked eyes with the Watcher. "If he was a true Son of Texas, he would never have ever let anyone to put that chain on him."

The Watcher roared and rushed Von Helm.

Von Helm vaulted to the top rung of the Arena fence as the Watcher advanced. Yanking the chain back, Joey gasped and hollered; "Whoa, whoa!" Guards and bystanders rushed forward to grab the chain, wrapping the chain around a free-standing fencepost in the Watcher's corner. As guards struggled to keep his Luchador away from the Comal County Crusher, Joey let go of the chain and stepped into the center of the Ring.

"That's where you're wrong." Voice ringing like a bell, the Promoter held out his hand to his Fighter. "We all say we'd never be taken alive—until someone threatens someone we love. Men will do all kinds of things to protect the ones they love…"

Remembering Joey's story, the Bath House Attendant jumped up in the crowd, agitated: "LoneStar Libre did it for his lil' spotted pup!" The crowd murmured sympathetically.

Sombre, Joey put his hand to his heart. "Those who love will sacrifice their own freedom, or even their own lives to protect what they love. Never Surrender doesn't mean never Sacrifice… ask the men of the Alamo."

A memory rumbled through the audience, a forgotten dream of Liberty… Joey glanced around the ring at the faces surrounding him.

"So you remember the Alamo?"

A hush descended on the crowd, as the sacred name was resurrected from the lore of the Hallowed Dead. Suddenly inspired, Joey proudly pronounced : "Tell you whut: in remembrance of the Alamo, I'll make a deal with you all. If LoneStar Libre wins tonight, he'll win more than just money—he'll win his freedom!"

The crowd roared.

He turned to extend his hand to his Fighter; moved, the Watcher shook on it, then subtly nodded, and Joey unhooked the chain.

Raising his Lone Star Flag-cape, the Watcher let it unfurl behind him, displaying his tortured body to his audience. The deep slashes that criss-crossed the oiled, armored muscles of his back spoke of claws and blades, and the ancient lacerations across his plated chest and shoulders witnessed to lethal force faced head-on. He gleamed like a flame in the firelight, his stout, muscular body becoming magnificent in its witnessed trauma. The Watcher flexed, and the audience clamored, impressed.

As he surveyed the applauding crowd, the Watcher saw the Public Servants of Purgatory, chained together for a janitorial detail. From the edge of the crowd, they watched the Arena, daring to dream that a chained man might be set free.

Behind the Mask, his eyes reflected their torment, lives without hope of freedom except for the few… the Watcher slapped his chest, then raised his hand to the Public Servants in recognition, and their eyes grew bright in a mutual understanding. With great reverence, the Watcher held his Flag Cape aloft, the Lone Star gleaming in the chill night; then he shook the padlock chain around his neck, as if to tear it off.

A murmur rippled through the crowd. From the edges of the Commons, at the end of the own chain, a wizened Survivor whispered back in awe:

"LoneStar Libre!"

The BrigadesMan jerked the chain, and the old man fell to his knees.

The Watcher growled, the years of injustice rolling through curled lips. He leapt to the Arena fence and shook it, snarling, and began to climb out. The crowd gasped collectively and an alarmed Joey leaned over to whisper in his wrestler's ear. Clearly angered, the Fighter smashed a fist against fence, then pointed a gnarled finger at the slave's guard in thinly veiled threat.

"Ha!" Desperate to get the Watcher back on track in the Arena, Von Helm mocked pointedly. "You'll never be free, LoneStar Liver—win or lose, you're a slave, and a slave is all you'll ever be." The Watcher's eyes glinted. From the margins of acceptable Purgatory Society, the Public Servants watched, suddenly hopeful against all odds…

"Speak for yourself, Candy Crusher," Coiling up the chain leash, Joey hurled an insult back at Von Helm as he left the Arena. The BrigadesMen closed the gate, and locked it shut. "You're the one going down!"

Fierce, Von Helm charged the gate, but the Watcher grabbed him from behind in a Sleeper chokehold. As the crowd shouted, Von Helm patted the Watcher's arm twice and whispered that ancient word, the code for a staged fight:

"Kayfabe…"

The Watcher patted his head twice in return, then shook the smaller man for effect and dragged him to the centre of the Arena. Boos and hisses followed them as Von Helm instructed quietly:

"Round One, Boxing Basics; Round Two, Shotokan Gankaku; Round Three, Jujitsu Grappling with Vertical Suplex to leg-lock finishing move." The Watcher responded with a pat, then flung Von Helm across the ring and into the barb-wire wrapped corral panel behind him. Just then, the bell signaling the beginning of Round One sounded—

Mr. Megaphone quipped: "LoneStar Libre didn't even wait for the round to start! But the officials didn't see it…"

"Cheater!" A drunken Hombre stood to yell, and some of the crowd stood with him. "Boo, Cheater!" Cans flew into the ring.

The Watcher snarled and beat his chest, pacing around the ring as Von Helm rose, pretending to be punchy from being blindsided. Strutting over to Von Helm, the Watcher picked him up by his belt loop, then flung him across the Squared Circle again. Von Helm clung to the rails dramatically as the Watcher paraded and growled.

"Ooh, that's gotta hurt! The Comal County Crusher is really having a rough start—is this the end for the Crusher?"

The Watcher picked him up, and put him in a headlock.

Dangling limply, the Watcher squeezed, once—twice—then Von Helm snapped a fist into his opponent's groin, and the Watcher released the little man to grab himself in mock pain. The crowd laughed and cheered as Von Helm popped a punch to the Watcher's mouth, who answered the challenge with a back fist.

Blocked.

Von Helm threw a right hook.

Blocked.

The Watcher opened a straight punch towards Von Helm's gut, only to be blocked again—and now the dance started. LoneStar Libre and the Comal County Crusher worked their way through a repertoire of punches and blocks, each one faster, each one more elaborate; haymakers, uppercuts, shovel hooks, a tutorial of basic boxing maneuvers blossoming into advanced techniques, each blow answered by an equally matched block, catch or parry.

Back and forth, they fought until at last the Watcher faked a jab, which unexpectedly connected with Von Helm's nose. Real blood flowed, and the audience yowled with delight.

What a shame; too bad you didn't pull your perfect snoz back in time. The Watcher snickered to himself.

"Ow, dammit—" Von Helm hissed through gritted teeth, wiping away blood. "My bad; lemme give you a receipt for that." He whipped out a fist to the Watcher's mask; the bigger Macho dodged the fist and grinned back at Von Helm through the flame print mask.

Good luck with that, Manlet.

The Chicken Egg Timer dinged, followed by the bell. Mr Megaphone chimed in: "That's the end of Round One—and the Comal County Crusher has made a comeback after a brutal round dominated by LoneStar Libre!"

Each man retreated to their respective corners to regroup. Survivors rushed the barricades to berate and encourage their chosen Champions, hopeful to goad them to greatness or denigrate them into depression. Beating on the bars, they screamed and cajoled as the Fighters did their best to ignore the noise.

Von Helm took an offered water, and looked into the stands for the Gambler. It had been agreed earlier that the HighRoller would give a signal to extend or shorten the fight, depending on any personal side bets the Gambler had going. The plan was to whip up the big money on the Underdog—Von Helm—and make extra dough in the last round. But he was nowhere to be seen. Von Helm knit his brows and hoped the old coot would show up soon; this was a bad sign if the Gambler wasn't in place for the final bets...

The other side of the Arena, Joey pushed past the howling throng to hand a bottle of water to the Watcher. The Fighter was surrounded by admirers and detractors, each with money to win or lose. Joey beamed.

"Good Job, LoneStar! Attaboy! Fight for your Freedom—and treats!" The Watcher glared though the rails at the enthusiastic Joey, who continued on, oblivious. "That's right—treats!"

Note to self: the Watcher snarled, *kick Joey's ass after this is all over.* The bell rang; Von Helm and the Watcher simultaneously sprang away from the rails.

Von Helm launched a flying tiger kick, but the Watcher swept a thick forearm to block it, responding with a snap kick to Von Helm's thigh. The little man jumped back to the a chorus of excited shouts. Now the focus shifted to a mixed martial arts style of fighting, as the fighters began to work their way through a modified Gankaku Kata—a sparring match featuring the forms from the Shotokan Karate routine, 'Crane on a Rock'. Von Helm's chosen routine was well known to both men, and allowed them to indulge a few personal embellishments to the flashier moves.

As their actions flowed seamlessly from one form to the next, the Watcher found it almost pleasant to engage in simulated combat with his well-seasoned opponent. The joy of fighting was flowing through his fingers as he matched Von Helm strike for block, and Von Helm offered him a few surprises along the way to make it interesting. The little Sheriff's love of martial arts made the Watcher almost regret that the round had to end…

Almost. The Watcher blocked a back-fist strike by Von Helm, answered with a lunge punch, then took down his opponent with a basic over-the-shoulder Jujitsu throw. Countering, Von Helm slipped the hold and swept the Watcher's feet out from under him. Bettors gasped as LoneStar Libre stumbled—then just as quickly, the tables turned as the Watcher did a handspring, kicking out both feet and planting them in a surprised Von Helm's chest.

Shouts erupted as the smaller Macho was knocked down, staggering up again just as the bell for the second round rang out.

The Fighters broke, and retreated to their corners once more, braving the vitriol of dozens of amateur ringside coaches. Suggested techniques and strategies were flung like fists, a virtual fight waged in a theoretical arena between all the onlookers.

In the Watcher's corner, hopeful winners beat on the rails.

The Lords crowded around, eager to eyeball the fighter. "Come on, Sliwa, just have your man crush his opponent, and stop wasting time with the fancy moves." Intrigued, Lord Leyden peered through the railing. "If your Servant wins, I'll offer you one hundred tokes and a load of corn for him. What do you say, Sliwa?"

"But I was gonna set him free…" Joey sputtered.

Lord Gunnar counter-offered: "I'll offer you fifty tokes more, and six months supply of Sugar Cane!"

A hot loathing filled the Watcher; it wasn't so much they were bargaining for him as if he were a commodity—it bothered him more that they spoke over his head as if he weren't there at all. Angered, he abruptly turned to roar at his bidders, and they jumped back from the rails, unnerved by his display of hostility. "This one needs a lesson in servitude." Lord Leyden spoke coolly.

In the other corner, one gung-ho Hombre passed a bottle of water to Von Helm:

"I got money on you, so stop pussy-footing around with this guy and knock him the hell out!" Von Helm wiped the blood from his nose and gave a sideways glance at the Watcher. Another Lord shoved a wet towel into the ring for Von Helm to clean himself up. "Get your mind back in the game… this guy has nothing to lose, but you're going to end up on the auction block if you don't bust this idiot's chops!"

Lord Li wriggled his way into the Von Helm's circle. "Hey fella, you've got a mighty fine fighting style, but it looks like you need some advice about fighting this big brute. Read this!" He slipped a folded note to the little Fighter:

> —*Keep Brother Wolf busy. Need five minutes more.*
> *Notice sent, change in plans*—*Raven*

Concerned, Von Helm quickly mastered his worry and passed the note back to Li. "Now, that's some dandy fightin' advice for sure. Thanks for the tip!"

There was trouble brewing, and the Gambler had sent word—extend the fight. Von Helm grimaced; "Change of plans..." In accordance with protocol, a message would also be sent to the Watcher, notifying him of the same.

"Keep him busy, huh?" Von Helm mulled over the thought of the Marshal beneath his boot heel, and it gave him joy. The little Sheriff's humiliating loss to the Watcher at Camp Forlorn still smarted; a healthy dose of payback might be just the thing to ease the pain.

"Long as we're at it, might as well make this fun." He stretched and muttered to himself, a mischievous gleam in his eye. "Time to taunt Brother Wolf, and see if he bites..."

———◆———

Whispers and a flurry of activity accompanied an unexpected delay for the start of Round Three.

Waiting for the fight to start, the increasingly apprehensive Watcher scowled and scanned the crowd again. Two prime operatives of the Betting Team—Habib and the Gambler—were flat-out missing, and any change of scene involving high-level personnel usually indicated a high-level problem. Sanders was still at his station, making Book and handling Purgatory Tokens, but Habib was no longer lurking in the shadows behind him, giving him advice, and the Gambler was absent from his expected seat in the BandStand.

Something's fishy... the Watcher worked his "Fives and Twenty-Fives", surveying his area in ever-increasing circles of five and twenty-five yards in an attempt to pin down the problem.

The problem wasn't with the Recruitment team. The last group of

Revolutionary Recruits was staging near the dock to make the run to the Campground, bags in hand and waiting for the scene to clear at the Campground entrance. There, a Ranger unit was questioning Agent Michaels regarding an earlier sighting of an extraordinarily tall, Silver-hatted Macho.

Likewise, Agent Michaels seemed in control of his situation; he was pointing towards the border of HighTown, in line with the ruse that Chief Emmanuel was on the run. In response, the Ranger unit leader was signaling to other Rangers on horseback, waving them towards HighTown. That would take the Shaney's men far from Pair'O'Dice, where the Afterling was hidden.

Anxious, the Watcher awaited a Security Team update on that particular mission from LandLord Li, the communications liaison for the Fight Team.

Prior to 'LoneStar's' first fight, Lord Li had passed a celebratory sausage to the Watcher. Inside the wrapper was written a coded message from the Security Team: the Wild Horses Hotel was now unguarded by Chartreaux's goons, who were escorting their hostages to the Bandstand —an old Carport now used as an open-air Pavilion for the betting tables of Friday Night Fights. Taking advantage of the drawdown in manpower, Rose's Security Team was preparing to move her to an evacuation point. If the drones were disabled, Rose could flee Purgatory with far less risk of a mechanical Follower.

The Electronic Warfare Team was working on that objective now. From their post beyond the Gate, the Electronic Warfare Team was all good; Li's last update indicated a positive report from Wilcox—the Catastronix test had been successful. With any luck, the bunker would be detonated and the drones could be neutralized if a decoy could lure them within range of the Jammer signal....

Looking to the Campground entrance, the Watcher assessed the associated Drone Decoy operation, under Goins' charge. Goins was sitting on a stump, glancing around nervously from time to time—a good indicator of drones in Goins' vicinity. The ALGOS were still trying figure out if Goins was a disguised Hostess, or not. If the drones were busy with Goins, they could be easily rounded up and herded towards the Jammer when the time came. All that was needed was a lure. But even if it all went to Hell in a Handbasket, Winston would be able to safely evacuate the Hostesses—and with them, Rose.

Fortunately, the Evacuation Team was already accounted... at last check, Habib had sent Lourdes off to join the Hostesses, putting them conveniently all back under Winston's command and out of harm's way. *Nothing against them, personally*; the Watcher was sure they were all fine Specialists, but he had no intention of having them in the line of fire when the signal dropped. *Sam and Lourdes have some combat skills, but the rest...* he shook his head. He was glad they were all corralled safely until time to evacuate Purgatory.

That evacuation would be easier now that the Insertion Team had successfully completed their takeover of the Gate. A broken bridle was tied to a nearby lamp-post, a sign to command: the Insertion Team had subdued Purgatory Gate Guards and taken control of the Gate and Livery Stable outside the walls. This stealth operation was accomplished during the mayhem of Shaney's noisy entrance. Impersonating Gate Guards, the Insertion Team would open Purgatory Gate so the Rebels could leave quickly, wagons rolling. With the Livery Stable under Rebel control, the extra horses in it were saddled and ready to ride. A quick, safe exit from Purgatory would be more likely for the Rebels now, thanks to this Special Operations success.

But what of Evangelo's secondary Special Operations Mission?

Sweeping his eyes back up the main drag, the Watcher noted a fancy iron lawn chair was empty at the Bandstand. The Watcher grunted with approval; Shaney's absence could be the first indication of success for Evangelo's second Special Operation: a covert 'Humanitarian Intervention Mission' to avoid Purgatory casualties during the Rebel evacuation of the city.

Just after the first round of fights, Chartreaux moved Shaney and her small security detail to the Silo inside Pair'O'Dice. The Watcher did a quick assessment of the Silo's concrete walls, swathed in the bright red leaves of fall Virginia Creeper; they were unscalable for all but the smallest Survivors, as the slender decorative vines needed no trellis. A leafy Live Oak grew near the base of the Silo, trimmed to prevent climbing of the adjacent tower, but allowing shade for Chartreaux's small courtyard; one sinuous evergreen branch overhung the nearby Commons Fence with an ominous noose dangling from it, waiting for Winston's hanging following the Fights.

From a security standpoint, Shaney's move to the Silo made sense. However, Sanders' intel suggested the move to Chateau de Chartreaux was not for security, but in response to the Ranger Commander's need for a bathroom break. Further up the road, the Watcher observed masses of BrigadesMen abandoning their posts to stand in lengthening outhouse lines—a confirmation of that mission's status. Even if they could stop vomiting, the hallucinating BrigadesMen would be in no condition to fight…

With Chartreaux's forces neutralized through less-than-lethal means, bloodshed could be kept to a minimum—a tactical and ethical success for Evangelo's Humanitarian Intervention Mission. The Watcher had to admit that Evangelo's idea was a twistedly compassionate stroke of genius; the little Marshal had confiscated the payday of El Trafico's now dead Assassin Team—vials of pure narcotic Stuff—and put them to a better use.

Or in this case, a butter use.

Evangelo had laced a gallon of melted, seasoned butter with the assassin's prize; Li then served it exclusively to the BrigadesMen as a 'peace offering' on his sausages—with a special order for Shaney. The effects of the adulterated food were nauseating and entertaining—and anything to even the odds and avoid unnecessary casualties was welcome. They would have made more to pass to the Rangers, but Li ran out of butter, and Evangelo noted the Rangers weren't allowed to eat while on duty anyway.

He imagined Shaney was regretting not following her own orders now.

With the Gambler's conspicuous absence, the Watcher wondered if the Betting Team had suffered collateral damage due to unintended consequences of Evangelo's operation. *Surely they were warned to avoid the delicious sausage delivery mechanism of the 'intervention'…* Unfortunately, there were a lot more dire possibilities that could explain the Betting Team's unexplained absence.

Their disappearance concerned the Watcher, who mulled over his plan of action: *end this fight quickly, get hauled off to Jail, and get a briefing on whatever that problem might be.* Now, it was time for the Fight Team to make that plan happen—and that meant it was time for the Watcher to lose. The Watcher grimaced, not from pain, but from disgust.

He hated losing. *Remember, it's not losing when you allow it to happen,* the Watcher opined, *it's just winning, disguised as losing.*

In order to protect his identity, the Watcher would have to retain his Mask, even while losing the match; but that plan had already been worked out. Von Helm would defeat the Watcher in the Arena, but upon attempting to unmask his opponent he would feign being 'knocked out' by his vanquished cohort, LoneStar. The insensate Von Helm would be toted off to the Commons for a medic, and the Watcher would be hauled off to Jail, fighting wildly and still masked.

And still a Loser.

He scowled. But it would be worth it to finally get this mission over and get the Afterling back under his own control. The Betting Team's absence was boring a hole in his already thin patience; if the reason for their absence involved Rose, then there would be Hell to pay...

still no update.

Suddenly, the Watcher didn't care any more if he lost the fight. *End it fast, get to the Jail—then get to Rose.*

At last the Bell for Round Three rang out.

Pushing back off the Rails, the Watcher spun and hit his fighting stance, expecting Von Helm to be within inches of his face; instead he saw the little Macho leaning coolly against the rails in the opposite corner as if nothing was going on.

Von Helm looked up and smiled from across the Arena. "How ya doin' there, Buckaroo?"

Trying to maintain the ruse, the Watcher growled and edged closer, expecting Von Helm to set up the finishing move, but the smaller man just kept grinning. Something wasn't right...

Perhaps he needs me to move in closer, to pass a message? The Watcher circled left, within earshot, and grunted, holding his hands loosely en garde, waiting for an update; seemingly oblivious, Von Helm admired his own fingernails and pretended not to notice his advancing opponent.

Rapidly losing what little patience he had left, the Watcher reached out to grab Von Helm to set up their finishing move. Von Helm deftly sidestepped him, sweeping the bigger man to the side. As he slipped past the Watcher, Von Helm slapped the Macho's backside. "You're slow..."

The audience roared with laughter. Seething, the Watcher turned and held up a warning finger, but Von Helm just chuckled, then did a standing backflip, to spectacular effect. He landed away from the Watcher, fists up, and the crowd hooted.

You just had to show out, you little punk...

The Watcher reached out once more to set up the Suplex, but Von Helm sidestepped him again, mocking—"Come on, it's like you're not even trying…"

The Watcher's arm flashed out to back fist Von Helm's head as he swept past. It was just a light tap, but enough to get the point across.

Von Helm staggered back, then laughed. "Oh that's not how you do it… *this* is how you do it!" He sprang at the bigger man, bursting into a flurry of punches directed at the Watcher's midsection, rapid-fire jabs. Blocking, the Watcher fended off blow after blow, only to have the little Macho lightly spring away from him once more, whispering—"Keep 'em coming!"

This was not at all how they had agreed to end the match… it was supposed to be short, swift, and result in the Watcher being 'knocked out' and put into a submission hold. But, bafflingly, Von Helm was refusing to set up for his finishing move. An overhead lift designed to get the actors in place, the vertical Suplex was a throw that would land Von Helm on the dirt and in position for a head-kick and winning leg-lock against the Watcher. But Von Helm wasn't co-operating…

Von Helm flashed a grin as he zipped past the Watcher again: "You know what to do—do it!"

Frustrated, the Watcher racked his brain; Von Helm had stuck to the script up to this point—what was different now? To the Watcher, the answer was obvious—Von Helm wanted to show off instead of sticking to the script. *I don't have time for this crap,* the Watcher snarled to himself: *time to end this sham.* He needed to get to the Jail—

Von Helm was dancing around him, stepping in and out as he jabbed at his bigger opponent. The Watcher grunted to himself: *let's make this convincing…*

All eyes were on the Watcher as he swung a haymaker and missed, then leaned into Von Helm's punch, taking a jab to the jaw. The Watcher reeled dramatically, then sank to his knees and toppled face down in the dirt.

Mr. Megaphone warbled: "LoneStar Libre is down! It looks like a knockout for the Comal County Crusher!" Groans and cheers swelled from the crowd as the Watcher rose once, then sank to the ground again. *Next time, stick to the script, you contrary jackass.*

Horrified, Lord Li motioned to Von Helm, subtly putting his hands together, then drawing them apart as if pulling a string between them— *extend, extend!* Von Helm gaped, then dropped to the ground on top of the Watcher.

"Get up! Fight me, you worthless Varmint—" he bent down to hiss in the Watcher's ear: "I need to you fight!"

So you want to drag this fight out just so you can shine for the crowd? Unaware of Von Helm's reason for lingering in the Arena, the Watcher grunted to himself and laid in the dirt, motionless. *Nope, we're done; I'm not letting this sham fight continue just so you can make me look like a fool.*

"Get up, dammit—" The Little Sheriff pounded the Watcher, trying to rouse him, but only got a half-hearted attempt at a block, then more feigned unconsciousness. Flummoxed, Von Helm looked up at the panicked Lord Li, who was shaking his head emphatically.

A determined look crossed Von Helm's face, and he leaned over to hiss in the Watcher's ear: "Go ahead and lay down, Loser. You might as well give up anyways—your purty gold ring arrived too late."

"One…" the Man with the megaphone counted excruciatingly slowly, egging the crowd on in breathless suspense.

"Your girl holstered my gun."

"Two…"

The Watcher's eyes flew open; Von Helm grinned. "Perfect fit."

"Three count, and—"

A craggy red fist smashed into Von Helm's shoulder, launching him completely off the Watcher's chest and into the corral panel. The entire Arena shook…

"Incredible—" The man with the megaphone shouted. "LoneStar's still in this fight!"

An ecstatic yelp arose from the Public Servants, cheering for their Chained Champion, much to the displeasure of their Guard. Bystanders surged forward Ringside, yelling and cursing; rattled, Von Helm found his feet as the Watcher came up off the dirt, roaring.

Von Helm somersaulted back, scrambling to duck an open palm strike where his own head had been only a split second earlier.

A palpable shock burst from the strike zone as the steel rail buckled beneath the Watcher's blow. Alarmed, Von Helm rolled to the opposite side of the Squared Circle, dodging another crushing blow as the Watcher's fist narrowly missed Von Helm's skull. Dirt and gravel erupted from beneath the Watcher's hand, his knuckles cratering the soil. Von Helm jumped up to run—

the enraged Watcher charged at the little Macho, grabbing him around the waist and ramming him into the corner of the connected panels.

Connector pins flew loose, and the Arena enclosure shifted off its foundation. The panels flew apart as Von Helm and the Watcher tumbled out of the Squared Circle.

BrigadesMen, Lords and Purgatory Folk scattered, leaving Von Helm to his fate. A brief but destructive chase ensued ringside, as the Watcher annihilated a taco stand and overturned betting tables, smashing them aside to hunt down and grapple a hollering Von Helm. The little Macho flailed as the Watcher yanked him out from under a table:

"Whoa, Hoss, Whoa! I'm just trying to get you to fight—"

Roaring, the Watcher snatched Von Helm up, heaving the smaller man directly overhead. Bystanders watched in sheer amazement as the Watcher bellowed, then spun, hurling his stunned opponent back into what was left of the now lop-sided Squared Circle. Agog, the crowd fled a safe distance as the Watcher hauled himself up to the top rail...

Launching himself off the rail, LoneStar Libre flew through the air, then slammed his outstretched body down on the dazed Comal County Crusher.

The crowd rushed what was left of the rails.

Finally in position for Von Helm's finishing move, the Watcher subtly released his opponent to allow him to buck the Watcher off and end the match with his winning leg-lock. The Watcher grunted to himself, irritated at Von Helm's unfathomable nonsense. *Like I'd ever buy that laughable lie about Rose 'holstering your gun'...what the hell are you playing at?* He silently snarled at the prostrate Sheriff. *If I really believed all your egotistical bullshit, you'd be dead.* The Watcher smacked Von Helm's head to get him going... *up and at 'em...*

...nothing.

The Little Sheriff just laid there.

"An amazing resurrection from the mat—" The Announcer gushed: "and with a flying bodyslam, LoneStar Libre crushes the Comal County Crusher!"

A cold sweat broke out on the Watcher's brow. *Oh Hell—I've actually killed the little bastard.* Alarmed, he shook his opponent, trying to rouse him; Joey rushed into the ring and splashed a lukewarm bottle of brew into the prostrate fighter's face. Sitting bolt upright, Von Helm sputtered, wheezed, then flopped down face-forward into a pile of dirt, groaning.

Mr. Megaphone exclaimed: "One—Two—Three, it's a Win by a Knock Out! LoneStar Libre's the Winner!"

The audience was in an uproar; bottles flew, and boots stomped. At the edge of the crowd, the Public Servants clapped for their Chained Hero; the old man cheered, and others joined him—

"LoneStar Libre! LoneStar Libre!"

Tacos and betting forms were strewn like confetti all around the Bandstand Area. It looked like tornado had hit the Arena—but strangely enough, Von Helm was still alive.

Head still spinning, Von Helm was snatched up by the BrigadesMen, who proceeded to haul him away to the Jail. As they left the Arena, Von Helm looked to Lord Li, who put his hand over his own mouth, dismayed. The LoneStar Revolution's carefully laid plan to win a fortune through fixed fights and underdog bets had been laid waste, along with the rest of the Arena.

Noting the exchange, The Watcher grunted to himself: *Von Helm's off-script behavior was a team effort…*

Von Helm had taken the dangerous risk of taunting the Watcher to keep him from ending the fight early, and to obscure whatever reason for the Fight Team's change in plans. A sinking feeling enveloped the Watcher… *so why wasn't I informed?*

Exuberant from all the pugilistic drama, the audience was shouting, riotous. Fist fights were starting to break out as bets were being called… the Watcher made note—in this chaos, they could make some contacts. *Time to get some answers.*

As Joey leaned in to attach the chain to the neck of his Fighter, he muttered: "So much for the plan." Bewildered, he threw the Lone Star cape over the Watcher's shoulders to ward off the cold, handed him his hat, then led him out of the wrecked Arena to sit ringside.

"But there still might be some money in it. As winner, you'll get part of the purse—we just have to cool our heels and wait for Boss Chartreaux to declare our winnings. Then I'll make a big show of it and you can be set free! The crowd will go crazy I bet…"

All around them, onlookers crowded to gawk at the Promoter and his Wrassler-Man, making communications difficult. Beneath the cape, Joey slipped him the Ring. Eager to have his voice back, the Watcher grabbed Joey's hand, then pressed the hefty Macho's thick finger to his own Neural port. "Hurry it up already…"

#MANCINI: What just happened here?

#WATCHER: Von Helm went off script. For some reason, he

didn't want the fight to end as planned... but he didn't inform me why. When I tried to end it like we agreed, he mouthed off about a certain little person—so I kicked his ass. End of story.

Sanguine, Joey nodded

#MANCINI: Good story.

The Watcher pondered.

#WATCHER: Unfortunately, I accidentally knocked him out cold. This puts a monkey wrench in our plans; we need to know next steps. Go get a snack from Brother Boar, and tell him I want answers, now. I saw him signaling Brother Coyote, so I know they're in on this together. I want details. If he doesn't tell you, tell him I'll wreck his sausage stand. I'd tell him myself, but I have Followers. I'm going to keep them busy here. Don't look up.

Nervous, Joey tried to not look up.

#MANCINI: Okay, I'm hungry anyways.

Snarling to ward off the clusters of curious onlookers, the Watcher disconnected, and Joey ambled over to the line in front of Li's Sausage Stand. Glancing warily behind him, he couldn't see any sign of those fabled drones, only a disgruntled Watcher. The crowd parted ahead of the Promoter to let the Winning Manager come through.

———◆———

As the spectacle unfolded in the Arena, Major Wyatt and his Ranger unit entered the Silo. A heavy, satin voice slid down the stair-railing, and landed with a contemptuous thud at the Ranger's feet.

"Tell me why you've returned empty-handed."

From the top of the stairs, Chartreaux loomed, his formidable figure backlit by candle flame. The supporting timbers creaked beneath his weight, and the Rangers at the bottom of the stairs earnestly hoped the massive wooden timbers would hold.

"We answer to Shaney, not you." Major Wyatt stated flatly.

The Big Boss almost seemed to relish their defiance of him. "She is indisposed in the safe haven I have so graciously offered."

"Then we'll wait until she comes out." Wyatt crossed his arms, and the other Rangers grunted behind them.

"You may wait," unmoving, Chartreaux cast his shadow from the doorway. "but you might wish to change your attitude. The City you search is mine, the Jail you use to house your prisoners is mine, and the roof you sleep beneath is mine. You might wish to reconsider your hostility to my hospitality, if you wish to continue receiving it."

The Major scowled. "None of us have to be here. I'd just as soon we head back to the Ranch, and leave this whole mess behind… we want to talk to the Commander."

"That's not my call." Chartreaux huffed.

"And why not?" Wyatt's voice rose.

The door to the water closet slapped open, and the Rangers jumped as a haggard Shaney swayed out, revolver in hand. "Dammit, stop arguing… can I not go to the bathroom for one minute without one of you bothering me?" Aggravated, she waved the gun. "Step back, if you don't want me to kill you."

An alarmed Wyatt threw his hands up. "My apologies Commander—I thought you were being held hostage in the bedroom."

"No, I'm being held hostage in the bathroom. " She staggered to the stairs and sat down on the bottom tread, delicately holding her head with her free hand. "I don't believe I've ever been this wretchedly ill in my life. My poor head feels like it's going to spin off my shoulders… I'm between bouts, so hurry it up. Report—Emmanuel?"

Wyatt looked uncomfortable. "Unlocated. He's not at the DragLine—we've searched every room."

"I'm so disappointed in you." Shaney's voice remained calm, but a glint of cold steel could be seen in her eyes, and Wyatt withered beneath the chill. "Locate him. I know I saw him. Next—where is my Fugitive?"

"A Search Unit is scouring Purgatory—four Rangers on horseback."

"That's a little better—but still not good enough. New info from our sources says she was on a place called Blackout Hill in LowTown within the last half hour. Go there and hunt her down—you know how to track runaways. Last—where are my prisoners?"

Wyatt pointed to Chartreaux. "That's the jurisdiction of The Boss and his BrigadesMen."

Confident, Chartreaux looked to Sugar, who was waiting in the wings. "Bring in the Captain of the Combined Brigades to give his report."

Sugar blanched. "There's a problem, Sir…"

Three men stumbled in, carrying Captain Bosley. Head rolling to the side, he reeked of the effluvia of the outhouse. "We found him ten minutes ago, passed out in the Porta-Johnnies, rambling about aliens and eggplants."

The Captain raised a hand and mumbled incoherently, then threw up on Sugar's black slippers. Sugar screeched, disgusted, as the BrigadesMan continued:

"But it's not just him—all the BrigadesMen are sick as dogs, talking crazy, unable to stand. Maybe it's an outbreak of dysentery, or the flu."

Chartreaux's eyes narrowed. "Why aren't you sick?"

The BrigadesMan answered with trepidation. "I don't know, Boss—we were guarding the Wild Horses Hotel, and were called in by Captain Bosley when other BrigadesMen started to fall out."

Shaney looked up: "Is there anyone sick besides us?"

"Come to think of it—no ma'am, I don't think so. Just BrigadesMen, and you."

Puzzling over the whole thing, Chartreaux asked: "Then who is handling the prisoners?"

"We need additional manpower for that detail—too many BrigadesMen are sick."

"Then call the medic on duty, you imbecile, if any are still left standing." Impatient, Chartreaux snarled and his BrigadesMen scattered. A few nauseous moments passed as Shaney contemplated the spinning walls of the round room. At last the crew show up with a round Macho in tow.

He blinked at Shaney, mesmerized, "I'm Curtis, Ma'am, and I heard you're feeling sick? I need to examine you, if I have your permission."

"Do whatever you have to do. I just want it to stop."

Shaney sat up. The medic looked at her eyes, and listened to her lung sounds and heart with an empty drink glass pressed to her back. "Well, you don't have a fever, so it's not infection, but you do have rapid heart rate, shallow breathing and dilated eyes; looks like you partook of too much party. Lay off the Stuff for a few days."

"What?" Shaney yelped. "I don't ever partake of the Stuff! Especially while I on duty—none!."

"I'm sorry Ma'am, I call 'em like I see 'em." Wisely, the Medic backed out before the patient could get mad. "Maybe someone slipped you a Mickey… " he shut the door and let her deal with it.

Unsettled at this new development, Chartreaux dismissed the rest of the group with a wave of his hand. "Wait outside. I must consult the Commander."

Glad at his deference to her, Shaney whispered confidentially to Chartreaux: "I've got a feeling someone deliberately spiked our delicious sausages. It's all I've had to eat today—and Li gave out a box of complimentary sausage wraps to the Brigades. We need to question Lord Li. Since most of your men are out of service, allow me to establish a task force, and set up a new entity under my unified command until this crisis is past."

"This is precisely why I need you in this Alliance." Chartreaux schmoozed. "I bow to your expertise, Commander."

"You sure know how to sweet talk a girl." Flattered, Shaney stood, still wobbly, and called in Wyatt. "Major, bring me a bucket: sick or not, I'll take command from the Balcony, and you will act as my Adjutant. Have your men bring in Captain Alderi to brief him as your field commander, and place him in charge of the Brigades."

Wyatt interjected: "Yes, Commander, but what do you propose we tell the BrigadesMen about this? Some of them are already grumbling."

"Make it a volunteer force—" Chartreaux stated. "But let them know that if they don't volunteer, they'll be put on mandatory Porta-Johnny patrol. Permanently."

Wyatt grunted in affirmation.

"Oh, yes! And let's give it a catchy name!" Shaney lit up. "Rangers is a tired old moniker anyway, and belongs in the cell with those who helped create it. We need something new—a name that indicates a new order..."

"Yes..." the Big Boss brooded. "The Order."

"Oh, that is perfect, Reggie! They'll be 'Enforcers of the Order'. And we can get Business owners and select citizens to sign up as 'Members of the Order'." Beaming, Shaney patted the Boss' beefy arm, Wyatt looking on with a dark jealousy. "And if someone doesn't want to be a Member or an Enforcer of the Order, they don't have to be; they can be a Public Servant instead."

"Precisely." Chartreaux noted Wyatt's ill-concealed ill will, and made plans.

"It's settled, then! 'Enforcers of the Order'... that has a lovely ring to it." Turning to Wyatt, Shaney commanded: "Major Wyatt, you are now Major General of the Enforcers. The Rangers are now dead; former Rangers will be officers, and BrigadesMen will be non-commissioned. Now, gather your Enforcers, and send a unit to retrieve our prisoners, pronto. Winston's to hang, and Dominic's going to join him tonight."

"What of Captain Evangelo?"

Her blue eyes flashed. "Turn him over to the Boss' custody. Raffi is going to wish he had been hanged… dismissed."

The entire entourage left, Sugar scurrying behind them. Chartreaux stuck out a gargantuan arm, and Shaney took it to ascend the stairs. Helpful, he waited for her as she holstered her weapon while he watched, amazed.

"I could crush you with one hand, and yet you are not afraid of me, Why?"

"You need me." She said it simply. "You have nothing to gain in harming me."

"An astute observation. Keep us needing each other and I will make it worth your while. As you can see, I have need of your leadership skills as Commander of my Forces—and you have need of my economy and manpower. Together, we can rule beyond the walls of the Co-op—and your Fugitive will allow us unbridled negotiating power with the Insiders."

Shaney gave a weak chuckle. "I like the way you think. If I wasn't so sick, I'd show you."

Chartreaux grunted affably and helped her climb the stairs. "I'm not normally a patient man—but in your case, I will make an exception."

They entered the Balcony Suite, and Shaney stopped to lie down on the bed, head reeling. "We have to find the lil' toot first—but we're hot on the trail." She tugged off her glove to reveal a platinum Ring set with a sparkling blue topaz. A notification to share a file popped up in Chartreaux's HeadsUp Display, and he accepted. "I received this update from James Generales while in the ladies' room… His ALGOS command unit found something interesting while they were scanning the woods around LowTown."

Her avatar popped up, and Chartreaux took a moment to surreptitiously download it for future use. Long, jet-black hair, bronzed skin, and a white bikini made it worth his while. His own avatar popped open and he quashed it immediately, but Shaney squawked: "Oh Reggie, leave it up for a minute, please!" She sighed as his holographic image beamed at her, perfect white teeth and perfectly tanned skin eternally gleaming from behind his news desk at the WeSpeex's world renowned JournoTainment Fact Center.

"Ooh, Reggie, you were so dreamy and authoritative, and just look at that hair!" She rotated the image to admire his manicured mustache and full head of coiffed dark locks. "That's a prime example of 'killin' good lookin'."

"One might consider that idiom to be literal in my case." Reflective, Chartreaux rubbed his bald, warty pate. "I used to hate this body, and what I have become. Now I embrace it fully—and so will everyone else, including you." He opened the image file timestamped from an hour earlier, and watched for a moment. "And why, pray tell, am I watching an armadillo root around in leaves?"

"Wait for it." Shaney said smugly. "Look where the little feller already rooted."

The big Boss grunted, impatient, then gave a hum of interest. Amid the myriad glowing yellow animal urine trails, the faintest glimmer of fluorescent green appeared. Chartreaux froze the image. "Interesting. This is on the ultraviolet band?"

"Actually, just at the very edge of that spectrum." Shaney mused. "Normally, this unit is calibrated for 365nm; I asked James to clarify, and as it turns out, that unit's light was miscalibrated and included 395nm, at the edge of visible violet light. Technically it's still invisible, but capable of bleeding over into visible range on glitchy units, so it's a risk for discovery. James doesn't want any Survivors but us to know about the ALGOS. That's why he's avoiding that range…."

He replayed the footage again. "So this is her trail, then?"

"Yes. Something about the Afterling is altered to make her glow green in that frequency; I found that out from hacking Emmanuel's ring. She's just like any other animal in estrous—she's still shedding blood, and that's why her urine trail has glowing green flecks in it; her blood must carry the fluorescence somehow…"

Shaney highlighted the glow: "The smart little critter knows enough to scrape and cover her trail, but a nosy armadillo uncovered it while grubbing for worms." Shaney became agitated. "Oh, how cruel that I'm sick—I do so love hunting and tracking!"

Chartreaux harrumphed. "Pardon my skepticism, but how did a city dweller such yourself become such an expert tracker of fauna?"

"Oh, I did it all the time as Head of the Human Resources for CognitoINCognito Incorporated! The Firm was always serious about employee productivity…" She sat up. "I'm just so happy to have my old tools back—now, help me get to the balcony. I'm going to adjust my WeLites to that frequency so we can scan for her. If I'm right, she'll be hiding in the bushes somewhere, like a plump lil' rabbit."

Chartreaux shook his head. "If you use your WeLites, the masses are going to see it, and know you are wearing a Ring. There will be questions…"

"I'll be discreet. I'll just keep it on to shine all the time, at a low intensity. No one will notice, and if I'm lucky, it'll catch her unawares." Shaney fiddled with her settings. "And since I have access, I intend to use it to hunt down that sorry snake Emmanuel, too."

"I don't think he's here." Chartreaux insisted.

"Well, you can take my word for it! I talked to Emmanuel myself, from his own ring—and Emmanuel indicated he had the Afterling." Shaney became huffy. "And when Evangelo came to see me at the Ranch, he gave me a bloody deputies' badge from Reunion Camp. Either Dominic or Emmanuel killed Azarian…"

"Did Evangelo say where the badge was found?" Chartreaux queried.

"Well, no, but Evangelo would never deceive me!" Indignant at this thought, Shaney dismissed it. "The DocuMental program shows he wasn't lying. Besides, I have two confirmed sightings of Emmanuel—one related by Sanders, from my own men before Emmanuel's assassins killed them, and another with my own eyes. I think the Chief Emmanuel is here."

"You're wrong." Heated, Chartreaux bristled. "We should investigate another subject—I have every reason to believe that the fighter 'LoneStar Libre' is Leona's Watcher, Saul Azarian."

"LoneStar?" Shaney would have laughed were she not so sick. "That caped rube down at the arena? That's no Azarian—his moves were all bluster and show. He's just another yahoo fighting for 'freedom'. Not that there really is such a thing…"

"Wrong. Because of your delicate condition, you missed this last round of the Championship Fight. The ALGOS have made a tentative match to his profile—a combination of martial arts moves associated with the B.E.S.T."

Alarmed, Shaney looked up from her bucket. "You're loco—nobody's left from that Team. I checked—"

"That's what the Consortium thought as well. Our information was based on your meticulous dossiers of each Survivor that has been processed into the Tejas Co-op. No surviving members of the B.E.S.T. were ever found—all were believed to have perished." Pensive, Chartreaux was pulling files. "It appears we were wrong."

The Big Boss swiped his wide finger across their shared display and a holographic avatar sprang to life; a ruddy young man with an athletic build, shoulder-length ash-brown hair swept back from a smug Roman profile with a neat, full beard. Chartreaux spun the image, and admired the lean. muscular figure, dressed only in a black compression shirt and biking shorts.

"Where on Earth did you find this file?"

"Not on Earth—on a Satellite orbiting the Earth, locked in the unreachable, everlasting Celestia Server, exists every employee file from every subsidiary of the vast WeSpeex Empire—CognitoINCognito, InfoMachiNations, RhoBiotix and DoggyDooRites, just to name a few. But until we can break back into the Mother Ship of all WeSpeex Corporate Knowledge, we must work through James and his limited access to a locally accessible mirror server he set up just prior to the Happening…" Chartreaux chortled. "Thanks to my persuasive wheedling with Supreme Commandant James Generales, I just received Azarian's classified internal dossier from James' redacted WeSpeex Employee Archive."

Incredulous, Shaney nearly let out a squeal of joy, but a fresh wave of nausea quelled it.

"Saul Alexander Azarian, intern and aspiring Agent of B.E.S.T.—the internal special forces group for CognitoINCognito Inc. James Generales considered them to be his own personal Praetorian Guard. Because they acted above the Law on behalf of Visionaries and their interests the world over, James named his Agents the 'Benei Elohim Security Team'—a group of amoral Guardian Angels to act as his 'Watchers on High'…"

"That would explain why the Judge insisted on calling Azarian 'the Watcher'!" Excited, Shaney nearly bounced off the bed. Regretting her sudden excitement, Shaney leaned her head against her forearm. "That sneaky old Battle-Axe! I thought Leona was just being pretentious, but she must have figured it out on her own."

"So it would seem." Chartreaux mused. "Their unofficial motto: 'What's done in the dark stays in the dark, and what's done in the light stays lit'.' They worked off the books to get rid of rivals, rescue hostages and discretely bring about regime change in Visionary-hostile areas such as Texas."

"Well, Azarian sure ain't that pretty now." Shaney clicked her tongue appreciatively at his animated avatar, bulging arms crossed over his chiseled pectorals. "So how come didn't I have this information?"

"No one had this information. Azarian was never officially inducted into B.E.S.T., so it wasn't in his file." The Boss smirked.

"But his internal dossier says he's an Intern III with the Department Encouraging Ecological Deep Sanitation." Shaney shook her head. "D.E.E.D.S…"

"As if the WeSpeex Empire would never obscure their true mission." Snorting, the Big Boss reminisced. "There were secrets within secrets within secrets… it appears even James didn't know of Azarian's status with the B.E.S.T. On the company roster, Benei Elohim Security Team Interns were considered top secret, their existence classified under the general internship program—not under B.E.S.T., but as 'Sanitation Crew'—to hide their 'dirty deeds' from official company records."

"So that's why we couldn't find him!" Shaney frowned, upset she had missed the clue.

"I see you are rightly impressed with my investigative prowess. So am I." Chartreaux leered.

"Oh Reggie…" Shaney eyes glistened. "I love you so much right now. I really mean it."

"Of course you do." He patted her hand sympathetically. Swiping right, Chartreaux pulled up what was left of an internal status report. "Azarian's final review was started, but never completed—the Happening interrupted our receipt of his test results. It would stand to reason he passed; had he not, Azarian would have been terminated along with his internship."

"Well, that explains the high drop-out rate among interns—or I guess I ought to say 'drop dead' rate…" Shaney quipped.

"Failure was never an option with the B.E.S.T." Chartreaux mused. "Aside from the final test result, Azarian did complete all his hours and clinicals for training; so technically, Azarian is a de facto member of the Firm, an Agent of B.E.S.T., and a Visionary in everything but name. But because of the Happening, Azarian was never formally added to the roster of the B.E.S.T.—and therefore never received his Visionary ID Tattoo. Not worthy to be in the company of the Fallen," the Boss sneered, "and forever just another loser among the Damned."

Chartreaux basked in having topped Shaney at her own game. "Fortunately, some of Azarian's original documents are still available in James' remaining CognitoINCognito archives—and I found where an anonymous party previously accessed these files, years ago."

"Perhaps it was Leona—" Shaney hummed.

"That stands to reason," Chartreaux harrumphed. "As WeSpeex Head Compliance Enforcement Officer, she was truly stellar."

"Now it all makes sense; I wish I had known this earlier—I would have recruited Azarian myself. What a waste of a great opportunity..." The Commander mourned. "We could have wrecked the world with the Watcher on our side, had we only known!"

"It appears Judge Leona didn't want anyone else to know the truth about Azarian, for that very reason. Perhaps she was concerned we would put Azarian to use for ourselves against her. I am certain that without the Watcher at the Reunion Gate, Leona's 'Sugar Sanctuary' of women would have never survived past the first year—they would have been breached decades ago."

"That prude started off trying to create a 'safe space' for Survivor Women. She confided to me once that if she got rid of the Warden, she'd be able to do it..." Shaney snorted. "Like Safe Spaces ever worked. She just ended up prostituting them out to Reunion instead, in exchange for continued power."

"Well, that's an interesting tidbit of information. So the Judge considered herself a Savior of Womankind..." Chartreaux's eyes glinted. "That explains her reliance on the Watcher—she intended to use him to protect herself and her women. Leona obscured Azarian's information from James, and altered the record, erasing all data entries on Azarian that might lead back to B.E.S.T. Fortunately for us, I was able to go through a change log to revert a portion of the record to an earlier version, and voila! Instant success—"

"So Azarian somehow survived his assassination... and now he's attempting to recover the Afterling from Emmanuel here in Purgatory! I bet he's got his own plans for power." Intrigued, Shaney opened up her Ring notes. "You know, I really could have used your snooping skills back in Human Resources at the Firm."

"My dirt-digging skills came in handy in the Firm's 'Journotainment Fact Center'—blackmail requires expertise." The Boss demurred. "Unfortunately, the bulk of Azarian's transcripts regarding his background, training and projects are permanently out of reach on the remote CelestiaServer. All we have left is this resume..."

Chartreaux filed it away under future projects. 'But if he truly is who I think he is, this Masked Man will bring some of his training as a Watcher to bear in any fight. Few martial artists have ever mastered 'energy transference'—usually delivered as an open palm strike—but according to his file, as an intern for B.E.S.T., Azarian was such a one."

Shaney was running profiles, making flowcharts. "Hmmm. Missing Afterlings, fires, civil unrest… it all sounds like something an Agent of B.E.S.T. would do—they were always super effective at disruption. But if you're right, Azarian has turned against the System!" She typed in a note. "Still, even if he escaped assassination, Azarian can't be running the show; he's been a ringless Prisoner in the Maximum Lockdown Prison at Reunion Camp, until week before last. That means he's been kept totally ignorant of the System in LifeAfter."

"Or he was a plant, and his status as prisoner was all a ruse…" Chartreaux growled.

Shaney paused to throw up in the bucket. "That's not what I wanted to hear."

"What you want is not what you need. You need the truth." Chartreaux narrowed his eyes, squinting at the hooded figure down at the Arena:

"I believe the Watcher has entered Purgatory."

———◆———

"Make way—Lord Sliwa coming through! He's got a Winner to feed!" Hands slapped Joey's back, tongues wagging with congratulations on the win. Joey nodded and shook hands as he pushed through the line, trying to figure out how he was supposed to talk to Lord Li with all these people around.

A hand tapped his back, twice then twice again, sending the signal. Joey turned to see a pair of kohl-rimmed, ice blue eyes above a red and turquoise floral print scarf. "Mind if I talk to you privately, ManTamer?" The lined eyes batted, twice, then twice again…

Through the crowd, Li caught the Promoter's eye, and nodded. Joey gulped, not certain where this might be going.

"Sliwa!" It was Lord Gunnar, shoving through the crowds towards Joey. "Hold on, I've got an offer for your Fighter; I'm willing to—"

"Back off!" DeLisha hissed. "Sliwa's mine, get your own hookup, you pervert!" A remarkably strong stiff-arm repelled Lord Gunnar, as the slender DeLisha grabbed Joey's arm in a vise-like grip and dragged him away from the sausage line, towards the Porta-Johnnies. "Come with me. This won't take long…"

At this pronouncement, Joey and DeLisha were showered with salacious catcalls from Lords and Citizens alike. "Wait, I gotta get my Wrassler-man a sausage…" Joey protested, but DeLisha persisted.

"Oh, I've got your sausage right here, Big Boy." DeLisha dragged Joey away from the leering crowd, and towards the lines leading to the Porta-Johnnies.

They surveyed seemingly endless queues snaking down the path toward the outhouses. Strangely, it appeared some unknown illness had swept the ranks of Purgatory's BrigadesMen. Everywhere, BrigadesMen were lined up, looking uncomfortable, waiting their turn. Some, having given hope of ever making to the privies, were heaving into bushes and clumps of grass. Others were lying in the adjacent commons, staring at the sky and watching the stars spin in ever widening circles of nauseous wonder.

"Uh oh… Change of venue—" DeLisha hauled Joey to the side, making a hard right down the alley. "We gotta find a place that's private. The BrigadesMen won't follow us if they think we're just hooking up."

Dragging the Promoter through a nearby HighTown hedge, the Dancer ducked into a yard. "Here—" DeLisha pushed through a gap in the thorny Bumelia hedge, hanging a silky turquoise sleeve on the branches. "This is the closest place I could find without a key." Delicately untangling from the branch, DeLisha pointed to a small clearing with a leaning utility shed. "Get in there quick, before someone walks in on us."

Ducking into the tiny building, DeLisha pulled the door shut. Tripping over rakes and hoes, they scuffled old gas cans aside in the dim interior of the shed. The Dancer leaned forward to whisper in the Promoter's ear: Joey pulled back, alarmed.

"I know you don't know me. But you've gotta trust me!" DeLisha looked harried. "Fenix Creciente, blah blah blah. I'm on your side!"

Wary, Joey listened.

"Two messengers were sent out, one for Wolf and one for Coyote—Me, and Lord Li. I think each message was different."

"Wait—we didn't get a message…" Joey whispered.

"I know! I was stopped. I tried to get the word to you before the last round started, but a Ranger detained me to search and ask a bunch of questions about the DragLine, dead El Trafico Agents, and Chief Emmanuel... I couldn't get away. I'm sorry!"

Loosening his tie, Joey took another step back to ponder the news from a more comfortable distance.

"The Gambler told me to find an enclosed space, to pass a message to you. He said if we were out in the open, some sort of drones could hear us?" DeLisha looked confused. "But there haven't been drones since the Happening..."

"Well, why didn't he just write a note?"

"He said this information was too sensitive to write down, just in case I got intercepted." Harried, DeLisha pressed on. "And I did, so it's a good thing I didn't have a written note on me."

Joey scratched his head. "Well, Brother Wolf is higher rank, so maybe his message has more important info... that sounds right. Okay, I'm listening. Hurry, 'cause I've got to get back to Arena. What's this message exactly?'

"Quoth the Raven:" DeLisha whispered, "Strut the Stage, so Foes ignore the Raven's calls for lost Lenore; Look away, or sorrow for your lost Lenore forevermore."

"Quoth? What's that even mean?" Repeating it back to himself to memorize it, Joey wrinkled his brow. "And who's Lorraine?"

"It's Lenore—and I don't know! I'm just the messenger..." The Dancer blurted. "The Old Man grabbed me and told to find you, and repeat it word for word. He said the Wolf would understand."

"So... tell Brother Wolf a pretty poem." Puzzled, Joey turned to go. "I guess I can do that."

"Wait, ManTamer." DeLisha reached over to touch the Macho's shoulder with a manicured hand. "If you're ever not fighting for your life, look me up at the DragLine. It'll be on the house. I'm free on Thursdays..." Batting those big eyes seductively, the Dancer leaned forward, hopeful.

Blushing, the Promoter looked down. "Sorry, but I gotta stay true." Joey stated gently. "I've got a girl waiting on me."

"Really?"

"Yeah... her name's Amelia." Dreaming, Joey mused. "She's a real peach... as pretty as one, and sweet like one too!" A soft look washed over his broad, plated face, making him almost handsome in the darkness.

"Oh. Well, tell her she's a lucky girl." Peeking out the shed window,

DeLisha tried to hide the disappointment. "In that case, let's get you out of here alive so you can get back to her… but you've gotta look the part."

Without warning, DeLisha grabbed his tie, planting a wet, red lipstick kiss on his cheek and rumpling Joey's collar before letting go. "There. Now you look like you've been given the DeLisha Special."

Joey sputtered.

Exiting the shed, Joey and the Dancer parted. Blatantly open, DeLisha sashayed back out to the Commons, greeted by scattered applause and ribald hoots. Edgy, Joey made his way back to where his anxious wrestler was waiting. Still surrounded by gawking onlookers, and attended by one half-baked BrigadesMan, the Watcher was pacing like a caged animal in a zoo.

Looking for Joey, the Watcher analyzed the crowd. Some were friendly, some hostile, but all were potential casualties in the coming battle. If they were smart, they'd run for cover and lay low until the action cleared.

But what of those who weren't free to run?

The Watcher looked to the chain gang, now being pressed into service to clean up the mess he had made of the Arena. Heads down, they were scooping up debris; a scrawny group of Hombres, they looked slightly malnourished and throughly demoralized. Every once in a while one would look towards the Watcher, only to be ordered to get back to work.

As the Guard looked away, a dusty Hombre mouthed the words: "LoneStar Libre…"

The Guard yanked the chain and the Public Servant turned back to his labors.

These men can't run. The Watcher frowned at the thought. They needed saving, but that wasn't his job. His job was to save Rose, and free the Asura for her; anything else was mission creep. It was, however, within the realm of the Recruiters to find able bodies to fight. Would these Survivors be considered fit enough to fight? The Watcher decided to delegate that decision to the Recruiters themselves—and that would fall under Von Helm's command.

Note to self: send word to Von Helm to make assessment and assign personnel to assist in Public Servants' Escape.

From the commons, Joey approached, the Watcher could see his eyes become more apprehensive with each step; and with every step, the Watcher could feel his own fire rise. Visibly nervous, Joey linked manually with the Watcher's neural port to message him beneath the cape. The Watcher steeled himself.

#WATCHER: Report.

Joey wiped his brow, hoping he remembered all the words. Through the Watcher's grip, Joey could feel an electric tension.

#MANCINI: The message was sent prior to the last round, but the Messenger got delayed by searchers. The Message is, "Quoth the Raven: Strut the Stage, so Foes ignore the Raven's calls for lost .. Lucille? Laverne?

Joey rolled his eyes upward, trying to remember.

#MANCINI: 'Look away or sorrow for your lost Le-something forevermore.' Sorry, I can't remember the name.

A wrenching despair seized the Watcher.

#WATCHER: Lenore. It's Lenore…

He felt a sharp fear at the recognition of the hidden message within the message—a reference to Edgar Allen Poe's alliterative masterwork, 'The Raven':

> *Eagerly I wished the morrow;--vainly I had sought to borrow*
>
> *From my books surcease of sorrow--sorrow for the lost Lenore..*

Lost… the Watcher's grip tightened on Joey's hand.

#MANCINI: Who's Lenore?

It hit the Watcher hard …'*sorrow for the lost Lenore*'.

Rose was lost.

A sick coldness fell over him. *Strut the stage so Foes ignore the Raven's calls for lost Lenore…* The Gambler needed a distraction to keep the Rangers and BrigadesMen away from the search scene—but the message to the Watcher arrived too late.

Von Helm wasn't trying to show off, the Watcher realized with a guilty pang—*he was following his updated orders.*

Due to the messenger's delay, the Watcher had been ignorant as to why Von Helm had been asked to drag out their fight. Now the Fight was over—and the search for Rose was still on. Behind the Mask, the Watcher's desperate eyes searched his HeadsUp display for any update of Rose's location data…

nothing.

Frustrated, the Watcher whipped his hand away from Joey and began to stride purposefully toward the Jail, Joey chasing behind him. Turning to snap at the onlookers crowding around him, the Watcher saw the glint of gunmetal from the Balcony—

grabbing Joey, he shoved his Promoter down, behind a seat.

A rifle reported, ripping the air as a high angle shot hit the gravel ahead of the Watcher's feet. It ricocheted into the trees that lined the Commons. Survivors shouted, Dancers shrieked and ran for cover; instinctively, Joey discretely moved a hand towards his pistol beneath his jacket.

Gun smoke drifted from an unseen shooter, wafting over the crowd.

A silhouette of a massive Macho stood backlit against the lanterns of the Tower. In one hand, a rifle smoked; in the other hand, he held a smaller version of the Arena Megaphone, cleverly crafted from a sheet of scavenged aluminum. Purgatory fell silent, except for one smooth, basso voice heard drifting down from on high.

"Leaving so soon, LoneStar Libre? That is what you're calling yourself now, isn't it?"

Behind the Watcher, armed BrigadesMen were forming a perimeter; glancing back, he saw Joey slowly raising his hands into the air, out of deference to the guard sticking a gun in his back. Chartreaux called down to the pair.

"No need to be in a hurry… In honor of your unorthodox win, allow me to invite you and your master, Lord Sliwa, to partake in a unique betting opportunity."

At the mention of betting, interested grunts answered from the crowd. Heads emerged from behind bushes and overturned tables—an opportunity to make a bet was always welcome at Purgatory.

"Your fighting style is unique, Masked Man… it reminds me of someone else, somewhere else." Chartreaux rumbled from the balcony.

Disgusted with his own lack of self-control, the Watcher silently berated himself. His loss of temper and subsequent actions had revealed too much to the ALGOS profilers—and now, thanks to the Watcher's indiscretion, a positive match may have been made with Saul Azarian's profile.

He knew the drill: ALGOS Operators were contacting New Alliance Leaders with questions.

Had this been in a more private setting, the Watcher had no doubt that he and Joey would both have been subjected to the same intense interrogation techniques Chartreaux had used on Evangelo and Dominic.

But LoneStar Libre was an instant Hero to a large crowd at Purgatory, and this setting was very public; the audience might not be so calm if the night's entertainment was summarily hauled off to Jail.

The fragile illusion that Purgatory was a free and fair place would shatter if the newly minted New Alliance forced an unfree, unfair action on Purgatory's New Champion. Chartreaux would need a clever story to convince the constituents that LoneStar Libre should be summarily executed for the sins Shaney had earlier attributed to others…

Behind Chartreaux in the Tower, the Watcher could hear the faintest sound of a feminine voice; *Shaney's feeding him questions.* That made sense—the Ranger Commander would know of the Watcher's dossier, as he had been a frequent escapee and Person of Interest. But even at this moment the ALGOS Operators might be reporting a possible profile match for Agent Saul Azarian, intern of the WeSpeex shell entity, CognitoINCognito Inc. That report would eventually end up in the hands of Shaney and her New Alliance.

The Watcher gritted his teeth with a grim determination. The moment was here: the System and everyone in it would discover that Saul Azarian the Watcher was the last of the B.E.S.T…

Menacingly jovial, Chartreaux pressed on. "Of course, it's possible this is just a case of mistaken identity. Why don't you remove your Mask so I may see your face for myself?"

The Watcher clenched his fists and shook his head.

Joey intervened. "Hey now, LoneStar Libre won the fight—that means he gets to keep his Mask! That's the rules for masked Wrasslers…" Grumbles and shouts arose from the audience, in a strange solidarity with these outsiders.

"Let him keep the Mask!"

"Yeah, LoneStar Libre won the right to keep it!"

Chartreaux surveyed the grumbling throng; the new societal order was hanging by a precarious thread of old tradition. In this fragile state, harsh measures could radicalize the New Alliance's subjects. Chartreaux recalibrated.

"Very well then. I admire your dedication to the Mask." The Boss continued: "Some men need a Mask—without it, they become weak. But in this time of War, we Purgatory Folk deserve to know who enters our gates. I'll give you a choice—you may remove your Mask, or fight to defend your right to wear it. Since you are newcomers to our fair city,

perhaps you are not aware of our traditions, so let me explain..."
Chartreaux's face was hidden in shadow, but the Watcher saw the glint of
his peg-teeth in the firelight.

"Here at Purgatory, we fight to defend our freedom. That is the beauty
of Friday Night Fights—those who say they would rather die than submit
to our System get to put up, or shut up. They do so by calling for a
Purgatory Death Match; no rounds, no rests, no holds barred. The Winner
is freed, and the Loser is dead... it's that simple. What do you say?"

The ALGOS were locked on, watching, analyzing. Purgatory waited in
suspense to hear the Fighter's answer, but none came.

"It seems strange that you have nothing to say, LoneStar Libre... it's
as if you can't speak for yourself. Odd." Chartreaux goaded from the
Balcony.

"Don't be insensitive." From behind the Watcher, Joey piped up. "He
don't talk because he don't speak good English."

"Pardon my arrogance." Chartreaux grunted. "That's a reasonable
explanation, Lord Sliwa. I'm so glad you finally showed up to Purgatory
after all these decades to offer your insights. Perhaps we can get to know
each other better later this evening. But for now, what do you say—is your
LoneStar Libre willing to fight to the death for his Mask?"

The Watcher's heart sank.

What if Rose was in trouble somewhere, waiting for the Watcher to
come to her rescue? But if he went searching for Rose, the drones would
follow, and find her as well. That was made clear in the Gambler's
message: *Look away...* don't look towards her. The ALGOS were watching
the Watcher even now, hoping he would telegraph Rose's location.

He had no choice but to stand and fight. But where was Rose?

The Watcher wished he believed in a God. *I'd pray for a sign, if I believed
in them...* desperate for some kind of input, he scanned his surroundings
one last time. In the deepening darkness, the Watcher was searching for a
guiding light—

A beam pierced the gloom as a silver crescent crested the edge of the
horizon, rising into a starlit sky. As it rose above the shadows of the trees,
the simple sweet chirp of a bird greeted the moon from deep in the
bowels of LowTown.

tsees... tsees...

A pause, then

tsees... tsees...

The Watcher recalled the last time he heard the familiar, nocturnal flight call of the chipping sparrow, under the stars with Rose, surveilling the abandoned strip mine. The call filled his heart with longing to be far away with the Afterling under a rising moon—but this little bird was not in flight, and she was not with a flock. She was alone; no bird answered back.

The Sparrow called again, twice, then twice again:

tsees… tsees…

tsees… tsees…

the Watcher felt a sudden thrill.

The familiar "double-double" pattern of the LoneStar Revolution's signal! His heart leapt up within him—

The Afterling was calling him.

Rose called to the Watcher again, and her plaintive Sparrow song tormented the Watcher's heart. He remembered what he had told her beneath the moon, listening to the Chipping Sparrow's call:

If you are lost, call to me, and I will find you.

Now his Little Bird called to him, lost somewhere in the overgrown trees of LowTown. Mind racing, the Watcher felt the hush of air drifting above him, the eyes of Rose's Hunters watching him…

To go to Rose meant death for her.

There was only one way to help: get word to the Search Team about Rose. But how? The Gambler's 'Digital Deception Transmitter' was jamming his own signal, and the Watcher couldn't transmit without direct link. Surrounded on all sides by guards, and under constant surveillance by newly alerted ALGOS, the Watcher needed a plausible way to direct link his Ring to the neural port on Joey's hand.

He closed his eyes… *what is the way?*

In a long forgotten memory, he could feel his Mother clasping his own chubby baby hands together in her own hands, praying to her own God. *The Way…*

He knew the Way.

Sensing a change in their Champion, the chain gang of Public Servants leaned towards him, seeking a sign of their own. The Watcher raised his hand in invitation to the waiting Chartreaux:

"What do you choose—lose your Mask, or fight to the death to keep it?"

So the Searchers need a distraction, do they? The Watcher nodded. *Fine. They asked for it…* he slapped his deep, plated chest, and the muscles rippled beneath it. Nodding to the Boss, the Watcher raised his fist to defiantly answer the challenge.

"So be it—LoneStar Libre declares a Death Match!"

Riotous applause swept the streets of Purgatory. Sweeping his arms dramatically, Chartreaux held up his hands and the crowd answered back with their approval. Malevolently benevolent once more, Chartreaux waved to his BrigadesMen. "Lieutenant Captain Corey—swiftly repair the Arena to the best of your ability, in preparation for the fight."

A hesitant voice answered from the group of BrigadesMen standing with their guns drawn on Joey and the Watcher: "Sorry Boss... Lieutenant Captain Corey is, uh, indisposed at the moment."

"What do you mean, indisposed?" Irritable, Chartreaux snapped.

"Um... he's having issues." The BrigadesMan pointed to the Porta-Johnnies.

Chartreaux's voice was menacing. "Then give the order to his Second-in-Command, Lieutenant Lapwell..."

The BrigadesMen glanced at each other. "Yessir, Boss. As soon as he comes out of the Porta-Johnnie, we'll tell him."

The Watcher could almost hear Chartreaux's blood boiling. "You have fifteen minutes to repair it while I summon Purgatory's Champion. Now get busy—we have a Death Match and a hanging to perform." Growling, the Big Boss turned on his heel and disappeared back into his Tower.

"Wait—who is LoneStar fighting?" Joey shouted as the door to the Balcony closed. No one answered; everyone was rushing the betting tables in anticipation of the Death match. A cacophony of excitement burst from the onlookers, eager to see more blood. Bets were being shouted, and the Lords were waving notes from the stands, exuberant at the chance to wager once more.

Time to send a message. Turning to Joey, the Watcher held out both hands to the Promoter, then clasped them in supplication. He could hear the faintest hum of the invisible ALGOS as they moved in closer to observe his actions:

"What is it? What do you want, Boy?" Joey cocked his head at the Watcher, playing along gamely. "You want a treat?"

No, you Dolt—groaning to himself, the Watcher shook his head, holding up his clasped hands again, before him. Flummoxed, Joey shrugged: "I don't know what you want..."

A familiar, melodic voice intoned from the crowd. "Pray."

Heads turned to see a man in an ornately embroidered suit and scarf, calling from the shadows. The man held up both hands clasped as the Watcher did. "He wants you to pray with him."

Joey's Guard snorted. "You! Hey, Dandy—the Boss wants a word with you—"

The trim figure retreated back into the shadows of the trees as another guard pursued him. Thwarted in the darkness, they searched the crowd in vain while the remaining Guards turned their attention back to Joey and his Fighter.

"Pray?" Joey blinked. "I mean, uh… sure." He turned to their guard. "You wouldn't deny a condemned man a last prayer would you?"

The Guard mulled it over. "Naw… I guess not." He stepped back.

Imploring, the Watcher held out his clasped hands before him; unsure of what to do next, Joey reached out and took both of the Watcher's scarred hands in his own calloused ones. Subtly, the Watcher pushed back a finger of his WeSpeex glove to uncover the uplink stone of his Ring, then shifted his Ring to link to Joey's embedded Neural Port.

Curious onlookers gawked at the sight; a murmur was heard from the Public Servants whispering one to another: "He prays…"

"I'm sorry," Joey cleared his throat awkwardly, "I don't know what to do. I never prayed before."

#WATCHER: Take off your hat, close your eyes and move your lips. Say Amen when we're done.

Joey obliged. A nervous titter erupted from onlookers as the two rugged men bowed their heads close together.

#WATCHER: Get this message to the Raven through Li: "A little Bird told me, search high in Low."

#MANCINI: High in Low? You mean high and low?

#WATCHER: High IN Low. Exactly that. Next—Send word to Brother Fox that Brother Coyote is to free the sheep. Brother Fox knows who has the Master Key to their chains—get that key to the Flock, and give them instructions to run out of their pen when they hear the Heavenly Trumpet…

MANCINI: Anything else?

#WATCHER: That's all—and thank you.

#MANCINI: Will do…

#WATCHER: Now say Amen to end it, then get a move on.

Uncomfortable, Joey hesitated.

#MANCINI: But shouldn't we actually pray? I mean, it don't seem right to pretend. Some of these people think this is real.

The Watcher peeked up through his Mask—all around, people stared. Some smirked, others gawked; but a scattered few Survivors removed their hats, deferential. With the Chain Gang at the edge of the Commons, an old Public Servant knelt in the dirt, alone, eyes closed, lips moving silently...

Grumbling, the Watcher acquiesced.

#WATCHER: Fine. Oh, God...

The Watcher scrunched his eyes shut again, dubious. The last time he had prayed like this, it didn't turn out well.

#WATCHER: Forgive our sin. Let us win. Save the Lost. Amen.

"Amen. That wasn't so bad, I guess." Affable, Joey replaced his hat, and the others in the crowd followed suite.

Above the Watcher the drones hovered...

Well if nothing else, that little display of Piety would be sure to confuse his profilers. Praying was something the mighty Saul Azarian would never do. *There are some bitternesses that never go away,* the Watcher mused, unclasping his hands to cast a doubting eye towards Heaven. *How about You be the Good Shepherd, and find my Lost Lamb, then we'll talk. You know, just like the bad old days.*

Looking to concoct a ruse, Joey turned to their guards. "I gotta get something to drink for my Wrassler-man..."

The BrigadesMen were looking a little grey, sweating slightly. One shook himself out of his stupor; "I'll go with you. I need something myself." The guard's partner mumbled and gazed down the barrel of his gun.

"It's like staring into infinity... I can feel it spinning."

The Watcher noted, and warily stepped away. *Drugs and guns make a bad combo.*

He listened for his Little Bird. He could still hear her call, and he wished there was some way to let her know that he had heard her call, and for her to wait...

I'm coming for you.

A few BrigadesMen were repairing the Arena, but they seemed to be moving slower than usual; meanwhile the lines to the privies had gotten longer. Surely someone in authority would be bound to notice that the BrigadesMens' ranks had been decimated by something resembling a psychedelic version of food poisoning.

Beneath a Cottonwood tree, DeLisha was talking to Joey now, leaning in close once more to whisper flirtatiously in the Macho's ear. Joey's Guard was hanging back, listless. In the firelight the Watcher could see Joey hand back the scarf the Dancer had given to him earlier…

With a dismissive wave of the hand, Joey was on his way back to the Watcher, leaving the Dancer staring after him…

———◆———

Back under the Cottonwood tree, DeLisha was abandoned once more.

Following a stop at Li's Sausage stand, Lord Sliwa had returned DeLisha's scarf with a perfunctory thank you and farewell. Now the ManTamer was returning to his Fighter, who was pacing around the perimeter of the Arena. With his fancy, feathered hat and noble brown polyester suit, Lord Sliwa was the epitome of a prosperous potential Sugar Daddy—and DeLisha had an opening, thanks to the Assassin Keller's timely demise.

DeLisha couldn't help but notice that the ManTamer had absolutely no interest in a Dancer alone beneath the falling golden leaves of the Cottonwood tree—but to be honest, it was hard for anyone to notice anything in all the hubbub surrounding the looming Death Match. Impressed with the fighter's savagery, Survivors stampeded the betting stands again, and Sanders raked in bets once more.

Standing apart from Purgatory Folk, the Dancer watched as the jostling crowd was swept away once again into an abyss of hollow pleasure. Taken with a disconnectedness that made all attempts at relationships seem futile, despair overtook the performer.

Good men like the ManTamer were not interested in DeLisha's company, and those Survivors who were interested were only interested in sex. DeLisha sighed; sometimes the makeup was a creative expression of beauty, but other times it became an obscuring mask, a disguise that overpowered all complex humanity with its promise of shallow sexuality. Just once, DeLisha wished someone could see the lonely human behind the lipstick and satin, a fellow Survivor struggling in this deadly, dying world—

Suddenly the struggle seemed worthless. Shivering, DeLisha wondered; *What good is life, when it is lived cold and alone?* A stiff breeze arose, causing a flurry of golden leaves to drift down, and the Dancer mourned in the decaying beauty of the moment…

a hard object landed atop the Dancer's head with a conk.

"Ow!" A golden leaf bounced off and landed in the dried duff below. DeLisha bent down to see that the offending leaf was wrapped around a hidden object; picking it up, prim hands unwrapped an antique tortoiseshell compact. Secretive, DeLisha opened it—

a note and five tokes fell out. Shocked, the Dancer quickly gathered them up, and unfolded the note: on one side, written in fat curly letters:

> *Jo sent me. pleese help—get this messag to wildland express ajents, I becam seperated from my frends. also pleese tell danser deleesha that jo rand on midnite street behind the green dor needs help, his nayber is the big man upstares. hire a gard with this muny and he reqests a cleen up on iall 7. he is a good man but very sick and he needs care. He sed deleesha is kind so pleese tell deleesha abowt mr rand. Thank yu.*
>
> *P.S. the anjels will reward yu*

On the other side was a line drawing, a strange brand-like pictograph of a Star with a bird upon it, and a note written in neat block letters:

> *-Blood chit: use only in emergency—return to WildLand Express for reward.*

Clean up on Aisle Seven—that was DragLine code for a dead customer.

DeLisha eyes grew wide, looking up into the Cottonwood, but seeing nothing except the moon rising low in the branches. "Jo Rand—you mean Queen JoLene? And who's the 'Big Man'? What the hell—" Immediately, the Dancer regretted swearing—"Oh, the Big Man Upstairs..." *and Angels?* "By Angels, you mean the WildLand Express?"

No answer.

This strange message, fallen from the sky, was more than just a call for help to the WildLand Express; it was an answer to an unspoken prayer. The note was from someone who knew DeLisha as more than just a prostitute: *DeLisha is kind..."* A little sparkle of warmth crept back into DeLisha's soul. "Alrighty, then, Big Man, if this is from you, send me an Angel who's not under surveillance..."

Searching the riotous crowd, DeLisha's eyes came to rest on the lean, eye-patched man, casually surveying the scene around the Arena—Lord Li's contact.

Making the sign—three fingers of the right hand held to the left shoulder—DeLisha took a deep breath, then waited for the Agent to look. He seemed to be searching for someone, looking around with an air of casual disinterest, but close observation revealed a careful pattern of scanning. Finally, his eyes came across the Cottonwood, the Dancer and the sign. Strolling nonchalantly, the Agent approached with a smooth, confident step.

DeLisha made the first move, pulling a Fo'Bacco cigarette from the neckline of the turquoise jumpsuit. "Nice evening. Got a light, Brother?"

"Always, for a Brother." The Agent flicked open a lighter and lit the tip—DeLisha took a deep drag, passing the secret bundle to the Agent. Turning against the trunk of the tree, the Agent flicked his lighter again to quickly read the note. A look of disbelief, then a rough fist grabbed DeLisha's collar to pull close.

"Where'd you get this?

Nervous, DeLisha pointed straight up into the branches of the Cottonwood tree.

Holding up his gloved hand, palm out, the Agent waved it slightly, revealing a small tear in the glove's ring finger, and the faintest glint of violet light beneath. He did this for several seconds, looking up into the branches of the grove. He shook his head. "Nothing..." At last he shoved the note into his jacket pocket, complete with its tokes and compact, turning to go. "I'll return with a couple of others. Go back over to your little pals and don't draw any attention to us, or this tree."

DeLisha grabbed the Agent's sleeve. "Wait—I need that compact and the tokes when you're done with it. They're to help someone in need."

"You're some kind of do-gooder?" The Agent studied the Dancer. "Trying to save the world, huh?"

The Dancer became defensive. "Somebody should."

"You did." The Agent grunted. He hurried away, leaving a wondering DeLisha beneath the golden leaves of the Cottonwood tree. Out past the public servants, Michaels caught a glimpse of a familiar silhouette past the lanterns of the Commons: a slender figure in a fringed poncho and flat-topped cowboy hat slipped through the entrance of the Campground—

Dominic was on the move.

———•—•—•———

VI

In the shadow of an Industrial District Pavilion, a pair of Survivors crept. Dominic whispered ahead to Von Helm: "Hold up, mi Amigo… we wait for our Brother here."

Von Helm sighed and stared into the darkness, using his Ring's WeLites function to scan for Rose once more. The Sheriff flashed its invisible ultraviolet light briefly into the interiors of the open barns, hoping for an elusive green glow to light his night; finding nothing, he turned it to the bushes thickly choking the spaces between the towering buildings. Shifting the load of his heavy backpack to a more comfortable position, Von Helm continued his search for the Afterling while his Mentor assessed Purgatory.

Surveying the Survivor City, Dominic cast a wondering eye at the hellscape of damage his Revolución had wrought. Coals glowed in the shell of Boss Waitie's burned-out cabin, casting eerie, flickering shadows down the street towards the other burned buildings; in the busy centre of the Commons, BrigadesMen struggled to push the Arena's wrecked corral panels back into a semblance of a square while others cleaned up the smashed remains of tables and food stands. He pushed back his hat. "Dios mio, you all have been busy…"

A blocky figure with black gear bag and a brown leather suitcase came lumbering through the brush and nodded to Dominic, hailing him Ring-2-Ring:

#HABIB: The Store is closed for business, and just in the nick

of time; a group of visitors has arrived—but all doors are secured, all personnel evacuated, all valuables removed or destroyed, and a red herring has been left behind, as discussed.

"Excellent. I hope you have included your silver tea set in your bug out bag..." Dominic murmured, preoccupied with his situational assessments.

Habib patted his suitcase; "Never leave home without it."

"An excellent philosophy." Dominic turned his head, and coughed into his coat sleeve, attempting to muffle the noise. At the sound, Habib grew concerned. "You sure you can handle this? You shoulda rested more..."

"I have no choice. Besides, your excellent tea helped immensely, and I can sleep when I am dead." Intense, Dominic shouldered his duffel bag. "Let's vamos, Gentlemen—it is time to commence this fiesta, and I still have a precious lost item to retrieve." Wending their way down a dark alley, the three Survivors made swift, stealthy passage through a back alley of LowTown, silent as they approached the broken down fence along the backside of the Campground. A nod, and a tip of the hat gave way to the signal, then allowance into the quiet wagon yard.

Except for a dying campfire by the entrance, all other fires had been doused; scattered clusters of seemingly drunken agents lay quietly next to their wagons, while the other agents watched the fights. Behind the scenes, handcarts laden with corn, sweet potatoes and other vegetables were being rolled through the back entrance of the campground, where their goods were offloaded by WildLand Express agents into smuggler wagons—food to feed the Revolution.

Another handcart rolled in, and the Agent pushing it thrust a hand down into a pile of dried beans to pull out a very nice little semi-automatic handgun. "I've prolly got twenty of 'em in here—I just rolled by and picked 'em up while the BrigadesMen lay there, stupefied in the grass." The Agent chortled. "It's like taking candy from a baby." He rolled the handcart into line with the rest, to be unloaded into the smuggler wagons.

As Dominic and his crew approached, a lanky Survivor patted the tailgate of one such wagon, bearing sacks of potatoes. A panel fell open, and Dominic, Von Helm and Habib loaded their gear quickly into the hidden hold, careful to avoid any suspicious actions that might draw the ALGOS away from Goins near the entrance if the Campground, some

100 yards distant.

Habib slid the Watcher's bag into the smuggler's hold last, pointing it out to Dominic. He whispered: "This belongs to your big Brute—you'll have to deliver it since he didn't follow the script and retrieve it himself." Clearly displeased with the outcome of the fight, Habib scowled. "Over three thousand Purgatory Tokens were in circulation on those bets—at least fifteen hundred could have been won by us—but someone didn't get the memo."

Moving between the closely parked wagons, Dominic checked each one for readiness. Horses were partially hitched to each of the eight fully loaded smuggler wagons, their road-ready harnesses hidden beneath blankets to avoid the appearance of an impending getaway. Likewise, their drivers lazed in the backs of their wagons, ready at a moment's notice. All other horses were geared up and ready to ride; the rest of the wagons would be left behind to facilitate a quick evacuation.

Each Agent gave a tap of the brim to acknowledge their leader, Dominic, and his second in command Von Helm. Dominic paused as they came to Von Helm's spry Blue Morgan horse, Steele; as he ran his hand across the steed's glistening coat, a visible wave of pain rippled across his mouth, and for a brief moment, Von Helm watched as his Mentor struggled to master his own sorrow.

"So many, lost..." Steele snorted, and Dominic was silent for moment.

"Maybe they got Charger out." Von Helm whispered sympathetically, stroking Steele's Silvery-Blue mane. Nodding grimly, Dominic patted Steele again, then moved on.

The trio approached a small, tin-roofed pole barn surrounded by thick brush; pushing through a perimeter of wax myrtle and ligustrum, they found a Brick Bar-Be-Que pit, coals winking from the ash. A tall figure huddled in bedroll beside the smothered fire, and a long, lantern-jawed visage peered out from beneath the covers. Dominic nodded to Sampson, pleased with the results of his Emmanuel masquerade, then motioned for him to cover himself once more. From a tree-stump table, Evangelo grunted a greeting, wrapped a blanket to quickly hide his suit; opposite them both, a heavy figure was shuffling cards.

"Welcome, Brothers. Care to parlay with us? The game is BlackJack."

The Gambler looked up from beneath his hat brim and shuffled the deck, then cut it, laying it upon the stump. The Gambler stacked the cards again as he opened a dialogue with Dominic.

#ANON: The Treasure Hunt continues, but with new hope— Brother Wolf just sent word that contact has been made by the subject, and a Little Bird told him to search high in Low.

At the word of Rose's call, Dominic passed his hand over his eyes, grateful just to know that she was alive.

#ANON: Brother Wolf has been informed of the all seeing-eyes, and knows to stay away. We have inventoried ten of Uncle Jim's Searchers inside the walls, thanks to careful observation. They have invested a great wealth in tech to retrieve this Treasure; it would be a great loss to them if any of them were destroyed.

Dominic grunted, deep in thought.

#ANON: We continue our search. However, no Bird call has been heard since—so the Bird is still in the bush, and not yet in hand. Six teams are dedicated to hunting.

Dominic stroked the sweeping ebony scales that adorned his upper lip and thought on Rose's recommended training—Asura were conditioned to seek out their Deva when threatened. As a Scout, Rose should be trained to use stealth and her tracking skills to get as close to the Watcher as possible, facilitating her own rescue. If the recommended teaching protocols had been followed by Tesoro's Asura Behavioral Committees, Rose's next moves would be easy to predict.

#SANTOS: The Bird should flock to its nest-mate when in dangerous territory—expect her to close the distance with the one who heard her call. Look where Birds would naturally roost.

#ANON: We will advise the teams. I am appalled to say that I myself may have heard the Bird mimicking an owl's call, but I did not heed it, thinking it to be an actual owl.

#SANTOS: That is understandable; the Little Bird can mimic almost any creature to perfection, almost too well.

The Gambler appeared mildly impressed.

#ANON: Intriguing—unfortunately I was too far away to get an exact location, but I heard the owl hoot repeatedly from LowTown. Now we must organize a Bird Hunt—Brother, have you seen the light?

Dominic pointed subtly to his Ring:

#SANTOS: We know about the Light, and we are spreading it wherever we go, in hopes of finding the Lost.

Riffling though the cards, The Gambler kept shuffling as Dominic messaged him.

#SANTOS: An update that may change our later route: I sent word from outside the wall to the our Home Camp advising them of our losses, but received no reply. We must prepare for possible bad news from the north.

#ANON: That is regrettable. We will consider that when planning our route; in other bad news, we lost big at the tables, as I'm sure you've been informed by your associates. An unavoidable delay of the messenger is to blame.

#SANTOS: Unfortunate, but we will survive.

#ANON: Visitors have searched nearby seeking a mythic Giant, but they have been directed elsewhere. We should expect more visitors to arrive, looking for you now you have moved. I would suggest you make your stay brief.

#SANTOS: Agreed—all key personnel will head to alternate locations once business here is concluded.

#ANON: Meanwhile, a Death Match is being prepared. Suspicions have been whetted about a certain Fighter's identity... the Boss wishes to unmask the Champion, and the Champion refuses, so a Death Match has been called. All eyes are on the Arena, allowing teams to search more safely.

Dominic glanced up with a hint of concern at this pronouncement from the Gambler.

#SANTOS: The usual opponent?

#ANON: In all likelihood, yes. Heavily doped and loaded for bear...

#SANTOS: I suppose we shall see if our Champion is worthy of his hype. Any other news?

The Gambler pitched the cards to the players.

#ANON: A trap is laid, and the Uncle Jim's Searchers will be drawn in. Give the signal when you wish the action to start, after we know where our Treasure is...

Dominic peeked at his cards, then motioned to 'stand' his hand.

#SANTOS: Of course. Where our Treasure is, there will our heart be also—and we as a whole cannot survive without our heart.

Concern cracked Dominic's cool facade at the mention of his Daughter. The Gambler lowered his eyes, unwilling to gaze that deeply into another man's soul.

The Gambler pitched out additional cards as the conversation continued. Habib signaled to stand his hand, but Evangelo murmured. "Well, I am no fan of the gambling vice, but I seem to be enjoying a bit of luck with this suit, so I think I'll take a risk. Hit me, Dealer." He seemed quite pleased as he tapped the top of the stump. "I've always wanted to say that."

Von Helm chuckled as he laid down BlackJack.

The HighRoller gathered the cards and shuffled them again, just as a tall slender figure and a slouching Macho came slipping out from between the wagons and into the dimly-lit circle. They flopped down on the ground.

A tense voice grumbled: "Deal us in." Pushing back his boonie hat, Mansour revealed himself; beneath her concealing scarf and hat, Sam stayed bundled up, anxious to leave again and locate the Afterling. She appeared to be utterly miserable as she opened her channel with Dominic:

#ELLISON: We're still searching, but no luck. We've used the lights discretely in all sectors but found nothing. All six teams report the same. House to house is next, but that will require planning, arms and covering fire… if I fail in this, I will resign my commission.

No hint of emotion was on her face, no drama in her statement, but her bitter disappointment at her own performance overflowed into her words. Stoic, she sat as stiff as a board, relying on her military bearing to mask her own growing sense of failure.

#SANTOS: Let go of that despair, and seize this moment; we have a lead in our hunt. The Wolf heard a Little Bird calling, and he sends word to 'look high in Low'—our Dealer here heard a Hoot Owl earlier this evening, but did not realize the Little Bird was calling to him. Still, he was too far away to get a good location.

Sam's jaw dropped.

#ELLISON: Wait—an owl? I heard one hooting from the Big Oak on Blackout Hill in LowTown, over and over again…

Excited, Sam leapt up from the stump, scattering dried leaves everywhere; nervous about the possibility of Sam being discovered by drones, Mansour pulled her back down.

From outside the circle, hurried footsteps approached, long legs wading through the dried elm-leaves strewn across the campground;

Agent Michaels strode into view, a glint of hidden triumph winking out from his leather eyepatch.

"I have a present for you, Judge Santos—she's not yet in hand, but I believe we have found a Bird in the bush…

He handed a small package to Dominic, who flicked it open; a folded piece of paper fell from the compact, along with five tokes. As his eyes came to rest on Rose's curly script, and gleam of uncontainable joy leapt into his smile. He leaned his head back, silent for a moment, then handed the note to Sam.

Sam covered her face, shuddering with relief.

#SANTOS: Excellent work, Brother Lynx! Draw a direct line between that tree and Brother Wolf. Tell the teams to search the trees in the general area along that path; the Little Bird is trained to fly to its friend when lost. Follow the Light, and if found, secure that location and send word back through a messenger—I will assign Brother Lynx for that purpose. Dismissed—

Dominic pointed to Michaels, and he tipped his hat to Sam. Thrilled to be back in the hunt, Sam motioned to Michaels, and rose from her seat again.

#ELLISON: Thank you! I swear to you we will save her. You can count on me—

Dominic grasped her hand warmly.

#SANTOS: I always could. Vaya con Dios, mi Amiga.

Tears filled Sam's eyes at the thought that this might be the last time she would see her Commanding Officer. She patted his hand, then turned away, unable to bear more. While Dominic messaged Michaels, Sam updated Mansour. He was busy gearing up for war, along with Von Helm and Michaels, who had opened one smuggler wagon to pull forth a trio of handguns. Mansour passed a revolver, then a short AR-15 to Sam, who expertly tucked the weapons underneath her long coat. Michaels distributed a semi-automatic pistol to Mansour, and took one for himself.

As Michaels distributed weaponry, he looked over to see Evangelo tallying bullets in his bandoleer. "Do you need any additional weapons, Marshal?"

Evangelo shook his head and pulled back his suit jacket to reveal his rig—two silver revolvers on either side of his tooled leather halter and one on his waistband. "I have enough firepower—but six more rounds of .45 ammunition would be most welcome. I must be prepared to face a hail of bullets, as I intend to call the Cat to account for his crimes."

Sam grabbed Evangelo's sleeve. "Now, you hold on one minute—you can't just barrel in there and arrest him in front of God and everybody!"

"Yes I can—and yes, I will." Evangelo kept loading bullets.

"But you have someone waiting on you—someone who needs you!" Sam blurted. Mansour shushed her, holding up a finger to the sky.

In the shadow of the Elms, Evangelo stopped, and looked up at Sam. "I wouldn't be worthy of her waiting, were I not a man of my word—and my word is the Code. I must do my duty as a Ranger to defend the Code, and return with Honor." His eyes looked past her, into a memory, becoming misty silver in the faint moonlight: "Honor. Duty, Courage…"

"Integrity, Justice, Loyalty… Truth." A reverent voice spoke as Dominic stepped out of the shadows, speaking the words of Evangelo's Ranger Code. He smiled ruefully at his Protege. "And the Truth is, we need you alive, Hijo—"

"Understood. But I cannot be a Man of Honor and let his accusations go unanswered. Chartreaux's hidden sins must be brought to light. He accused us of the crimes he committed. This is an affront on the Honor of all who follow the Code, and I will not let it stand." His eyes flashed, an edge of steel.

Dismayed, Dominic answered. "It is a noble endeavor, but we have no additional manpower to spare." Undeterred, the Marshal kept loading bullets into his bandoleer.

"One Ranger is all that is needed."

Evangelo loaded one last bullet into his revolver and flipped the cylinder shut. "You yourself stated I am the last Ranger. If so, then I have an obligation to speak out on behalf of this villain's victims. Whether or not I live to take him in, all will know of his crimes. And live or die, I will return Honor to the name, 'Ranger'."

In the dying light of the campfire's coals, the assembled Survivors regarded Evangelo with admiration and fear: the last of his kind, the Believer in his Oath.

"Go ahead then, Ranger." Dominic clapped the little Marshal's shoulder with a resigned grace. "I will await your return with Honor."

"Thank you, friend. Tell her…" Evangelo reached up to clasp Dominic's hand. "tell Destiny I defend her Honor, even as I defend my own."

The assembly watched the Last Ranger stride away into the night.

Mansour cleared his throat roughly, then touched Sam's shoulder as she stared after Evangelo. "Do you need a moment?"

"No. I need to do my job." Not looking towards him, Sam wiped her eyes, and secured her weapon. "Let's go, Team—"

Leaning against her partner once more, Sam lead the way towards the LowTown Oak, Michaels trailing a distance behind the Constables. Watching them go with a heavy heart, Dominic dismissed a pensive Habib, who headed off to tally assets with the Gambler. For the moment, he was alone by the glimmering campfire.

He opened his HeadsUp display on his Ring, and checked into the Xirxes simulator one last time. In local host mode, he entered Private Chat Room Seven, and unlocked the digital door with an encrypted key. It creaked open realistically to reveal the holographic love nest he had so recently shared with Dr. Iyer, or as he preferred to call her, *Saisha, my plum*. A note materialized in his hand; kissing it, Dominic tucked it beneath an aromatically enhanced digital gardenia, laying both upon the velveteen dais where they last made simulated love.

It was never as good as the real thing. Dominic mulled, *but it was enough, just to hold you in my heart.* Should it all end tonight, she would know to look here…

His moment alone was ended by his Second in Command.

#VON HELM: The Brotherhood is ready when you are.

Sealing his virtual bower, Dominic stifled a cough, then reluctantly entered the real world once more.

#SANTOS: Carry on. All preparations are in place, now we await the rewards of our Treasure hunt, and the results of the Death Match. Go do your rounds, and report back to me with any changes.

"Oh," Suddenly remembering, Dominic pulled a small skeleton key from his pocket, and handed it to Von Helm.

#SANTOS: Brother Wolf has requested you deliver this key to our fine friend at the Booking Table; ask him to discreetly take this to less fortunate sheep such as himself who need to leave their pen when the trumpet sounds. They are to be added to our fold. Meet me back here for the commencement of festivities.

Von Helm scowled.

#VON HELM: This ain't a charity. It's one thing to liberate someone, it's another thing to take them in. Those Public Servants

are skinny, old, and are gonna be a hindrance.

Measured, Dominic answered back.

#SANTOS: Perhaps so; but you'll find a way to make them work. After all, you've always found a way to make even the most fragile of Hostesses fit in with the organization, Besides, it wasn't request—it was an order, direct from Brother Wolf.

Finished with the conversation, Dominic leaned against a tree, pretending to be working plans on his HeadsUp Display. Von Helm stood by, brooding, until at last Dominic asked:

#SANTOS: Now is not the time for mourning, but I share your loss—there will be a moment for grieving. Until then, let us settle our hearts on the mission ahead as retribution.

Von Helm became brusque.

#VON HELM: Understood—but that's not the issue. Permission to speak freely?

#SANTOS: Why the sudden formality? You know you always have permission to speak freely, Hijo—

Experienced in such matters, Dominic braced himself for the emotional torrent that usually follows such a request.

#VON HELM: Why not me?

Dominic pushed back his hat, and held out his hand, motioning for the little Macho to continue; Von Helm took a deep breath and looked to the Arena, where a Masked Man with a Lone Star Cape swaggered..

#VON HELM: I've been with you for nigh on thirty years—you called me your right hand man, like a son to you. And yet you told me nothing about your own Daughter, or your plans for this whole shebang.

A shadow of pain dimmed Dominic's eyes.

#SANTOS: Even I did not know of her until just the last few weeks—

#VON HELM: But why him? Why is he the one? Why not me?

Grunting in affirmation, Dominic crossed his arms beneath his poncho. He could feel Von Helm's tension boiling just beneath the surface.

#SANTOS: It stings, doesn't it? You have been there for me all these years; you have been rough and ready, giving everything I asked, and more. And yet, in time of your greatest trial, you have been denied this new role to play—one you feel could have made up

for your enormous loss and indescribable pain. You feel I should have given that role to you.

In deference to Von Helm's dignity, Dominic did not look directly at him, for he knew that unwanted emotions were steaming just below the facade. Jaw clenched, Von Helm listened...

#SANTOS: But she is not mine to give. She was already given to Brother Wolf by Another, the One who led her to him. She found him, and she chose him. That choice is not mine to undo.

#VON HELM: But he's not fit! He don't even want her—

Fists clenched, the little man was fighting an overwhelming sense of indignation.

#SANTOS: I believe you are wrong; but I will not be able to convince you of that. You are in a great deal of pain, and you are looking for someone to make it stop. She is someone new who would distract you from that pain; but that is not what the Author of this Tale has written for you. There will be others—

#VON HELM: It's not just that! He's just... he's not one of us, but he struts around as if he is—and you treat him like he's the Anointed One! What makes him so special? Why him? Why does he get the Girl, the recognition, the fame—"

Circumspect, Dominic gazed through steepled fingers.

#SANTOS: So this is not really about her, then. It's about him.

#VON HELM. Damn straight. Why him? Why not me?

He held out his hands to the sorrowing Dominic, begging for what he believed was rightfully his.

#SANTOS: Hijo, you know all I have is yours. Can you not rejoice that I have found what was lost to me? Can you not have the patience to see how your story will play out?

Dejected, Von Helm dropped his hands limply to his side, and turned away, dissatisfied.

#VON HELM: Alright, I'm done; I just couldn't die and leave it unsaid between us... and you've told me what you think.

Dominic placed an understanding hand upon Von Helm's broad shoulder.

#SANTOS: Trust me. There are plans for you that will give you a future and a hope—just be patient, and you will see. Now go, and prepare for your own future.

Beyond the low light of the coals, the sound of whispers and footsteps caught their ears. Weary of his own turmoil, Von Helm perked up.

#VON HELM: Gear up—some agitated folks are coming this way.

Two Survivors entered the clearing. "Begging your pardon Sir, but we have a special delivery". Through a brushy hedge, a scruffy Agent approached, heavy feed sack in his arms, whispering low. "You ain't gonna believe what hitched a ride in a sack of silage—" Dominic's face lit up with hope.

The scruffy man set down the bag, and bundles of dried corn husks erupted from the bag as a pert nose poked its way out. Dominic's face fell as the rest of Kendra's face peeked through the opening.

"Glad to see you, too…" Kendra hissed.

At the sound of her voice, Sampson roused, rubbing his eyes. "What?"

"No, no, it's just…" Dominic recovered his demeanor, "we weren't expecting your company, Brother Jay."

"Yeah, well I wasn't expecting my company either. I have an urgent message for the Gator."

Dominic nodded to the scruffy Agent, who hurried off with Von Helm to retrieve Habib and the Gambler.

"What?" Alarmed, Sampson jumped from his bedroll up to whisper into the feed sack. "How?"

"I stowed away in a handcart. I do it all the time—no sweat." The feed sack whispered back. "Now you—why are you wearing that ridiculous outfit?"

"You're not supposed to be here!" Sampson glared into the feed sack.

Dark eyes glared back through the corn husks. "Sez you. I have my reasons… now get me Brother Gator. I have to get back to my mission."

Sampson clutched at the sack "What mission?"

The scruffy Agent ducked back through the hedge, followed closely by the Habib, Gambler close behind him.

"Birds of a Feather…" Habib grunted, peering down into the bag. "Well, whatta ya got for me?"

"The Egret sent this private message for you…" a slender ivory hand passed a square of folded paper to Habib. At the sight of the Gambler, Kendra wondered: "Huh… I'm surprised to see you here instead at the betting tables. And just for the record… things can't go boom if someone forgets to put batteries in the remote."

"Preposterous!" Indignant, the Gambler's protested. "I would never forget such an important detail…"

"Ha! She says you forget that kinda crap all the time, Brainiac." Kendra tried to crawl out of the bag, but Sampson shoved her back in. She persisted: "You forgot to put the batteries in, and we don't know where any are—but she said she'd deal with it. While she's doing that, she asked me to bring this message to Gator. So what does it say?"

Habib looked up with glassy eyes, shaking his head in disbelief. "It says goodbye…"

The Gambler snatched the note from Habib's hand. He read it hurriedly, a note written in an elegant script:

> - *Gator* ~
>
> *Tell the Raven: since there's no other way to keep our secrets secret, I'll be the one to do the deed. Thanks for the wild ride…*
>
> ~ *Egret*
>
> P.S. *Spy vs Spy, Baby.*

"You've been had, you gullible little guttersnipe… " Incensed, the Gambler muttered low to Kendra: "The note was a ruse to send you away. She's planning to detonate the Bunker manually, but that won't leave time for her to get out alive…"

Habib bolted from the clearing.

"Oh, Hell naw—" Kendra gasped. "Not without me she doesn't." She started to wriggle her way out of the sack but was stopped by a big hand.

"Nope." Calm, Sampson stuffed Kendra back down into the sack again. "I outrank you again, and I say you're done. Gimme a piece of rope, Jack." The scruffy Agent reached into the back of a wagon and retrieved a short length of twine, and Sampson tied the burlap bag shut.

The feed sack hissed at him. "You've got no right!"

"Sorry, but you're gonna blow our cover running around."

"Excellent job bringing the message, Specialist. You are dismissed." Dominic patted the feed sack. "Brother Bear, you may resume your duty as guard." Satisfied with this order, Sampson threw the feed sack in his bedroll, then leaned back against it, using it for his pillow. The feed sack kicked him, and the Giant sighed, contented.

The Gambler hailed Dominic.

#ANON: I'll handle this inconvenient mess, you sound the signal to cue Brother Eagle—remember the plan.

He left without fanfare, hot on the trail of Habib.

Keeping a low profile, the Gambler darted through the trees, vigilant for any signs of followers. He considered using his active camouflage cloaking device, but like all tech, it had a limited life span, and its decaying components were wearing down. *Better to save it for when it's needed most.*

Current conditions were favorable for stealth—in the hubbub preceding the Death Match, men were moving quickly, trying to repair and prepare, so his movements didn't garner much attention. Likewise, Habib seemed to escape notice; without his familiar fedora and sports coat, no one recognized him in the dim light. Hugging the fence line, the Gambler followed in Habib's stealthy wake, until he caught up with the MoneyMan.

Up ahead, barely visible behind an old refrigerator, the Gambler noticed that the Dump Access fence panel had been dismantled and laid to the side. He wondered what they would have that was large enough to need the gate down.

He was fumbling around blindly for the door in the pitch black trash-canyons surrounding Bogie's Hut. Habib flicked out his knife, unsure of who was tailing him.

#ANON: It's me, you fool. Put your toy away or I'll be forced to neutralize you.

#HABIB: You and whose army?

#ANON: Mine. Now, move out of the way so I can get us inside.

Habib stepped away as the Gambler knelt to punch in the access code on the keypad beneath the doormat. They slipped inside, closing it up behind them. The Gambler then unlocked the hatch, and slid down the ladder, followed by Habib.

#ANON: Leave the hatch open for now, so you can leave quickly; The hatch keypad is rather touchy, and the Egret may not be cooperative.

As they crept down the corridor, they could hear the sound of someone rummaging though drawers. A soft, harried voice was murmuring: "No… no… dammit, BillDad, where is it?…" Lourdes' voice trailed off as she heard the sound of their footsteps.

#ANON: I suggest we stop here, or she will kill us. I'll make

contact; don't let her know you're here until I call you in. When you do talk to her, just whisper, and we should remain undetected by ALGOS this far down.

The Gambler softly tapped out the code on a metal wall. A tap answered back, then the sound of a round cycling into chamber of a shotgun. He grumbled: "That's the proper response, but not for me—put it away."

"How'd you find out I was here?" She grumbled back. "Never mind… where did you put the AA batteries?"

"We're out."

The Gambler stepped into the dimly lit living area. All around the room, components were missing, scavenged by Wilcox; the area was a shambles. Lourdes appeared from around the corner of a wall, a shotgun in hand. Her other hand was cradled in a fresh sling, rewrapped and made immobile.

"Well maybe if you stopped drinking like a fish, you could keep track of things. But if you want to die an early death from alcoholic dementia, then don't mind me…" she sniped. "not that you ever do."

"Impertinent as always, Lourdes. Since you are so busy telling me how to conduct myself, perhaps you'd care to share how you got here?"

"Stealth and insubordination." She continued to shuffle through drawers.

"So how do you intend to use all your wisdom to detonate the GOD Pod?"

"If you must know, I intended on using C4 and det cord if I couldn't find the batteries, but this place is a wreck, and I can't locate the key to locker, either." Lourdes replied coolly.

"C4 and det cord… that's brilliant, except for the part where you die. Is that part of your plan too?"

She looked perturbed. "It is if I can't find another way… there's no way I'm letting this tech fall into Chartreaux's slimy hands."

"Commendable. How'd you score this job?"

"Let's just say I heard Winston and Wilcox discussing logistical problems—and as you taught me, I recognized that one person's problems are another one's opportunities."

She gave that smug little smirk once more. "Your Catastronix Manual came just in the nick of time, but left none to spare. Wilcox and Winston went into the back workrooms to prepare the Mobile Jammer for loading into the Wagon they had secreted in the brush earlier. I took the opportunity to abscond with the remote and the girls, taking them out the access tunnel to the Jammer safe. Kendra knew the access code, so she was able to open it for us—and from there, we stole the horse with a brilliant plan in mind. We left instructions with Destiny that my team would do the job to blow up the tunnels as long as no one interfered with our getaway. Of course, Gunny had no objections, seeing as how he was all tied up."

"So I heard, Where is the rest of your team?"

"You'll find out. Thanks to Araceli's gift for pilfery, we acquired not only the supplies for a perfect ruse—we also gained a pelt plus a multitool in the process. That was fortunate, since we needed the multitool to make a quick access for a horse. That fence panel wasn't going to remove itself." She wrinkled her nose at the Gambler. "But I stupidly left without making sure YOU had done YOUR job. How could you forget to put in batteries?"

"Save your haranguing for later." The Gambler glowered. "Move on to finding a solution. If you are going to get your lures for the ALGOS into position, we need to hurry—time is running out."

Irritated at his condescending tone, Lourdes chided: "Consider yourself complicit; you could have avoided all this trouble by sending the Technical Manual for the Catastronix device earlier. Why didn't you?"

"I had to write it first." The Gambler studied Lourdes. "But enough second guessing every move I make. What of Habib?"

In the darkness, the MoneyMan blinked, surprised at the mention of his name.

"He's still in love with Sam. Frank's never going to get over her... I know that now. I offered myself to him, and he turned me down." Lourdes sniffed. "I'm not Araceli; I'm not spending the rest of my life hoping he changes his mind. I've sent Habib a farewell note via Kendra, and if for some reason he manages to stop mooning over Sam long enough to think of me, he'll be locked out, forever unable to forget my heroic demise. Besides, the rat detained me for spying, then left me behind, and I intend to prove he can't just walk away from me like that."

"That'll show him." The Gambler said dryly. "I realize there's no trying to convince you otherwise; it's clear you've made up your mind, and that's your right to choose your own fate,"

"Really?" Lourdes appeared slightly crestfallen at this supportive pronouncement. "Oh—I hadn't expected you to be so egalitarian."

"Absolutely. In deference to your self-determination, allow me to help you get this detonation done. A fireball might be just the thing that's needed; there's a key to the explosives locker hidden beneath the sofa, if you care to search it. You'll need to hurry, as I have business to attend."

"Business… business… it's always business with you people," Lourdes muttered. Laying her shotgun to the side, she knelt down to look under the couch. Sweeping her good arm side to side under the low sofa, she peered beneath it. "I can't see anything up under here—where exactly is this key?"

"The same place as your shotgun…" The Gambler snorted as Lourdes looked up. "In my hands."

"You thieving liar—give it back!" She scrambled to get up.

Gun trained on Lourdes, the HighRoller called over his shoulder into the shadows. "That would be your cue, Accountant."

Habib tipped his cowboy hat as he walked out of the darkness. "Hiya, Chickie."

"Oh this is rich—both of you are in cahoots now. Perfect." She glowered at them icily. "I suppose we might as well get this over with." She turned her back on Habib to confront the Gambler. "Since you're so smart, I imagine you have a better way blow this Bunker?"

"In all probability, yes. But if I can't find an alternative, your plan will do." The Gambler waved to Habib. "Habib, get her out of here."

The MoneyMan grabbed Lourdes by the wrist and pulled her with him into the corridor. "Wait—no! You can't do that!" Shocked, Lourdes tried to twist out of Habib's grasp. "Frank, don't let him; the Revolution can't survive without him!"

"That's very flattering." Preoccupied, the Gambler mulled over his options. "But the truth is, we are all expendable. Now, if you'd like me to have a chance at surviving this blast, leave the doors open on your way out, and get ready to evacuate the Hostesses. Lourdes, once you get clear of the gate, you know where to go. Get them there."

Lourdes was fighting Habib, struggling to pull free as she strained to keep her voice low. Desperate, she hissed at the Gambler. "What about Her? What am I supposed to tell Her?"

The Gambler gave Lourdes a lingering look, and for a fleeting moment, his face teetered on the edge of almost tenderness—"Tell Her I'll see Her in the stars…" His coarse, aquiline features became arrogant once more. "Game on."

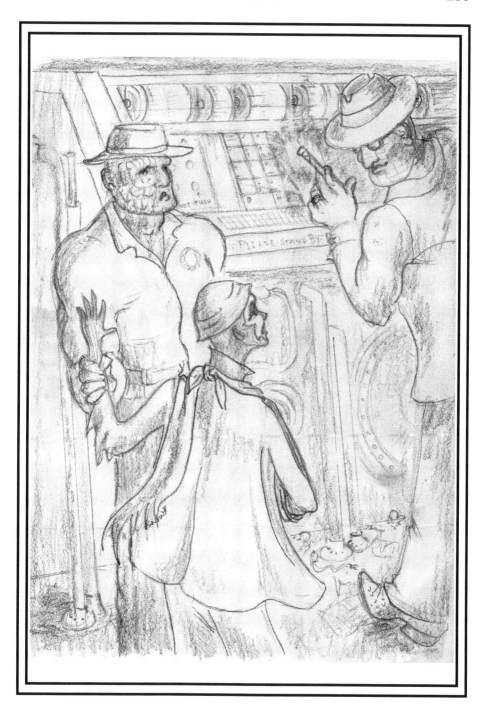

The Wall flashed down, cutting them off. "No!" Livid, Lourdes beat on the wall with her one good hand. "Dad…"

Grasping Lourdes' wrist, a grim Habib hauled her down the corridor, back towards Bogie's Hut and into the mayhem of Purgatory.

A timid knock came at the door. Chartreaux lifted the massive timber which barred the door, and it opened to reveal a trembling BrigadesMan flanked by two newly-minted Enforcers. Chartreaux barked: "Make it quick."

The BrigadesMan swallowed hard. "The Jail is locked. We can't make entry, and when we looked through the bars, it appears to be abandoned…" He looked towards a shocked Shaney, hoping for mercy,

"…and the prisoners are gone."

"My prisoners? All of them?" Shaney's eyes glimmered with tears, mist before a gathering storm.

Chartreaux grabbed the terrified BrigadesMan by the collar, lifting him from his feet. With two strides, the Boss hauled him through the french doors, and held him at arm's length, dangling the helpless man off the Balcony. A collective gasp was heard from the crowd far below. Chartreaux snarled quietly:

"You have failed."

Struggling to breathe, the BrigadesMan nodded; Chartreaux shook him, and the man flailed like a rag doll in the Boss' brutal grasp. "This incompetence will end. A change in management is underway—"

Face distorted, tongue protruding, the BrigadesMan was red, grotesque in his suffering and terror. Shaney leaned forward in interest as the Survivor gaped, trying to breathe, suffocating. She finally whispered: "I think they're ready to listen, Reggie."

Chartreaux flung the BrigadesMan off the Balcony.

Broken, the hapless BrigadesMan pinwheeled down to the Courtyard. A shout for a medic arose, and the sounds of fear were heard once more from the Citizens of Purgatory. Unnerved at this display of merciless strength, Shaney's men backed away.

"I will only lay this out once. Take notes." Chartreaux turned to Shaney's shaken men. "You will use this upcoming fight as cover to discretely target persons of interest—Lord Li, Lord Sliwa, and any

WildLand Express personnel that can be found alone and apart. Surround the Fighter. Do not attempt to take them until the fight is underway, and do not alert their compatriots. These men will be used as hostages to compel their peers to submit. We don't have the manpower to take down the entire WildLand Express—and I am now down one more."

At the thought of his losses, the Big Boss's voice became quiet, but his eyes glowed red with rage. "His sacrifice will not be in vain—let his memory live as an example of incompetence. Now go."

Wyatt crept a glance to Shaney, uncertain.

"Well, go on, Wyatt, we don't have all day."

Wyatt stammered."Y-yes, Commander, right away—" Scrambling, the unit beat a hasty retreat, a bemused Shaney observed Chartreaux with growing interest.

"Hmm. I gotta hand it to you, Reggie—your Leadership style sure is handy."

"Size matters." Chartreaux smoothed his ascot.

Waving a languid hand towards the Jail, he schemed. "Now Commandant Generales must be dealt with. This is Insurrection, but we will say nothing to Generales about this development. I've sold our New Alliance to James as a way to bring everything in the Co-op completely into System Compliance, and bypass the Consortium's insufferable insistence on Outlaw autonomy. But our ability to control Purgatory must be beyond question, or James will annihilate us—and once word reaches the Consortium of our outreach to James, they with attempt to depose us unless we depose them first."

"Well, how do we know the Consortium isn't behind this whole shootin' match now?" Sick again, Shaney pulled off her hat to fan herself, exposing her sleek, perfectly shaped head atop a graceful neck traced with fine, rose-gold scales.

"It's entirely possible. That would explain Azarian's presence—the Consortium always had an interest in him, even after Judge Leona laid claim to him. If he survives this Death Match, perhaps Leona's mute brute can be persuaded to reveal something about those who have brought him on board. But if he doesn't, no matter—I will make Azarian an example to other would-be rebels." Chartreaux gazed out over the city. "Imagine Azarian armless, legless and impaled—a living warning, wailing above the Gate of Purgatory…"

Chartreaux waited patiently as Shaney struggled with another heaving round of illness, then resumed his thought: "Insurrection is a snake; to stop it, we have to crush the head. That Head will be cunning, motivational, and dedicated…"

"Chief Emmanuel? We keep seeing him, but never finding him…" Shaney's keen eyes narrowed,

"That's because Emmanuel was never here in the first place. It was all an elaborate misdirection, a sleight of hand from a master Magician—the kind of Magician that can make a man appear or disappear into thin air." Brooding, the Boss rubbed his chin. "As brilliant and dangerous as Azarian is, he is not the mastermind behind this plot. There's only one man in the Tejas Co-operative capable of creating such an elaborate scheme to overthrow the System—and make a seemingly impossible Jailbreak while doing so…"

Exasperated, Shaney lifted her head from the bucket:

"Dominic."

———◆———

Dominic…

Winston watched as a blue pancho'd figure disappeared into the far tree line behind the Campground. *Dominic's in motion, and any minute now all Hell will break loose.*

From his perch atop the Gate's parapets embedded with the Insertion Team, Winston could view a fair chunk of the Main Drag, The view extended to the Hanging Tree, with its long branch overhanging the Pair'O'Dice fence, and the noose which dangled, waiting for him.

Not today, boys, Winston smirked to himself.

Winston wondered how the other Ultimates in the Consortium were going to take the news of Chartreaux's coup against him. *Probably the same way the Ultimates are going to take the news about me helping start a rebellion without them,* he thought grimly—with fire and fury. The Consortium might not have drones yet, Winston mused, but they had other options that were every bit as deadly. He kept a wary eye on his surroundings…

Behind him in the corral, he observed the Mobile Electronic Warfare Unit. Thanks to the Gambler's tech manual, the Catastronix Mobile Jammer's access panel had finally been unlocked; fortunately, the factory default admin password had never been reset. On the way out, the mysterious device was uprooted and hidden in Shadow's smuggler Wagon.

Shadow pranced, nervous and ready to roll, with all his equine compatriots safely stowed in the now-liberated Corral. Hidden in wagon's secret hold was the Jammer, with a slightly-addled and injured Destiny. She was still traumatized from her attack, but hiding in the cart seemed to make her feel better.

Winston frowned at the abuse of his Hostesses, and silently vowed revenge. It wasn't just Destiny, although she was the most egregiously wounded; Lourdes had been manhandled, and Araceli had received that nasty gash on her sleek, rounded thigh… he turned slightly green at the thought. Winston wasn't sure why the sight of her blood affected him so —he had rendered first aid to hundreds of patients at Purgatory, so why this queasiness at Araceli's wound?

Winston decided to not think about it. *Think about something else, anything else…*

Where to set himself up as a lure for the ALGOS?

Just inside the gate, Winston spied an enormous Bois D'Arc stump in the Commons area next to the Pair O'Dice fence… *set up a shooting position there*. Winston made the executive decision that he would be the Lure to bring up the ALGOS. It was risky, but brass cojones would be required for this operation, and his own cojones were the only ones he was willing to risk.

He gave a rueful chuckle; he had no doubt his mother would be proud —it sounded like something a Trung would do. Mother had always been vocal about her family's history as warriors in Vietnam, and equally proud of her Houston, Texas Heritage. True to his roots, Winston kept watch over his territory, looking for any sign of trouble. What he couldn't see was any sign of his mutinous Hostesses.

There was plenty of other action. A mixed group of Rangers and BrigadesMen was riding from tree to tree down by LowTown; Agent Michaels was conferring with what appeared to be a pair of drunken Survivors, and Marshal Azarian was pacing with Joey down by the Arena —but Winston saw no Hostesses.

No Araceli.

Beyond Joey, he could see Von Helm lurking down by the gate of the Campground, waiting for his signal. Winston subtly snarled; the Sheriff's presence was an odious reminder of their first encounter. As the Number Three Ultimate for the Consortium, Winston had been working undercover and was on the lam from Araceli's former LandLord when they both stumbled into Von Helm's Camp. Welcomed, then challenged by Von Helm, Winston decided to fight…

it didn't end well.

Von Helm landed a sidekick, and Winston slammed to the dirt with a loud 'crack'. Cradling his broken arm, Winston rose to fight again, only to see a sobbing Araceli on her knees before Von Helm, her hands on his boots, offering her shirtless, smiling Victor anything he desired, if only he would stop the fight…

Anything.

Declaring victory, Von Helm magnanimously offered Winston a position as Agent with the WildLand Express, saying he was impressed by the tall man's persistence. Winston had no choice but to reject Von Helm's offer of Agency; his dangerous covert assignment at Purgatory demanded Winston turn down all other offers. But he did have a choice to make regarding Araceli—

Winston walked away.

He left Araceli with the WildLand Express, saying she had chosen her Winner. Then Winston bandaged his own wounds and went his own way, leaving behind a weeping Araceli and the failure she represented.

His fury at that memory was mitigated by present reality. The Watcher's long-overdue serving of humble pie to Carlos Von Helm was bittersweet for Winston, tainted by the horror of Camp Forlorn's demise. Now Von Helm and Winston were on the same team, just fighting to stay alive. An itch crept up inside Winston, a need to know that everyone was safe. Where were the Hostesses? Where was…

It bothered him that she was bothering him.

Usually when Araceli was out of sight, she was out of mind. Of course, she was always out of sight in a secure area where Winston left her. Whether she was left behind in the able company of an entire horde of sworn agents at Camp Forlorn, or later ensconced in the walled garden of the Hostess Club, Araceli had always been in a safe, Winston-approved zone…

Leaving her behind with the WildLand Express was the best choice at the time, Winston justified; before Purgatory was a Hell of a Town, it was just Hell.

Winston made it a Town.

Anointed by the Consortium to take Boss Diego's place, Winston immersed himself in the taming of Purgatory and when it came time to retire Old Diego, he did it graciously and efficiently. That task aside, he proceeded to make the Purgatory a haven for Survivors—and one particular Survivor came to mind.

Araceli flared up in Winston's dreams. He doused her with the cold memory of Camp Forlorn, only to see her to rekindle the next night. Tormented by his own obsession-rejection of Araceli, Winston troubleshot his emotions, then engineered an ingenious solution to deny Von Helm the victory and allow himself to see Araceli's light without feeling her heat:

Winston would contain Araceli's flame within the Gilded Lantern of Purgatory's Hostess Club.

He worked hard to make that dream a reality. As soon as Purgatory's fence was secured and sanitation was installed, Winston demanded Von Helm remand Araceli to the newly fortified Hostess Club. Von Helm was forced to comply with that request if the WildLand Express wanted to do business with the biggest town in the Tejas Co-operative; Winston was now Number One Boss at Purgatory.

Araceli's move to Purgatory was for her own safety, Winston reminded himself; the weekly updates from Camp Forlorn were just not enough to keep him from wondering about her welfare in that rough camp. But with her relocation to Purgatory's newly refurbished Hostess Club, Winston saw her lovely face; relenting his anger, he considered opening his arms to her once more. That idea was crushed when Mansour informed Winston that Araceli was now a Specialist with the WildLand Express, recruited by Von Helm himself to embed as a spy in the heart of Winston's territory—Purgatory.

Winston let his displeasure be known. As was his right as Boss and Ultimate, Winston partook of the Hostesses' charms, but he never called for Araceli. When finally asked why by a puzzled Sam, he simply told her to ask Von Helm.

Well, Sam can waltz on down to the Campground and ask Von Helm in person now. Winston wondered if the little Sheriff's presence had anything to do with Araceli's current rebellious state. It was possible she was seeking his attention as well—with the Afterling in his sights, Von Helm no longer seemed interested in Araceli. *Just as well.*

A fierce annoyance consumed him at the thought of her mutinous behavior; it was in character for Lourdes or Kendra—but Araceli? He shook his head. *She's out of control, unhinged by our final encounter.* That was the only logical explanation for her defiance of Winston's command, and for her ardent embrace of that moonie little cowboy, Agent Montague.

A sneer crept to his face, but he reeled it back. This was an obvious and laughable attempt on Araceli's part to induce jealousy, but Winston knew it would predictably end in tears and heartache for the scheming little seductress. *Montague will make promises, make love, then ride off into the sunset, just like any good cowboy should.* Araceli would then morph back into her usual self; crying, making origami animals, and telling stories for the entertainment of all.

For some reason, this tragic ending to Araceli's ridiculous rodeo romance made Winston feel better. Maybe then she would give back the prize she had stolen from him. He grumbled at the thought… she had given back his stolen compass, only to pickpocket his beloved Wunder-Man Miniature Action Figure from his chest pocket. Mint in its minuscule box, it was the only present Winston had ever kept from Araceli; he liked the fact that she said he reminded her of the invincible Wunder-Man.

The action figure was much like the one Father bought him for his sixth birthday, before the old man left to go back to his third consort and her new baby. Tiny arms akimbo, signature 'W' on his chest beneath a plastic three-piece suit, Araceli's Wunder-Man differed in that he came with the highly coveted "Slide Rule Of Reality"—an ancient object of great power that fit neatly into Wunder-Man's patented Action-Grip, allowing him to engineer circumstances any way he saw fit. Winston hummed the theme song to himself;

Wunder-Man, Wunder-Man,

Everywhere, Everytime, Wunder-Man!

He's the Man with the Plan—

the Amazing, Sublime

Wunder-Man!

Father told him it was a collectible, and like all good gifts, to never take it out of its box. But the young Winston took it out to admire it, and accidentally flushed it down the toilet.

He never saw it—or his Old Man—again.

Winston absentmindedly felt of his pocket, and noted the empty space next to his Father's compass, the place Araceli's Wunder-Man had resided—until… Winston frowned again. That would all end soon enough.

He was going to get all his toys back.

Still, schadenfreude at Araceli's inevitable lost romance didn't stop the nagging anxiety Winston felt, not knowing to where she had fled with his prized toy, or even if she were still alive. He lowered the binoculars and messaged Wilcox Ring-2-Ring:

#WINSTON: Any word about you know who?

#WILCOX: For the ninth time, no. Look, I'll tell you if I hear anything; between you and this chatty pink one asking questions, I hardly have time to think.

Behind Wilcox, Destiny blinked out of the dark hold of the smuggler wagon. Wilcox had put her in charge of listening for the faint, high-pitched hum that indicated the jammer was activated; in the event in the ALGOS were attempting to hack it, the hum would modulate with the interfering frequency, changing pitch.

#WILCOX: But in other news, I do get a good, clear signal for the general beacon server—Brother Crow has released the hounds, and they have found a safe position away outside the interference radius. We can broadcast live when the cue is given.

#WINSTON: Great news—send word to Brother Fox that we are ready, and prepare for the end game. He's to sound the signal when we crank up.

Gunny's suggestion to tie the beacon server around Oskar's neck was homespun genius. It was remarkable how easily Gunny had been able to establish communications with the cub Ring-2-Ring, and the intelligent creature was able to be trained quickly without audible commands.

With the Chupacabra on a long chain, Gunny took Oskar with Sassy to a tree at the far of the corral, and allowed the cub to climb in the branches, outside the range of the jammer signal. This allowed the server beacon Oskar carried to act as a digital repeater from a higher point, and also allowed Gunny to take his beloved Sassy out of harm's way near the gate. The old Soldier simply couldn't bear the thought of any harm coming to his cherished bloodhound.

Winston grunted smugly to himself. He *probably feels the same about Sassy as I feel about Araceli.*

His face fell in a sudden, freudian shock as the words echoed through his hollow heart:

…I feel about Araceli…

I feel…

The fiery abyss opened before him.

Winston wavered on the knife's edge between oblivion and obsession. The familiar blistering heat of her flame returned, and Winston grabbed his chest: *damn it all to hell.* Now was not the time for a mental breakdown. Every thought was being engulfed by Araceli, just like it was before he forced himself to leave her behind at Camp Forlorn—

she was taking over his mind again. There could be no safe handling, there could be no controlled burn; any contact with Araceli lit an all-consuming fire in the tinder-dry forest of Winston's dead emotion. He stamped out what he could, and made himself think of the battle ahead, putting the binoculars to his eyes once more.

A commotion was rolling up the road from LowTown: "Get ready—" Winston turned to his Rebels manning the gates. "LoneStar Libre's opponent is headed his way."

———◆———

VII

———◆———

In the midst of the maelstrom, the Watcher centered himself, the calm eye of the mob's storm. All around him, outer voices assailed:

"You're gonna die!"

"Nobody's beaten the Executioner, nobody—"

"It was a set-up! It's how they execute people here!"

"You shoulda just given Chartreaux the Mask, and walked away…"

Cracking his knuckles beneath the thin, fingerless gloves, the Watcher felt the Ring. *Her life is in here… her memories…*

he opened his HeadsUp display and swiped up to his favorites file; a holograph popped up, Rose frozen in split second of time, on endless loop. Beneath forever stars, the small golden woman knelt in the craggy palm of the Watcher's red hand, her lips pressed to Oskar's warty chupacabra ear:

"I love you."

It mattered not that the Watcher could not feel love for Rose; radiating through her recorded words, he still could feel her love for Oskar, and it was an amazement to him, the purity of that alien emotion… inexplicably, her voice crept through his neural pathways, lighting a trail of warmth through the coldness, vining into the dusty cracks of his soul.

Hada Pequeña—how do you do this to me?

He forgave himself the voyeurism; the borrowed moment was the closest he had felt to love since Mother, and he allowed it to seep into his heart. The Watcher held them in the palm of his hand, watching the tiny pair, the cub's eyes squinched shut in bliss as Rose whispered again and again:

"I love you."

He felt her welling up inside of him—the reason to fight... *the reason to win.* Would that reason die tonight? Suddenly fierce, he closed his fingers protectively around the image.

Unbidden, Miyamoto Musashi chided him from the depths of his inner Dojo:

> *"The only reason a Warrior is alive is to fight, and the only reason a Warrior fights is to win."*

Conflicted, the Watcher realized that Dominic's assertion—that Rose was his reason to fight and win—clashed with Musashi's advice of 'live to fight—fight to win..."

> *"Do not let yourself be guided by the feeling of lust or love."*

Musashi had never failed him in his life's path; he could not afford to be distracted now, even in philosophical realms. Relenting, the Watcher swiped, and the image of Rose slipped through his fingers. Musashi exhorted:

> *"Everything is within. Everything exists. Seek nothing outside of yourself."*

To ensure his survival, and hers, the Watcher had to turn away from Rose completely, and turn into himself. Focus would win this battle; twice ten thousand days of training had led to this place, where more than just a prison camp depended on his survival: Humanity itself could only live if he lived.

Humanity was out there, perched in a tree, calling to him; he needed to ignore her to save her.

Beyond the throng of onlookers, the Watcher could feel footsteps beyond the crowd's edge, boots in the dirt, coming down the hill from LowTown. Synchronized steps surrounded a heavier step, a cadence of muscle and bone syncopated with a gravity that obscured all others. There was a bounce to each heavy step, a confidence that indicated a much larger opponent, one with the physical prowess to match his confidence. As the footsteps drew closer, a deep, rumbling voice could be heard bellowing through the sharp howls of the mob.

"Your Executioner comes, LoneStar Libre!"

The Watcher breathed deeply, inhaling the essence of alcohol, addiction and men; the sharp scent of fear and bloodlust filled his nostrils, and it gave him a sense of peace. He heard Joey whisper from behind him, in awe.

"It's time."

Opening his eyes, the Watcher saw a bald head bobbing above the crowd, scaled and covered in scars. The Opponent and his entourage stopped just out of sight, behind the bandstand, where he was surrounded by his own fans.

Every eye now turned to the Silo and its reinforced metal Balcony. On this platform, high above the unwashed masses, Boss Chartreaux appeared, leading his fragile, glittering Commander Shaney. She waved to the fighters, then smiled at the Watcher and winked. He felt an unwelcome blush wash over him.

Resplendent with his ball-tipped cane and swathed in a billowing khaki duster to ward off the evening's chill, the Boss resembled a monumental wizard. Chartreaux swept his humongous arms wide.

"Welcome to Purgatory Death Match!"

The Arena shook with the crowd's frenzy. Faces leered from every side, lusting for death, but not their own... only the somber expressions of his fellow rebels and the wan faces of the Public Servants reminded him that there were those in the audience who earnestly hoped for his survival. Was a Little Bird watching, hidden among them?

The Watcher looked to his equipment, in place next to the Arena: He had divested himself of his Bowie Knife, as he was unwilling to take the chance that any weapons might be confiscated before the fight. Joey was juggling the shopping bag, filled with the Watcher's weapons and items from the Emporium, plus the car door the Watcher had scavenged earlier...

All in due time.

Mr. Megaphone stepped into the clearing, coattails flapping in the chilly breeze. "Good evening, High Rollers and High Ballers! It's the moment you've been waiting for—Purgatory Death Match!

Wild cheers shook the Arena. The Watcher stood and flung back his cloak, slapping his chest and limbering up.

"Let's meet our Fighters…" He pointed to the Watcher:

"In this corner, weighing in at approximately two-hundred and ninety pounds, and six feet tall, hailing from parts unknown—one part WildLand Wolf and two parts Texas Tornado, the Mysterious Masked Macho: LoneStar Libre!"

The Watcher opened his arms to the crowd, spreading the Lone Star Flag Cape behind him. Beneath the brim of his black oilskin hat, the golden eyes of his hood gleamed in the light of a hundred lanterns. The Watcher flexed every muscle, reveling in the virility flowing through every fibre….

Shouts rattled the trees, echoing from the far deeps of the Lake. On the borders of the Commons, the old Public Servant held up his shackles and shook them, shouting…

"LoneStar Libre!"

Survivors jumped to their feet, roaring it back. Infectious, the Servant's cry passed man to man, waving their fists—

"Libre! LoneStar Libre!"

Vicious, the Guard gave the old man a swift kick to the shin, and the Public Servant went down, clutching his leg.

Lunging to the rails, the Watcher roared, grabbing his own chain to shake it in answer to the old man's war cry. He pointed to the beefy Guard, and roared again. No words were needed—the message was loud and clear. LandLords slid down in their seats, uncomfortable with the prospect of LoneStar Libre as a free man.

The Watcher checked the chain… the prop was set to break away if grabbed, so he didn't have concern for it being used to choke him—but he was concerned about his personal jamming device being torn off. Unwilling to remove the jammer with drones hovering overhead, he reached up and discretely tucked his bandana and hidden jammer beneath the stretchy neck of his mask for safekeeping.

A tiny crumb of dirt fell out of the bandana into his hand, soil from Rose's little Flower. He thought of the Child, and of the bloody scene about to take place. He waved a brief farewell to the unseen waif: *Go to your Mother, little Child. Stay with your Mother…*

"And in this corner—"

A behemoth stepped from the back of the Bandstand, accompanied by four guards.

"Weighing in at approximately three-hundred and seventy-five pounds, measuring six feet, eight inches tall—"

Cracked, oozing plates of gunmetal-grey skin formed a leathery helmet, encasing a skull dominated by heavy brow-ridges and a bony jaw. A lumpy, cap-topped head topped a pyramidal neck, sloping down to bulging deltoids and rippling biceps. Stripping off a grey flannel shirt, the fighter exposed a barrel chest protected by rock-hard pectorals; a narrow waist and trim hips topped well-muscled, long legs, clad in leather chaps and steel-toed work boots. Suddenly Evangelo's soft, tire-tread soled moccasin-boots seemed less than adequate to the Watcher.

"He's the Killer Driller from Katy, the undefeated Champion of Purgatory—"

The opponent whipped out a couple of jabs, demonstrating his reach and lethal speed. *Reach*—that was the key. But that trait alone didn't explain why was this man was undefeated...

"All Hail the EastLake Executioner—Jip McMasters!"

Jip McMasters—the man who kidnapped Destiny and murdered Boss Zhu at the order of Boss Chartreaux. Hot anticipation filled the Watcher; this was a man who needed killing.

Pounding his chest and bellowing, Jip entered the Arena: the crowd whooped, and he whooped back.

"Time to Purge Purgatory!" Applause and laughter greeting this declaration from Jip's fans. He swept off his gimme cap and held it over his heart with great mock solemnity. "I dedicate this fight to my next victim, the chunk of ground beef formerly known as 'LoneStar Libre'."

The audience clapped, and Jip chuckled, tossing his hat into the crowd.

"Alright, listen up—" Mr. Megaphone called from outside the Ring: "these are the rules of Purgatory Death Match: No rests, no rounds, no holds barred. No weapons, no whining, no mercy. Last Man living is the Winner. Any questions?"

"Yeah... you got a will, LoneStar?" Jip laughed, and the crowd laughed with him. The Watcher growled.

"Teams, prep your Fighters."

Joey handed the Watcher a bottle of water; the Watcher sniffed it, then took a tentative sip, testing it for any unwanted additives before taking a swig. Finding it clean, he drank it, then handed the empty bottle back to the Joey with a pat on the back.

In the opposite corner, a rangy old Hombre wrapped Jip's hands in cotton strips, as Jip surreptitiously slipped what appeared to be rough-edged brass knuckles onto his right hand. "Hey!" Joey hollered: "He's got knucks—"

Chartreaux glowered from the Balcony. "Jip, do you have brass knuckles?"

Jip spat and shook his head as one of his managers gave him a shot glass of Brew; the Opponent downed it in one swallow, grimaced, then wiped his mouth. "I swear." He grinned at the Watcher, revealing jagged, broken teeth.

"There you have it." The big Boss waved a dismissive hand. "I applaud your honesty, Executioner. Carry on."

Gleeful, Jip's Guard laid down the gear bag to pull forth a length of rubber tubing, an empty syringe, and a full vial of amber liquid. Another man retrieved a Budweed cigarette, and lit it for the fighter, placing it between Jip's lips. The Executioner leaned his head back and sucked in a great breath between clenched teeth as the BridageMan injected the Stuff into Jip's left arm…

A cold sweat broke out beneath the Watcher's mask.

"Oh! Pardon our inhospitality—" Shaney warbled from the Balcony, a beatific smile on her lips; "don't be rude, gentlemen; offer our guest a chance to partake. You would like some, wouldn't you, LoneStar Libre? It's a tradition here at Purgatory, to use it before fights. I heard there's nothing as sweet as the taste of the Stuff…"

Her voice sounded like the voice of angels. Rattled, the Watcher shook his head.

"That's a pity—you should be more respectful of Purgatory Tradition." Shaney chided the Fighter, and a rapt Purgatory listened.

"The Stuff is a potion of unparalleled power. I'm sure you know it gives a man strength and speed—something you might need in this fight. They say it's a secret recipe, crafted by the ol' Witchy Woman of Reunion to save the man she called son, when he went afoul of the System."

Still pale, Shaney leaned against the rail of the Balcony, her spangled western shirt open to her waist, high, hard cleavage glittering in the lamplight. "Legend has it she sold the recipe to Judge Leona of Reunion as a ransom for the man's life—but in the end, all her love meant nothing to him. He ran away, and left that Witchy Woman behind to take the punishment meant for him!"

At this dramatic pronouncement, a shocked hush fell on the crowd. A drunken Survivor muttered, indignant: "That ain't right..."

The Watcher's hand involuntarily twitched, and Shaney saw it; a brief, victorious smirk flicked across her full lips, before she caught herself. She cast her disapproving stare at him, shaking her head. "For shame... what sort of man lets another die for his own sin?"

Her eyes snared his through the veil.

This is all my fault.

The Watcher's heart began to race as the old familiar guilt came rushing back. He flung it away, and clung to the mantra his mentors taught him when the night terrors came. *I didn't kill my Mother.* He breathed out, and added a new line to the mantra: *I didn't kill Abuelita...*

It hit him with a jolt. *No, Sentinel Montel killed Abuelita.*

And in a rush of guilt, the Watcher's only real friend, Montel, had killed himself. An unexpected tsunami of hopelessness and anger swept over the Watcher—the injustice of being robbed of both his adopted grandmother and his friend, both killed by the same hand.

"Poor, abandoned Abuelita." Chartreaux wagged his jowls: "But even if she is not remembered by the heartless fool who abandoned her, we honor her memory here at Purgatory. Every time we partake of these gifts, we remember this poor Public Servant woman. We owe her for far more than just this glorious potion—the Witchy Woman of Reunion also created Reunion Brew and its successor, Reunion's Finest."

The Boss swept a hand across the ocean of debauched faces surrounding the Silo. "Every vial, every bottle in the Tejas Co-operative is the work of her hands. But none of this would have existed were it not for that ungrateful bastard she called 'Son'... the Watcher of Reunion."

Tongues wagged, the judgement of sinners on one of their own.

Behind his mask, the Watcher's mind raced. *All this madness is because of me...*

Musashi spoke from the inner Dojo once more:

"Do not regret what you have done."

The Watcher steeled himself. *This is a psy-op;* not only a means of taunting him, these psychological attacks were an attempt to create a narrative and turn the crowd—and himself—against the Watcher. An epiphany sparked in the Watcher's mind: overwhelming guilt led Montel to kill himself, robbing the world of his goodness. The best way to honor

Montel's memory would be to deny guilt another victory. He just had to stay centered…

"Surely as a last act of penance you should join us in honoring Abuelita's memory, LoneStar…" Chartreaux's words rolled, an unstoppable wave of celebratory condemnation. The big Boss waved his arm, and Sugar stepped forward to the Arena, a silver-plated jewelry box in his hands. The attendant opened the lid, revealing a gleaming syringe of sweet golden poison, needle glinting against black velvet in the firelight.

Shaney leered above him. "Go on… take it." She licked her blood-red lips.

The Craving rolled over him, brutal and swift—*so close*—

From far and away, the song of his Sparrow called to him, begging to be heard.

tsees… tsees…

He heard it again, louder this time, insistent in her call, and his heart answered back, a shaft of light piercing his spiritual fog:

my Little Bird is watching.

With an abrupt fury, the Watcher slapped the box out of Sugar's grasp.

Shaney's leer twisted into disbelief as the crowd scrambled for the loaded syringe, trampling it into the dirt. Cheers turned to groans as a LandLord held up the broken syringe, the drug trickling away into the mud beneath their feet.

The Watcher roared a Victory, one only he could truly understand—

Chartreaux grumbled: "You have chosen, LoneStar Libre—and like all your other choices, it is a bad one. Die with your choice."

"You can do this." Joey muttered under his breath: "You don't need no drug… but I'm trying out that prayer thing, just in case." Taking the Cape from the Watcher's shoulders, the Promoter suddenly snapped it, unfurling it to let it fly as he strode out of the Ring:

"LoneStar Libre!" Anxious applause rose from the back of the crowd; Joey stepped out of the Arena and took his seat under the watchful eye of his Guard.

A hush fell over Purgatory as the Boss raised his ball-topped wooden cane, Shaney leaning against his shoulder with casual ease. With Purgatory at his feet and KingMaker by his side, Chartreaux exuded a raw power found only in those who take power from others. He pointed his rough wand at the Watcher.

"Before we begin, I'd like to propose a toast to the Prize—Life." Shaney handed the Boss a glass of Reunion's Finest, the golden corn liquor first brewed by Abuelita… "LoneStar Libre, I believe you may be the only Man left in the WildLand who will appreciate the fact that my structured blank verse is not yet another tired example of rhyming iambic pentameter." Chartreaux raised his glass:

"Here's to Her—green, glimmering Life; the hope of all Humanity—" the Watcher froze as Chartreaux mesmerized the crowd with his melting patois: "the glowing prize of the Winner, and the dream denied to the Damned."

Green, glimmering Life—A sick realization descended on the Watcher.

"I will savor Life in your stead, 'LoneStar'." Chartreaux raised the goblet of golden liquor to his turgid lips.

…they found Rose

A savage growl erupted from the Watcher's mouth. Blazing eyes fixed on Chartreaux, the Watcher coiled, and leapt towards the rail to spring out of the Arena—

The Bell chimed to start the round.

A swift motion registered in his peripheral vision, and the Watcher twisted in midair to evade. Sparks exploded, followed by a shock of pain, showers of stars raining down. The Arena spun in slow motion as the jagged edge of Jip's brass knuckles connected with the Watcher's right brow.

The fabric of the Mask tore, but the Metallilume beneath it held. Blood seeped through the shredded fabric of his Mask as a brazen bell gonged in his brain. Lunging forward, Jip's lead arm flashed out, attempting to grab the Watcher's neck chain; turning, he swept Jip's hand away with a forearm block, then spun out of range.

Distracted…

Dominic had warned him; even when she was not present, Rose was a distraction. Chartreaux's poem about Rose had been a deliberate ploy by Chartreaux to draw the Watcher's eyes and thoughts from his opponent. He re-centered his mind:

Let nothing exist but the Arena.

Anticipating a combination move, the Watcher dodged Jip's follow-up to the straight left jab—his opponent's right cross. The Watcher slipped his head under the cross, as Jip's fist brushed past the horny scales of the Watcher's crown. He baited a fat target for Jip, luring a left hook…

The Watcher turned his body and slid his head back from the hook, evading; the gargantuan fist, nearly as large as the Watcher's head, whipped past his ear with blinding speed. He heard the wind in his ear and the draft of air that followed in its wake…

Jip's left ribcage was unguarded as the missed left hook's momentum twisted him forward. Cool, the Watcher contracted his core then unwound, delivering a brutal spinning back kick to his opponent's unguarded liver.

The kick was solid, and should have caused excruciating pain. Instead, Jip staggered, then laughed. "Take your best shot—" Jip quipped, backpedalling away."I'm feelin' no pain."

A black boot snapped out, a lethal lead leg kick. The Watcher bobbed to avoid the kick, but it clipped his shoulder on follow through. Warm blood spurted from the gash, arcing to follow tip of a nail embedded in the toe of Jip's steel-toed boot.

A faint whimper-whine was heard from the Live Oak beneath the Balcony, the sound of a small animal in distress…it was the same cry the Watcher heard when Henderson killed Rose's companion dog, Barnaby. Now he heard that familiar muffled wail from the trees nearby.

No one else seemed to notice the odd little noise. Intensely focused, the Watcher ignored his own blood, and the creature who might be making such a noise in reaction to his injury. *She's near.* But for now—*pay attention to nothing but the Arena.* The Watcher kept his concentration upon his seemingly unfeeling opponent.

"I bet you're ugly as homemade sin under that mask…" Lightning quick, a massive fist whipped out to grab the Watcher's Mask, just above the ear. The flame-print grimace stretched into an obscene leer as Jip's fingers snagged a loose wrinkle.

Closing the gap between himself and Jip, the Watcher stepped forward, smashing his left fist into his foe's nose while simultaneously raising his right arm high in a high outside block. He swept Jip's arm away, then ducked under the taller man's arm…

As the Watcher passed under his shoulder, the Big Macho twisted, throwing down a single-fisted hammer blow at the Watcher's head; the blow glanced off the Watcher's thickly muscled back, and the Watcher barrelled through the opening and away.

"So you're just going to run like a little punk…" Jip wiped blood and mucus away from his broken, bubbling nose. "I mighta known." He swung a haymaker. As he dodged Jip's punch, the Watcher assessed his rival, mid-move:

Feelin' no pain… that was the reason Jip was the undisputed Champion: he couldn't be pushed back by pain. Pain was a warning, and most fighters avoided it, so it could be used to direct action—but Jip wouldn't respond, because he didn't feel it.

Years of the Watcher's experience with the Stuff confirmed Jip's statement—a careful combination of alcohol, budweed and the Stuff could create a short-lived, functional high that increased speed and endurance, while deadening pain. The downside was addiction, withdrawal, and potential for adverse effects. Unfortunately, none of those downside effects were going to be in play in the next half hour, unless the Watcher could induce cardiac arrest in his big opponent, which was highly unlikely. But the lack of pain also could translate as a lack of situational awareness, and overconfidence…

Time to exploit that immunity to pain.

The Watcher's eyes narrowed as he increased the distance between himself and Jip.

"This ain't no play party dance—" Jip took a couple of jabs, whipping at the air with a nervous energy.

The Watcher kept his distance.

Bottles were thrown into the ring, accompanied by jeers. "Fight, you pussies!" One bounced off the Watcher's arm, but he didn't seem to notice. Another hit his opponent on the head, and the big Survivor swatted it away with an angry scowl.

"I ain't got all day, punk…"

The Watcher held up his hand and wordlessly beckoned to Jip: *Bring it.*

Jip spit. "Ladies first, LoneStar Libre."

From the vault of memory, Musashi instructed the Watcher:

> *"When you decide to attack, keep calm and dash in quickly, forestalling the enemy."*

The Watcher bounced in slightly closer, hanging just within his opponent's reach. Jip gave a short-legged hop, the preamble to a kick. The Watcher stood still.

Jip's leg flashed out, aiming where the Watcher's head was—then wasn't. A slip to the side, and Jip's foot lashed empty space where the Watcher had been.

Move the target with the launch—keep it small…

Maintaining balance, Jip lightly touched his toe down, then snapped another body kick out where the Watcher now stood;

—another miss by millimeters as the Watcher deftly turned his body to subtly slip past Jip's kick once again. Adjusting his trajectory midair, Jip's fearsome boot came down in kick's follow-through, gashing the Watcher's shin, and the Watcher answered with an inside kick to the knee of Jip's lead leg.

Jip took the kick to the knee, impervious. The Watcher snapped another kick with the same leg, and Jip blocked the kick. Whipping out a right hook, Jip leaned in; the Watcher's head bobbed away from Jip's strike, and the Watcher kicked out another inside snap, aiming for the big Macho's shin. Jip moved his leg back, away from the Watcher's flashing foot—

The Watcher's foot came down between Jip's ankles.

Ducking inside the 'shell' between his Opponent's guarding arms, the Watcher moved in close. Too close to punch, Jip brought his arms down to try and clinch his opponent; rocking back on his leg as if to kick, the Watcher could smell the stench of the Executioner's sweat, and feel the warmth of Jip's fetid breath on through the Mask as his opponent chuckled:

"Lights out, LoneStar!"

NOW—

Pivoting off the faked right kick, the Watcher planted his feet firmly and speared his right elbow upward into Jip's throat.

Cartilage snapped.

A shout of disbelief arose from the crowd as the Watcher extended his arm, backfisting a crushing blow into Jip's temple. Heavy bone buckled beneath the Watcher's bony knuckles…

Jip staggered back, involuntarily flailing a roundhouse against the Watcher's upraised forearm. The Executioner was wheeling away from the Watcher, arms extended, head thrown back as if in ecstasy; feet in a solid stance, the Watcher opened his mouth wide, the pure force of his energy flowing through his body, a living fire—

Cry splitting the air, his open left palm smashed upward, into the hollow below and behind Jip's ear.

Through the Watcher's hand, the wave of Chi poured, a hammer of energy penetrating flesh and bone. It shattered space and matter, rushing from the Watcher's body and into the body of his opponent—

Blood spattered, a fountain of life spraying the energy away from the Watcher, through Jip and into the air beyond... a forceful pop was heard, then a thud, as Jip's lifeless body dropped to the dirt of the Arena.

A stunned silence fell upon the crowd, leaving only the trailing edge of the Watcher's piercing cry to die on the wind; he exhaled it, pushing all the energy out with it.

Joey leapt forward, only to have the Guard wave a gun. "Halt!—"

From the corner, another guard came, with Lord Li before him, hands raised in surrender...

the four guards from Jip's entourage raised their rifles to the Watcher. Chartreaux's trap was sprung.

Blood trickling from his head and his gashed leg, the Watcher held his fighting stance, unmoving except for his eyes rising to the figures in Balcony. Keeping their distance, one guard gingerly prodded Jip's lifeless head with a wary toe... it slid a little to the side, the base of the shattered skull disjointed from the neck. Fearful, the Guard raised his eyes to the brooding figure watching from the Balcony.

"He's dead, Boss."

"Pity..." Chartreaux grunted, "but that was to be expected." The Boss extended his ball-tipped cane; an odd hum arose as the ball began to glow. Too late, the Watcher caught a glimpse of a silver-alloy bracelet beneath the Boss's shirt cuff...

An insidious heat burrowed into the Watcher's gut, intensifying rapidly. He tried to step aside, but the pain followed, excruciating, unstoppable.

"Do you like it?" Chartreaux grinned through narrow teeth, his toad-like visage cruel as he wielded his cane against the incapacitated Watcher. "It's a gift from a friend, a downpayment in exchange for bringing you and your little friend in..."

The Watcher attempted to move, but the vibration reverberated inside him, a current he couldn't shut down.

"I have a question for you—and if your remember your Latin from our dear old Alma Mater, surely you will be able to answer it:" Cold, the Boss sneered from his Balcony:

"Quis custodiet ipsos custodes?"

Gnashing his fangs, the Watcher tried to spring forward, but staggered, every nerve overwhelmed as he raged, unintelligible.

"Wrong answer." The Boss nudged the toggle. "The question is, 'Who watches the Watchers'?"

The Marshal clutched at his midsection as a seizure of pain overtook him.

Chartreaux smirked, "The answer is: me."

The Watcher could feel his blood heating, scorching nerve endings throughout his body; this was the pain of the Afterlings, their torture becoming his own. Snarling and gnashing, the Watcher fought to stay upright.

Titillated by the sight of the agonized Survivor, Shaney licked her lips and dangled her own gifts over the railing of the Balcony. "You should have taken up the Warden's offer for citizenship, and quit while you were ahead."

Sweating, the Watcher gave her an evil glare.

Chartreaux intoned from the Balcony: "Lords of the WildLands, and Citizens of Purgatory: I present to you the Man behind the Mask—"

A guttural groan erupted from the Watcher's cracked lips as he sank to his knees; from behind him, a BrigadesMan grasped the top of his mask to snatch it away.

The Watcher's fist flashed upward to snag the Guard's wrist; throwing him over his shoulder, the Masked Man smashed his tormentor into the dirt. Wrist broken, the BrigadesMan flailed, pulling the bandana and the protective jammer with it. Unnoticed, the talismans tumbled to the ground...

At the Watcher's defense of the Mask, a shout arose from the Chain Gang and the Lords in the Pavilion. Angry at his victory denied, Chartreaux edged the toggle forward on the SHIVA device. The Watcher groaned, his body twisting.

"No matter. Die with your stupid Mask. It cannot hide the truth and it cannot change who you are: the notorious criminal, Prisoner #7..." A wicked sneer leaked across Chartreaux's face:

"Saul Azarian—Watcher, of the Damned."

Gasps arose from the audience at this pronouncement at the infamous Watcher in their midst. They stood on their seats to stare at this Masked Man and the Weapon tormenting him. Displeased with this societal disorder, Chartreaux snarled to his subjects: "Welcome to the New Order. Now, if you all don't wish me to use this weapon against you, take a seat and enjoy the show; I intend to find out just what Prisoner Azarian is doing at Purgatory, and what his role is regarding this unrest in our fair city."

Citizens and Lords alike took an uneasy seat, confused and concerned.

Chartreaux glowered at the writhing man: "I hear that a certain small golden woman may be traveling with you… point her out to me, and I will let you die quickly."

The Watcher ripped his chain away; with a mocking grimace, he held it aloft in an angry fist, then extended a gnarled middle finger to the Balcony…

Chartreaux tapped the brass slide again, and the Watcher fell forward onto his hands again, his scarred face contorted in agony.

"You continue to make poor choices. Since you are unwilling to show me where she is, perhaps one of your friends would care to speak up on your behalf." Chartreaux pressed the toggle further. The Watcher opened his mouth, emitting a strangled moan: Joey sweated, and Lord Li's eyes darted, seeking guidance in his HeadsUp display, but finding none. The Guard pressed a rifle muzzle into Li's back. Out in the Commons, Li could see each Agent waiting for a sign that the Afterling had been found, so the party could commence; but no sign came.

The Boss waited for an answer, but the only answer was the sound of the Purgatory gong chiming repeatedly, the same double-gong signal, over and over…

"No?" Chartreaux feigned surprise. "No help for the Most Wanted Man in the WildLand?"

"They could help you, if they actually cared." Shaney said sympathetically.

"Or maybe they'd just like to watch you explode." The Boss nudged the toggle, the ball's tip glowing brighter. The Watcher howled—

A shot ripped the night.

Chartreaux's left shoulder erupted with blood as a bullet tore through the bulging muscle; the ball-tipped cane flew from his hand to land in the branches of the Hanging Tree below. Stifling a shriek, the Boss grabbed his wounded arm in shock as Shaney pulled him back into the safety of the Silo.

The Watcher collapsed in a heap.

Pistol in hand, Shaney searched her horizon for any muzzle flash, but saw only a drift of gun smoke. She shouted from the Balcony Door: "Show yourself, you sorry son-of-a-bitch!"

A sharp voice rang out, as clear and piercing as the shot which preceded it: "You shan't have him!" Nauseous with pain, the Watcher glanced up, alarmed at the sound of a lilting, feminine voice:

A light flickered as a small figure appeared on a rooftop of a tin-roofed shop neighboring the Silo. Hovering above Purgatory, it shone as if lit from within; an uneasy murmur rose from the crowd, anxious, unsure. The voice spoke again, coming from everywhere and nowhere, multidirectional.

"I am she whom you seek—"

Swathed in deer furs, the ethereal vision raised delicate hands to pull down a doe-eared hood away from a painted golden face with large, dark eyes. She flung back her cape, revealing a soft arm, then a curvaceous frame draped in thin brown fabric.

Shaney yelped for all Purgatory to hear: "It's her!" Floating sparks of blue began to drift towards the vision.

The Watcher lifted his eyes to see his Goddess on the Berm, beckoning him once more; she seemed slightly blurred, as if seen through a fog, then became clear again. The Silver Chain about her neck glowed, tied with a ribbon of light, and her eyes were brilliant, black emeralds. Raising her hands, she tugged on her stocking cap—

long black coils of glossy hair sprang forth, billowing down past her tiny waist to her full hips and rounded thighs, living testimony from a world thought dead. The Call of the Wild, the Song of the Moon, Deer Woman beckoned from her shadowy perch, luring her seekers. She danced on the breeze, hands stretched out to the yearning masses, full breasts straining against the softness of her dress:

"They told you I was lost; but seek me, and you shall find…"

Speechless with rage, Chartreaux raised a bloody hand to point at the vision.

Rose raised her fist into the air, flickering with an electric glow. "We will be Free!"

The Watcher sprang up out of the dirt and onto his feet:

Deer Woman disappeared.

Purgatory sucked in a collective breath—then all hell broke loose.

Survivors rushed the Pair'O'Dice fence, running towards the last location of the Afterling, trampling and fighting, every man for himself. The Guards gaped, uncertain of what was taking place… Shaney was applying pressure to Chartreaux's wound as the Boss shouted commands from the Balcony, but none heeded—

With a sudden savagery, the Watcher whipped his chain around him in a tight circle, smacking the padlock into the faces of his encircling Guards. Blood sprayed as it caught the hapless men unawares, and they fell at his feet.

Joey nodded to Li, then twisted to bash his own Guard in the nose with a hammerfist; Li stomped on his captor's instep, then elbowed his Guard's ribs, knocking the breath out of him. A vicious struggle ensued, as high above Purgatory, sparks began to gather, humming, analyzing...

Running to the rail, the Watcher prepared to leap the Arena rail after Rose.

Shoving his fist into the Guard's face, Lord Li shouted over his shoulder to the Watcher: "All that glitters is not Gold!"

The Watcher kicked another Guard away, then shrugged at Li, puzzled.

"Not Gold!" Li shouted again as he dodged a fist., louder this time, as if louder would make it clearer.

Baffled, the Watcher shook his head: *Not Gold. Not a small golden woman?* If what he saw wasn't Rose, then what was it? He looked overhead; the drones were still hesitating, not pursuing the woman—

"Hold your position!" Li gasped, then swung a roundhouse punch to finally knock out his opponent.

Hold Position. Li obviously had information the Watcher didn't—yet. *Protect this piece of ground.* Was Rose nearby?

Kicking the body of his guard away, Joey gave a mighty heave and tossed the scavenged car door into the ring, then grabbed their gear and flung open the gate to the Arena, Li right behind him. "Suit up, Wrassler-Man. It's technology-bustin' time." Joey threw the Watcher his cape, and the Watcher quickly put on the signal-blocking gear, then slapped on his hat.

He turned to Li for answers—

Reaching into the top of his sock, Li pulled out a folded paper note— the blood chit.

#LI: Your Package is nearby. Brother Lynx passed this note to me just before I got rolled up by the guards. We just don't know exactly which tree she's in—she hidden herself away, and not even the ALGOS can find her. Stay put, and prepare a safe extraction zone because Brother Fox says she is making her way to you...

The Watcher glanced at the note, reading Rose's added plea to help Jo Rand... he shook his head, marveling. In true Rose fashion, she had gotten in trouble and ended up saving someone else instead. Tucking the note into his jeans pocket, he looked to the surrounding grove for any sign of the Afterling. He tried to whistle to find her, but heard nothing except his own bird call.

Back to back with Joey and Li, the Watcher prepared to hold his position against all comers.

Now, to find my objective. Closing his eyes briefly, the Watcher took a deep breath, inhaling the night air. At edges of blood and sweat, he caught the scent of his prey: the odor of warm fruit-bread mixed with sharp fear. He felt a surge of power rise in response to her unintended signal; somewhere nearby, Rose was lurking.

As the rest of Purgatory chased Rose's image, the drones hesitated, not pursuing—*they detected an anomaly, perhaps?* What could be causing them to not pursue? He reached instinctively for his beloved bandana and its Gambler's personal jammer, the DDT. *Gone*—his eyes settled on the ground in front of his feet:

There in the dirt lay his bandana and the Digital Deception Transmitter. Now unprotected by the Gambler's mobile jammer, the Watcher's unique identifiers from his embedded nanobots were summoning the ALGOS. Soon, Saul Azarian would be located by those who had hunted him since the day of the Happening.

The Watcher grabbed his bandana and DDT off the ground, pulling them on once more to disrupt his own identifying transmissions. Stealing a dead Guard's shotgun, he rose to face the threat. The sparks edged closer…

He raised his car-door shield.

"Hey! Stop right there, you airborn garbage cans!" Incensed, Goins jumped up as the attendant blue pinpoints glows began to drift towards the Arena: "Oh no you don't!" A shout burst forth from the fearless Survivor: "Come back and fight me!"

The sparks moved towards the Watcher, and a ripple appeared above the Commons.

The sound of metal hitting high-impact composite was heard as Goins flung a pipe wrench into the darkness overhead, connecting with the unseen demon. A thin bolt of blue pierced the darkness, then a crackling web of blue lightning arced, netting around an unseen electric sphere some fifteen feet overhead. The Watcher held out his hand to Goins, shaking his head frantically, then ducking behind the car door shield as a heat round pinged against his shield, tracing a fiery trail through the half-darkness of the Arena.

Damaged, the metallic ball spun to the dirt—grinning triumphantly, the cantankerous Goins bellowed: "Fight ME, you stupid pieces of hi-tech sh…"

The smell of ozone and burnt flesh spattered into the air as Goins crumpled to the ground, convulsing in the radius of the drone's electrocuting web.

An outburst of horror was heard from the Campground.

Michaels ran from his observation post, trying to get close, but unable to get past the web of electricity.

The Watcher blasted the Drone, and it rolled away from Goins, allowing Michaels to rush to to the electrocuted Agent's side. Desperate, Michaels grabbed a branch to pull the smoking, jerking body out of the road.

The damaged drone sparked and arced, spreading a protective net of high-voltage danger around itself. One curious BrigadesMan approached it warily, trying to assess the threat.

"Stop! Stay back!"

A bellicose voice shouted as a familiar, tall Hombre ran up from the gate, shotgun in one hand, Halligan in the other. The BrigadesMan turned his head, confused…

"Chief?"

Winston ran, Chaos running before him; "Stay away! Don't touch it—"

"Chief? Chief Winston?"

Chief had arrived on scene. Winston raised his voice—"Don't touch it Cooper, don't—" An explosive shock rocked the Commons as his BrigadesMan accidentally stepped into the sparking circle and was knocked back, lifeless.

Drowned out in the pandemonium of the moment, the wounded Chartreaux snarled at the return of Boss Winston. Bleeding, the big Boss shouted from the Balcony:

"I'm glad you could make it, Winston. The Hangman awaits, you traitorous malcontent… Enforcers—mount up and take down Winston!"

But at this command, a sharp crack in the facade of the New Order appeared; some jeered at Winston, and others stayed silent, unwilling to commit either way. But many more BrigadesMen rallied to their former Boss, heartened by his courage and gladdened at the sight of the man they once followed into Hell—

The men of the old Municipality Brigade cheered, glad to see their

Chief; an officer shouted, pointing at the sky: "What the hell are those things?"

"ALGOS—they're ALGOS!" Still running towards their fallen comrade, Winston waved his Halligan, warning away bystanders. Winston dragged Cooper away from the ALGOS and two of his BrigadesMen began resuscitation, just as Winston had trained them…

Some in the crowd scratched their heads. "What's an ALGO?"

"Drones—" Backing towards the gate, Winston tried to explain quickly. "Killer Robots—"

Angered at the BrigadesMen's embrace of Winston, Chartreaux turned to Shaney in a cold rage: "I am documenting these faces—when this is said and done, your men will round up these insurrectionists…" Still clutching his bleeding shoulder, Chartreaux leaned over edge of the Balcony.

A heat round hissed in the dirt at Winston's feet as the ALGOS began to circle, pausing to receiving new information, reprogramming…

The skies above Purgatory rippled as drones deactivated their optical cloaks, revealing glowing red balls of heat and light hovering over the anxious faces of the crowd.

No longer lurking unseen, nine ALGOS bobbed in synchronous harmony, all at the same altitude above the Commons. Curious onlookers gawked beneath the floating orbs. An old Hombre looked up drunkenly from his bottle and pointed at a drone: "What the ever-loving f—"

A hot tracer of light hit the drunk's forehead, and his skull exploded.

Winston barked: "Take shelter, now!" Firing his shotgun at the orb, he dove behind the Bois D'Arc stump.

At Winston's order, bedlam engulfed Purgatory. Citizens and LandLords ran for cover; screams resounded as the drones scattered over the helpless crowd, heat rounds spattering. Survivors fell, combusting as they writhed in the dirt. The ALGOS hummed and spun towards Winston—

Grim, Winston raised his shotgun and prepared to die.

From behind his tree, the Watcher blasted in the cluster of ALGOS, and a drone spouted blue lighting. It pivoted on an invisible axis, a multiple heat rounds streaked through the air towards this new threat—

The bullets lodged in the Watcher's armored steel door-shield, melting the outer metal. The glass webbed as the shots his, but couldn't penetrate the thick, coated glass. The Watcher fired again, and another orb crackled.

Tracers targeted the Watcher with precision, and he twisted, ducking behind the tree as a fresh hail of projectiles spattered the Commons. The tree trunk in front of him ignited; smoke and lighting arced as the wooden fence behind them caught fire. Joey and Li huddled behind the Watcher's Shield, guns drawn…

Bobbing in a deadly dance, the drones separated into three groups of three. The Watcher grabbed Joey's hand:

#WATCHER: Tell Li to get ready—they are preparing to split up and take us all down at once. One group for the crowd, one group for Winston, and one group for me…

Li whipped out his pistol as the drone groups parted. Joey bared his teeth in an unaccustomed snarl. "Time to play a little Death Ball…"

In the far distance, Purgatory heard a thrum of hoofbeats, and a high voice calling in the night: at first so far away, it didn't seem real.

"Come to me!"

Heads turned, and servos whirred. The ALGOS fell silent, turning their deadly gaze from their targets towards the voice in the distance:

The voice was a woman's voice.

The hoofbeats grew louder. Now all could see a small Tobiano Paint Horse and his petite Rider drumming up the road from the park—incredulous, Winston watched as the pair raced towards the gate, running, running for their lives. A slender woman was riding, the Watcher's missing deer's pelt pinned around her shoulders as a cloak, her fur hood partially hiding her face from onlookers.

A cry was heard from the commons, as Agent Montague rushed out to see his horse racing through the dirt streets of Purgatory. He tried to tear his eyes away, but could not… beneath the furs, a tangerine print dress gleamed like a flame, and a glimpse of a fluttering orange headscarf was seen. As the Horse barrelled through the street, they hear the Rider cry:

"Andalé!" She stood in the saddle, and the deer pelt fell away from her burnished face, firelight dancing in her dark eyes, scarf waving like a banner, fist raised in defiance. "Come to me! Follow me!"

The ALGOS hovered, targeting the fur-clad, feminine rider—unlike the previous vision, this woman had a heat signature. The drones pivoted with their uncanny grace, and moved smoothly towards the Horse and Rider.

"The Afterling can ride?" Shaney gasped with delight. "Hold your fire!"

Uncertain in the dark, Chartreaux leaned forward on the balcony rail, still trying to staunch the flowing blood from his wounded shoulder. He called out to an unseen listener, somewhere across a digital divide: "Pursue, but hold fire until my call. If it's the Afterling, she must be captured unharmed!"

Winston's heart stopped.

Araceli raced towards the gate; the ALGOS gave chase, moths drawn to her flame. A broadcast signal through the encrypted comms server to his popped up in Winston's Display, a message meant for Wilcox—Team Whiskey:

#GOLF: WHISKEY—activate, activate
#WHISKEY: activated

Behind Winston, the Gate opened; his Ring went dead as the hidden Jammer came alive with a pop. Within the radius of the activated Catastronix Jammer, his HeadsUp display went dark, leaving only the vision of Araceli flying through the streets of Purgatory. Close behind her, ALGOS were pursuing and behind them, Enforcers were riding, pouring out the entrance of Pair'O'Dice, guns drawn…

Tense, Winston waited as Araceli raced towards him, his heart set to explode.

From the other side of the Commons, a slender Hombre whooped in a mixture of fear and joy. Finally recognizing her, Montague held out his arms as Araceli flew by, awestruck at the sight of his Beloved Woman upon his beloved Horse. "La Reina!" he called to Araceli, waving his broad-brimmed hat: "Queen of my Heart—"

She gazed over her shoulder to beam back at her Lover. Araceli pulled the reins back and the Paint launched into the air, a heavenly Steed; amazed, Winston stood still as stone, watching Rider and Horse ascending as they flew over his head.

ALGOS hit the Jammer barrier.

Static shrieked as the Drones activated their audio deterrent, one hundred and twenty decibels of brutal noise mixing with the terrified cries of bystanders in the Commons. The air around the drones was buzzing, blue lightning crackling as ALGOS entered the Catastronix's signal radius. A thunderclap resounded as all nine ALGOS simultaneously deactivated, hitting the invisible energy field of the Jammer. Storms of light and fury shattered against an unseen wall as the ALGOS fell dead at Winston's feet…

But all Winston could see was Araceli flying above him.

Caught up in the Horse's waving, multicolored mane, Araceli was alight, uncontainable, the Fire Winston could not tame. He raised his hands to her as she flashed over him—

Winston noticed the hole in Peanut's belly, small at first, a precision wound in the beautiful Paint's white-rimmed underside. He watched in mute horror as the hole widened into a geyser of vaporizing blood, propelled by an ALGOS' expertly placed, low calibre incendiary round.

The Horse screamed as shredded entrails spurted out the wound. Sturdy legs stiffened as Horse and Rider descended, their perfect flight arcing towards catastrophe. Dread seized Winston—

As the steed landed, Winston heard a cannon bone shatter. Another sound rent the Commons, just as terrible; Montague cried out, his heart shattering with his Horse's leg.

Araceli pushed away as Peanut fell, trying to clear the saddle, but her bare foot caught in the stirrup. Peanut rolled, thrashing and whickering, and Winston heard her bones crush as Peanut rolled upon her ankle, a cracking sound, like twigs breaking. Her shriek tore everything apart—

Throwing away his Halligan, Winston vaulted over the dying Horse; pulling his knife with his free hand, he slashed at the stirrup, cutting it free to drag a dazed Araceli away from the frenzied animal and back towards the Purgatory Gate. Her deer pelt cape fell away into the bloody dirt beneath the rolling horse.

"Imposter!" Livid at the deception, Shaney yelled to her men: "Don't let her escape!"

Shaney's Enforcers lunged forward, pursuing the imposter Afterling and her rescuer. Winston shouted to the Insertion Team as he sprinted towards the Gate: "Return fire!"

The Insertion Team scrambled to take firing positions at the parapets atop Purgatory Gate as the team of Enforcers advanced. Clutching a bleeding Araceli to his chest, Winston ran, shielding her with his body, flinging his arm over his shoulder to blast at their pursuers. One bullet grazed his shoulder, another his thigh, and still he ran, running for their lives to make the Gate—

Montague stepped into the breach.

Hat thrown back, both hands filled with hot death, the Cowboy wept as he fired. One Enforcer fell dead, shot through the throat. His revolvers roared again, and another Enforcer groaned, arm bleeding. Montague raised his pistol, then a shot pierced his left shoulder, blood staining his gingham shirt—

"Mi Corazon!" Twisting free of Winston's grasp with a remarkable, sudden strength, Araceli tried to run back through the Gate to Montague, but stumbled, her foot still tangled in the dismembered, bloody stirrup. Her broken, bare foot crumpled beneath her, the little bones jutting out through the mangled flesh of ankle and foot.

Shotgun blasting at the remaining Horsemen beyond the Gate, Winston lifted Araceli again to haul her into the Corral. The Enforcers wheeled their horses, unleashing hell through the closing Gate once more. Blocking their way, the bloody Montague fired again—

A storm of lead descended. Bullets riddled his lithe body, and Montague's final shot whizzed wide into the starry sky; the Cowboy jerked as he fell, sprawling onto the blood-stained deer pelt next to his beautiful Tobiano Horse.

Topping the parapets at the gate, angry Agents returned fire as two of their own staged to retrieve Montague. Shaney's Enforcers retreated into the Commons, sheltering their horses in the Bandstand to dismount. Purgatory descended into War.

Shots erupted from the dump as a team of WildLand Express Agents emerged from the drifts of trash to answer the challenge. Citizens and Lords watched in awe as a scarf fell away from the face of one tall, slender figure to unmask Sam, flanked by Mansour and Michaels as they raced to take position on the battlefield.

"Get Montague!" Furious, Sam yelled, returning suppressive fire with her Beretta: "Leave no man behind!"

Shots pinging around them, two Agents slipped through an opening in the gate and raced into the danger zone—Ludwig and Pritchard from the Insertion Team. Ludwig flung the bleeding Montague over Pritchard's shoulder, then blazed out return fire from his pistol as he and Pritchard stumbled quickly back through the open gate to the cover of the Corral.

Pinned down, the Enforcers cursed, suppressed by Mansour's covering fire. Proficient in the use of small firearms, Mansour fired efficiently, economizing ammunition and waiting for openings to make measured shots. He was careful to avoid crossfire, constantly assessing teams and logistics. Taking cover behind an overturned semi-trailer just inside the Dump's boundary, the team made good use of the long structure, running from one end to another to shoot at unsuspecting opponents.

"Get ready—evacuation will be under way shortly. We'll pin down the shooters while the wagons roll." Sam heard footsteps running in from the dump; she hissed to Michaels; "Handle whoever that is, by whatever means needed." Michaels nodded curtly, and racked the slide of his 9mm once more.

Hands linked, a heavy Macho and a willowy, long-legged Survivor were dashing between the trees. Lourdes running behind him, Habib stopped to tap out the signal from behind a cottonwood, once, twice…

"Aw, screw it…" Habib yelled to Sam's team: "Hold your fire!" He ran up to take cover. Mansour looked up in surprise to see Habib ducking down, running towards them, a harried Lourdes in tow: "Tell us what the hell is happening here."

Michaels ran up to meet them, updating: "Santos and Von Helm are with the wagons and Agents, ready to roll to the gate. Azarian, Joey, and Li are holding position at the Arena, providing covering fire, staking out the nearest location we can figure for the Package. The ALGOS are deactivated down by the gate, thanks to the Jammer—but unknown how many more out there. Casualties: Goins dead, Montague dead, Diaz wounded, and she's by the front gate with Winston."

"The Package's location is unknown?" Lourdes' face clouded. "Araceli wounded?"

"Her foot was caught under the horse when it rolled." Michaels stated flatly.

"And Goins… does Gunny know?" Lourdes seemed shell-shocked.

"Not yet. Keep it that way for now; he's out with the Comms Team."

Subdued, Lourdes nodded. Habib was uncertain about to the significance of that last exchange, but he figured he would find out soon enough. They followed Michaels through low brush towards the semi-trailer, where Mansour and Sam were concentrating intensely, firing in a seemingly random pattern. Lourdes cringed inwardly; this was a recipe for a sullen meltdown from Habib.

Strangely enough, it never came. Habib crouched next to Mansour. "Whatta ya need?"

Mansour ducked back as a bullet whizzed by. "We need to get the wagons through the gate—and to get them out, we'd need overwatch."

"Overwatch? What?"

Sam fired again, then whispered to Mansour: "Explain to civvies." She poked her head around the corner again, too busy to talk.

Leaning into Habib, Mansour muttered: "Overwatch—we need someone to pop some shots into their position from a higher angle, but the guys at the gates aren't high enough. Unfortunately, we don't have an Angel of Death from on high to snipe their position."

Habib mulled it over. "I've got one…" He whispered to Lourdes. "If I set you up with a rifle somewhere high enough, can you take a shot into that cluster of thugs over there?"

Studious, Lourdes considered the possibilities."With a stand or a tripod yes—but I'll need help."

"Leave that to me." Habib turned back to Mansour. "Any of you got a rifle?"

"Take this." From beneath her long coat, Sam pulled the battered AR-15. "Thirty rounds. What position, Lourdes?"

Her cool green eyes swept the dark horizon. She looked behind them and frowned. The Jailhouse Roof was no longer accessible—she scanned Purgatory. "There—" Lourdes pointed to one of the mountains of trash rising twenty or more feet above the dump. "Get me there, and I'll make it worth your while."

"Consider it done." Habib pulled his snub-nosed revolver, then pulled Michaels aside. "I'll send word when we're in position. Just hold on, until I can get her in place." Lourdes was already heading out, creeping through the brush. Habib took one last look at Sam, firing away from her position next to Mansour, and she briefly looked back at him, her eyes burning with that heat he had always adored:

"Thanks for everything." He tipped his hat, and walked away, never looking back.

Sam let out a deep breath, cleared her mind, and turned her attention towards Michaels. She whispered over her shoulder."Give me a SITREP on our Package."

"Everybody's searching Pair'O'Dice, looking for the Package; LoneStar Libre and crew are holding their position inside the Arena, no takers. They look like they're just cooling their heels, but Brother Wolf says the Package is very nearby, and he's covering that area. Covering fire from the dump will continue to pin down any Enforcers who move, and the sniper will engage when they move out providing cover for their search. I've sent word they are to look for their Little Bird in the trees next to the fence, parallel to where she was seen, and to get ready for the Brothers to roll momentarily."

Michaels jerked a head toward the Watcher : "As soon as they make a pinpoint location, they'll broadcast on Channel 145 so all units can co-ordinate. Brother Wolf's team will set up a perimeter, and he will extract her."

"Good. I can't believe no one's spotted her yet..." Mansour tapped Sam's shoulder, and pointed; she saw a muzzle flash from the Bandstand, and answered it, then turned back to Michaels without missing a beat.

"I also need an update on enemy movements from that side. It's bugging me that I don't see anyone engaging Brother Wolf and his team —that means the enemy is busy elsewhere. Can you get me a report from our operative over there? That Dancer who showed you the note..."

"Yeah. Give me five minutes; I'll sneak through Industrial and up the other side. I've got to return that compact anyway—minus the note, of course."

Sam shook her head. "I can't wait to hear this story... whatever it was that happened our there, she turned it into a mission of mercy and a spy mission, all at the same time. I've got to hand it to her, though—she came through in the clutch."

"That holographic image?" Curious, Michaels grunted; "If I hadn't been an amateur holographer back in the day, I would have been suckered in, too... but the shadows and light were slightly off. How in blue blazes did she find a projector?"

"It found her." Sam smirked. "But as for the rest, let's just say I planned her big debut from the moment I saw her, and it worked like a charm. Now this little golden Genie's out of the bottle, and there's no putting her back." A burst of gunfire sounded as Mansour laid down bullets around the bandstand. "Word of the Afterling will spread through the WildLand, and societal unrest will spread with that word. This reaction tonight is just a taste of what will happen across the Tejas Co-op once word gets out."

Michaels gazed out with his one good eye across the Commons, watching the horde of Enforcers and Survivors scrambling through Pair'O'Dice, searching for the Afterling. "Yeah, if I was that kind of man, I could see how she might inspire that kind of reaction; but to be honest, it's not much different than the reaction you Ladies have gotten from every Breeder at Purgatory over the years," Michaels mused. "Once these oversexed maniacs calm down, they'll join forces to take control the same way they did with you Hostesses. Society will eventually get its act together, and your revolutionary disorder will give way to systematic exploitation."

Displeased with this observation, Sam grumbled as she reloaded. "Fine. We'll be way ahead of them—and in the meantime, we'll take advantage of their chaos to get the upper hand. Now be a positive thinker, and go get me that info."

Michaels made his way down the fence, through the back alleys of the Industrial District. As he passed the scorched earth of Goins' last, sacrificial act, he couldn't help but agonize: the loss of the abrasive Agent left a gaping wound in his psyche. It wasn't that he missed Goins; but he felt remorse that he couldn't apologize for doubting. Goins' bravado was not false—it had all been true.

The Commons was now fairly empty of non-militarized personnel, except for the occasional sick BrigadesMan and several trapped onlookers.With the threat of ALGOS and gunfire in the Commons, smart citizens had fled to Purgatory's margins, or wisely taken shelter in their own houses. Cognizant of the danger, Shaney and the wounded Chartreaux had abandoned the Balcony as the firefight raged in the Commons. From the base of the tower, henchmen ran back and forth, sending messages and commands. Wary of being spotted, Michaels slunk through the brushy hedges lining the Main Drag, stopping briefly to assess the Fight Team.

Li, Joey, and Azarian were now just outside the Arena, taking cover behind an overturned beer cart, bottles strewn everywhere, holding weapons they had scrounged from their dead guards.

Outfitted in his cape and bearing his Bowie Knife, Marshal Azarian resembled some wild Texas action figure—except for the part where he was wielding a car door as a shield. The Watcher had taken his neck chain and looped it through the inner wall of his scavenged car door, padlocking it to make a sling; looping it around his left forearm, he gripped the handle, using the rolled up window as a make-shift riot shield. With the flamboyantly hatted Joey hunched behind him, and boar-helmeted Li covered the team's 'six', they were a remarkable looking crew, watching the Silo and scanning the trees.

Marshal Azarian raked his eyes around the perimeter, holding up one hand to surreptitiously search the skyline, He caught sight of Michaels, stopping his search to briefly give nod, then tapped Li on the shoulder. Michaels' HeadsUp display lit up.

#LI: You rang?
#MICHAELS: I'm on the move for a contact. Ignore.
#LI: Will do. No sign of the package, but the Wolf has caught the scent, somewhere close—keep us and our environs out of line of fire.

Michaels nodded and slunk away once more, slipping into the grove of Cottonwoods where he had last seen the Dancer. Entering the grove, Michaels stumbled upon a group of wild-eyed DragLine Queens trembling in the grass behind a large Cottonwood; they gasped as the rugged Hombre with an eye-patch raised his hands: "I'm looking for DeLish-"

he saw stars as a heavy Cottonwood branch hit him on the back of the head, sending him face first into the pile of Dancers. They kicked him away and he rolled over to see someone who resembled DeLisha holding a branch over him. Lipstick wiped away, collar disheveled and scarves missing, the person looked like DeLisha, but... different.

"Oh my God, I'm so sorry—I thought you were a Ranger!"

"Dammit, do I like like a Ranger?" Michaels growled, rubbing his head to glared up; the Dancers scattered like leaves in the wind, leaving DeLisha to face Michaels alone. DeLisha cocked the branch back, prepared to strike again.

Michaels grunted. "Put it down, I ain't gonna fight you—and if I was, that wouldn't stop me. I just came here to get a movement report."

"Oh—" DeLisha lowered the branch, swinging it with a casual grace, whispering: "A group of five or so are moving along the outer, lake-side fence of Pair'O'Dice; it looks like they may be trying to sneak up on the gate. Another two groups, about ten each, are searching Pair'O'Dice for that strange girl we saw earlier. I tried to get a message to Li, but there was too much gunfighting going on, and I didn't want anyone to see me talking to him..."

"Naw, you did it right. I'll get this information to command." Michaels stood up, and drew out the compact with its tokes. "I also came back to return these. What are you gonna do with them?"

Tucking the compact into a pocket of the rumpled turquoise jumpsuit, DeLisha pointed towards LowTown. "I'm gonna hire me a guard and I'm gonna go find and help this sick man in LowTown. It's time somebody did something besides drink and gamble around here, and if the Big Man Upstairs thinks I'm good enough to do it, then I'm gonna do it."

"Huh." Drawing himself up to his full height, Michaels put hands in his pockets and looked the de-dragged Queen up and down. "I'm a man's man—but I'm willing to make an exception in your case."

"And what in the hell exactly do you mean by that?" DeLisha snapped.

"It means I'll be seeing you again." Michaels walked away into the darkness, leaving an unnerved DeLisha behind him.

Creeping along the hedgerow between Pair'O'Dice and Main Drag, Michaels scanned the hedges, looking for any sign of the Afterling. She had to be hiding somewhere in this area... he cast up a glance at the Silo, then froze:

On the side of the Silo, clinging to the vines beneath the cantilevered shadow of the now-empty balcony, a barely visible figure climbed stealthily towards the open French Doors. Michaels ducked behind a bush as the small, sturdy figure of Marshal Evangelo pulled up on the platform, then swung his legs over the upper railing to leap into the Balcony.

Evangelo held his breath: it was time to face his greatest foe.

Quicksilver, Evangelo drew his gun, shouting for all to hear as he leapt behind the shelter of the doorframe:

"Reginald Chartreaux!"

No answer came back. He flung his shoulders back, steeling himself. "Lillabeth Shaney!"

From far below, the eyes of the crowd looked up to Evangelo.

"I am Captain Evangelo of the Tejas Co-op Rangers..."

A rack, then a blast from Chartreaux's 50-caliber hand cannon answered through the open doors. Shaney's entourage looked up from their search in the streets at the ruckus. Unfazed, the little Marshal continued: "By my authority as a Ranger, I am charging Boss Reginald Chartreaux with the kidnapping and rape of Destiny Rogers. With co-conspirator, Commander Lillabeth Shaney—"

Another shot blazed through the door, taking a chunk out of the concrete doorframe. Studying the hole, the Marshal calmly assessed the weapon—*a .50 calibre semi-automatic with a seven round capacity*. "... he is also charged with the murders of Boss Jack Zhu, Hizzoner Norris, Agents Walters and Mercedes of the WildLand Express, unlawful imprisonment of Boss Winston, kidnapping of the Hostesses, three counts of Arson and conspiracy to murder Director Santos of the WildLand Express..."

The next blast hit nearer, pinging off the metal decking of the balcony, but the little Marshal never blinked.

"Destiny Rogers is innocent of any crime. You are the criminals; come out with your hands up, and face your victims—the Survivors of Purgatory!"

Whispers and accusations floated up from the commons.

Evangelo heard the sound of running footsteps in the streets; protected by the tree and the metal balcony, he was safe from fire for now, but it wouldn't be long until Shaney's Enforcers would be in range. He needed to hurry this along...

The little Marshal removed his hat, and draped it across the end of his gun, the edge of the brim peeking into the doorway.

Another blast, and the concussion of the shot sent the white hat sailing into the courtyard below. Undaunted, Evangelo ascended the rail once more, and quickly climbed out onto the vines again, to the hidden side of the Silo's walls. Heavy footsteps stomped towards door, and shouts were heard as Shaney's security team ran upstairs.

Evangelo scrambled atop the conical, vine draped roof of the Silo, and waited to ambush Chartreaux. He heard the Boss' gun click—then a curse, and a click again. Evangelo knew that sound—

Jammed.

A frustrated groan followed, then Evangelo heard the Boss mutter: "All right, you have me... I'm coming out with my hands up. Don't shoot a wounded man..." Suspicious at this sudden turn, Evangelo waited as Chartreaux stomped out onto the Balcony,

Shaney was wrapped in Chartreaux's bloody, bandaged arms.

Cheek to cheek with her own arms about the Boss's massive neck, she dangled in front of him, a human shield. Taken aback by the sight of the pale and obviously ill Shaney, Evangelo shifted on the metal roof, trying to get a better angle for the shot. The metal roof creaked...

From the Balcony, Shaney looked up to see Evangelo, half-obscured and precariously balanced on opposite eave of the conical roof. "Well, look at you, all dressed up like a Dandy!" Wrapped around the grim Chartreaux, she pouted: "So you're that mystery man I saw by Li's sausage stand earlier... funny, I never would have guessed you had it in you to commit a mass poisoning."

The crowd below them murmured at this pronouncement.

"I-I only did it to incapacitate you—" Taken aback at such a terrible charge, Evangelo felt compelled to answer in his own defense: "I did it to keep you and innocent BrigadesMen out of harm's way."

"So you made me sick so I couldn't join the fight?" Bemused, Shaney batted her eyes at him. "Well, that's mighty chivalrous of you, Raffi. I suppose this means you wouldn't shoot a helpless woman, would you?"

Gun still trained on the pair, Evangelo felt his finger twitch.

"Who knows, maybe you would; maybe the Ranger Code really was all a lie." Shaney smirked. "Or maybe you just forgot it..."

She spoke the words and her voice rang, a silver bell:

"I swear before what I hold Holy, to do my Duty as a Ranger and to live the Ranger code, for the System and for those I serve: HONOR—follow the Ranger code, DUTY—protect the weak, the innocent and the defenseless..."

Evangelo's spirit reeled.

"I'm weak." She pointed at herself, then at Chartreaux. "And he's defenseless."

"But not innocent; you are a liar, and he is a rapist and a murderer." Evangelo said it with cold contempt, and all of Purgatory heard it.

"Well maybe the Code is just empty words to you, then. Go ahead and shoot if you want. But you'll kill me in the process—is that what you really want? Or do you want to kill me just because you're angry you're going to die a virgin?" Shaney spoke the word with venom, and a titillated crowd leaned forward en masse:

"Incel."

The audience gasped.

Evangelo set his jaw firm. "If the choice is between you and death, I'd rather die a virgin."

"Have it your way." The Commander laughed coyly. "But while you're busy playing Ranger here, real Rangers are taking the gate back from your bunch of wanna-bes. I don't know what Game you're playing, but it's over." She nodded towards the entrance to Purgatory; from afar, they heard shouts, and panicked screams, above a strange, shrill growl...

with a jolt, Evangelo remembered the words of Sam:

"But you have someone waiting on you—someone who needs you!" He felt a sudden surge of fire. *Destiny...*

Destiny was at the Gate, and her rapist was here, within reach of Justice. But try as he might, Evangelo simply couldn't bring himself to shoot Shaney, even to get to Chartreaux...

Footsteps were stampeding up the stairs, into the Balcony suite;

victorious, Shaney's lips curled into a savage little smile as she pulled her arm from behind the Boss's head. The glint of her silver muzzle flashed in the faint moonlight. "Jig's up, Raffi…" She squeezed the trigger—

Evangelo kicked his feet out from under himself, sliding off the edge of the steep Silo roof.

Her repeater roared, flinging hot lead into the empty space where Evangelo had just stood, puncturing the Silo's tin chapeau. Dangling from the opposite eave of the roof, the little Marshal was hanging by his fingertips, toes of his boots hooked into the scarlet vines of Virginia Creeper which thickly wrapped the Silo.

Evangelo was out of sight behind the Silo. Shaney couldn't make the shot; she swore beneath her breath, attempting to see him, but unwilling to let go of Chartreaux for fear Evangelo would somehow find a way to shoot back at the Boss. He heard the screams from the gate again, this time more panicked;

"Come out Raffi—" Shaney's voice dripped with sweet venom. "Time to die a virgin."

Without warning, the entirety of Shaney's security detail burst though the french doors, crowding out onto the Balcony, and it groaned beneath their weight. Major Wyatt shoved towards Shaney, attempting to pull her away from Chartreaux. "I'm here to save you, Lillabeth!"

"I don't need you to save me, you ninny! I need you to shoot Captain Evangelo—" Shaney pushed Wyatt away, still clinging to an alarmed Chartreaux who barked:

"Back up! Back up—The Balcony can't support us all!"

Purgatory watched in breathless suspense as Marshal Evangelo clung to life by his fingertips, enemies on one side and a thirty foot drop on the other. Agitated, Shaney was snapping for her men to get off the balcony, carefully backing up into the Silo suite once more. Wyatt leaned over, trying to get a better shot at Evangelo. The Balcony creaked dangerously as one support strut broke free beneath it.

"Beware, Commander—" Chartreaux hissed: "your men are making the Balcony unstable…"

A sharp, gurgling cry was heard from the gate; then all heard the sound of Evangelo whispering a prayer—"Deliver us from Evil…"

"Oh, you and your ridiculous prayers." Shaney laughed. "There's no God, just like there's no way you can take us out and save them too, Evangelo—"

"Get thee behind me, Satan."

Evangelo kicked his feet away from the roof, clinging to the delicate red Creeper vines. He gave another swift kick, and the vines swung further... tearing away from the wall, the vines broke free, and Evangelo swung away from the roof.

Shocked at his audacity, Shaney took the shot—and missed as Evangelo swung from the vines beneath them to fling his full weight to the Balcony strut just below her feet. Overstressed, the metal shrieked as bolts sheared and the Balcony separated from the Silo...

Shaney flung her arms in a chokehold around Chartreaux's neck, shrieking: "The Balcony is fixin' to fall!"

With a mighty heave, the little Marshal swung free of the strut beneath the Balcony, swinging to another creeper vine, then through the branches to rappel to the ground. Another strut snapped, as Chartreaux barked: "Get us off this Balcony!"

Evangelo rolled, grabbing his hat as he tumbled by, headed for the courtyard shed. Balcony sagging, Shaney fired again, but Evangelo ran, obscured by the limbs of the Hanging Tree. Lightly leaping onto Storm's blanketed back, Evangelo cut the reins free from the post in one swift motion.

Precariously off balance, the Balcony shifted beneath Chartreaux's bulk as he attempted to make his way to the French doors without breaking the rest of the Balcony free. A bolt sheared off, whizzing into the air; clinging to the Balcony rail, Wyatt drew his gun, finally able to get a clear shot—

"Hold your fire!" Shaney shrieked: "Hold your fire—don't hurt my Baby!" Leaping down from the Boss' arms, she grabbed Wyatt's gun, and the Balcony groaned, sagging further as Enforcers scrambled to get off the dangerously unstable structure.

Evangelo pulled back on the reins and Storm cleared the Pair'O'Dice fence with an easy bound. The gathering crowd shouted as Evangelo barrelled through, knocking down Lords left and right.

"Stop!" Shaney wailed to her men in the Commons: "You'll hit my horse!" Unchallenged, Evangelo galloped away on the stolen Storm, guns blazing, urging the horse towards the gate. Enforcers ducked inside the Silo, racing down the stairs.

Angry, Shaney stumbled through the French Doors as she grabbed ahold of Wyatt's collar:

"Get men and run to the Gate—Evangelo's got my Baby! I need Storm back, whatever it takes!" She thrust him away from her; flustered, Wyatt ran out the door, his posse hot on his heels. She started to run down the stairs after him, but stumbled, still weak from the effects of Li's drug-tainted sausages.

Waving away Chartreaux, she hauled herself up and staggered back out to the Balcony but the whole structure swayed, sending bits of metal spiraling down into the tree below. Retreating once more, she flung her hands over her eyes, disgusted, trying to not give in to tears.

They all heard another shout from the Campground—

"Move'em out!"

Following the lead of Ranger-gone-rogue Evangelo, whoops and hollers echoed through Purgatory as WildLand Express agents rode down the main drag, shooting into the air; the sound of rattling wagons wheels and thundering hoofbeats filled the Commons. At the head of the column, Von Helm led the way, riding atop a galloping Steele, followed by agents on horseback and eight loaded wagons. They tore through the streets, heading for the Gate, and the sound of battle.

As they rolled by, a panel fell open in the back of the last wagon, and a poncho'd man somersaulted out of the hold with a gear bag. Dominic flipped up onto his feet and ran to join the Watcher.

Shaney's men in the Bandstand shouldered their weapons.

A suppressing shot pinged out from a high angle, somewhere out past the Dump—it clipped the leg of one of Shaney's Enforcers down by the Bandstand. Hands dragged the swearing Survivor back under a bench, and the Enforcers hunkered down as more fire came from Sam's team. One eased around around a bleacher, gun in hand, to take a shot at the escaping wagons, but a barrage of fire from Sam's suppression Team rejected that notion. The last Wagon rattled through the Gate, and fresh sounds of sporadic gunfire accompanied savage shouts.

"The time has come for you to make good your promise; I have given you an army, Watcher, and now you must use it to set my Daughters free." As he ducked behind the overturned beer cart, Dominic smiled exuberantly, tossing the battered nylon gear bag to the Watcher. "Start with Rose."

Throwing the bag to the ground, the Watcher unzipped it, first strapping his 12-gauge bandoleers across his bare chest, then slinging the Mossberg Mariner across his back—*welcome back, my beautiful Marie*—and his Remington V3 Tac13 Semi-Auto 12-gauge. *Ah, sweet Sindee…*

He clipped it into the quick-grab holster behind his back. Out came his bugle; he slipped its faded cord around his back, hiding it beneath his cape. Over this the Watcher slung his make-shift car-door shield, a protective shell for his back. He quickly shoved their shopping bags into the gear bag, and prepared to zip it back up.

"Hold up, Compadre"… Dominic reached in and withdrew a blanketed bundle. He patted it—"now you may continue. " The Watcher flung the bag at Joey, and the hefty Macho slung it across his shoulder. Dominic nodded. "Now, to find my daughter."

Unheeding of the sniper, Shaney shouted to her men pinned down in the Commons. "What are you waiting for?" She pointed at the slender man in the blue Poncho. "Go after Dominic, you—you…"

She stopped mid-sentence, then pointed again, this time down, towards the Hanging Tree. She squinted, then held her hand up, palm outward, the faint violet light from her Ring cast its activating glow. Astounded, Shaney stretched forward, reaching from the Balcony:

"You!"

The Watcher looked up to see a sparkle of green, glimmering life; a flash of luminescent eyes and a strand of oddly glowing green hair, high in the branches overhanging the fence separating Pair'O'Dice from the Commons. Too late, Rose lowered her eyes, hiding her face in her furs. Tucked into a fork in the Hanging Tree, fifty feet away, a bundle furs was now barely visible between the leaves;

she appeared to be stealthily inching towards Chartreaux's mysterious, ball-tipped weapon dangling from a branch high above her.

"La Fugitiva!" Eyes wide, Shaney jabbed at the Live Oak below the Balcony. "The wiley little varmint's in the Hanging Tree—and she's after your Cane, Reggie!"

"Ha!" Chartreaux shoved the Commander aside to shake his bleeding fist at Rose. "The weapon is useless without the power source, you impudent little clonemonkey." Sneering, Chartreaux mocked the Afterling. "Congratulations on risking everything for nothing."

Clonemonkey? The Watcher snarled and racked his action, raised Sindee and squeezed. A slug whizzed by Chartreaux's ear, pocking the concrete wall behind him; the Boss ducked inside as the Watcher opened fire from the Commons.

"What's the matter Azarian? You don't like me calling your so-called 'girl' a clone?" From within the Silo's balcony doors, Chartreaux needled the Watcher via his fancy megaphone. "Perhaps it's too close to the truth for you? She's not even a real girl... just like any Fighter who wears a Mask is not a real Fighter."

Growling, the Watcher took another fruitless shot to drive back Chartreaux, before turning to take aim at the Bandstand once more. He hit an Enforcer, and a severed arm went flying into a tree.

"Stop shooting up my men, you jackass!" Shouting down to the Watcher, Shaney handed the Boss his reloaded .50 auto, which she had helpfully cleared of the jammed round. Wounded arm dangling limply at his side, Chartreaux fired a round in the direction of the Watcher. It blasted into the dirt at the Watcher's feet.

Across the road, they heard a shout; in the shelter of the Hanging Tree, Survivors were gathering, pointing up into the tree, gawking, and staring. The DragLine Dancers were mingling with a small crowd of LandLords and Citizens. Some bystanders were attempting to scale the fence into Pair'O'Dice, hoping to escape the bullets—others were milling beneath the high branches, looking for a way to pull down Rose.

A few lobbed bottles to try and knock her out of the tree; she ducked into her cape, cushioned from harm by the thick fur. Curious, lascivious, or both, this crowd was turning into a mob. Across the main drag, the Hanging Tree loomed, the Watcher's Prize hiding in its evergreen branches... The Watcher started towards her.

Her saw a slender hand appear over the Boss's shoulder, and the glint of light on a silver barrel; the Watcher dove behind the concrete water trough as another shot was fired, and a divot of dirt went flying up. He heard a shriek. *Rose?*

"Oh I'm sorry, did that frighten you?" Shaney fired a random shot towards the Watcher and shouted to Rose: "You afraid I'll kill your big ol' ugly friend?"

Taking the cue, Chartreaux took another shot at the Watcher and it chipped the edge of the water trough. Survivors around the tree looked up, listening to Chartreaux. "I doubt sincerely she cares about him, much less any single one of you beneath her..."

Shaney's voice became sweet once more. "How about this, lil' darlin': you come down out of the tree and I'll stop."

Don't talk to strangers, Rose... especially this one. The Watcher noted; Shaney was a master-level manipulator, a psychologically toxic wordsmith with no mercy, and no limitations.

"But it's up to you… if you want all these people to die, you just keep it up, Missy." Shaney fired a bullet at the edge of the crowd, and a Dancer squealed as the crowd stampeded beneath the tree. "See?" Shaney whined in an accusatory voice. "Look at what you made me do."

"Stop!" a panicked voice was heard from the branches of the tree— "Don't—don't hurt them…"

"Then stop making me shoot. It's that simple." Shaney retorted.

Well, Hell. The Watcher groaned to himself. *That's just great… Rose is dialoguing with Devil herself.* Pinned down by multiple shooters, The Watcher fired a blind shot back at Shaney just to shut her up, driving her and the Boss into the Silo once more.

The crowd beneath the tree was jostling, trying to get away from the bullets, but still trying to catch a glimpse of the Afterling. Above them, the Balcony dangled by just a few bolts.

"Careful there, Watcher…" Chartreaux threatened from behind the door jamb. "You'll get your little Chippy and her unarmed admirers caught in the crossfire. Or maybe she needs to realize you're just an indiscriminate killer who really wants to kill these poor oppressed war refugees."

Oh good, let's blame me again. Tired of the drama, the Watcher pointed to Dominic then the bag. Joey tapped the Judge's shoulder, and he looked up from his work,

"Hold tight, Compadres." Ducking bullets from the Bandstand, Dominic unwrapped the bundle to uncover what appeared to be a industrial sized reciprocating saw; he pulled it out and placed its power bracelet on his wrist. "I have a burning desire to see what these can accomplish…"

Joey and Li gawked. "Holy Moly, Judge Santos… what's that?" Joey looked closer at his mystery weapon. "Are you going to saw them to death?

"It's the future, mi Amigo, otherwise known as 'crowd control'." Dominic said, pleased with the prospect. "The same weapon as Boss Chartreaux's cane, this 'Super Heating Internal Volatility Activator' is an energy weapon disguised as a working power tool and smuggled into the Republic during LifeBefore. We picked it up from the same people who brought us these ALGOS drones. I have more of them, but I don't have time to train you, and the others are back with the wagon anyway. For now, this will do… allow me to demonstrate."

The Watcher grunted. He wanted to use it, but he was too busy shooting in two different directions at once—at Chartreaux and the Enforcers in the Bandstand.

Using the beer cart as cover, Dominic turned the saw end of the SHIVA device towards Shaney's men at the Bandstand. Cranking the collet on the muzzle of the silver barrel all the way left, Dominic opened the choke wide, then pushed the sliding brass toggle forward on the haft of the long gun. Apprehensive, Li stepped back as a hum was heard.

No effect at all occurred, other than Shaney's enforcers letting loose a storm of bullets. The Watcher returned fire to the Bandstand with the Mariner, as Dominic ducked back behind the cart. Beneath the Bandstand a hat, complete with head, rolled out into the street, and the shooting stopped for a moment.

"Perhaps I need to adjust the aperture..." Dominic fiddled with it, then poked it around the corner again. This time an Enforcer yelped and jumped back. "Ah—broad spread equals short range." He tightened the aperture once more, then aimed towards the Bandstand again...

A portion of the wooden underskirting burst into flames. Shaney's men scattered as the flames spread, and Lourdes' sniper bullet killed one as he ran. Surprised at the flames, Dominic stifled a cough and grabbed his ribs. "Well, that was unintended, but handy. However, that is not where I was aiming..."

"Maybe it needs to be sighted?" Joey offered while taking potshots at the fleeing Enforcers.

"Perhaps." Dominic ducked behind the cart once more to play with it.

Down by Purgatory gate they could hear the battle raging, shouts and curses spattering in the darkness. From the Commons, the sound of Sam's crew exchanging gunfire with the Enforcers could be heard dying down. Dominic noticed the change—the dynamics of the battle were changing on distant fronts, and it was time to join forces.

"Now, to hurry this along and help our friends—let's see if we can make it hot for Chateau de Chartreaux..." Dominic raised the SHIVA saw-rifle to his shoulder, and squeezed the integrated trigger-grip, listening to the melodic hum.

A small, twiggy bush caught fire near entrance to Pair'O'Dice, and the ancient wooden gate went up in flames.

Dominic smiled with satisfaction. "Alright, then, Gentlemen, let us begin. Cover me, Compadres." Joey and Li came out from behind the cart with their pistols to take aim at the Balcony. Seeing them, Shaney and Chartreaux hung back, out of line of fire. A sniper bullet from afar drove the point home, chipping the doorjamb…

Dominic calmly strode out into the Main Drag surrounding the Commons, SHIVA device shouldered. As he approached the Water trough, the Watcher fired a shot, and all heads turned to look his direction. The Watcher stepped out from the behind the trough to take his place at Dominic's side, a smoking Sindee in one hand, his car-door riot shield on the other.

"Good Evening, Amigos. I am Dominic Santos of the WildLand Express, and I am here to rescue my daughter and avenge the murders of my Agents at the hands of Boss Chartreaux and Commander Shaney. You though—" Dominic pointed to the gathered crowd beneath the tree. "I have no quarrel with unarmed bystanders. I have opened the gate for you, and I suggest you head through it to Pair'O'Dice and safety." He waved towards the gate. "Go now, and you won't be harmed. Do so quickly, before I change my mind…"

Aiming the directed energy weapon at an isolated tree nearby, Dominic squeezed the trigger once more, and a branch of the tree combusted. Alarmed, the Dancers scurried toward the charred remains of the gate. Others, however, lingered, incensed by the prospect of the Afterling.

"Very well, let me convince you to leave." Dominic opened the aperture wide, and gripped the haft of the gun tightly; the hum modulated to a lower, buzzing pitch.

Grumbling and shouting, the crowd suddenly moved away from the tree, as a wave of discomfort washed over them. Dominic smiled graciously as he walked towards the tree, the Watcher with him. Dominic swept the weapon side to side, and the group of Survivors stepped back with each sweep. Joey and Li pushed behind him, brandishing their weapons.

"Muchas gracias—Hija, Father's here to pick you up. Come down."

As Rose's Extraction Team advanced, the small sea of Survivors parted willingly, jumping back as the SHIVA device heated their innards to less-than-lethal levels. Dominic planted himself beneath the noose of the Hanging Tree, and whispered to the Watcher as he held the crowd back:

"Watcher, sound your signal, then grab your date—it's past curfew, and I want her home."

Reaching behind him, the Watcher lifted his Golden Horn to his lips, then blew his call. The brassy peal split the smokey veil that obscured the sky; it rang out, above the Silo, past the Commons, all the way down to the Jail, where the Public Servants heard the trumpet blast. With a mighty shout, they threw off their chains, and Sanders fired the shot that set them free…

Slinging his horn back behind him, the Watcher walked beneath the tree, gazing up into its branches. High above him, a delicate face peered down, eyes glowing in the moonlight. He beckoned to her, and she nodded her head, then pointed towards Chartreaux's ball-tipped Cane.

"Oh absolutely—just let me get this, and I'll be right down."

He scowled and shook his head emphatically, and pointed at her again, then at his own feet. *You. Here. Now…* Rose scooted out onto the branch, "Of course; this will only take a minute—it's on the way."

Chartreaux bellowed from the Balcony bedroom door: "Leave my Cane alone, you trollop! I will flay you alive—"

The Watcher blasted a shot through the branches of the tree, and it hit the underside of the balcony, ricocheting off into the night sky.

Bystanders ducked and he heard Shaney cursing."That's not meant for you! You've got no idea what you're doing—if you handle that thing wrong, you'll kill us all!"

Undaunted, Rose crept forward carefully, calling out to the Visionaries in the Silo as she went:

"I shan't let you have it. You can't be allowed to terrorize these innocent Survivors with such a terrible weapon." In response to Rose's impassioned cry for justice, a beer bottle bounced off her leg, and she winced. A drunken Survivor smooched at her:

"C'mere… c'mere, you lil' tart!" The grubby Hombre grinned a gap-toothed smile at Rose, and lobbed another beer bottle her way. The Watcher smashed his face.

"Well, I'll be dogged—you really are that dumb, aren't you?" Shaney snorted. "These 'innocent Survivors' will tear you limb from limb unless someone controls them."

Certain in her virtue, Rose ignored Shaney and kept climbing down the branch. Growing impatient, Dominic hissed over his shoulder at her: "Time to go now, Hija… leave it."

Stretching, the Cane was just beyond her fingertips' reach. "I can't. They will use it to destroy people's souls—just like they use them to destroy the souls of the Asura. Please—I promise..." Rose inched forward on the slender branch, struggling to grab it. "I'm coming!" She tried to sound cheery, but it was not easy while poor oppressed Survivors were tossing bottles and bits of gravel at her. The Watcher snarled, a vicious growl that could be heard by everyone—including Rose.

He waved his shotgun and the crowd jumped back. *I'm done with 'crowd control'—it's fixin' to be mass casualty...* Grumbling to himself, he raised it, and they rushed away.

"Almost got it..." Rose reached out as far as she could; her hand closed around the tip of the Cane's shaft. "Okee Dokee!"

The Boss leaned out the doorway to fire off a shot. The Balcony groaned as another strut came loose, and the balcony dangled precariously by its last bolt. Agitated, Shaney drew Chartreaux back just as a strut snapped. "Don't step out there again you lunkhead—"

Something small and silver ran out from between Chartreaux's legs, leaping out to the topsy-turvy deck of the dangling balcony... a groan of ancient steel was heard as the last ounce of structural integrity sagged beneath Princess Precious Sweetums' dainty paws.

The world stopped as Chartreaux thrust Shaney away. "What are you after—" Shaney snapped, then saw it—

Oblivious to all else around him, the big Boss held out a shaking hand. "No no no, kitty, come here kitty, come here Precious—" Defiant, the kitten yowled, angry with the chaotic world around—then leapt sideways to the Balcony rail.

A hideous metallic shriek was heard as a beam twisted, and the balcony crashed to the ground in the courtyard below.

Rose froze as the iron deck smashed past her, narrowly missing her to break a thick branch. A man's leg was crushed beneath a fallen metal beam, and she heard shouts as the crowd clambered to get away.

Amidst the mayhem, the Afterling heard a mewling cry; it sounded like a baby, lost and alone. She turned her eyes upward, and saw a small grey ball of fur. It spit and hissed at her.

"Princess Precious Sweetums!" Shocked, Chartreaux jabbered: "Any of you vile hooligans harms my Precious and I will rain death down upon you all!"

"Perhaps we can come to an agreement." Dominic said cheerfully, training the SHIVA device upon the spitting feline. "You call off your men, and I won't fry your cat. That seems fair enough."

"Oh Father, no—" Rose reached out to try and comfort the little beast, and it clawed at her. "We can't hurt this darling little cat!"

"Well certainly that kitten is not worth any more that you. I'll be glad to trade him. Chartreaux should consider it." Dominic seemed mildly annoyed.

Agitated, the Watcher grunted loudly and grabbed Joey's hand. Joey cleared his throat: "And, um, the Watcher says he will personally roast your Princess Precious Sweetums like a marshmallow unless you let his Princess Tippie-Toes escape unharmed…"

"Princess Tippie-Toes?" Rose hissed softly at him, embarrassed.

The Watcher gave a gunpowdery, sideways smirk.

"Fine." Chartreaux glowered down, eyes malevolent with unbridled rage. "I'll give it all up to save my darling Precious."

"What? Are you insane? You can't do this—" Shaney yanked on the Boss' arm.

He caught her by the lapel and shook her; the Boss whispered into Shaney's ear, and she ducked back inside the tower. He turned back towards the French Doors, just beyond reach of bullets:

"You have me." Chartreaux threw a meaty arm across his forehead in a rather dramatic fashion. "I'll withdraw our men, if you will allow my aides to retrieve my innocent little kitten. Tell your people to hold their fire, and you may go ahead and leave…. Just don't hurt my Princess Precious!"

The Watcher gazed upon this performance with suspicion.

"WildLand Express; hold your position, but hold your fire on innocent bystanders—for now." Shiva device still trained on Shaney's men, Dominic pointedly called to Rose: "Vamos, Hija!"

Rose began scooting down last forty feet of the branch and towards the Watcher, careful not to slip and fall into the bystanders.

Out of the Silo and through the gate Sugar and Spice came, calling as they went: "Here, Kitty, Kitty—" Sugar split off from Spice and jogged over to the PickUp Truck Planter. The Watcher's eyes followed him, suspicious, as Sugar leaned against the tailgate, fiddling nervously with something in the bed of the truck.

"Here, Kitty, Kitty… " All other eyes were on Spice as he approached the tree, wiggling his fingers enticingly to Precious, muttering low: "you wretched little furball-horking demon spawn…"

Precious hissed.

Openly rebelling at this weakness, Shaney's Enforcers grumbled as they withdrew to a position just within the Pair'O'Dice fence. Wary, Joey and Li moved in tight formation with Dominic, forming a protective circle around the Watcher and his intended catch.

Urgent, the Watcher clapped his hands—*Come. Down. Now.*

Rose wriggled towards him faster, inchworm style.

Wandering back over from the Pickup Truck Planter, Sugar sidled up to Spice and whispered in his ear. Abruptly, both Hombres turned on their heels and leapt through the burnt fence into the Silo courtyard with Chartreaux's men.

The Watcher racked his shotgun, motioning frantically to Rose— *NOW*—

Suddenly, the hum from the SHIVA device stopped; the smile disappeared from Dominic's face, as the Watcher's HeadsUp display went dark.

Grim, Li hissed to Joey: "We've lost all Communications."

Unpleasant reality set in as the SHIVA device became cold and lifeless once again. "Dios mio—the SHIVA device has shut down..." Dominic murmured to the Watcher: "and that means the Purgatory Jammer is back up!"

"What an ironic shame." A deep voice sneered from the darkness above. "You're the ones who prayed, but we're the ones who've called down the gods." The Watcher looked up to see Chartreaux giving a savage sneer from the French Doors of the wrecked Balcony once more: "You are pathetic and gullible. Thank you for allowing my 'innocent bystanders' time to invoke the gods' wrath."

The Watcher blinked—*the old PickUp Truck Planter hides the Main Purgatory Jammer!*

Shaney gasped with delight.

"Make a note for future reference; I don't negotiate." Chartreaux raised his gun towards the mewling kitten.

"No!" Rose shouted, horrified.

He pulled the trigger.

The bullet whizzed wide, and the little cat tumbled from the tree, caterwauling. Fur singed, Princess Precious Sweetums darted away into the crowd.

Chartreaux gloated as a pleasantly surprised Shaney openly ogled him from her bucket. "Princess will be back, and she'll learn to come down from trees when Daddy calls. You only wish you could train your little clonemonkey so well, Watcher."

The Watcher snarled.

"Now, with that out of the way..." Chartreaux pointed to Dominic: "Welcome back to the Bronze Age, Gentlemen. Men of Purgatory—Santos' terrible weapon no longer works. Get the Afterling!"

Cheering, Shaney's Enforcers surged through the burnt gate. Shaney commanded as they ran: "No guns! La Fugitiva must be taken alive, and we can't take a chance on a stray bullet!"

The Horde roared, rushing forward. Clinging for dear life, Rose tucked herself into a fork of the branch as her Protectors' guns roared back, and the entire scene degenerated into bloody mayhem. Rocks and bottles flew; lead sprayed, and gun smoke billowed.

Below her, the Watcher had slipped his Remington back into its holster, unable to reload. He had replaced it with his Bowie Knife, slashing with one hand, smashing his shield into the crowd with his other, repelling them.

A knife-wielding Hombre reached through the crowd to slash back at the Watcher, then weaving back into the mob around him. She gasped as the knife-man pressed forward again, slicing a gash into the Watcher's shoulder...

Suddenly the mob seemed less human to her. "Leave him alone, you Devil!" Angry, she swung the ball-tipped cane at the knife-man' head, but she was too high up to reach. Frustrated, she tossed the Cane at knife-man, a blunt spear, and the heavy metal tip bounced off the Hombre's felt hat. The knife-man grabbed his head and glared up at the Afterling:

"You little bitch—"

The Watcher's fist smashed the knife-man in the face, then sliced the blade across his opponent's throat. He shoved the dying man back, and grabbed the Cane from beneath his bloody feet. *This has some reach.* The Watcher sheathed his knife, and began to swing the Cane like a long handled mace, crushing skulls with a barbaric glee.

Perilously close to running out of ammo, and fighting in the half-darkness of the lantern-lit Purgatory Night, Dominic, Joey and Li warded off the last remnants of mob. They opened up the clearing again.

The Watcher glared up into the Hanging tree, and the Afterling recoiled for just a moment; hands black from gunpowder and red with blood, he beckoned to her once more. Slinging his car-door shield back behind him completely, he held up his arms; *Come down, NOW—*

"I'm sorry. I wasn't trying to delay..." Her eyes glittered with tears. "I just wanted you to have the Cane, so they couldn't ever hurt anyone with it again." Adjusting her small bag beneath her cape, she prepared to inch down the rope, and into the Watcher's arms fifteen feet below. She gingerly stuck out a leg, then gasped.

Rose was glowing. She looked down at her hands, confused, then looked up, trying to see anything that might cast such a light—but she saw nothing.

The crowd gazed on her, temporarily dazzled; her face, her legs, her slender fingers, all fluorescing, growing brighter, then fading, as if a light touched her from a great distance, then passed in the night.

All tech was still down; nothing was working, and yet—the Watcher could feel it on prickly edge of his senses—something was piercing the Jammer's electronic veil. He was abruptly, keenly aware of a whisper in the darkness. Not the buzzing sound of a drone, but something different, something he had never heard before. He heard the hiss of razor-thin wings slicing the air.

"Oh—" Rose flinched, then touched the side of her neck, dazed. She swayed as she pulled her hand away, holding up her fingertips. "I-I'm… Staring at them for a moment, she looked confused, voice trailing away…

Suddenly limp, Rose began to slide off the branch. Alarmed, the Watcher reached for her, straining to catch Rose as she fell—

He felt it zip past him, an unknown entity, small, quick. Still reaching for Rose, the Watcher lashed out to strike the mysterious object with the ball-tipped cane.

He saw the flash before he heard it—

A crunch and a hiss as the spherical weapon's components connected with the ethereal object's power source, sparking into conflagration. He saw a brief glimpse of a matte black shape, triangular and thin, as the payload materials ignited. Above the blinding light, Rose fell tumbling from the Hanging Tree, and the entire crowd leapt with the Watcher, reaching for the Prize.

The Glider Drone fused with the Cane's SHIVA device—and exploded.

The Watcher rolled and caught Rose, sweeping her into his arms. Crouching on the balls of his tire-tread moccasins, he slammed her against the trunk of the tree, his arms tight around her. Wrapped in his Metallilume-lined cloak, the Watcher turned the insulated car-door against the blast, and he became a living Shield; the fur of her cloak's hood smoked as he buried her face against his neck.

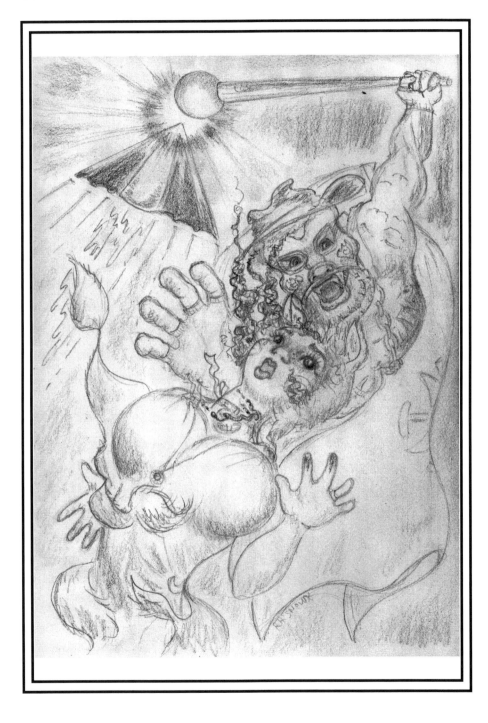

He heard a collective shout as everything disappeared. Concussion and fury became the world all around them, a concentrated electro-chemical flash blotting out all other sound and light—

and yet, all the Watcher could feel was the warmth of Rose's soft skin against his scarred flesh, her smooth cheek against his neck. He pulled her in, tighter, covering her with himself. The blast evaporated with a pop, then crackled into oblivion; the noose fell to the ground, its dangling rope burned from the flash.

The Watcher stuck out a finger, then raised his head, pushing away from the tree trunk.

Several Survivors in his immediate circle standing were now knocked out or dazed, lying on the ground—another appeared to have been blinded, stumbling. The blast radius was limited to less than ten feet, a hot, quick blast. The tips of his thick ears were singed, and the backs of his hands had some small burns, but otherwise, the Watcher escaped the conflagration relatively unharmed. Relieved, he released Rose, reluctant to let go when she was so quiet and warm against him...

Unmoving, Rose slid from his grasp into the dirt beneath him.

Further outside the immediate blast radius, Dominic was fist-fighting some hulking Macho; still further out, Joey was grappling with two skinny Hombres who were trying to reach Rose, and Li was firing into the Commons, answering some unseen shooter; but all the Watcher could hear was Rose, speaking from the night before, in her little room in the loft of the Wild Horses Hotel:

"They did it to punish Love! Oh Saul!" She had cried, full of chocolate and angst, flinging her arms around his neck: *"I can't bear the thought of what they might do to you if we are captured! I can't! I can't..."*

I can't bear the thought—

He shook her slightly, and her head rolled to the side, exposing a faint trickle of blood from a small hole in her neck.

I can't...

He pulled Rose in close, trying to feel her breath on his cheek, but there was none.

I

can't

Joey was talking to someone about Rose not looking so good, and Li was shaking the Watcher—

An attacker rushed from his left, but the Watcher didn't seem to notice. The world was strangely calm, outside of himself; he could see himself quietly trying to rouse Rose, even as he smashed the face of the stranger with a flashing backfist. The Hombre fell senseless as the Watcher attempted to gently wake Rose with one hand, patting her face, which had taken on an odd grayish tint in place of her usual golden-pink undertone. Uncoiling from her hood, her glossy black hair spread out, loosing itself to lie in a puddle beneath her head.

Nothing.

Lifting her to his chest, he cradled her in one arm, gathering hers up with the other. Her arms splayed to the sides, slithering away from his own, limp, open...

Dimly, as if very far away, Dominic shouted over his shoulder: "Get her to the Gate!"

a dark energy was coalescing in the Watcher, concentrating—

he felt the flash in his soul before he heard it, roaring as the world faded to red.

Suddenly his legs were moving of their own accord, pumping, flying, the prairie rolling beneath him as he hovered above the earth, each stride a mile, each step an eternity. Rose was on one arm, his shield on the other, covering her from fire as he ran, the world rushing by.

An arm appeared from over the Watcher's shoulder, throttling him in a chokehold; he broke off the hand, twisting it at the wrist to rip the sinews and crush the bone, then flung it away into the weeds. The arm owning the dismembered hand spouted blood as it fell away.

Beyond the Watcher's consciousness, an Enforcer thrust a shotgun into the Watcher face. He seemed to be moving in slow motion, almost peaceful as the Watcher twisted the shotgun out of the Enforcer's hands. The Watcher beat him to death, two short strokes to the head, smashed like a melon beneath the wooden butt of his own shotgun. All the while the Watcher was running with Rose dangling from his embrace...

A group of five Enforcers appeared in his field of vision, closing fast; someone fired a shot, and he felt the blast incinerate the air by his ear. Tucking his head behind his car-door shield, the Watcher smashed his way through their wall of flesh, slashing with the raised lower edge of his shield to cut them apart. They scattered before him, evaporating as a red mist hanging in the cold night air... he felt their entrails slip beneath his moccasin-boots as he trampled them into the dust.

All the world was narrowing down to one pinpoint of light, one single

Rose blooming in an eternal Fibonacci sequence; he could hear the voice of Rose inside his head, singing over and over:

There's a meadow in a valley, where the skies are fair

Even though I've never seen it, I know that it is there

Her song filled his mind, and the Watcher wondered why he had never sung the song himself. He never had to—Rose sang it, and that was all he had ever needed.

A bullet ripped through the metal edge of the car door shield, exiting the other side. Effortlessly, the Watcher slung his shield to the side then stooped as he ran, scooping up a stone to fling at the BrigadesMan. The stone sailed lazily through the air, earth joining flesh between the shooter's bulging eyes as the BrigadesMan sank gracefully to earth.

The Watcher was suddenly transported back in time to his first glimpse of Rose, only mere days ago. He remembered the stone he flung, believing her to be his enemy, and he recalled her little life-saving bike helmet with a scuffed pink heart sticker. But even though the helmet saved her life, she carried the scar, inflicted by his own hand...

Farther, faster, he flew, but the gate still seemed to be miles away, Smoke curled upwards from the burnt houses of HighTown, ghosts from the Hostess Club rising in their pall, up from the now-abandoned tunnel where he had once kissed Rose—

Far behind him, he heard feet running, and shouts, and the sound of gunfire—the bloodlust of battle, the thrill of the fight. The noise of War now rang in his ears, ascending to the high places of his consciousness, almost overwhelming the song of Rose and the memories of Life lived on the cusp of happiness. Always one more moment away...

from his memory, Rose's song of Life vaulted over War's dirge of Death:

Oh my dream has never failed me though I searched my whole life through;

There were times I almost found it and those times were with you...

the memory cracked open his soul, and the music poured out.

And I know that I will find it someday

....

His Mentors were wrong.

There was only one reason to fight, only one reason to live, and Rose was the reason. With her, Life was music—without her, life was just noise, an empty gong. He couldn't go back to Life without her glorious music, the melody of Freedom, the cacophony of Love...

Even if he had never sung of Love himself, he had heard it in the Song of Rose.

The Watcher ran howling beneath the waning crescent moon. Behind him, he could hear burst of gunfire; before him, Purgatory gate opened to the WildLands, the abyss of Eternity yawning.

A dull rumble quaked the earth beneath the Watcher's feet, and he briefly stumbled. Buildings shook, rusted panels of tin tipped off the edges of their precarious perches on rafters to open rooms to the stars. Glasses shattered, falling from ledges and shelves...

Another boom, and then the entire dump heaved into the sky as a fireball burst forth from the entrance to the Bunker. Bogie's hut disintegrated into a thousand putrid shards as drifts of trash came tumbling down around it, avalanches of refuse, cans and bottles launching rolling into the streets. Leaves were blown from the PickUp Truck Planter's fig tree as the concussion rolled through Purgatory; Survivors fell to the ground, Dancers shrieked...

The Watcher flew on the wings of morning, bearing Rose through the darkness, beyond the Gates of Purgatory.

Joey and Dominic entered ahead of him, Li firing back towards the Bandstand as he ran, providing cover for the Watcher, Sam and her team. Lourdes ran ahead with Habib, elegant hands stained with gunpowder, shaken by the explosions.

Blood spurted behind Michaels as he stumbled, shot though the calf; Mansour dragged him out as Sam returned fire. Li backed in with her.

Running through the crowd, the Watcher heard Winston call out: "Status check—are all accounted?"

"One last group!"

The Jailhouse Team were cheering from the parapets, firing into bandstand, holding back Shaney's Enforcers as a great shout arose from Purgatory itself. Sanders and the last of the Public Servants ran for their lives, at last unbound, running towards freedom, shouting as they ran—

"Libre! LoneStar Libre!"

Grey eyes bright, Sanders raised his rifle towards the sky, running as fast and as free as he had run in the days of his youth, before the chains came. The years fell away with every step, and Sanders became younger, stronger, more beautiful than the world had ever seen him, a man who had always been free—

A shot pierced the fine pashmina scarf; its hue changed, champagne to sangria. Eyes lifted to the open sky, Sanders fell just outside the Gate, free of Purgatory at last.

As the Watcher ran by with Rose, Sampson lifted Sanders, bearing him to the casualty wagon. To the side of the Wagon stood Gunny, holding watch over the earthly shell of Goins, Sassy lying mournful at his feet.

"My Lulu…" the old man wept.

Beside him, Araceli sat with Montague's cold body, her crushed foot wrapped in a rag. She was trembling, gritting her teeth, while Kendra poured out liquor over the blood-sodden rags to try and sanitize the wound. Unnerved, a wan Winston averted his eyes and shouted to the assembly:

"Status check—are all accounted?"

Lourdes was searching, cool eyes now wild with a strange light. "Wait… the Gambler, has anyone seen him? Anyone?" They shook their heads. Lourdes started to bolt through the Gate: "I'm going back…"

Dominic grabbed her hand to stop her: "No—there's no going back." He called to Evangelo's team:

"Close it—block the Gate!"

Lourdes turned so none could see her weep; the Jailhouse Team swung the gate shut, jamming boards into the mechanisms; a heavy wagon loaded with dirt and rubble was hastily rolled in front of it to prevent the block any exit by horseback. Joey and Li swung into action, a pit crew to disable the wheels and block the gate.

Winston called to Wilcox, who was hanging partway out of the hold of the Catastronix Wagon. "Shutting down in two minutes—we'll need communications back up when we split up on the trail." Wilcox nodded, and ducked back into the hold to tinker with the Catastronix. The Wagon was surrounded by gore, parts and pieces of shredded bodies lay in the roadway, and two more lay mangled inside the corral, torn apart by some vicious horror.

That horror was now lying meekly with his ladies. Destiny sat on the tailgate of the open hold, her arms around a hassling, bloody Oskar.

Sighting the Watcher running, Oskar leapt out to lope along beside him.

Not slowing, the Watcher ran through the Corral gate, vaulting over a wounded Agent, bounding up to an open Wagon bed. He tried to lay her down, but his arm stayed twined around her. It seemed to have grown that way during this last eternity together…

Grim, Winston grabbed the Watcher's arm and pointed to the wagon. "Get her on the bed, let us look at her—" Dominic ran up behind him, holding a dimly-lit lantern aloft in the darkness.

"Prepare to move out!"

The Watcher laid her down upon the boards, her limp body rolling in his encircling arms. Face hidden beneath her hood, she was covered in gore from the Watcher's run; nonetheless, all could see where a thread of blood trailed out of the pinprick hole in the side of her exposed neck. It oozed, a trail of dark red blood, already coagulating.

Dominic's face darkened, "Dios mio… " He looked to Winston, and Winston shook his head, whispering.

"Don't say it."

Beneath the wagon, Oskar howled.

Everyone was reaching for her now—Von Helm shoving though the line, his forearm wrapped in a bloody rag; Evangelo standing in tense prayer, Sam, reeking of sweat and gun smoke, and Mansour, hanging back to watch in silence…

Winston tried to pry the Watcher's fingers loose. "I'm going to resuscitate—let go—"

I can't…

The Watcher was frozen next to her, grasping the edges of her deerskin cape. Winston barked: "Let go!"

The Watcher's hands began to shake. *I can't*—

Reaching around the Watcher, Winston grasped the fur ruff. He pulled her hood back, revealing—

A pair of luminous black eyes blinking up, embarrassed.

At the sight of so many around her, dumbfounded at her apparent resurrection, Rose tried to hide her face beneath the hood again.

Sam shook her head; "You… you're not…"

"I'm so, so sorry. I'm not dead… I'm just cataplexic." Silence answered Rose. She pulled her hood down, hiding her face.

"Something shot me while I was in the tree, but I don't know what or how. It burned, and then…"

Dazed, the Watcher pulled her hood away, clutching it by its floppy deer's ears so she couldn't pull it over her face again.

On her neck gapped a hollow, pinprick puncture; an ugly, unnaturally empty-looking puncture wound slightly pink around the edges. Gently touching the wound on her neck, she wiped away blood, staring at the crimson stain on her fingertips. She murmured:

"I tried to move, but I couldn't. Then he knocked the breath out of me when he slammed me against the tree, and with everything going crazy, I...I just, you know—freezie flopsie.."

Mortified, Rose held up her hands, trying to hide herself. The Watcher wrenched her up from the wagon bed by the collar of her fur cape, and she stammered: "You r-really should check for pulse first..."

He tore the Mask away and pressed his lips to hers.

From atop the disabled Gate, gunfire still raged; from within Purgatory, the Forces of the New Order were regrouping, reloading, preparing to give chase. But here, within the circle of his arms, the world stopped moving; the sounds of war faded. Nothing existed but the light in her eyes, the rise and fall of her breath, and the throb of her heart beating against his own:

Life!

At last she gasped for breath. "Wait! I don't need to be resuscitated!"

He wasn't listening.

Beyond the Watcher's consciousness, his bittersweet celebration at Rose's life was tempered by the specter of death; war was still unfolding its bloody banner across the midnight sky. A visibly shaken Dominic called out to Winston: "Casualty count?"

Winston came, carrying a groaning Araceli, Kendra fast behind her. Gilberto and the new recruits rallied around their former Boss, helping attend casualties. Winston called out to Dominic as he strode by. "Nine wounded—Seven with minor wounds—King, Throckmorton, Peters, Von Helm, Stills, Luck, and Ghambi. Three with major injuries—Michaels, Diaz, Sanders. Two dead—Goins and Montague. Missing—the Gambler."

"No!" Grimacing, Araceli pushed Winston's arms away: "I must stay with Ricky—" Bloody foot flailing, she wept, still fighting to break free.

"You can't remain with the dead," Winston stated flatly. "You're alive, and you're coming with me." He said it more to himself than to her; Araceli shook her head and wept again. He laid Araceli next to Destiny in the hospital wagon, and Kendra jumped in beside her to hold her.

Dusty and quiet, a Dark Macho came up to the hospital Wagon, crumpled hat in his hand. He spoke softly to the wounded woman.

"Ma'am, my heart is truly broken… Ricky wasn't just my partner, he was my friend. But I'll never forget what you did for him, never." Agent King's face started to crumple, but he straightened himself out. "You made his dream come true. He made this for you. Here—" pressing a small item into her hand, he trembled slightly, then replaced his hat, and walked away.

Araceli cracked apart her bloody fingers to gaze at a tiny wooden heart, Agent Montague's last act of beauty. Closing her hand tight around it, she whispered. "Mi Corazon…"

Winston was starting to show an odd strain on his face: "Do we have anything for pain?"

"I gave her four shots of Reunion's finest, then doused her foot. It should kick in soon. But if all else fails," Kendra pulled a stub of a budweed cigarette out of her pocket, "you know I always carry a little something extra…" Sampson scowled at it, but Evangelo bowed his head.

"That is the purpose for which God intended His gift."

Leaning over his daughter, Dominic whispered. "Medic, the wounded are triaged, but your hands will be needed as soon as you recover."

"Oh, Father, I am ready now!" Hearing Araceli's anguished groans, Rose started to sit up, but the Watcher pushed her back down. Dominic shook his head:

"You are wounded, Hija. Until we know all the effects of your injury, stay with Marshal Azarian."

"Oh it's just a teensy scratch. I feel shaky, but that is all—it will pass, I promise."

As he passed, Winston whispered to the Watcher: "I'm no medic; I'm just trained in basic first aid, but it looks like a self-cauterizing injection wound, just like you said one would be used for a tracking payload." The Watcher returned a grave nod to Winston.

Dominic squeezed Rose's hand, then walked away; "Stay by her side, Watcher. Angels unawares…"

Enlightenment dawned as the Watcher remembered the Gambler's same words. *Angels unawares—Watchers on High, the Guardians Angels of the System's Universe.*

It all led to this. All the training, all the death, all the sorrows—it all led to this one moment of life. and now more than ever, he had to be the B.E.S.T… the Watcher pulled the Mask back into place. Any minute, more drones could come—and now, they were coming for Rose. A payload had been delivered…

Rose had been tagged.

Grim, Dominic called up Evangelo. "Shepherd, pray over the missing, the wounded and the dead—our fallen will ride in the Honor Wagon until we can bury them down the trail."

Kendra wrapped Sanders in a blanket as he gurgled, his eyes searching. Lourdes climbed up, and laid his head in her lap, the blood from his new clothes staining the slave rags Lourdes' had taken to disguise herself. He tried to reach beneath the coat she had given him. Habib leaned in to take his assistant's hand, struggling to contain his emotion. "Is there something you wish to say?" Sanders nodded slightly, then gasped for breath. patting his own pocket. Lourdes reached beneath the coat and felt a mid-sized, heavy bag—at the sight, Habib's eyes grew wide.

"The betting pot!" For the first time, Lourdes saw a glimmer of tears in Habib's eyes. "The whole thing… you stole the entire pot from the betting tables! You did it, Mike—"

Smoothing Sanders' noble brow, Lourdes spoke soft words until at last his eyes lost their luster, and she closed them with a soft hand.

Laying in the last shots from the parapets, the gate defenders pushed back against the few demoralized stragglers still shooting from within Purgatory. Joey and Li made rounds securing the wagons, while Von Helm rallied his troops into formation. From their truck-bed wagon, the former Public Servants of Purgatory joined with the kinsmen from Reunion, and others of their lot. Beneath the watchful eye of Von Helm, the new recruits were gathered, ready for their new lives—

Occasionally the little Sheriff looked over to see the Afterling, but quickly averted his gaze when the Watcher looked his way.

"Marshal Azarian, it's time to give the signal—" Dominic emerged from the Corral atop a joyous Charger; he stroked his Horse's mane, whispering: "Now we ride, mi Amigo…"

The Wagon jerked, rolling forward. Sweeping Rose out of the Wagon, the Watcher found Oro, and lifted Rose into the Golden Palomino's saddle, hauling himself up behind her. Oskar gamboled beside Oro, glad to finally run, and the assemblage marveled at the sight of the barbaric Watcher riding his magnificent Horse with the Afterling in his arms, a Chupacabra running by his side…

The Watcher's hand found hers, and he laid eyes for the first time upon the gold and pearl Ring. It shone like a full Moon, and he wondered if that was why the Child chose it; *does it remind you of your Mother in the Moonlight Meadow, your Little Flower at her Feet?* The Watcher felt a breeze touch his bleeding cheek; he did not see the Child but it was enough just to know she was near.

His eyes turned to the Child's mother, facing away from him in the saddle, her fragile fingers twined in his as he gripped the reins. Swept away in the moment, the Watcher was overcome by a feeling too deep for words, one he dared not name for fear it would shatter his heart. What the future held, he did not know; death, life, hope, or despair; but in this moment, it didn't matter anymore. Here, now, he held all of it in his arms, and the Watcher felt he could never want for more.

He linked Rose's old Ring with her new one. Rose admonished: "Oh, it's not working yet—I think they are still jammed." He grunted and linked anyway, wrapping his sinewy hand around her small one, then set his Digital Deception Transmitter. It would be needed in the coming days…

A small window opened in his right top HeadsUp display, a legacy function running silent beneath the sheltering umbrella of his own personal jammer, the Digital Deception Transmitter. Running the network analysis, he could see an unknown signal testing portals and channels.

From inside Rose, the Telometrix Instant Recognition System was seeking a way past the Digital Deception Transmitter and out through Rose's Ring.

#WATCHER: Talisa, block this signal and isolate it. Analyze.
#<3 TalisaBOT: *I'm on it, Saul.* **<3**

The Watcher slammed the digital door shut.

Now Rose's data began to flow from her embryonic nanobots, communicating with the matching receiver-bots embedded in the Ring perched on his own gnarled finger. Once more, he felt Rose's warmth spiraling through his nerves, and entering his soul as her scent curled around him. The Watcher felt a strange new emotion, a fruit of a Living Vine:

Credit where credit is due, Unknown God—you saved the Lost.

He remembered his Oath to Evangelo.

Thanks.

Reining tight, the Watcher wheeled his steed, galloping towards the assembled wagons and horsemen. From his flank, Evangelo cantered alongside the Watcher, bringing up the rear on William as he escorted the hospital wagon with its precious cargo. Fancy suit now stained with gunpowder and gore, he clasped the Watcher's hand in joyous reprise: "Never Surrender!"

The Watcher grinned in return—then gunfire erupted from Purgatory Gate once more as defenders fired a volley to repel pursuers. Evangelo rode back to his team, shouting commands. Horseless personnel were loaded into holds, sitting on sideboards, armed and ready.

It was time for the Revolution to escape into the WildLands

As Evangelo broke away to rally the wagons, he saw Destiny lying against the other Hostesses in the bed of the Wagon, trying to warm Araceli. Face still bruised from her terrible attack, Destiny groped for Araceli's trembling hand, trying to comfort her injured friend. Even in her distress, she emanated a loving beauty; the soft cream sweater and hat made her unseeing eyes appear as if they were the most silver of snowflakes.

Evangelo blushed and quickly turned away.

"Marshal?" Hesitant, Destiny whispered to him, as he cantered by; surprised, he turned William to trot back to her:

"I'm sorry Ma'am, I m-mean yes?" As sophisticated and dashing as he had been in Ruby's beautiful suit, Evangelo suddenly felt awkward once again, fumbling his words.

"I don't think we were ever properly introduced." From the safety of her friend's arms, she called to him. "I'm Destiny."

"Oh…yes. I know." Evangelo blushed down to his toes. "I'm sorry Ma'am, I mean—Destiny, I… " He said it and he didn't die; " how did you know I was riding by? Can you see me now?"

"Not yet, but someday I will. I asked Kendra to let me know when you were riding by; I just need to tell thank you for today."

Disappointed with himself, he frowned. "I don't see why. I failed. I didn't arrest Shaney or kill Chartreaux."

"Maybe not today, but another day will come." Destiny murmured softly. "Instead, you came to my rescue, even though you had another mission. You gave up killing Chartreaux to save me."

Evangelo's bloody, powder-burned hands gave testament to his battle at the Gate. "I heard you scream, and I came as fast as I could—but even then, Oskar had already killed most of the villains on his own." At the mention of his name, Oskar belched up a bloody badge.

Destiny continued. "But you remained true to yourself, and you defended my Honour. You told the world I was an innocent woman. That means so much…" She thought upon it. "I haven't been called innocent by anyone in a long time."

"It will be different from now on, Ma'am" Pensive, Evangelo urged William forward, then turned one more time towards the slender pink hembra. "Destiny. You are Destiny."

He galloped off.

Destiny listened as the Last Ranger rode away, then whispered to Kendra. "He's never really been my lover, has he? That was all just a pretty story Araceli thought up to make me feel better, wasn't it?"

Araceli grimaced and shook her head; "No! It was real—love was real!" She wailed once more, more from a broken heart than her crushed foot. It echoed off the walls of Purgatory, causing the the nightbirds to scatter. Unable to bear the sound, Winston abruptly spurred his horse and galloped away to the head of the column, as fast as his horse could carry him.

The cry still echoed. Winston still heard it.

"Maybe so." Kendra squeezed Araceli's hand as she shook violently beneath the heavy blankets. Kendra glanced ahead to Sampson, who was checking Shadow's tack. He nodded to the sleek Hembra, and Kendra turned up her nose just to make sure he didn't get any more ideas than he needed. "But it's like Afterling says—if it happens, it won't be just a pretty little story anymore, it will be a pretty little truth. So I suppose you better make it happen…"

"I suppose you're right. I-I'm just not ready yet." Destiny retreated back into the fortress of her friends, holding her hand out to Oskar: "Oh please come here, Oskar, and help us keep Araceli warm?"

Oskar whined up at Rose, and she whined back: "Go ahead, sweet baby, I'll be right here." Oskar grinned, then jumped into the Catastronix wagon with the Hostesses; sobbing, Araceli hid her face in his warty shoulder, and the cub reached up to pat her arm tenderly with his bloody, recurved claws.

Dominic riding by his side, the Watcher galloped to the head of the line, blood-stained cloak streaming behind him, the Flag of the Lone Star Republic. A shout swelled on the breeze as he rode down the line, Survivors' voices rising up out of the blood and dirt to take hold of the skies—

"LoneStar Libre! Libre—"

Pulling his Golden Horn from beneath his cape, the Watcher turned Oro to the front and blew his call once more.

It echoed off the walls of devastated Purgatory, ricocheting from the shallows of along the shore and across the open waters of the Lake, far beyond his sight… gunfire died with the last brassy note as the last of the defenders leapt from their parapets and rushed to the waiting wagons. As the wagons started to roll, the Watcher tapped his Palomino lightly in the flank with his boot, and the Horse sprang away from the walls, riding beyond the reach of Purgatory's Jammer;

The HeadsUp display of the Watcher's WeSpeex Ring flickered back to fully functional life, white text inviting him to connect with Rose. Scrolling through her settings, he hacked her ring once more; the notification ping sounded, declaring Saul Azarian as Admin of her new Ring.

Exasperated, Rose shook her head at his piracy of her tech. Her curls slipped their bounds yet again, tumbling wild from beneath her hood, untamable and free. Overwhelmed by her hair, the Watcher gently grasped a thick handful and lifted it to his lips, burying his face in her fragrance once more.

"Deva, what are you doing?" Rose whispered, tugging on his bloody fingers half-heartedly: "Let go—"

He grinned triumphantly and turned up the volume on her Ring. From their coupled hands, the Watcher activated Rose's external speakers, and Saul Azarian's dry Texas drawl roared to life:

#"Never."

The Watcher laughed, and Rose heard him through her own ears for the first time; his ominous chuckle sent a shudder down her spine. Oro dancing beneath him, the Watcher tightened his arm around her, then turned to Dominic and nodded. Dominic raised his hand and raced to the head of the column, shouting as he went:

"Fenix Creciente…"

Answering Dominic's call, the Watcher raised his Bowie Knife, the blood-stained blade a beacon, Lone Star Cape unfurled on the Texas wind. Every eye turned to the Watcher; every ear waited to hear his war cry.

He had the Power; but the Watcher knew—true Power knows when to yield.

Patting Rose's arm, he pointed to the Army of the LoneStar Revolution, waiting for the words. Suddenly shy, Rose looked over her shoulder to see the Watcher crack that devilish smirk of courage once more, that same smile he gave her the day she sashayed away to those same words…

#"Tell them—"

Giving him a brilliant lopsided grin in return, she raised a defiant fist; then with eyes bright and hair wild, Rose roared a shout to shake the foundations of the World:

"We Will Be Free!"

One mighty leap, and their Steed bounded forward, bearing them towards a darkling dawn.

Epilogue

#GENERALESII: So you're saying she got away?

The text flickered, its signal being interrupted by some unknown counter-signal near to its source.

#CHARTREAUX: No, you saw—she has been marked. She is being tracked.

Leaning back, the Supreme Commandant arranged his chess pieces, and motioned for his Rakshasa to make the first move. The young man rubbed his perfect, unblemished brow, golden-tanned skin glowing. He touched a chess piece before removing his hand.

#GENERALESII: But you're saying she got away.

The young man reached out again to move that same chess piece; the Commandant smacked his small tanned hand with own large ivory one, the white hair of his muscular forearm in stark contrast to the smooth, almost hairless arm of the neutered hybrid. Hurt, the Rakshasa pulled back his hand, drawing it under the satin cuff of his heavy velvet robe. "That touch used your turn—if you touch a chess piece and remove your hand, you can't go back. If you want to play, you must play by the rules." The Commandant turned his attention back to his conversation. Chatreaux answered him:

#CHARTREAUX: I'm asking you to look at your objectives. You wanted your Asura located, and she has been located. You asked for her co-conspirators to be identified, and they've been identified—Azarian is a positive match, and must be dealt with according to his training. You asked for Purgatory to be turned over

to your control, and it has been done. Not only that, but we have enacted martial law and taken two-thirds of the LandLords under our wing, to be permanently secured in exchange for their loyalty. You have now have plantations and personnel—and allies to crush Consortium control of the Damned. Thus secured, you may begin shipping valuable flesh to any area you need, worldwide, for any purpose you see fit, whether for labour or entertainment.

The Supreme Commandant scratched his white-haired chest beneath his own velvet robe, distracted from his pleasant break by this unpleasant interlude with unpleasant people. He always found Chartreaux tiresome, even before he mutated. Now, he found the reeking, oily Devil to be unbearable... He sighed and made his own move, pushing his bishop forward.

#GENERALESII: But you're saying she got away.

Chartreaux persisted.

#CHARTREAUX: No, she will be tailed, to lead us to the rest of their rebels—and they will be destroyed. She will be returned to you, alive or fresh-frozen, your choice, with appropriate shipping.

The Commandant harrumphed.

#GENERALESII: She must be returned alive. Asurinol shortages are becoming a reality, and she is the only renewable resource for the future. The only truly renewable resource is female. All others are... limited.

He looked at the Rakshasa sitting before him, so beautiful, so terminal, an evolutionary dead end without the means to procreate themselves. The Commandant continued:

#GENERALESII: I also expect a full accounting of every disabled drone—my teams must be able to activate and fully recharge each **ALGOS** back to full capacity, or you will pay for every damaged unit. That, and I need a full report on the **SHIVA** device you saw in the rebels' hands. I want to know how they came to be in the hands of prisoners.

#CHARTREAUX: The **ALGOS** have already been gathered and sent to your drop zone. We'll get a report out right away for the weapons, but may not be able to determine make and model without a close image.

#GENERALESII: I will be sending my own operatives to provide oversight in your search. Azarian is a problem that will need to be dealt with from the top level. While you are busy searching for my Asura, you will take control of the Co-op. Seize the means of production, and bypass the Consortium; you will find their allies, and remove them from the scene. Then we can maximize agricultural and industrial productivity for all, and increase the well being of the Society world wide. In exchange for your co-operation in this matter, you will be given up-to-date weaponry and vehicles for your personal use only—but you will not receive full payment, or the freedom to travel out of the co-op until you secure the Asura. The destruction of your custom SHIVA device makes it far less likely for me to trust you with this technology.

A pause, then Chartreaux answered back:

#CHARTREAUX: Very Well. I will inform Commander Shaney of our exchange.

The Commandant stroked his short white beard, smoothing it beneath his smooth hand.

#GENERALESII: Why don't I tell her myself? Bring her in. I wish to see her.

#CHARTREAUX: Apologies—she is busy recovering her beloved pony, which was stolen by one of her vassals. Fortunately for all, the yokel left it behind, tied to a post with a note. Otherwise, we would all be suffering from her wrath...

The Commandant chuckled, and the Rakshasa jumped, startled by it, unaware of the conversation.

#GENERALESII: Ah yes, Lillabeth's love of all things horsey. I know her addiction all too well; many's the time I've paid handsomely to feed that addiction. Give her my regards. Tell her if she wishes to keep receiving my regards, she will get me that Asura. Otherwise, you both will be terminated. Dismissed.

The HeadsUp display went momentarily dark. Pondering, the Commandant removed the marble chess pieces and swept them into a matching, velvet-lined box. He handed it to the Rakshasa; "Put these away, and go draw my bath—I must prepare for the evening debriefing. Armies don't run themselves." Eager, the young man nodded, his glossy brown hair matching shining brown eyes. As the Rakshasa slipped out of the room, the Commandant dropped his robe to dress, revealing his perfect, muscular body, a testament to the power of Asurinol. What James had hoped would replace Humanity had instead become a gift to Humanity. *To be used judiciously of course…* it was such a limited supply.

Now Society had discovered the secret to extended, vigorous life—Asurinol—there was no need to create more humans; there was only a need to create more Asurinol for the humans that already existed. If a way could be found to replicate Asura females naturally, that would help immensely; but James was beginning to rethink the Exodus Objective. A controlled breeding program in Tesoro was ultimately the best idea.

He admired himself in the gleaming mirror which adorned the walls of his magnificent seaside cabin. "Not bad at all for a one hundred and four year-old man…"

He wondered what his Father would have thought of Asurinol.

Javier was never truly on board with creation of the Asura, but he had become weary of the constant battle to save the Earth from an out-of-control Humanity. Having given his authorization for his son James to run the company as he saw fit, Javier took his retirement and set off to hike the world. His disinterested approval of a "peaceful Humans breeding program" had allowed James to create the Asura—and in turn, to birth the Kali Yuga Project outside Javier's knowledge.

What the old man never knew, never hurt him. The last time James heard from Javier, he was hiking the Copper Canyon of Mexico, exploring, as distant and inaccessible as he had always been.

James decided it didn't matter what Javier would have thought. The Old Man had never shared any of his other private thoughts at any depth… *why wonder now?*

His reverie was interrupted by the sound of howling and hoots coming from the heavily fortified Training Compound next door…

Aggravated by the din, the Supreme Commandant peered out his window to see a troop of seven umber-skinned, red-headed Rakshasas pile into the courtyard and jump a running Deva. The youngest, a toddler, screeched with delight; emerald eyes afire, he leapt atop the pile while the older youths wrestled the larger man to the ground.

Scowling, James opened up comms:

##*Supreme Commandant to Lt. General Jefferson*##

#GENERALESII: Your whelps are running roughshod over their tutor again.

#JEFFERSON: Yes, I'm sorry Sir, I'm attempting to regain control now.

#GENERALESII: Don't 'attempt'—do it. If I have to do it, you will be controlled with them.

#JEFFERSON: Right away Sir.

He wondered if this breeding experiment had been worth it.

Progeny of one of Dr. Iyer's precious salvaged proto-Asura embryos, these unruly, unaltered boys were the last hope to create an unrelated breeding line of Rakshasas to breed back to the prolific "Zoe" Asura line.

Jessica was brought back with the last three surviving proto-Asuras as consorts for the Commandant's inner circle. Considered to be inferior to the Zoe line for breeding, these proto-Asuras were restricted for use as sexual objects. But as the reproductive catastrophe of the Asura unfolded, James had gotten the desperate idea to try and breed them himself at his own compound.

What a complete waste, James mourned. On advisement from Dr. Iyer, James parted them out between his most trusted associates. He gave the stunning red-headed 'Jessica' to his Adjutant, Lt. General Jefferson, as a reward for loyalty and to tap into Jefferson's vigorous, unrelated gene pool. But true to the proto-Asura's short-sighted and irreversible 'reproductive governing' gene, Jessica had only produced males before her untimely death. She had aged suddenly, falling apart to die in the devastated Jefferson's arms...

Now the grieving Lt. General was saddled with the task of training the products of their union, and it was clear the man was in over his head with his rampaging sons. James would have gladly neutered them to be put into the lineup of pleasure Rakshasas. Unfortunately, these hellions had to be preserved, as the other two proto-Asura were infertile.

Now it was up to Jarrod's breeding program to produce a girl from the Zoe line. If one could be produced, Zoe's daughters could be bred back to Jefferson's Rakshasas. This union would create the basis for the ultimate F1 cross—James' original vision of 'Domesticated Human' who could be sent to the Colonies for the purposes of repopulating the Earth with a kinder, better humanity.

But Jefferson's boys were still too young and time was running out. Five years ago, the last of Zoe's cloned Asura were hatched; Jefferson's oldest son was still only fourteen, and by the time he would be capable of siring a child, only the last generation would be left to complete the task of producing a daughter...

Pensive, James observed the wave of testosterone rolling about on the lawn; these brats were supposed to be the future of humanity. *They need to be brought under control.* The boys would need to be removed from Jefferson if he couldn't train them. James shook his head. *Don't get attached*—that was the only way to deal with the short-lived, fragile Asura and their unexpectedly difficult sons.

Speaking of which, time to check in on my own son... still buttoning his uniform—a simple, green woolen affair with brass buttons and a stand-up collar—the Supreme Commandant started his next dialogue.

##James Generales to Jarrod Generales##

He waited a few minutes, finishing his dressing. "Jarrod has no respect for anything but his own likeness..." The Elder Generales grumbled to the mirror. "At least I've been there for him, unlike my own absentee Father; but what else could we expect, considering his simpering 'Mother' spoiled him completely." Pressed and dressed, he became irritable, and resent the message with an addendum:

#answer your damn messages
#this is your Father

A few seconds passed, then at last a return message popped up in the Commandant's inbox.

#like I could have never guessed

"Live Reply" popped up, and the Holocam activated to reveal the cold blue eyes of his Son, a languorous, deadly Lion in his den. Clad in a silk tunic and a Renaissance Faire hat, Jarrod leaned back against the divan, his golden-pink skin glowing beneath the lights of his studio. Behind him, a naked Asura cowered beneath a satin sheet, her glossy tumbled curls partly covering her supple golden body.

"Can we hurry this up? I'm busy holographing my next installment of "The Wicked Wives of King Henry the Eighth..."

The Elder Generales bit his tongue in an effort to be civil. "I'm glad to see your projects are coming along well. The Arts are a necessary component of civilization; however, we have a crisis to address."

Jarrod preened, staring at his own image in a gilded Mirror, running his elegantly long fingers though his golden-brown beard. "What is it? Another Asurinol shipment needed for the good of the Society? Some randy old man can't make it another day without a beautiful boy from Teroso?" Jarrod smirked. "Tell them to wait in line."

"No." The Elder Generales glared. "You are missing an Asura, and she has been spotted running amok in the Co-op."

"That's impossible." Jarrod replied without looking away from his own image. "All our Asura are accounted, and none are missing. This is just another baseless rumor from the dirty, delusional Damned."

"You are incorrect. Our intelligence indicates one escaped from Harvest somehow, and took up with a prisoner at one of our Facilities— our ALGOS made a positive identification on a former intern of the Firm." The Elder Generales gave a fierce look into his holo-cam, hoping to impress the gravity of the situation upon his son. "This is an extremely dangerous situation."

"Oh really? And who exactly did they say she was running with?" Jarrod kept his voice deliberately cynical.

"Saul Azarian." Beneath the calm, the Elder Generales was measured, analyzing his son's reactions. "You may have heard of him as the Watcher of the Damned. He has an interesting history—perhaps you should take time to read up on him. I'll send you his dossier."

"What's so special about an enslaved junkie?" Genuinely contemptuous, Jarrod asked with a carefully maintained air of disinterest.

"We have discovered that Azarian is the last remnant of our 'Benei Elohim Security Team." The Elder Generales said it with a hint of intrigue. "Unfortunately, Azarian never completed the final test, or we could use him at higher levels." The Commandant stroked his white beard.

"Oh yes… your fabled 'Guardian Angels' Security Force. But that shambling hulk? No wonder he failed out…" Jarrod waved a dismissive hand. "I'm not concerned. He'd have to be a superman anyway to save the Asura—they can't fight their way out of a wet paper bag, much less escape from Harvest. I'm sure it's a rumor. Don't let it bother you."

"It bothers me because my drones have captured her image, and proven one of your Asura is missing. We sampled her— #TMA673CdF…" James Generales pulled up her image in their shared display. "It says she was assigned to you."

A hint of distress appeared in his son's diffident eyes. "Oh, oh, yes I remember her—she was decommissioned early due to infertility. I sent her out, and the group was attacked by Chupacabra. We found the breach in the Electric Perimeter fence, and fixed it. But we thought she was dead!"

"Why was this not reported?"

"Oh it was—I'm sure of it." Jarrod lied. "It must have gotten misdirected somehow."

"Well, un-misdirect it and send the report again. There are issues, major ones—the Damned are aware of the Asura now, and they may have consorted. Once that starts, there will be no containing the Damned; they will want what they believe is rightfully theirs."

"It's no loss—the Damned can't reproduce, and even if by some miracle they could, neither can she." Jarrod sneered. "The little tart was barren."

"They only have to get it right once. And even if they can't reproduce females, they can produce males—and you of all people should know how dangerous unaltered Rakshasas can be." The Elder Generales glared at his son through the Ring's lens. "Fortunately, she's been tagged, thanks to our latest re-purposing of ancestral tech. But I need her stats… send me everything you have on this Asura, tonight. She will be brought back —I am sending a team of hunters to get the job done." James leaned forward into the camera.

"Speaking of which—how goes the breeding program?"

"Oh, all's well, as can be expected. The little buggers continue to crank out quality males, but as you know, they have never made a little girl. But no worries—we'll keep shooting for the moon! Never give up hope, etcetera, etcetera…" Jarrod smiled winningly at the naked Asura behind him. "Isn't that right, Pumpkin?"

Terrified, she nodded her head, and the Commandant made note.

"I'm glad to hear you are still working on it. Send me a full report—I believe an audit may be in order." The Elder Generales grey eyes grew cold. "I'm sure it will all be perfect. Isn't that correct, son?"

A pallor crept over the younger Generales. "Of course, Father. You know I always aim to please."

"Yes, you should." The Supreme Commandant switched off his cam, and Jarrod's HeadsUp display went dark.

"Damn him!" Livid, Jarrod turned to the Asura: "Out! Out, and don't bother me again—I have work to do."

She looked hurt. "But you said we were shooting a scene…"

"No! It was all a ruse, you simpleton! Besides, Shakespeare never used female actresses for female roles—he used boys, glorious boys!" Jarrod railed, flipping her out of the sheets. "Know you nothing? Now shoo, Lorraine—I have work to do. Go back to being a fat little housewife—or if you want that kind of attention, go work on your postpartum figure and bring in some money for House Generales."

She blinked back tears as Jarrod scooted her out the door, huffing. "At least Rose could make me laugh—too bad she was such a pain in the ass." He slammed the door. "That little scamp. Such a money maker, too, with a hell of a body—for an Asura. I can't believe she's actually fallen so low as to give herself to that Monstrosity…"

Whirling, Jarrod exploded, and a shockwave of rage flashed around him, a palpable surge of vitriol. "You stupid Asura!"

Across the room, a vase fell to the floor and shattered, scattering its red roses across the marble floor. He kicked the shards out of the way with a heavy boot. Apoplectic, Jarrod yelled at the Mirror: "How did you miss that, you idiot?" He grabbed his own head, hands laced into his dark golden mane. "Azarian—'The Watcher'—come on! He practically told everyone he was with the Program!"

He closed his eyes, and searched. "Maybe you'll give him away, Rose…" Probing the outer reaches, could feel her at the edge of his consciousness, just beyond reach of his feelers…

Nowhere. Was she blocking him? He reached for a slender translucent-red rod, and attached it to the stone of his Ring—

Nothing. Grimacing, Jarrod fiddled with the rod, turning it, before flinging it down in frustration. "Stupid Eitherior… what a waste of tax dollars, James. If you're going to make a physical transference device, make it work."

Incensed at inconvenient technological conundrums, Jarrod shoved the Eitherior device back into his work cabinet, and locked it tight. Muttering vehemently under his breath, Jarrod paced nervously, then barked into his golden Ring:

"Leland! Bring in my deliveries."

A dutiful voice answered: "Right away, Governor Generales."

In response to the order, light steps scuffled down the polished wooden floorboards of the hall; a knock rapped softly, and the carven door opened. A coppery, dark-eyed Rakshasa directed a scuffed cargo-hauler drone into the spacious bedroom. Worn tires rolled effortlessly across the edges of the cowhide rug and the three-wheeled robot hummed, raising the lid to its integrated cargo hold.

"Deliveries for the Church of God in Texas are presented here for your inspection. Out of those, three are deliveries for House Generales, as follows: gifts for Chaundra, from Major Cassius of Angelo AirBase—a box of ammo and a bottle of Dublin TeXas Red Creme Soda; gifts for

Kamiah, from Sir Davis of Fredricksburg UnderFarms, two boxes of ten-penny nails and a jar of Peach Salsa—"

"Exquisite… " Lifting the glass bottle up to the light, Jarrod admired the brilliant ruby hue of the sugar-cane soda, then popped open the salsa jar. The perfectly preserved, spicy-sweet aroma of peaches and peppers filled the room with promise of breakfast toasts to come. "Send the boxes to their respective department, then add these delicacies to my private reserve; schedule Chaundra and Kamiah for four client hours, each."

Not done with his tally, Leland raised a finger. "… and gifts for Pearl, from Captain Montez of Citadel Colony, a 200-count case of Chili-Lime Twangerz."

"Really? Twang?" The Governor of Tesoro wrenched open a box and fished out a packet of the flavored beer salts. "With salt in such scarce supply, too—" Ripping the foil packet open, Jarrod dabbed some of the glittering red powder on his fingers, then licked them with relish. "This will act as payment for an army. Schedule Pearl for an entire evening. Captain Montez is a man of good taste."

"Yessir. Anything else?" Meticulous, the young man swept back straight, dark locks from his forehead, and tapped his heads-up display to enter data.

"Inform the illustrious Dr. Iyer I'm sending in our medical team to crank up the All-Mother in time for our Dia de Los Muertos Spook-tacular Marketing Masquerade. We need our original Asura trotted out for investors to ogle on the HoloCam, and the All-Mother does me no good if she's looking frail."

Leland glanced away from his HeadsUp Display with a discreet concern. "Begging your pardon Governor, but Dr. Iyer stated in her last report that the All-Mother is no longer well enough to entertain clients, even in a virtual setting."

"Hogwash… tell Dr. Iyer if she wants her daily rations to keep rolling in, she'll find a way to prop up what's left of her 'daughter'. No one wants that worn-out wench for anything but ceremonial purposes nowadays; but with enough makeup and a mask, the All-Mother can handle smiling and waving in the Chapel for a few minutes at least. Investors want Proof-of-Life," Jarrod groused. "Now get dressed and prepare to accompany me to the ballroom. We have guests to impress, and I need you to make notes on who's who with whom. We've got to scrounge new client contacts for our Asura to make up for that gaping hole in our income stream."

"Replacing Rose has proven challenging," Leland replied coolly. "Her clients are still unhappy with her departure…"

"They'll get over it." Distracted by flavor, Jarrod waved a hand. "Schedule a team meeting, and tell Team Pink to show up motivated. Hannah is due for labor and delivery next week; set up her and Lorraine for extended workout routines. We've got to get them back in shape and back in the game within the next four weeks if we're to meet quota. We'll bring Amelia back into rotation once her black eye heals up, and give her Rose's stage routine."

"Yessir. Anything else, sir?"

"Set up my office for an all-nighter after the ballroom meet-and-greet. Hook me up to an espresso machine set on endless refill mode—I have reports to write, and it couldn't come at a worse time."

"Will do." Leland tapped in his final entry, then the slender Rakshasa swept out the door again to dress for his evening as attache to Tesoro's glamorously intimidating Governor.

Irritated at his unexpected workload, Jarrod comforted himself by tallying tribute packages, sent from Tesoro Hopefuls far and wide. He opened the package of roasted Coffee Beans from House Hermoso, flown all the way from Bogota, up the treacherous route though Mexico; *We really ought to thank Adelaide... Tesoro gets these for free now.*

Jarrod ran his fingers through the beans, checking carefully for hidden hate-notes or embedded bullets from his nemesis, the elusive, hated Hanuman's Mace. Finding none, he stuck his nose down in the package, and breathed in their fragrance, energized by the addictive bouquet of real, live Coffee…

That last note—pinned by a knife stabbed into a pillow in his laundry —had set him on edge. An internal ally of the Asura had somehow escaped the New Initiative's political purge of Tesoro, and that meant he would need to redouble his surveillance measures of the Asura, the Rakshasa, and their admirers. He sincerely doubted it would be an Asura, though… *pathetic, sniveling little bundles of fat, sugar, and tears….*

Contemptuous, Jarrod threw off his silk tunic and replaced it with his own uniform; a dark blue, nineteenth century Italian Calvary officer's uniform, resplendent with cords and a white bib, brought in as a gift from one of Rose's admirers. He had it tailored to fit his tall, muscular frame, adding gussets and lengthening the cuffs with scraps from other suits—it worked out quite well, as long as one didn't mind being historically inaccurate.

Jarrod pondered his loss. She was the reason he named 'The Yellow Rose Lounge' after her, to showcase his finest star. Rose's admirers had always paid the very best in goods, just to experience the rush of real love, streaming from her fingertips, pouring from her heart, whether it was in spoken word or song—the gifts of the Asura, come to life in its greatest practitioner—Rose.

"Ah well, it's worth the loss." He scowled into the mirror, stroking his beard, then pulled up his HeadsUp display again, and hailed the Warden.

#GENERALESIII: Ron, wake up. I know it's late, but we have news.

He continued to dress, finishing off with a ribbon and golden medallion befitting a King; fortunately for the King, the Warden was responsive, and not dragging his feet.

#HOWELL: What? This better be good—I got a Hembra on hold while I'm dealing with you.

#GENERALESIII: Give me an update on your Hit Squad.

#HOWELL: Not much to tell yet from the last update, except that I have a recon team due within the next hour. No communications from the squad since four this afternoon.

#GENERALESIII: Well, find out. I just heard from the Commandant himself; we've got trouble. He used his drones to find my Asura—and Azarian's with her.

#HOWELL: There's no way in hell Azarian's alive! You and I both heard from Chief Emmanuel, saying he killed the bastard.

Jarrod brushed back his tawny hair, and admired it.

#GENERALESIII: That was a lie. It's as I suspected all along… Azarian spoofed Emmanuel somehow, and lied to throw us off track. Father just told me Azarian was in the Benei Elohim Training Program, but never completed the final test.

A tense pause followed.

#HOWELL: Crap. Are you sure?

#GENERALESIII: Yes—the destruction of my rapid response team proves it: only someone with those skills could have brought them down. Now your Hit Squad is missing, and I'm willing to bet that Azarian is at least part of the reason you haven't heard back from them.

#HOWELL: We need to deal with this now; first, the Commandant is sending in his tech—that means Boss Chartreaux

has made an alliance with the Commandant. My contacts at Purgatory will be under scrutiny now, and this means we're going to have a lot harder time dealing black-market magic at Purgatory. Second, Azarian is out there, and he's got someone helping him. I think you're looking a the rise of a rival gang at the very least, or perhaps even an uprising—so give me some high-octane weaponry. If what you're saying is true, then Azarian is dangerous as hell. I always knew He was trouble, but…

Jarrod snapped.

#GENERALESIII: If you thought he was so much trouble, then why did you deputize him in the first place?

#HOWELL: Hell, I didn't know Azarian was a Benei Elohim trainee. Leona didn't tell me a damn thing. I thought he was just a prisoner… besides, he wasn't ever supposed to be a real deputy—he was just supposed to walk out there, get the Asura, and get killed. I figured she'd come to him and then we'd off the beast. Even I didn't know what all he was capable of.

#GENERALESIII: Well, we're about to find out. Father is sending a complete file—and if we're lucky, a magic bullet will be in there, to help us take this savage down. Now, I've got to get to down to the Ballroom at the Magnolia Club. It's Vienna Waltz Night. New clients are waiting to be wined, dined, and blackmailed, and I need to schmooze if we're going to get more goods and weaponry.

#HOWELL: Make sure to synchronize your calendar with mine again—it still keeps resetting to Reunion time instead of the proper day, and you and I need to co-ordinate the new client escorts to and from Tesoro. We have a colony in San Angelo that wants to schedule a rush shipment of Asurinol next week.

#GENERALESIII: Well it won't happen his week. Our Heliscram 9 "Bison" was shot down while trying to recover the Afterling, and I can't spare another. But if your rugged riders salvaged parts from the wreck, our mechanics could repair the one in the shop to get it running again. Message me as soon as you hear from your recon team; I need to know what's going down in Purgatory. Over.

Shutting down the beacon, the Warden leaned back in his chair, and put a hand to his forehead. A concerned voice asked him: "What's the problem, Warden?"

"Nothing you can help with. You're dismissed, Darlene; I've got to work. You'll get a double ration of food in the morning, full pay for a partial night's work—it's not your fault I have to call off early."

Athletic and sleek, the Hembra gathered her faded skirt and stood from where she knelt at the Warden's feet. "Oh, thank you, Warden…" A guard came to escort her back to her barracks.

"Yeah, I'm a real treasure." The Warden rubbed the back of his neck. Curr whined beneath the desk, and the Warden patted the fat yellow hound absent-mindedly. A knock came at the door, and a barrel-shaped Sentinel poked his head into the Warden's sparse office.

"Pardon, Warden, but your Recon Team has returned."

"Send them in."

Walking through the door came three dusty Survivors, smelling of horse sweat and night air. They removed their hats, deferential. He waved them in, still sitting behind his desk. "Give me a report."

"It ain't good, boss…" A rough Hombre shuffled his feet and shook his head.

"Spare me the commentary. Give it to me straight, and let me deal with it."

"Alright then—we can't make contact with the Hit Squad, weapons are missing from the Heliscram Wreck, and Camp Forlorn was burned to the ground. Dead bodies everywhere. Something's bad wrong; but we found someone that may have some inside info to help us. While we were scavenging, we found a fella locked in the cargo hold of one of the WildLand Express smuggler wagons—he says he wants to make a deal."

"Send him in."

They opened the door, and a tall Hombre walked in, smoke and death following in his wake. The Warden stood, aghast: "Clemson? Paymaster Clemson?" Suspicious, he cast a wary eye to the Agent. "What's your racket?"

"I'm here to get rich." Singed from head to foot, the thin man grinned from ear to ear. He doffed his sooty hat. "I heard you have an opening, due to the untimely death of Chief Emmanuel. But I want assurances before I tell you everything I know."

"So the Chief's dead?" The Warden waved to his men. "Give us some privacy, boys—right outside the door will do." They closed the door, leaving The Warden alone with his informant.

"I hadn't heard from you in a while—I began to wonder if you were still interested in working with El Trafico or not." Intrigued, the Warden leaned forward, reaching into his desk to pull out a bottle of Reunion's finest.

"I'm always interested in fine goods." Clemson poured himself a shot and held it up to the light to admire the golden liquid. "I have information about the Afterling. I tell you who has her, in exchange for a cushy apartment and a pretty Hembra or two here in Reunion. The more you give me, the more I tell. In exchange for your generosity, I'll do for you what I did for the Director and Von Helm—manage the books and help distribute the wealth."

The Warden thought on it for a moment. "Give me a sample, and I'll see if you're worth the cost."

"Oh, I'm worth it all right." Clemson took the shot glass, and swilled it down. "You might like to know about a little plan by Director Santos to take down the System, called 'The LoneStar Revolution'. Azarian's leading Santos' army—and he's got the Afterling with him." Clemson threw down a small piece of leather—on it, a five-pointed star emblazoned with a bird rising out of a fire, above a broken chain. "There's also a thing called an ALGOS. I don't know what the hell it is, but Camp Forlorn and everybody in it is now nothing but a heap of ashes."

The Warden's eyes grew wide. Easing himself into his seat again, he stared through his steepled fingers at the former Paymaster of the WildLand Express. He handed Clemson the bottle. "ALGOS… and the Watcher leading an army, huh?" The Warden brought the badge closer to read the inscription:

"We Will Be Free…"

He opened his HeadsUp display, and called in his men.

"Get ready to ride—" He looked out the window into the WildLand night. "But first set up our new Paymaster here in Leona's old quarters— and send in Darlene as a welcome gift. She's already dressed and ready, and she owes me half a night anyway."

Tired, they hurried out, Clemson behind them, and the Warden pressed the hidden beacon once more to open a new channel. He fiddled about for a bit, swearing at the tech, but it finally clicked, and he punched in the number code. An odd notification tone rang several times, and he listened as a pleasant voice answered.

"Little Joe's Tire Shop. Leave your name at the beep and we'll get back to you."

"Yeah this is Ron with a message for the Consortium. We need our shipment early; the Commandant is on the move, and with good reason. There's a Revolution brewing, led by our worst nightmare..." He paused, examining the leather badge in his hand.

"... Watcher, of the Damned."

———◆———

END—BOOK VI—WATCHER OF THE DAMNED

Once upon a time in pre-apocalyptic Texas, R.H. Snow fused experiences as a firefighting, storm-chasing bard to bring the sci-fi western series "WATCHER of the DAMNED" to gritty, exuberant life. Snow's post-apocalyptic Texas saga combines bleeding-edge action with heart and humor to create a Tall Texas Tale of life, love and liberty after pandemic world's end. This book is a paean to the Survivor in us all, and a tribute to all who fight to be free.

Seventh-generation Texan R. H. Snow is a singer, sketcher and gamer living with a family of other rescued humans and animals. Snow does not have a Chupacabra… yet.

Contributors:
David Snow—Weapons and self-defense
Roxanne Morris—Cover Art, character continuity edits
Daniel Snow—Worldbuilding and storyline development

Beta Reader:
Arthur DeVitalis
Arthur DeVitalis is a journalist, photographer, podcast host, writer, and gardener. Though Canadian-born, he got to Texas as soon as he could at the age of six. He graduated the University of Texas. Today, he writes for newspaper publications in Texas and Colorado. He resides in Whitney, Texas, with too many pooches.

Design and Layout:
Cynthia Davis
Cynthia Davis is a native Texan who has enjoyed a successful career as an artist in multiple mediums with an emphasis on graphic communications. She resides in Whitney, Texas.

Melanie Calahan, Self-Publishing Services
Melanie was born in Texas, and she is part owner in a company that specializes in editing, formatting, and cover design.

Publishing House:

Rosa De Oro, a Texas Publishing Company. Rosa de Oro is a boutique publishing house in Central Texas, specializing in Faith, hope and love—and the joy of all things Texas!

REFERENCES

———•—•———

Fundamentals

TEXAS HISTORY MOVIES
https://www.tshaonline.org/handbook/entries/texas-history-movies

Rose's knowledge of Texas History is encompassed in the pages of the 1986 reprint of the Texas Sesquicentennial Edition of the schoolyard classic, *Texas History Movies*.

THE VIRGINIAN: A HORSEMAN OF THE PLAINS
https://www.gutenberg.org/files/1298/1298-h/1298-h.htm

Epic and adventurous, *The Virginian* is the first-ever Western Romance— and Rose's ONLY idea of Romance.

THE RUBAIYAT OF OMAR KHAYYAM
https://www.gutenberg.org/files/246/246-h/246-h.htm

Filled with beautiful imagery and dark despair, the *Rubaiyat* has lured lovers for centuries with its jaded joy—and the Watcher is among them.

THE KING JAMES BIBLE
https://www.gutenberg.org/cache/epub/10900/pg10900-images.html

The One, the Only. Whether he believes it or not, the Bible is the foundation of the Watcher's malleable morality—because it belonged to his Mother.

GO RIN NO SHO—*The Book of the Five Rings*, Miyamoto Musashi
https://www.academia.edu/7011243/Miyamoto_Musashi_Book_of_Five_Rings

DOKKODO—*The Way of Walking Alone*, Miyamoto Musashi
https://terebess.hu/zen/mesterek/musashi.html#a1
Everyone needs a guiding hand—and if your hand is holding the sword, Musashi should be the hand to guide it.

Foraging

DR. MARK MERRIWETHER VORDERBRUGGEN
Foraging and native plants of Texas. The greatest living Authority on foraging in Texas! Author of "Idiot's Guide to Foraging" and creator of "Foraging Texas" Buy his bandana and know what your ancestors knew! www.foragingtexas.com

Flora

THE ANTIQUE ROSE EMPORIUM, Brenham, Texas—-Growers of Rare, Own-Root and Old Garden Roses.
https://antiqueroseemporium.com

"Caldwell Pink" Rose: There's a reason Survivors grow these beautiful roses—because these roses are true Texas survivors!

Food

DUBLIN BOTTLING WORKS, Dublin, Texas—Keepers of the Sweet, Celebrating 120 Years of Sugar Cane Sodas in the Lone Star State!
https://www.dublin1891.com/s/shop

Dublin Pure Cane Sugar Sodas: A Bottle of Sweetness in a bitter world, Dublin Pure Cane Sodas are prized by Survivors for their pure deliciousness and quick energy.

FREDRICKSBURG FARMS, Fredricksburg, Texas—Three Generations

of "Texas Real" Farming
https://www.fbgfarms.com

Peach Salsa: Sweet, spicy and sassy salsas for Survivors who savor the flavor of Texas!

TWANG, San Antonio, Texas—Welcome to the Flavor Factory!
https://www.twang.com

Chili Lime Twangerz Twang makes food and drink Fun with Tex-Mex Flair! With salt scarce, and spices even scarcer, Survivors fight for the taste of Twang - if they can find it...

Friends

MIKE S. MILLER
https://www.facebook.com/MikeSMillerArt

BAM! POW! Leaping from the pages of our favorite Comic Books, it's Artist and Storyteller Mike S. Miller! Even in the distant dystopian future, Survivors are fans of his Indie Comic Hero, Lonestar… and all his many other wonderful works.

Fun

FORT PARKER STATE PARK, Springfield, Texas
https://tpwd.texas.gov/state-parks/fort-parker

On the banks of the winding Navasota River, a shining Sycamore Tree awaits.

JUNETEENTH GROUNDS, Booker T. Washington Park, Limestone County Texas
https://visitlimestonecountytx.com/booker-t-washington-park/
https://www.lcjuneteenthorganization.org/

More than just a safe haven for lost Afterlings, Booker T. Washington Park is the Birthplace of Juneteenth, and gathering place for generations of freedom-loving Texans!

OLD FORT PARKER
https://oldfortparker.org/

A great place for gun battles, Outlaws, and Lawmen—and a haven for Texas Shooting Sports.

REUNION GROUNDS, Joe Johnston Confederate Reunion Grounds, Limestone County, Texas—
http://www.thc.texas.gov/historic-sites/confederate-reunion-grounds-state-historic-site
Reunion Camp wasn't always a camp—it was a glorious summer getaway for war-weary veterans and their families, and a stage for grand battle re-enactments.

SHILO, Limestone County, Texas
https://smallcountrychurch.wordpress.com/

There really is a little white Church called Shilo! For over 100 years it has bloomed amidst the roses on a little country backroad, serving with love. There is no street address—just directions to an intersection   but like the Good Lord Himself, if you seek it, you shall find…

SPRINGFIELD HALL
https://www.springfieldhalltx.com/

Tucked away in the Central Texas, Riverbottom Woods is a Sanctuary for wayward travelers—and a testament to local Liberty.

Firepower

Texans LOVE guns.

BOND ARMS

https://www.bondarms.com/

Browning North America
https://www.browning.com/

COLT
https://colt.com/

DESERT EAGLE
https://www.magnumresearch.com/

DPMS
https://www.dpmsinc.com/
GLOCK
https://us.glock.com/en

HECKLER & KOCH
https://hk-usa.com/
HENRY REPEATING RIFLES
https://www.browning.com/

KELTEC
https://www.keltecweapons.com/

MARLIN
https://www.marlinfirearms.com/

NORTH AMERICAN ARMS
https://northamericanarms.com/

STURM, RUGER & COMPANY
https://ruger.com/

SMITH & WESSON
https://www.smith-wesson.com/

TAURUS
https://taurususa.com/

REMINGTON
https://www.remington.com/

WINCHESTER
https://www.winchesterguns.com/

———◆———

Firearm Accessories

MAGPUL
https://magpul.com/

———◆———

Made in the USA
Middletown, DE
30 August 2023

37625149R10236